This
Black

How a Boy Tripped Over His Feet and Accidentally Saved His People

By
Ajali Shabazz

The first Afro-futurist, heck, the first novel ever written about the New Radioactive Reality, brought to each of us following the initial explosion, melt-through, melt-down and the continuous hemorrhage of planet extinguishing nuclear isotopes from the destroyed Fukushima Daiichi Power Plant.

ISBN-13: 978-1549776144
ISBN-10: 1549776142

In Loving Memory of
John, Shirley and Adrian Beggsmith. I kept my promise,
because that's how you taught me.

Acknowledgements

All Praise is Due to Allah for seeing me through more than I need to say here, as He knows. His Divine Intervention came to me through the Person of Master Fard Muhammad, who came to me through the Person of The Honorable Elijah Muhammad, who came to me through the Person of The Honorable Minister Louis Farrakhan, who came to me through my Beloved King, Zaahir Muhammad. Nothing in my life has ever been the same and won't be until the day I die, which will be never, as through their truth? I've forged my own immortality so I submit, lovingly, freely to The Best of Planners.

Allahu Akbar.

I Thank my amazing son, Elijah, whose birth turned the lights on in my soul, and whose patient ears helped me do a much better job of being a compassionate person. Everyone is a better learner who can learn from the youth.

I, also, joyously Thank Sister Donata, whose initial assistance made this a far more interesting book than it would have ever been. And Thank You, also, Sister E-Queen, for being such a wonderful anchor in this turbulent storm, called 'The United States'.

An extra intense Thank You to all the piercingly beautiful friends I made on Facebook and Youtube, with Facebook being the initial forum where I learned I could string together a couple sentences and folks would actually read them. I Love You, ALL – FIERCELY.

Finally, an essential THANK UUUUU to every Black Person alive and every one of Our Ancestors. You've each fueled my ability to create in ways I never contemplated I was able to employ until I better understood that We each are talented, gifted or clever, not despite being Black, but

B
E
C
A
U
S
E.

This is for You. This is for Us, and forgive any imperfections, as I didn't have an editor due to financial constraints. Though, even if I did, this work of sheer Love will never be as beautiful as a one of Us, no matter what temporary state that being may find him/herself within; though, I humbly pray my love in action proves You deserve the best of whatever this world has to offer, if you take action, also, to become the champion you seek...

INTRODUCTION

I know and knew quite quickly, that upper cross to my face, after the fall into the void, made me ponder the randomness of fate a whole lot better. Things like that will change a man and I was still a boy. Yet, in the end? Was all that's happened since been only about accidentally tripping over my own feet; oh, and then being decked by a bully (actually, a whole bunch of stuff too plentiful to mention in one paragraph happened over those 5 days, and that's the reason writing this all down will be one heck of a chore) – was it about bumbling fate or could any of it have been about me?

This is not a novel. It's a history book, but – I'm not a professional historian. So, please. Don't interrupt my seemingly random stream of thought, nor let me interrupt myself, as I may never get through writing this not only mandatory assignment, but I accept – I might not make it through this essential documentation of how and why we finally won. Considering my lack of formal training at being a writer, let alone a historian, penning this history could be the worst on purpose endeavor I've ever embarked upon. However, I'm supposed to do this. I am commanded to do this. A history book written by not a deliberate scholar, but by accidental me.

Let me repeat, I wasn't supposed to fall, nor get clocked in the kisser, thus making this entire grueling effort perhaps the result of happenstance, not choice, which isn't the best motivation for working diligently, when you don't know if you're supposed to be doing what everyone assumes you should do, because you do it so well – by accident.

I'll tell you what I do so well in a moment, but...

I vow this monumental undertaking will be finished, no matter how reluctant I am during the torturous process. Mark my warning, therefore. My name isn't Professor John Henrik Clarke, Dr. Amos Wilson, James Weldon Johnson, nor Ivan Van Sertima. And although I'm well read (meaning I've read plenty of books, never written one, though), I ain't Richard Wright or Chinua Achebe. I'm going make mistakes. Lots of them. Seems that's how I started and it'll be how I end – at least in composing this testimonial.

Now, the best history, in my estimation, presents the bare facts. But these facts are about me, the accidental, highly reluctant to write about it, hero. That's gonna be embarrassing, as I'm not sure how much I should be revealing to the random and not so random judgment of those who'll read this, including you. Who could relish the idea of strangers possibly finding me guilty of having flaws I never meant to confess? Flaws that brought me here. Flaws that brought Us, all, here. Everyone has flaws, but? Maybe, I'd be more enthusiastic if I only had virtues.

Oh, well. Looks like I'm gonna hafta wing it, even though – I don't have wings! Ha! A little God humor there. Ah? I haven't mentioned that part, yet? I mean the wings, not the humor... so? By the way...

I'm a god...

Who's getting ahead of himself. Told you I don't know what the heck I'm doing. But here's a pleasant interruption. My lovely wife (I am so fortunate) has just entered the room with my morning tea as I recline on our large but nothing too fancy queen-sized bed, eh... writing. Yes, gods perform mundane tasks and we're normal sized so we sleep in beds exactly like yours. And here is my wife standing beside me, while I write, my normal sized pajama-ed body wrapped up in the bed linens, though there's no typewriter and/or pencil or pen to be found.

There's a whole bunch of 'deity things' that may seem magical to you which I'll have to explain later. Gods are patient and I highly recommend practicing the same if you have the nerve to read this book to figure out how to become one, yourself.

A god, I mean. Not a terrible writer.

Making my morning tea is a tender routine my other half does for me each dawn, as she can – and I dearly appreciate it. Though, I usually appreciate it in silence. A simple nod is exchanged between us, and sometimes not. It's an almost imperceptible 'thank you' that in no way conveys the depth of what is done. And done for each other continuously, as I'm given to doing for her, in my many ways. Now tea may not seem at all romantic, but both of us are free to choose our idea of what's tender. In our realm, with nothing but gods (and some – uh? Let's call them – mortals – who are voluntary servants, although she and I have none. We have just friends, neighbors, who we in turn help with their big chores) – no mass media dares give us instructions on the personal matter of how to love. Nearly omnipotent beings make for lousy pets and the most disobedient of robots as we don't take kindly to mass programming.

Nope. We don't. Those days are over.

Her short buoyant afro, sculpted in soft coiling nappy peaks, (she told me her hair's a 4c, but I have no idea what that means) – her coif is still crumpled a bit on the right side from rising less than an hour ago, dusted by this morning's light, still streaming through the circular window, directly behind me. Her face, expressionlessly handing me my cup, unreadable as is my own – speaks volumes that needn't be shared 'cause we're old enough to know how to read quietly to ourselves. For she's a full god, also, and we immortals are steeped in the maturity that comes with the job, whether on purpose or not. If you can't cut this divine gig, then you don't.

Me? I was born for it. No accidents involved.

Jepkemboi. That's the name of my deep dark skinned beauty, with eyes like no woman I've ever seen. Have no illusions, however, reader. By no means is she the most physically captivating woman I've ever met; but these days in 'Heaven' (for lack of a word you'd understand more readily) – these days are simply better, as, We literally see the beauty inside, first. Women have no desire to prove their value through their surface charms – charms to which we men are still helplessly addicted, although, We be gods. That said, what self-respecting man or god (which is, ultimately, a thoroughly self-respecting man) – which of us enjoys enslavement? If men don't like following somebody else's romance rules, well? Fighting against that magnetic attraction to the sisters, we brothers used to trivialize their sacred role. We attacked, we raped, we demeaned that which we should have sheltered, and didn't. Couldn't in that trap. All were devalued and diminished. But we, men, with our greater physical strength, we have a higher sacred responsibility, beyond all, to keep our women safe, especially if that means from us, their brothers.

Uh-oh. That was a lot, huh? Well, I told you, I'm winging this without wings, having only started today – and here I've aimlessly rambled on, and it's only page 8.

So back to the external flow of my life's blood, Jepkemboi. Radiant from the soul outward, she is the reason my own individual home is called 'Heaven'. Yup. A home like this doesn't happen by accident, either. Nor do we maintain it by blundering along, or does it exist by itself. I do what is necessary by her and radiating outwards from her – what's right for my nation, joyfully, as does everyone else....

Don't get the wrong idea, though. No one's forced to comply with some moral code everyone secretly loathes. There's no police because there's no need for police. Why should there be when nobody wants to commit a crime? We don't have 'poor huddled masses' as even the most brilliant and celebrated clean up after themselves, while it turns out? The huddled masses weren't huddling voluntarily. Freedom raises everyone's intelligence quotient to genius.

And as for dressing respectfully? There's no dress code in this existence, either. If a sister or brother wanted to run down the block in a thong, nobody would stop him or her because each onlooker would feel such anguish for that person, knowing he/she has the right to make even asinine decisions, if they so choose. However? Everyone would instinctively know something profoundly wrong had to have happened to that person to make them focus on the least powerful of their gifts. I'm only predicting, as no one's ever felt the need to streak down the block or across a football field (yes, yes, we have sports, though they're not distractions because we pay attention to everything else, now) – I'm predicting, We, the community, with sincerity and love, without needing to consult one another, would visit that person's home, individually or in groups, to show that begging for attention divine being that he or she has all the world; for this world works for everyone, as the sadness of one is the sadness of the whole, eventually.

We've learned that, firsthand, you have no need to destroy what feeds you true love. Simply didn't know before, 'love' is an action...

Thus, the goddesses are safe from womb to grave in the haven of our protective devotion. They trust us, their gods, fully. Why, you've never seen so much jubilant deference between both sexes, and what a daggone relief! We've discovered powers no one ever realized had been there, all along. We'd had no idea of Our innate, personal mightiness due to being formerly overwhelmed by the negation of never ending negativity. Who knew back then, if we'd have shut the heck up, and worked united, we'd have already been super people...

Sometimes, for those unfamiliar, I capitalize 'We' and 'Us' when referring to We, Gods, because like one would capitalize a proper name, or the pronoun 'I', WE protect Ourselves better as One.

But, oops! I'm going too quickly, again. I was talking about my Jepkemboi. She isn't mine, of course, like one would own a chair or a pair of shoes. She's her own being, free to leave anytime she feels she must; same with me – however, joyfully we're happy in this marriage after having met what seems lifetimes ago, and we're both committed to weathering all storms. Now, after 2 years of

9

wedded bliss, she's delightfully 5 months into carrying our first child – which is the crux of my problem...

Oh, my, this is a fine cup of tea. It's green tea, but so potent, compared to what I used to drink decades and decades ago. It must be the variety she's grown on our own homestead, up on the roof farm that fans out onto the terraced hilltop, beyond. Such a skilled agrarian she's become, after learning, like most of Us – who knew not a thing about how to do for Ourselves. She's germinating, cultivating, enriching and harnessing life, not only in her womb, but in the womb of the Earth. She taught herself the lost art of coaxing the soil to not only sustain us, but with the assistance of those friends, our neighbors, on this and their little farms, the entire community has no need for supermarkets. There are markets to purchase all manner of goods (some gods don't care for farming, like I don't care for writing), but? We barter for equal trade, not sell for profit.

She's standing beside me, as I recline, propped up on the pillows. I'm patting her little belly bump, as family and friends do, while they all tend the fields, or relax in our sunken court garden. Now, I nod with a warm smile that I feel, not one I'm compelled to give, as she's returning one of her own, subdued but full of understanding.

Look. I know this seems rather randomly personal – especially for a supposed 'dispassionate' history book, but my son, yet for me to hold and guide, his new life has the greatest bearing on how I choose to chronicle my own life, and how I choose not to – though I wouldn't tell you what I don't want you to know, if I decide, um?...

Not to tell you? Yes, that would be silly, because, then? You'd know what I didn't want you to know and I'd have to explain why, eh......? Let's scratch those last couple sentences and barrel on, if possible, why don't we?

Perhaps getting it all out, a bit at a time, will guide me in the right direction before I hit the deadline my superiors have set for me. One doesn't wiggle out of doing as commanded by these men. I mean, I *could*, but this is HEAVEN! It's ALL GOOD. How – like no one would go streaking butt bare – how could I possibly overlook the command of the One called 'The Alpha and The Omega', who has as many other names as there are H_2O molecules in the clouds, air and water, combined, but? That still hasn't made me rush to the job, and now there's no more time for delay. I've got hundreds of pages to write in perhaps less than 3 weeks. Maybe days if the wrong or right person comes inquiring. I'm a god, yes, but I ain't Theeeeeeee GOD. That said, no matter what the dire consequences of trudging forward, even embarrassing the heck outta myself with exemplary poor writing skills (as you may have already detected, you annoyingly avid and piercingly precise bibliophiles [and I know 'outta' is not a real word]....) – no matter my even sorrier true story, forward I must trudge. Sheesh.

Therefore? I am Akhenaten Ra, the Librarian Keeper, one of many in the committed service of Knowledge Protectors from every discipline. There are Military Protectors, Commerce Protectors, Science Protectors, but my branch of service specializes in gathering information for posterity's enrichment. I, 17,059th in the line of librarian succession, I myself, have retained this duty, this distinction for a short 97 years; whereas the longest holder of the office was the man just before the one who directly passed it onto me. My teacher (who ascended to the role after that longest Keeper) – my teacher was the esteemed Dr. Kattan, who had no initial intention of conferring the title onto me, whatsoever – at first. He may still, given my reluctance to make a written record of my experiences – he may still regret the transfer (I'd ask him, but then I'd have to admit that I've only started writing this history). As I alluded to, preceding Dr. Kattan, ranged the career of the most famously distinguished senior Protector of all, as he maintained Pre-Heaven for an unprecedented 437 years – he was the brave Mumia Sirius Negus Ra.

I do have my own distinguished claim as the youngest Keeper of all, having begun at the tender age of 12, which would be a source of pride, as I'm continuously told I've done well, yet? How can I claim pride for an accident? Those who weren't there are full of praise, but, I know starting so young was a handicap as I was never fully prepared for the job like someone who'd had a prior calling. I've never even finished my schooling beyond the 9th grade. Yes, a god is what I was created to be, however, Librarian Keeper simply, *literally*, fell into my lap. Or maybe I should say – I fell into its!

Also? Perhaps because of my lack of previous awareness of the profession altogether, I've put off doing what others before me accomplished straight away. Other Librarian Keepers, it appears, couldn't wait to chronicle their discoveries, having trained for years prior to accepting their responsibilities. They painstakingly detailed each encounter with exacting accuracy, leaving a collective cavernous vault of information; whereas, I've recorded mine on thousands of post-it notes, which I attach to whatever I'm standing near and there it remains until Jepkemboi very patiently collects them into an accordion folder I'm staring at this second. More like an accordion encyclopedia, 17 volumes in one. Yes, yes! I've brought this dilemma onto myself. I admit it! So the astute reader might understandably conclude I'm taking up space with useless fluff, like in a grade school book report packed tight with run-on sentences. Or like a cheap novel where I earn a penny for every rambling word, rather than getting straight to the meaty dripping with gore facts. To that I'd answer a vehement, um?

Maybe...

But despite my delay, this could never be some boring testimony from a salaried dullard who no longer remembers how to spell 'passion', let alone what it feels like. This is my life I'm chronicling and my life's been edge of the seat harrowing!

No. Really. I'd tell you the chapters to skip to, but I don't know what they'll be. Plus, if I have to do all this work, then somebody's gotta read it!

Not to mention... I don't get paid for this. See, money's not needed in Heaven. But, dedication is.

Making my own dedication in critical condition and on life support in this pro-bono work of recounting the tale of The End, which has been Our People's Beginning. Where do I start with this unprecedented testimonial? No other Keeper ushered in Heaven. It was all Pre-Heaven before, which was...

Hell.

No other Keeper had to retell this transition so it can be understood by those still in their own Pre-Heaven, who'd never imagine such a change remotely possible. Heck, none of the previous Librarian Keepers themselves knew We'd eventually win! Completely understandable considering the history we're all acquainted with. Even if you live in another reality, Hell's always the same – a seemingly endless yadda, yadda, yadda stream of oppression, with no hint there's a rhyme or reason. That there's a plan. But, don't fret –there is.

Then there's that kicker that my mistakes are as integral in the outcome as are my triumphs. My self-reflections and concerns are inextricably meshed with the accurate whole picture, because accident or not? The Beginning happened faster due to woefully unprepared me.

Alright. To some more facts. With this authority I fell into? I have the solemn honor, the unavoidable duty to collect every authentic piece of knowledge that will continue to contain the evil from which We, the Original People, We the Black, the Brown, the Red and the Yellow, were only recently delivered from enduring any further. I must keep that evil within the boundaries of its self-imposed Hell, with IRREFUTABLE FACTS made IMPERVIOUS through WISDOM. I don't mean to shout, but this era, being the end of Our 6,000 year sojourn from a state of unconsciousness to Far Planning Deities, requires respect for the enormity of what We've accomplished, and sympathy for those who are still struggling in their own dimensions with what they may believe is hopeless. That was Us, once, too. And that may be you, still.

But back to me, huh? Lest my fumbling prove that this will be yet another agonizing torture device, called a 'book'. I assure you, if you still reside in the more limited lower 3 dimensions, you have never met a librarian of the like that can challenge my office, unless you've met me or one of my predecessors. That's possible as we do get around and around and around.

And around.

There's an awful lot of dimensions out there, twisting about each other the more of them you discover. I can't explain the dynamics since this is history. The science I leave to The Alpha and The Omega, or to the Science Keeper; who, unlike me, has a long and detailed line of books I highly recommend – although your own dimension may keep you from considering that knowledge relevant, but they, nevertheless, detail 'The Plan', atom by atom...

My own regular non-periodic table duties are decidedly not those of your typical pedantic recluse, stalking bookcases in some suffocated library, whose manner and voice have become dustier than the volumes he maintains. And not to malign those dedicated professionals – mind you. However, I'm certain not many could lay claim to the skirmishes I've been through on behalf of a collecting so vital it's saved Us from extinction and the Earth from obliteration. For not only is it the solemn duty of the Keepers to gather a record of all truths and all lies, no matter who is responsible for the birth of either, but, I doubt any common librarian, including all the other prepared Keepers, have been tossed into spiraling vortexes to be jettisoned out onto planets ruled by metal incinerating gases. Yes. A definite lack of formal training, there, I confess, and probably youthful bravado, but? Whatever the cause, I'm pretty certain I'm the only one who's been shot and left for dead 3 separate times, stoned just once, poisoned by a hundred vipers after being tossed into a pit of the same; and none but me has had both arms, legs and only a merciful one time, had their tongue ripped out, along with the rest of my various and painful to lose parts getting hacked at on too many occasions to want to recall. On the job training some would say. Others? On the fool training. Most accurately, it's been a hands on (and hands chopped off) detailed education.

OH! By the way. YES! Losing body parts is EXCRUCIATINGLY PAINFUL. Not to mention the near burnings (I managed to escape those just in time, as I wouldn't want to know what it feels like to have my eyeballs set aflame) and that pitiless hanging... Whew. The more I think of it all, the more I remember. Took me decades to get the swing of this job, giving you a humble appreciation for the gentle things in life, like this delicious cup of tea. (I sip, still smiling, though my wife has left the room).

Indeed. Indeed. And all that BEFORE I became a full god.

Don't mistake me, now. What I'm about to share, merely the beginning of my duties, is not bereft of that which makes life a splendor worth cherishing. Don't feel sorry for me because what you may have never been told is that gods are Fully Hue-man, with all the emotions, thoughts, highs and lows that anyone has. We merely can understand the complete picture the more of the picture we hold in our range of vision, because in all situations, We defend hope. Thus, despite the danger, despite having no choice but to perform my responsibilities, this duty has perks and peaks beyond description. Actually, I have to admit – I've thoroughly enjoyed most of this profession that fell on me, even if accidentally. There are truths to be found in the depth of danger you could never conceive until you get there. Plus, no one could help but rejoice at the rising of a twin star sun on a most agreeable, if not this one, planet, swirling about the horizon in other dimensional panorama like a sky wide liquid kaleidoscope. Even if the level of methane gas in the atmosphere finally made me drop dead from asphyxiation. Because of this duty, I've born a hushed by awe witness to the proof of Allah's Perfection.

Therefore, I greet you, reader, with the words of Peace in Paradise in the Arabic language, 'Asalam Alaikum!' May every Gift due you be yours and swiftly, as they are yours but to claim should you be currently suffocated not by the air you breathe, but by tyranny that suffocates your soul, and should you be convinced, as We were, nothing will ever change. There is a plan by a Man with a vision of everything.

Call me Brother Amen. No challenge to The Almighty intended, given my references to Allah, as only HE knows everything. If I knew everything, this book would be done, and it'd be called, 'Allah's Final Word'.

Feel free to use the name for the Original Creator you prefer as many among Us still have varying names for Our Original Maker, which may be surprising;

but gods, as I said, are as complexly different from one another as mortal you are from your fellow mortals! We've simply learned how to walk as one being, without the useless bickering over nothing (I mean, truly, what was all that fighting from Pre-Heaven about when the choice was simply good or evil?) We've mastered everyday civilization, together, learning to run faster than the speed of light as a unit, differences in tow, and with ease.

Kinda.

We don't actually run faster than the speed of light. I was speaking metaphorically. Which reminds me to add...We're not perfect, you know – or have you read my book?...

This a regular People's History of Black Us, who became universal friends. That's it in a nutshell. We're common folks who learned how to do better, and I'm sure you'll remain present to discover the why and how, so mayhaps you can copy it – and? All Praise Due to Allah, exceed Us. Gods don't mind their betters. It's a 'God Thang' and one day, you'll understand, 'cause that's the plan for you, too.

In my 97 year career, my duties are mostly pleasant – researching the mountain range of inventions Our People have created – accomplishments which were never documented; or I witness how completely We love, despite Our enemy's obsession with portraying Us as brutish. I'm not a Peeping Tom, but I study the family trees of Our entire Greater Family. It's Our nature, historically, to share with one another, no matter the oppression heaped upon Us. Which is another amazing reality of this job that keeps me going, though, I hafta repeat – I didn't start this with a desire to do it as a profession. I didn't know it was a profession, never having heard of such a strange vocation. I've always loved reading, and reading history perhaps the most – but, I did love science fiction, too. I just never imagined I'd *be* science fiction-history – making the books I'd read look like beginner readers for 4yr olds. On career day, long ago in what We all took for a normal school, the vocation I am now bound to uphold, didn't roll off the tongue after being asked, "What do you want to be, young man?"

I wouldn't have ever answered, "Let's see? Lawyer, doctor, fireman, bus driver? Nah! I wanna be a continuously dismembered Librarian Keeper!"

"Excuse me, Tyree?" my teacher would have said, using the name I was called then. Having interrupted his resolve to endure boredom by having another day he'd teach without teaching, he probably would have testily replied, "This is your future, child, not a comedy show, unless doing stand-up is your answer!"

Ah! Like all adults, and me, now, with millions of lifetimes of knowledge condensed into one mind, if I could have known then what lay ahead for me, ahead for everyone, I wonder? Would I have done things differently? Would I have still ushered in 'The End' if I'd known it would then become so much tedious paperwork, afterwards? Who knew Heaven would have paperwork and that this paperwork would mean sharing imperfect me in a history that will last the centuries, into my descendants' lives beyond? That's a long time to carry the weight of being embarrassed about yourself, your dad or by then – your great, great, great to the power of forever – grandfather...

Chapter 1

It usually begins with words, and these words began with:

"You wait till we get outside, punk, 'cause I'mma kick your..."

They rolled off my tongue like I was speaking them under water. An underwater waking dream, and I was sure that 'punk' bit might have been enough unneeded pressure to keep me submerged a minute too long. But out it was tossed, along with everything else I'd said before - little air bubbles popping out my mouth; only these sank, resting heavily upon me, Modern Black Boy, Tyree Jackson, European year, 2012AD.

I suppressed the urge to flinch, anticipating a swift blow to my face for daring to call such a very large, (not to mention) older, equally modern Black Boy - and probably a lot better at fighting - for daring to call him, a 'punk'. It was as if it wasn't me doing the speaking, although I could clearly feel it was my lips doing the moving. That was that underwater feeling, as if I was sloshing with the tow, my muscles responding a moment after my attempt to move them. Yup. My brain sent the command, and my lips, what felt like 5 seconds of delay later, obeyed, remotely performing the task I demanded of them, without wavering once the signal was finally received.

They just didn't like the sensation of drowning, nonetheless of being forced to lie.

But, no matter how deeply submerged I had become in a decision I wished I could take back, at that moment, leaving my history classroom, buffeted within a crowd of "Ooooooo"ing and Ahhhhhh"ing students, I threw the 'punk' tsunami at my opponent, determined - not allowing my lips or any other part of my body to reveal what I actually felt - that I, modern or ancient, but oh so new Black Boy in this inner-city Black Boys and even DANGED tough Black Girls public school, I had picked a battle with one of the biggest, scariest boys in the class, hoping it would help me to survive within the depths of what the world considered the most frightening place on Earth.

A Black inner city neighborhood.

Why, I could scarcely believe how convincing I sounded and appeared, with a calm, assured saunter, crowd surrounding both me and my target, out into the end of the day hallway. Despite my carefully masked feeling of terror, I'm sure I appeared a seasoned, battle ready brute. In hindsight, I think, 'Didn't we all, despite what lay beneath, just because?'

What had I been thinking?! Here was this boy I'd only seen for the first time, just 3 days before; and now my success or failure in Public School 47, Newark, New Jersey, depended on an all or nothing throw-down that I'd instigated myself. I was brand new to the detailed day to day of that city, and, prior to my move there, had only come to Newark to visit my grandmother during the holidays, and never during the long summer vacations. That would have been too much time spent with 'bad influences' (as my parents insinuated but were too polite to say point blank).

I was sorely missing my friends – way, way, back in serene upper middle class Black Atlanta (with plenty of rich Black folks thrown in here and there throughout the community). Friends had warned me, "In the hood? They shoot babies for lookin' at you the wrong way..." That un-coincidentally coincided with, 2 months before this day I'm recalling – before I'd ever heard of this school, or this boy, (what was his name?) – that's when I knew what must be done to survive. Or so I had desperately concluded.

Humbly, I add? I wasn't a bully. Never. As I've said I was a considerate card carrying book lover, which the tone of my writing can't hide, although - I realize this history might have a greater appeal if written in a simpler style. I'm constantly reading other people's writing so I'm more than acquainted with the differences between a ten page book report, an encyclopedia and a magnificent novel, but? Well, you, reader, will come to understand as I said, my assorted imperfections, 'cause I'm beginning to think? I should start by deleting this paragraph... In the meantime I ask your indulgence as I have no time for editing. Here comes 400 pages, mistakes and all. To heck with my developing a consistent 'style', as long as it makes some kinda sense, so:

I may have never finished formal schooling, but back then I'd always scored amongst the best in my class – and that class had been in the best of schools. Plus my upbringing made me comfortable with myself, meaning? I was a bookworm, but I was in no way a nerd, any more than I was a bully. I wasn't boastful about knowing a lot and even confessing that I did know a lot in this personal history isn't easy. It's just true. Or why would I have already confessed one of my first glaring childhood imperfections? Making rotten choices, like picking a fight...

I also had a cozy kind of face that was enough on the side of not ugly and far enough from the nosebleed side of too handsome, keeping me usually out of 'Dang, you ugly' insults, or earning anybody's 'He's so fine' envy. I didn't fully notice it until later, but the majority of people felt comfortable with me, and I, son of loving parents, felt comfortable with the majority of people. I would have done quite well in any school, as I'd had in the one I'd only just reluctantly (very reluctantly) left. Despite the fact it had been a private, top achieving 'Institution for the Future Black Leaders of the World' – it was still populated with boys and girls, who are universally ravenous for fun. Looking like a nerd, (though technically I was) – that wasn't an issue for me in this new school as nerd-ism wasn't part of my family's visible DNA. We made 'smart' look as normal as having a nose and mouth.

My problem, which had brought about this sink or swim remedy, was that all those books had had a permanent effect on my academic level that couldn't be hidden, not completely. See, whereas, according to my age then, I should have been in the 7th grade, my curiosity had satisfied this cat and might have killed it, by placing me a full 3 grade levels above where my 12 years of life would have ordinarily gotten me. But after much begging and pleading with my mom to please, "Good LORD!!" don't put me in a class with such GIGANTIC children – my begging skills had landed me right there in the 9th grade, rather than the 10th, only TWO WHOLE levels above my age range.

Thus, now? Nerd or not, coke bottle glasses couldn't have announced my 'weirdness' any more than if I'd worn a sandwich sign that read, "Apply Boot to Poindexter's Rear End, HERE." My problem was spatial – me being, obviously, a whole lot shorter than the average height of the students that would now, still LOOM above me, even if they were only 2 years older.

Side note: No, I didn't wear glasses, though nobody who did then would need them, now. Here. In Heaven.

Side question: Why do parents so soon, even Us, gods, why do they forget what life as a child is like, where 2 years of difference between children seems the same distance as what's between a pebble on the moon and a cup of molten magma from inside the center of the Earth?

The reality of my family's move, during these, undoubtedly not-yet-a-deity days, had sunk in and stuck like a hypodermic needle the minute our impending destination and new schools had been unexpectedly revealed by my mom. Immediately, peaceful me desperately embraced the new warfare ready me, complete with battle strategy, which I'd perfected watching Youtube videos on "How to Fight'. Thus when the moving trucks pulled up to haul away the evidence of my former life – in that upper middle class suburb, distinctly called, Sandstone Hills in Atlanta, Georgia, I had pre-decided, in this new school? I would have to pre-pick a fight.

Using all my book enhanced ability to think beyond my age, and at that pre-fall into the void time (more on that later, I promise), I realized execution called for nothing less than stealth, making it easy to be covert when you're not just smart, but terrified to boot. From the day I'd arrived in that school, in mid April, with its dim ancient brown bricks on the outside, impervious white tile within, incognito, I had begun watching the crowds of students, checking out the probability of engaging this one, whilst mulling over the damage that that one might cause. It was an assortment of 'too easy', 'too goofy', and/or 'too tremendous', all mixed up with my own undersized proportions that made nearly everyone mostly 'too *tremendous*'! I could have leisurely extended the sizing up for months longer, happily, as I didn't really want to go through with it. But, as this wasn't my mom's fresh baked chocolate, chocolate chip cake that you savor – securing my own self protection was more like needing to breathe than lingering over dessert. This dilemma called for caution, but the caution demanded action.

Why, I had already gotten into a 'This is my seat' stare down in homeroom class, that first day, with some snarl-eyed fellow students, and one of the many tough-eyed girls. I had snarled appropriately back – or should I say, 'glowered' coolly, keeping my ground, and the situation had ebbed away into nothing. Okay, I did change my desk, so, I knew, eventually, someone would challenge my ferocious charade; and though my dad had taught me to fight... um... kinda... um...

...well? I wish he'd videotaped those couple times, as he'd taught me whenever he hadn't been working, which as the years had worn on, had become almost all the time – up to those last months, during his long unemployment and deep frustration...

On top of that, I'd never been in the middle of actually having had to use those dubious skills. Someplace where (I was certain) others would've been practicing their skills regularly.

Or so I'd assumed that these children would be darn near professional class boxers, 'cause they were Black, remember? Nobody snarled, glowered, and/or backed it all up with beat downs better than them.

Right?

I'd have never thought I'd have been without my dad for one on one advice, and support, even if sporadically. Yet, that new reality, was mine. Although my mom was okay, or used to be okay to talk with? What I faced, during that point in my life, was not in her tea and cream realm of expertise. This was man stuff, and from then and on, all the advice I would get from the most important man in my life was whatever memory I could hold onto fiercely. There wasn't any busy schedule to interfere, yet? No telephone call, no email could traverse my father's then latest, and final realm. No one returned for even a court mandated visit from his new permanent address, even if he wanted to...

So, with head and heart treading water, confidence sinking slowly, I had settled on this tall, yet not too tall, strong, but not bulging-ly strong, deep, deep black, Black Boy. His darkness made his somewhat smallish physique more imposing, but for a reason to which I was oblivious. If you had have asked me back then, I would have sworn I hadn't chosen him because his deep hue was extra intimidating. I'd merely had a sense something about him was believably striking enough to fit in well with my aim...? Aim? Nah! My desperate PRAYER of seeming hog wild enough in a fight with him that I'd look fearless to the inevitable crowd that would gather (that was gathering), everyone cheeringly convinced, (forever, I hoped) of the danger of messing with "That crazy boy, Tyree."

I had precisely observed, over the previous days, this boy... what was his name? Amazing, at the moment, I barely remembered my own amidst the rumble of the crowd, egging us combatants on, above the riot of slamming lockers and my own louder colliding emotions within.

Howard! Yes! His name was Howard. I had noticed that Howard had no accompanying posse, despite being convincingly imposing. As the other children would wander into rotating classes, tossing noise with them as easily as they tossed their books upon their desks, my pre-designated target rolled in, but disconnected from the conversations, sitting down usually near the middle of the class. I saw he moved calmly, with no hesitation that might show a nervous nature, and this would work in my favor. It wouldn't look like I had

21

picked on a loser, making me seem like a chump. But most importantly, on top of needing someone tough looking, with whom I could have the fight of my life, utilizing every ounce of strength, every offensive, defensive tactic I could remember, including using them all at once in an insane flurry to save my life? I most of all needed someone who wouldn't have good buddies who'd startle me with unexpected kicks and punches that sealed my fate as carrion for easy picking by everybody else for the rest of my P.S. 47 days.

So, if I could, with calculation, endure just one fight, then the other boys, and those unique girls, might leave me the heck

A
L
O
N
E!

Being older now, which on this day, I would have been delighted to know I would become, why, I realize even clueless twelve year old me knew I didn't hate Howard. In the still of my, despite all that reading – in the still of my young mind that hadn't connected yet with the right words for my feelings, I wondered about this boy, walking the hallways, alone like myself, and whose Blackness was as silent its owner. A blackness so complete it was a question both disquieting and intriguing. A demand that felt like the answer at the same time. I knew before I could explain – in another world, a less brutal one, I and this Howard might have become the best of friends.

No gay, though. Gods don't go there because Our Creator commands it for easy to understand reasons if you are a god; so, we're hyper sensitive to its wrongness. I could explain further, but that's for another book. Suffice to say, if we would be nice to the thong sporting Sister or Brother running down the street, we'd feel no need to be mean to those way, way off The Straight Path.

Settling on Howard wasn't personal. It was frightened. A rational frightened calculation, as the parts that were rational in me didn't hate him. It was finally, at the end of every consideration, my survival that came out first. Being 'friendly' had to move to the side. One day, sooner than I could have known, my demanding realities would flip inside out, making the impossible the commonplace, the complex, the simple. It was going to be one heck of an 'Uh-duh' moment, however for right then? Who knew what lay ahead? It was me protecting my future that day in the history class, and I was my one and only best friend.

When the final class of that third day began, before Mrs. Finn had arrived to teach, I took my seat right behind Howard. The day before, when I'd decided on picking my fight with him, I'd changed my seat from the very last row (the definitive 'non-nerd' row), several in back of his, complaining that I couldn't quite see the blackboard. I had squinted convincingly, hiding my 20/20 vision. Mrs. Finn, who was dryly explaining the origin of democracy in Athens, Greece, focused the crux of her attention on the sudden appearance of a late student entering the class. She waved me forward with a distracted yes, as she pointed annoyingly at a pile of tardy slips on her desk for the late student's notice.

Sitting in my new spot, I knew this was close to my last chance to get some kind of fight between myself and Howard going before it got to the start of the weekend. It was Thursday and the rest of the morning and early afternoon had gone by without an opportunity to set off anything believable. I'd seen him around, but he'd never been conveniently near, and even if he had been – I couldn't just deck the guy. It had to appear as if he was annoying me, not that I was actually 'Crazy Tyree' due to some mental instability, apparent 'cause I'd attacked somebody from well across a room for 'no good reason'. I needed a verbal jump-off, and now this chance, before Mrs. Finn arrived, might evaporate with no argument begun. I couldn't let that happen as that day's homeroom close call had been augmented with further narrowed glares from random boys, throughout the day, confirming my need to prove myself good 'insane' and quickly. Yes, it was only Thursday, but I couldn't risk waiting any longer to pick someone if I became picked instead. I had to find an excuse, not too dumb, not to awkward, but what?

I gazed out the multiple lumpy coats of beige paint slathered windows, which had been so distrusted on their outside, they had been prevented from escape with heavy prison-like metal grates, through which one could see no comforting future for the windows or the viewer as they and I looked hopelessly out at the no higher than 3 stories soot gray and soot brick houses of outer Newark, drowning in concrete and lazy architectural design. I, used to the reassurance of greenery, felt duteously hopeless, turning my attention, instead, to the boy before me, who was no more encouraging than the view; no more encouraging than my current dilemma.

Howard was absentmindedly tap, tapping on his desk with his pencil, lightly and rhythmically, playing the drumbeat to some song only heard in his own head, as I hurriedly wondered, 'What can I say to piss this guy off and look kinda respectable? Insult his sneakers?'

Nah. His sneakers were a brand new high top mildly famous basketball player endorsed brand. They were nicer than mine.

Tap.

"Call him stupid?"

For no reason? Uh, that sounded... stupid.

Tap.
Dangnamit! I couldn't concentrate. Couldn't focus with that annoying tapping...

tapping...

Tapping!!

That was exactly what I needed!

"Yo! Mongoloid!" Way little me blew out my first air bubble, my eyes fixed into slits, channeling my anger at my true problems to sound like a convincing anger with him, "If you don't cut that racket out, I'm gonna punch your lights out!"

Now, reader, understand that my actual language was a might cruder than this, but as your parents, teachers and that wonderful librarian (no insult intended to you, librarian, at the beginning of my chronicle... uh, oh – shouldn't have reminded you, huh?) – but as that wonderful, fabulous librarian who recommended this book sooooo kindly to you would have never let you near it, history or not, if I wrote a verbatim accounting of my expertise with profanity – I won't begin to tell the exact filth that spewed out my mouth that moment, but those air bubbles sank from the dirt of it. Not that cursing was natural for me or anybody in my family, but with the streets full of 'experts', both in Sandstone and Newark and everywhere else, those 7 words were a familiar second language to me, better known than the French I'd taken at Medgar Evers, which I'd aced. I only used one cuss word that day. That moment. Pick the one you prefer.

After my last bubble popped out of my mouth, the mumbling around us had lowered to a couple hushed, "Whoa, did you hear that?"

Howard, who had been staring ahead at the blackboard, then turned around, real slow, and focused on the source of this assault. He frowned, and his face took on an angry expression. He seemed quite at ease with anger.

"Whatchu say?" he demanded, lingering for a leisurely visit with the word 'say'.

I suddenly had this uncomfortable, instantaneous suspicion that maybe I had not picked such an 'easy mark'. But, gulp? It was a might too late for backing out.

"I said," and performed my own slow motion emphasis, "cut the racket. What? You deaf AND stupid?" 'Oh, that was a good one to call him stupid', I thought, congratulating myself, despite drowning in fear.

The quiet in the room thickened to a sludge, with only low groans of amazement, giggles of approval, and the whoosh of various sized butts (mostly fat in those days) sliding about face on chairs to get a better view of the sudden entertainment in the middle of the class.

I took the upper hand by adding, "You got a problem with that, then I think a butt kickin'll teach you some respect!" I had wanted to say 'manners' but figured that wouldn't have sounded 'authentically tough guy-ish'. I didn't really know. 'Did tough guys use a word like 'manners'?' Funny how at an improbable moment like that, silly stray thoughts enter your mind.

Before an outraged Howard could respond to whatever I'd said, Mrs. Finn's nasaled voice boomed into the room as she entered and shut the door behind.

"Good Afternoon, class! Shall we begin on the right foot, today?!"

All the students, with a couple moans of disappointment, and the two combatants, stonefaced, turned forwards. For that 'hopefully' newly born 'Crazy Tyree', the whole, woefully short lesson, (were there ever such speedy minutes that flipped by, more like seconds for me, who, although I may not want to write a history book, I adore learning history just a little less than I love eating my mom's aforementioned chocolate, chocolate chip cake) – I could hear my heart racing in near rhythmic synchronization to the clock's ticking.

Still? Too much time was zooming by to not imagine the blows coming my way once the bell rang, in just 2 minutes! I could feel the impending pain as my ears swore they already heard a series of crunching sounds, to which my eyes added their imagined spritzes of red squirting from my pummeled, used to be

25

kind of nice face. I began to dread that the crowd I had hoped might cheer me on, would very soon be celebrating the mercilessness of Howard's revenge all over an IDIOTIC Tyree who had dared to use him to carry out some foolish, foolish

FOOLISH

and horribly mistaken plan.

What the heck had I been thinking?!

It's not easy to feel confident about a plan if you can't count on the other person's cooperation, 'cause you never went over the details with him. It's funny afterwards how you never remember what true fear is like. But, I remember that fear, though. For me, my blood felt like molten lead sloshing inside dry veins, pooling red hot at my feet. I would have put good money on a bet that getting hit by a train would have been easier, because at least it'd have been over quicker, without any potential humiliation.

I consoled myself, knowing this one stomping, as long as I wasn't the stompee, was all I needed, or I could face a long line of those who were undoubtedly tougher, stronger, and came with friends. Unfortunately, I'd made up my mind weeks ago. At that point I was merely along for the ride, or as it really felt – the drowning.

The end of the day bell mechanically trilled, longer and louder than it had seemed to yesterday. I sprang up like Ali and back into the game I'd started and would finish seamlessly. I turned on Howard, who had also stood up promptly from his seat, a full head taller than me. That's when I added, quickly as we made our way out of the room in a tight circle of the curious, "You wait till we get outside, cause I'm gonna kick your butt!" That sounded like what a bully would say. Right? I had no idea. I wanted to sink in my molten ocean of fear, hide under the table and pray nobody would find me.

"Well," Howard growled, "we'll see about that! The only butt kickin' ", he said looking down on me, "will be yours at the end of my foot!"

'Ooo. Good one,' I thought, '*He sounds like he knows what he's talking about...*

...gulp.'

26

Out loud I was all, "Ha! Meet me in the courtyard in 10 minutes, and eat my fist, PUNK!"

For good effect, amid the hoopla, I shoved my way past Howard, who shoved right back. We stopped and glared at one another while someone pushed us closer together, goading us on with the whispered cry, "Fight! Fight! Fight!"

From inside, obviously noticing the stalled crowd, Mrs. Finn called out, "What's the hold-up? Now, move on guys! No congregating in the hall!"

"Hey," said a young chubby boy, "Wait for outside! Don't get the teachers in on it!"

For, in the crowded jostling, and cajoling of nearly teenaged youth, which had reached a rippling pitch of contagion when wind of an upcoming battle spilled into all available ears that were glued close enough to another person's telling lips, a couple of teachers stepped into the traffic jam with warnings of coming detentions if students didn't break it up and go home.

Howard and I separated, looking cool-ly mean at each other, and I was accompanied to my locker by a couple of obvious fight lovers, who apparently didn't want the adrenalin rush to stop too soon. Because of their company, they brought me a bit of relief from my pounding terror, which in that crowd had gotten quite the life of its own. Howard disappeared down the hall and around the corner to where I guessed his own locker probably stood. He had no hangers on and with my own's first comments, I figured out why. These guys thought they were getting a front row seat to a future car wreck and it would be happening to somebody else's car – with me the lone driver and the only passenger.

"Yo, dude! You's crazy! Whaz your name?" The young chubby boy, wearing an elaborate Boca Raton t-shirt, and the most enthusiastic grin of all, addressed me while speaking fluently with his hands.

"Tyree." I said it with contrived anger, maintaining what I considered a steady, but appropriately seething expression. Though I seemed to move with an eagerness to get going, I rifled elaborately amongst my books for items that I did not seem to find.

"Yeah? I'm Reggie! Yo, ain't you scared? You're just a little dude and that guy looks like he's gonna kill you!"

27

Several murmurs of agreement were voiced by four other boys who'd remained with me to soak in more of the upcoming confrontation. Or slaughter. Books and homework, for the moment, were forgotten.

"Scared?!" Crazy Tyree cried indignantly at the pathetic suggestion. "Size don't mean nuthin'! That punk'll be cryin' for his great, great grandmommy when I get through with him! I don't take kindly to nobody messin' with me!"

"Whoa!" The collective sharing of approval went round in nods and looks between themselves. Yup. This boy was stark raving mad.

"Well, we'll meet you out back!" said Reggie, and with the others, headed off to their lockers.

I was left alone for yet another one of the shortest moments I had ever known. No clock keeping time; just my trembling heart.

There was a slowly thinning crowd buzzing about the corridor. Most of the remaining students were indifferent to my presence, having not heard about the fight, and or not caring. Even if they did know or care, they could have had better private concerns than wondering if this was some new boy's final moments alive. After all, I thought, didn't kids carry guns in these schools? Or hide them outdoors... close to the courtyard? That after all was what those cold white plastic metal detecting sentinels warned me about, each time I saw them at the very entrance into the school. This was a dangerous place or why spend so much money to put them there? I watched the students file beyond them, up at the end of the hall, chatting amongst themselves, while the most doughy faced, non-threatening armed policemen, who were oblivious to the children they absentmindedly observed walking without protest through the two detectors – while the cops chatted about some reality TV show my mom would never have let me watch, nor would she have watched herself.

The detectors guaranteed no firearms inside a building of children, or at least that's what I understood. Still, the sight confirmed for me how utterly far I'd fallen. My old school didn't have those. This day, I was in a place the world despised and for what I suspected had to be a good reason. I mean, I should know as my other school was all Black, too, but it wasn't like this one. Medgars Evers Prep was privately owned, and supported with grants from the U.S. government for being such an excellent educational institution.

I had a frozen moment, standing there immobile for a bit, like I wasn't there at all. And I knew, if I never came back, no one would have missed me.

28

But, finally dragging dutifully along, I forced myself to get on with the goal of saving my butt, backpack slung sloppily on one shoulder, making my leaden footed way, on a late afternoon, to the exit, greeted by a warm, cloudless blue sky, walking beyond the school building, past the neglected shrubbery to the courtyard, that continued on to the back parking lot.

By the time I'd gotten on that side of the school, I had become so numb with swirling emotions, that forget just drowning – I had already inhaled a lung full of water and was now floating upon the suffocating ocean like I was watching myself from outside my body. Yet, that's when another growing emotion struck me, seeing my small brown self stride across the yard despite everything. I could scarcely believe it, but coming up to that gathering of people in the basketball court, rising from the exhausted tumult of my feelings, I sensed an almost hidden pride in this determined boy who answered to my name. I was Tyree, Brave Manchild, brave enough to face his own beat down.

The expectant students, about 15, were assembled in a random broken circle at the end of the small court, with two fairly rusted hoops on either side. The teachers had quickly abandoned the school to get into their cars and head home to more familiar, less infamous territory. They'd no idea a group of children they expected nothing from would, that day, hasten the prophesied turning of the tail into the head, the head into the tail, all begun by my insane desperation and thorough ignorance of self. The teachers scrambled, politely enough, while the few bolder ones, along with the custodial staff who were paid more than the educators, and the couple of cops, remained inside the building, concentrating their attentions elsewhere. They weren't paid to actually care. No salary could pay for that much pretending. You had to be trapped and desperate, like me, to hang around.

I took a frozen moment to scan the faces still so new to me. They nodded eagerly and some came over to slap me jovially on the back, as if they knew me; yet I suspected they more wanted to discourage me from backing out of their soon to begin entertainment.

There was a gleeful goading all around, with a few talking about other concerns.

Maintaining my bully act, I punched my fist into my hand, several times, seemingly furious and eager. I could only hope it looked believable.

"Man! When he gets here," I said, for Howard wasn't there yet, "he's got some serious butt whooping coming his way!"

"Why you so mad at him?" asked one particular dark mocha girl, with a rich echoing voice, all without an actual echo. You had to hear it in real time to understand, and she added, "Whad he do so wrong to you?"

Nyisha. I knew her name as I had noticed her, in my homeroom and some of my classes. Also at the lunchroom table, my very first day, she had made quite the impression, talking and laughing easily and effortlessly with her friends. There was something extra about her. She wasn't outstandingly pretty, but she had a uniquely serious face blanketed in satin skin that made me want to listen. It was her almond shaped eyes, rimmed with a near carpet of lashes that guaranteed my attention. One in a million eyes that radiated a strong no nonsense kindness, and gave anyone the sense that though Nyisha could be, she didn't have to be one of the rugged girls. She didn't have to be because her presence was impressive enough. So?

It was that indefinable balance that caught my curiosity.

However, I didn't know her. Best to figure, even the sweetest could be carrying an explosion of "In Yo Face, Boy!" There wasn't anyone in this school I felt I could take lightly.

"He pissed me off! Tha's what!" I responded, immediately regretting that my first exchange with her was one of an angry charade. I wanted her to like me for me. The Sandstone Hills me I used to be.

"Oh!" she said, with cool sarcasm, tilting her head to the side, turning back to her girlfriends.

Reggie, arrived with back pack nearly dragging on the ground, belly bouncing slightly more than the folds of his green t-shirt as he came up to the crowd, and retorted in defense of his entertainment, "Yeah, Nyisha! Man's got a right to teach a brother to show some respect!"

'Reggie to the rescue,' I thought, but rescue to what?

"Yeah!" seconded several boys who equally didn't want their live video game getting switched from Friday Night Fights to the Cinderella Channel.

"I ain't no punk!" I added for effect.

"I ain't call you no punk!" Nyisha stated flatly. "Just everybody be fightin' like there ain't nothin' better to do with their time. It's stoopid!"

"He's not here to fight no girl, girl!" Reggie, scrunched his face to heighten the effect of his disdain and won instant affirmation from the other boys, with grimaced lip snaps from the girls in defense, but no further verbal challenge.

'*He's good at that,*" I thought.

"Hmpf!" the afro-puffed Nyisha did blurt out, but adding no more, eased back into her clutch of female friends.

'*Whew!*' I internally exhaled, feeling a strange sensation of relief in the middle of muffled dread, mixed with that morsel of pride I intended to cling to till the bitter end. One fight a day was about all I could handle.

This universal posturing (unbeknownst by this name to even undercover egghead me or the gathered children) continued for a moment till the crowd became quiet with a growing....? A growing? Hmmm. What was that sensation? A growing? Ah!

Impatience.

Their tantalizing anticipation, not shared by me, but by my mannerisms, had begun to slowly seep out to a deflated disappointment, coated with a reluctance to let go of what was supposed to be live spectator excitement. Why, weren't they missing some favorite TV shows for what was supposed to be happening already?! I'm sure the thoughts that many had of mothers, older sisters, brothers, grandparents, and 'others' wondering why their walk home from school was taking so long, filled many a mind, if they were lucky to have somebody fret over their whereabouts, at all.

Now their impatience bubbled over, boiling, ready for some action, fast!

"What the?...." someone chimed, "Yo! Where's Howard?!"

I, still in exemplary acting form, said, "YEAH! Where is that li'l twerp?!"

Surprised faces and disbelieving comments caught fire around the circle for a full one half minute. Just as some considered leaving, risking missing out on the action, two girls came running round the building (of course there was a side exit, shod in heavy rusting chains, as the City of Newark could barely afford teachers, let alone 2 more cops and a whole 'nother metal detector for a side exit) – the girls came up to us, breathless and yelling,

"Hey!"

They gasped and dropped their bodies over to clasp their hands on their knees, while panting.

"Howard!" Breath. "He ran" another breath, "his butt home!"

"Whoa," said a great many, in their own individual styles as the credits rolled on this real reality show.

And just like that, Tyree Jackson, ME, Modern Alive Black Boy, felt the ocean of fear ebb instantly away, replaced by flowing blood, that told my body parts, they were safe once again, for the first time, I realized – in months.

=

There had been more pats on the back, faces widened with happy amazement that each had a whole new twist to share tomorrow, far more dramatic than a plain fight. Those happened regularly, but this? Where one amongst the student body had had the nerve to be forever painted as a chicken? A fight could take second place to that.

And everyone seemed to agree with a roar at Reggie's

"Man! That dude musta clucked his way home!'

My own leisurely long walk home, then, unlike the other solitary couple of days, was now accompanied by four of the boys, who had been in the courtyard, including Reggie. I strode boldly, as I was supposed to be a tough guy; my usual shyness I put at bay, except, I wasn't a braggart. I kept my body language mildly reserved since I didn't know any of these guys and didn't want to act like a jerk. Jerks came in bully size, too, and nobody liked them.

I did feel confident knowing I'd landed safely on my feet, even if by forfeit. I had acted my way out of being someone else's target practice, and if Howard ran home then surely that was the end of the story. If these had been my Sandstone Hill friends, I would have asked them to check me for whiskers, 'cause I must have been a cat who'd hit the ground from 20 stories up and walked away. But these boys weren't my far away friends who accepted me as a regular guy, rather than as a bruiser. I had to maintain my facade, which for the moment was fresh, exciting and hadn't cost much. Why, the relief of easy escape from what I had been dreading for so long, dulled my ache of homesickness. I was beaming. I was safe. I was victorious by default, yes, but most importantly I was in one un-pulverized piece for today, and more likely, for tomorrow and the next. That flood of fear had turned into a cool, splash.

We erased the blocks, with the guys eagerly asking me where I was from – "Atlanta."

"I got a cousin down there!"

Why I didn't have a southern accent – "Lots of folks in the south don't, either."

33

"Oh."

If I had any brothers and sisters – "Yeah, my older sister, Kyerah."

"Whoa, dude, that's it?! I got me 3 younger sisters, one a baby and my mom makes me look after them ALL!"

And, where I lived now – "On Carson and Garvey."

"Whew! That's rough."

The boys groaned in commiseration.

"Hey," said one, named James, a tall skinny boy, "isn't that the street with that weird haunted house with all that witch doctor voodoo mess out front? Ouff!"

That last word was a verbal release of air 'cause Reggie had jokingly elbowed the boy in the gut.

Reggie laughed, "Dude, what are you? Five?!"

Guffaws rolled out, like the money of rich men with all the time to spend it. But I couldn't help but notice, the laughter didn't seem entirely carefree. Nervous rich men is never a good sign.

"Yo, man!" belted Terrence, a tall, lean caramel boy, who, to enthusiastically face us, was practically walking backwards in his high tops, tongue pulled out 'cause there weren't any shoelaces to hold them in. Wanting to change the subject back to the fight, he gave commanding flips of his hand downward to gain my and the other boys' attention.

"I wish," he exhaled and spoke at the same time, "I couldda seeent that skirt wearin' Howard running home! I'd a paid a ticket to watch that!"

But the minds had moved on.

"Ah, boy", said Reggie, "you ain't got no money to pay for nuthin'! Can't even buy yo'self some shoelaces!"

I had noticed, in school, wearing no shoelaces seemed to be fashionable for a few, but not most. And no one in this group besides Terrence was sporting the 'look', so?

34

They all snickered at Reggie's lighthearted rebuff, while I just smiled. I didn't know a thing about Terrence enough to laugh at his expense.

"How you gonna say that, negro?!" he retorted, "when my sneakers alone cost mo' than your entire wardrobe?!"

More laughter.

"Ha!" shot back Maxwell, a boy taller than everyone, who added, "tha's cause yo family be living on rice and beans for months at a time, pretendin' they got some serious bank when they step out the do'!"

That fast round of laughs agreed Maxwell's joke had spiked it. James added, "And they's probably knock-offs, anyway!"

"Ah, no, they ain't!" Terrence protested, vigorously while pointing down at the more than clearly visible Jordan logo on the side, making him hop awkwardly along to keep up with the group.

"JORDAN'S??!!" they all mocked, not needing to say more. Even so uncool suburban kid me knew – nobody still wore Jordan's!

These laughs, they came and went as the blocks fell behind with our pace that showed no hurry. Then our group whittled down to 4 at Benstone Blvd, 3 at 234 Arbitron Pl., 2 at Sutfern Circle and finally to Reggie, who bid a "Yo, see ya tomorrow!" as he turned up an unknown block, which was missing the street sign at the top of the post. With the life preserver relief I had painlessly received from ending all the terror of the last couple months, and now between my victory and my entree into a new group of possible friends or good people to know, I had been fairly floating off the ground...

only to end flat, with my next step, that hit my block, Carson Avenue. The way back towards the school had been lined with moderately well kept, small homes. Plain, undecorated, and definitely not of the rich, nor the famous, but surprisingly tidy. It was only that garbage strewn about the gutters and lawns, as though the people who lived within deserved no better because they were Black – that was the only embarrassing aspect; since I knew the color of the neighborhood was not the reason for the refuse, as not only my old school, but my entire Sandstone Hill neighborhood had been just as Black. Sandstone, by sharp, sharp contrast, had been an unrelentingly clean showcase for the economically mobile Black classes. Thus, I doubted I'd be inviting the old gang for summer visits, to my new hometown. Actually, most of my old crew I

35

hadn't even bothered to tell the address of where I'd moved. I'd noticed, they in turn, hadn't asked.

Though, if I had lived on one of those tidy if peppered with discarded empty french fry boxes and crushed Coke cans Newark blocks, maybe my complete horror might have been kept at a tolerable level (which means no inner shudder every time I turned the corner onto Carson, visitors or not). Maybe. I might have even tried to sell my old best friends on paying a me a visit, as the city wasn't half as bad as the news reports made it seem. Plus, I could have impressed them with being an authentic tough guy. Sadly, Carson was a stone cold mostly unemployed step way down from even common, hardworking, still employed Black People's Newark, and its devastation came screechingly to life the minute the right side of the street came into view, where my new dilapidated residence sat, amidst its equally destitute brethren.

But, then? Across the road from my abode? Was that curiously all out of time and place gigantic house, whose mention had gotten a gust of air pushed out of James by an elbow.

It was an urban tale of two realities. The contrast of crushed dreams on the right, versus the left, where dreams, despite the threat, refused to go down for the count. Or at least that's the way I'd always thought of that 'haunted' house.

I liked and knew the owners of that place and thus understood it wasn't haunted in the least. Just very big. Very. And 'different'. Add another 'very' for a more accurate dimension. It was my neighbors', the Kattans, home, and it was their other side of Carson that had always made visiting my grandmother not too bad, and even quite the adventure, as the Kattans were family friends, who regularly invited us over for assorted gatherings.

Straight in front of the wreck of my current home, this sprawling dwelling, just off from the corner end of the block, its grandness, which was grander than even the homes I'd been familiar with, now served to remind me of how far my family had fallen when it was compared to (and I couldn't help but) – when compared to our current little hovel, shrinking back, so tiny within the row of the rest of the houses on my side, in the looming glare of the Kattan edifice's magnificence.

Did I call it a house a few lines back? This wasn't a house. This was a mansion, and I don't mean 'Mc'.

Its presence soothed me, since I'd no longer be traveling anywhere remotely plush and/or startling; but with James' hesitant inquiry, I wondered, should I be embarrassed about that place, too? I'd known it was said to be haunted, as my grandmother, longtime resident in the community had told me, and today James had confirmed the rumor lingered, but whether or not there were any ghosts there didn't bother me. It was now having nothing on this block worthy of others' admiration.

That bothered me plenty.

For starting on my side of what I'd always assumed was the sole sad half of these two realities, came that painful introductory sidewalk, buckling threateningly upward, with neglected cracks and fissures, all out of proportion to what a two legged creature could comfortably manage. As one stepped cautiously from angry slab to jagged outcropping, there stood a line of two family wooden row houses, set back from the sidewalk, on either side of my own. The first one was boarded up and abandoned, then came ours, about 7 occupied others after that, and then, a length of burnt out hovels, 4 ruined brackish frames deep, which ached to be torn down, until one reached the next group of droopingly occupied and un-incinerated dwellings, way down the block till you reached the other corner. Children and grown-ups relaxed upon the desperately unadorned porches, enjoying their unemployment, with benefits or without.

I sighed a breath, seasoned with pain as I opened the creaking gate, connected to a rusting Acme wire fence that surrounded all the houses, recalling my mom's reminder that,

"At least we're not homeless and it's not Detroit."

Between the gate and the front door, on the side of the concrete walkway, cringed an expanse of sparse, choking weeds that threatened to grow taller than me, maybe overnight. One could have assumed that each individual weed had triumphantly strangled any grass that had dared to grow here, with only hard red earth and a few mute clumps of dandelions to witness the crabgrass' rampaging crimes.

Dandelions. They weren't weeds to me.

They'd always been one of my favorite flowers, indomitably speckling even the most tended lawns of Sandstone. I'd admired that sort of determination, back then before I realized determination could meet its match. Yep. They had been my favorite.

37

All the houses down the row, including mine, were painted either yellowed white, or anemic green, smeared with streaks where rain water had cascaded over full gutters in its own determined rush to reclaim the tottering structures in the name of Planet Earth. Up my pathway and all the others, but mine seemed particularly neglected, were separate flights of crumbling brick steps. Then sat our porch, beneath an awning that intended, one day, to murder anyone unlucky enough to be standing underneath at its appointed hour of execution. There were a couple of rattan lawn chairs there, but since no one dared sit in one, given the looming threat, the rot claimed chairs looked to be the only victims on the porch's day of mayhem, that was surely on its way.

I know, today, despite its dejected specter, it wasn't the ramshackle of the house that really troubled me most of my new life on Carson. It was moreso the ramshackle my family had become, barely getting by without my dad. That was the complete tale, the contrast between, not just a not haunted, not a house mansion across the street, and my new barely better than a cardboard box residence; but, it was the contrast between the ignorant bliss I used to know and my new starkly cruel existence. It was this dilapidated wreck called my life that was told in a tale of two realities between 846 and 847. 'Cause compared to my former splendor in suburbia, compared to that former life with my in-house best friend I called 'dad', 846 was worse than a walk into a dump. It was the drop into Hell itself.

Funny. Getting rid of my fear of physical danger in school let me suddenly recall that the Devil remained in a two-story detail I couldn't scare off by calling it a 'punk'.

With the little I knew then, I'd have sworn Sandstone had been Heaven. It's beauty was woven into the muscle and blood of my heart, rolling with verdant Kentucky Bluegrass lawns straight to the curb, with no thought for a sidewalk, buckling or not. Ha! Funny how both Carson Ave and Sandstone did not encourage casual strolling, but for strikingly different reasons. My old house (which I refused to relinquish as mine, though the new owners would have insisted it wasn't, until I'd ripped open my chest to show them a beating replica of what they'd thought they'd bought) - my house had a sweep of color rippling blooms bordering the perimeter, meant to be seen in a passing vehicle, only, with wide and towering hedges that equally framed the carpet of green in mathematical artistry. You could cut your fingers on the edge of those hedges. And my old house wasn't plopped down in the middle of some war zone like an abandoned cabin lost children came upon in the woods before they were eaten. My real home had been in a neighborhood, a community that echoed

38

and shouted its bucolic promise of bliss from corner to corner, veranda to veranda. Whether it fulfilled that promise, or not, you were surely guaranteed to be reminded of its possibility.

That was before the car crash. Before, moving in next to my new row housed neighbors, one of which we shared a common outer wall with. Though one neighbor and her parcel of children next door was pleasantly noisy, the other middle aged couple had acquainted me with more variations on 7 little curse words than I'd have ever known I'd grow sick of hearing. They were among those profanity experts I'd mentioned; and they seemed more comfortable with angry shouts than any compliments I'd imagine the two might want to say to one another instead – since although we couldn't hear soft words through the wall, they couldn't have had much time to say them in between the constant stream of cussin' we did hear. Often, the couple would be outside sitting on their non-murderous porch, giving anyone within a 2 block range a completely free lesson on why marriage sucks. But most of the time they were indoors, giving us private tutoring through the wall. That thin sheet rock barrier had been such a money saving convenience for the construction company who'd built my Hell.

Before opening the door, I took a look across, as was my habit, to drink in the other house... excuse me... the MANSION on the other side of the street. It spanned the length of 4 or 5 row houses on my side, separated from my buckling sidewalk by a newly tarred stretch of roadway that glistened with light dappling asphalt. The Kattans had paid for that, themselves.

All that grandeur just a few steps away, yet an ocean between the two in difference...

Why, that structure was so striking, the very air that blew from one side of Carson to the other changed as it embraced its 4 storied Victorian Old World magnificence.

No, really. I'm not kidding. The air DID change.

It seemed to take its sweetened time to hover about the structure's 6 mill paneled gable rooftops that jutted up against the sky in a desperate grasp to save the air from the agony of returning to the less deserving surroundings. All outside its boundary was gray, heavy, but about that house, color and vibrancy remembered their meaning.

I had noticed the air's change about the house from as far back as I could

39

remember when my family came for our visits to stay with my grandmother. We always wound up visiting the Kattans, and inside or outside that mansion, life became brighter, cleaner, more sustaining and durable, as long as you didn't look back, where you'd instantly recall, you were still in Newark.

For me, the doctor's and his wife's home, meant to be a school, but the school had never been begun – it wasn't merely across the street. It sat in another country, in another promise, maybe greater than the whole town of Sandstone. I thought about what James had said and had wondered if it was the change that made some believe it was haunted. There were other factors I'll mention in another chapter, but for this second and that day, and as usual, I was enthralled with the transformation. It's not that it was dramatic or one could take a picture of it – which I had tried on numerous occasions and the photos confirmed it was an ordinary house, since in the pictures, the colors appeared the same as the colors around any building.

That still didn't expunge how a quiet part in your perception, like you see an image coming up from behind you before you can identify it – how colors swirled around that house, taking on an intensity they did nowhere else. I mean it w-a-s that subtle, like looking for the difference between tints on a dry sunny day and the same tints an hour after a rain. Green is still 'green', blue still 'blue', but the moisture made it richer and that house was a saturation of hue drenched intensity. That definitely spelled 'weird', which is easily translated by even grown-ups into 'haunted'.

But, for me, it'd always provided a calming certainty that anything was possible, ever since I could remember, looking at it across the street from my grandma's livingroom window. With the death of my grandpa, 9 years ago (whom I couldn't remember), my parents had begged her to move to Sandstone, but she'd refused to leave her collapsing structure of a rental apartment, no matter how my parents pleaded that we had plenty of room. She swore living near that house kept her arthritis at bay. When she went for trips longer than a week or two, her joints would start aching again without relief until she returned to her Carson Avenue. I didn't believe that one, myself, but she was grandma. Everybody left her claim kindly alone.

I would peer out at that mansion, sometimes with her, by myself or sometimes with mom, taking note of the colors as they blossomed over on that side of the street, which had no other house or structure on the whole block. I would attempt, in aimless childhood curiosity, to find the exact place where the colors became warmer, alive. Though, I could never pinpoint if it was a gradual change or dramatic, it seemed like both, sometimes. No matter where it started, I had no doubt, there was a change.

No one in my family took it remotely seriously, nor really discussed it. When I had mentioned it to my grandma, she'd nodded, told me briefly that her neighbors believed the house was haunted, smiled and then had started on about her arthritis. That got me quiet, fast, and I soon stopped asking her about it at all. Kyerah? Well, she was Kyerah – all jokes. Then my mom, more enthusiastic, would confirm, indeed, positive energy could affect whatever it touched through multi-dimensional transcendence. But when I asked her what that meant, she'd always told me I'd understand better when I was older (and boy, she wasn't kidding. I got to understand that and more, real quick). My dad, who I think refused to acknowledge the possibility at all, had laughed and patted my head, amusedly. He was a nuclear physicist, one of the few Black ones in the world. As a matter of a fact, before his death, he'd been appointed Chief Executive Engineer of Lochan, Marchlin, Ganderheist, the nuclear industrial giant. He was mathematically, scientifically so exacting (the 2 subjects which weren't my best – OKAY – they were my worst), so for him? Such phenomena had no place in a rational world. Only scientific verification and occasional boxing strategy did.

My mother had grown up living next door to that house. She met my father when she had left.

As for all the voodoo stuff that James had mentioned, yes. There were various masks covering this archetypical European style dwelling, aplenty. Strategically placed and flattering, the masks dotted the front visage with alternating plaster reliefs of warrior ferocity, encircled with precisely painted Kente motifs, which I knew to be writing from Ghana, because they'd been painted by my own mom, when she had been an aspiring teenaged artist. The Victorian intention submitted to the authority of the Afrikan additions handily, as there were too many – covering it at each joint and juncture – too many for the original design of the house to dominate the mansion's Afrikanized aura. The whole edifice had been crafted into something new and reinvigorating, to itself and the world lucky enough to find it and be open to the refreshment.

Dr. and Mrs. Kattan, deeply smooth skinned Black Afrikans, were from Senegal. They'd originally bought the house 45 years ago to open a school that, as I'd mentioned, had never gotten off the ground, for some unknown to me grownup reason. I, personally, could have confirmed to James, before the elbow, they weren't creepy or magical at all, but were typically predictable adults, doing ordinary dull grownup things, which the Kattans assured me I would, also, dutifully do at some time in the distant future.

They weren't kidding, but on I write...

41

However, that day, that afternoon, wrecked family or not? I did, again, believe a future would happen; whereas just an hour ago, it had seemed unlikely, no matter the now imperfect reminder across the street. Even if my own future lying before me, right then, seemed so much more difficult to achieve triumphantly, I knew it would happen. I knew that I was not only clever enough, I'd been brave enough that day of my pre-picked fight, and if the very air could, be cured somehow, in a way I didn't understand, despite my entire block being the shame of a city that itself seemed constructed of shame – if I could be the master of my destiny, choosing whether to be a punching bag or a victor, then maybe one day the pain of life without my father would be healed and good as new, too. Or as good as something I couldn't predict – like a boy who could have pounded me into the ground, fearfully running home, instead.

If only I could tell when that healing would begin, better than I could see the change in the air's color.

I opened the door to my own light dimmed home and entered the place that at least kept me from being homeless and was, supposedly, much better than living in Detroit, although? Detroit, I learned and will explain in another book if I get a chance, was nothing like the newspapers reported – anymore than Newark   was,   or?

Anymore than they reported about how awful all of Black Us were supposed to be...

When I'd reached the uppermost landing inside, past the apartment downstairs, where a Haitian family lived, I removed my sneakers, as was my family custom, set them in the wooden cubby, and then unlocked our front door next to the cubby.

It was small, inside. Remarkably small. And dark, as the main window caught only the brief north by northeastern light of the morning, since the street was at an angle. So it caught that light very briefly. This was late-afternoon, early springtime. There was a plain brown carpet covering the floor and though the furniture was lovely, it was large, misplaced, and made the limited space seem stuffed since the apartment had been built for two, most comfortably, or two with room for one smaller person, maybe. My grandma's furniture had been old and worn, so we had substituted with ours as best we could. We sacrificed spaciousness for necessity, habit and hope that we'd move someplace bigger, soon. Minimizing the still hard to ignore sloppily painted walls and cracked ceiling in the living room, there was the big screen TV (which wasn't allowed to be on very often and never during a school day), 2 wrought iron inn tables, and an antique leather portmanteau used for a coffee table in front of two plush green couches with lots of quirky pillows. The furniture changed from room to room, but the cracks, the shoddy workmanship in each one remained monotonously predictable.

And then, at the end of the long sofa opposite the door, peacefully resting, sat my grandma, dozing. She didn't snore, her chest merely rose and fell, gently. The indirect light from the window behind, cast her tussled silver hair in a luminescent glow, which lay, on her shadowed face.

As the door clicked shut, her head came up from its sleeping nod, slowly.

"Oh!" she started, kindly but without expression, "Hello, Tyree! You're home." My grandma's voice had a light girl-like tone.

"Hey, Grandma."

"Tyree's home!" she called out to rustling noises emanating from an area curtained off to the right, continuing, "You're a little late, Tyree. Was everything okay? Have you got homework? How was your day?"

These were her usual routine questions, with the first added in as an old family tradition, I'll explain, sooner or later – a tradition, that moment, I felt safer ignoring. With a yes, in my best gurgle speak, I knew that was enough for her. And, Ruby Larchmont asked no more, remaining seated on the couch for the entire brief exchange. The couch, on the far end, was grandma's 'spot.'

"Yes, mom!" came my own mother's voice, with a hint of exhaustion, and then she parted deep crimson chiffon curtains that hid the rest of the apartment to step into the living room. She came out with a distracted look, but soon melted into her own usual routine smile as she grabbed me – she was still taller than me in that day – she hugged me in an open-hearted embrace. I confess, I returned it a little stiffly.

"Hey, mom," I said, automatically, with not much emotion on my part. This had become my own new routine, and it was hard to break, despite having had one little victory, today.

"MmmmMMM! Hey sweetie! How was your day? You're a little late," she frowned, continuing, "Was there some trouble?" Luckily, I correctly guessed she'd ignore tradition, given all the other family issues, and if she had or hadn't noticed the difference between her warmth and my distance, she gave no sign.

My mother was an attractive woman in a way that was purely, African – or AfriKan as the Kattans wrote in their invitations. She was solidly built for a short-ish woman, but not at all fat, with a wall of cottony, slender locs falling to the small of her back, that haloed her well defined square chin-ned oval face. There was nothing aquiline about her wide and buttoned nose. Nothing European in her thickened lips; whereas my grandmother, her mother, was (in the popular jargon) high-yella'd, with features uncannily similar to a regular woman's version of Lena Horne in Lena's later days. In contrast to her generously featured daughter, grandma had a small but pointed nose and less dramatic lips. No dreads, but a wash of tendrils, full of hair straightened not by a hot comb, but by rapes from generations back and still visible on her head and in her skintone. But, just like her daughter, all her features conspired in a successful plan to make her undeniably lovely.

And while my mom's skin was a deep honey walnut, my grand's was an extra cream coffee. I, myself, with my mom's same Ibo derived Afrikan face (only such knowledge of where our features came from was no longer ours to know, due to matters beyond our control) –I was, and of course still am, cafe au-lait, though these god-days have removed the cream.

With finally my sister, who then emerged through the curtains and bopped me decisively on my buzz-cut head; she was a roasted almond with the skin left on, topped by a similar cascade of loc-ed, nappy wonder. Our gradations of brown were a talking, emotive, life infused panoply. Yet, inside our souls', inside our minds' perception of self, our Blackness was intensely deep and deeply equal, automatically. No question. So much so, that no one in that house, not my mom, grandmother, sister or even detail studying me noticed any difference between. We simply were Black. As natural as enjoying a cool drink of water from a glistening crystal glass, on a sizzling summer day. Every day.

"Hey, li'l bro!" Kyerah said to my, "Ow!"

Ordinarily, I would have gotten into a playful tussle with my sister, age 15, with less incentive than this, but where I'm beginning this history, and these next pages wherein I'll share the reasons, I didn't have the desire to joke around, let alone wrestle frantically. In the times before then, we'd have batted at one another, laughing with contrived rage and snarls 'til mom or dad would either jokingly or annoyed (depending on their level of exhaustion) break it up and tell us to do to something "fraught with less hazard." That would have made us all laugh, especially dad or mom, that one could use the words 'fraught' and 'hazard' in the same sentence with a straight face. We would have ended in more joviality, mostly everyone in a rolling, tickling romp. But those days, I hadn't felt like that for a while.

"Quit it!" I said, though without true anger, knowing my sister would do as I asked. She was, unfailingly, joyful times or not, a pretty good sister – for a girl.

"I was funnin', knucklehead!" she protested but indeed ceased after delivering one last playful swat - very lightly, before our mom, sans dad, gave her an understanding, wordless frown.

"You know I'll look out for you, super little, little," and yes, she added one more emphasized 'little', "... brother, even if my good sense tells me better!"

I smiled begrudgingly, my energy, though reduced, enough to deliver it as a veiled threat.

"Well," mom said, "How was your day? And why are you late?"

"Am I late?" I answered, innocently, acting surprised, while thinking, '*Best to keep the reason to myself.*'

"I must have lost track of time!" I said.

Mom grinned, fixing her gaze on me, but then she relaxed as we all walked into the kitchen. My reputation as a good son was working out well...

My grandma remained seated on her spot, not participating in the continuing conversation, as wounds from more than 70 years ago had rendered her shy, even in the midst of those who loved her without hesitation. She did smile and laugh during undeniably happy occasions, though with skittish caution. She had always been this way, talking only rarely, for as long as I or anyone still living could remember. I'd asked both her and my mom what had made her so, but no one could or would answer, and grandma mostly denied the difference in her ways with a sad giggle, that I knew meant, "Hush...." She was quiet, yet gentle, a little nervous, but not in a madly depressed way. Simply, resolutely silent, and to this day I don't know the exact why, what or who that had stolen her enthusiasm – I still don't know, except in the small memories she revealed that didn't tell much. I could discover more as that is my ability as a seasoned Protector, if I wanted to, but I'm immortal because of my stronger ability to think of others and respect their privacy. Well, mostly, I'm respectful, depending on who it is, or what they've done...

But, I'm still not only not perfect, I'm not from a perfect family, either. Heck, don't let anybody fool you, but no gods are perfect. That's a myth to stop you from believing you can become one, when only the One has no flaws, and He made Us with HIS image.

But I'm tellin' a history here, so...

My entire childhood, long as I can remember, the whole family, though sometimes frustrated, nonetheless, accepted my grandmother as she was, even my dad who'd married my mom despite the warning that daughters ended up like their mothers. I could tell grandma frustrated my mom at times and I could see that frustration on rare occasions, but I guess that was a mother, daughter thing. Primarily, we never demanded what Grandma didn't seem to have. We accepted when she offered her company, but mostly we resigned ourselves to hiding our pain at seeing someone we cared for so much, lost inside her own.

So, just three walked, without rude intention, into a kitchen permanently held hostage by, what would have been in another home, a moderately sized wooden dining table with 4 high backed chairs that had the audacity to demand even more space than the table, all in a kitchen that exclusive real estate brokers would have described as a nook. There were school books and papers spread out upon the side of the table nearest the wall. And the wall,

46

along with the others in the living-room, was nearly barren, except for a calendar depicting smiling Black children, and equally, but less professionally, beaming snapshots of our family, from up to 4 generations back. The further back the more black and white and the less 'Say Cheese!' chromacolor.

There had been one large painting in the living-room of a very young, and stoic Renee Jackson, almost depressed. Honestly? I didn't get it, but it was my mom's self-portrait from her young adult years, which I found to be a sharp contrast with the person I called my 'mom'. That wall hung canvas of another 2 dimensional woman, painted in light snuffing drabbery, leaning exhausted against a dirty burnt sienna wall, was even more bereft of hope than my grandma seemed to be. That painting was of someone I had never had the displeasure of meeting, until my dad died; and that introduction to that massively forlorn mother? Mercifully that acquaintance lasted only briefly, though at the time I thought she'd never leave. Now, once again, I only knew her as....

"Was it a good day, hon?" she stopped my thoughts, looking at me with joyful, yet not as corny as say as a 50's TV show mom's eyes, as she cheerily went to the sink. That was normal her, except for that bunch of mercifully over and done grieving her, that had visited for such a long while, months ago.

"It was cool," I answered, not willing to reveal anything about the day's complexities. How could I have expected her to understand that sometimes fights are needed? That sometimes ya had to pick one? She had never understood pugilism before, winching the few times dad had given me lessons, maybe because she was a woman or because she knew her husband was a better nuclear physicist than a fighter. Either way? Best to keep even today's non-fisticuff adventure to myself, lest I hear an earful.

Actually, those days I was keeping most things to myself, as I had found talking had done nothing to change what happened when the final decisions got made, and lately those decisions were never made in my favor. I had learned, pulling out one thread of truth, or questioning why this whole thing had happened like it had, led to an unraveling of all the threads, beyond my ability to mend what I assumed had started to repair itself in the first place by simply ignoring it. It had become obvious to me there were questions no one was prepared to answer, without in turn disintegrating to shreds all over again.

You'd be right to conclude my grandma wasn't alone in her hoarding of pain, after all. We were merely better at pretending to be boldly disconnected. I could feel it in everyone, mother, sister and me, in carefully placed 'ahems', or a casually brushed off or distracted, "Cool!" Followed, predictably, by a protracted silence. Then, during the hazardous shredding, came the look at an 'important' bit of nothing on the floor.

But unlike Grandma, our emotional shrouds had been sewn up only about 6 months ago, after the tears over Mr. Jackson's demise had dried up. And the reason for our sorrow was no secret, even if no one ever discussed it. Though my sister and most especially my mom, after crying for what I feared would be forever, they had finally gotten back to something resembling regular family life – and I preferred 'regular' over the painful uncertainty of a mother wracked with grief – still, the loss clung to everything we did as nothing we did came easy any longer. That's how I knew my best personality trait would be invisibility since unraveling their threads were dangerous as they were umbilically sutured to my own; and nobody, not even my father had ever taught this boy how to box female agony, and especially, although he had taught me respect, he'd never taught me how to withstand feelings of my own that boys aren't supposed to have.

I plopped my backpack on the table.

"Cool, huh?" my mom inquired as Kyerah resumed her seat in front of her own homework, "Only cool, love?"

She had filled one of the twin stainless steel basins with soapy water, looked back and popped gently but firmly, "Back-pack off the table, young man! Who knows where that thing has been?"

"Yes, ma'am," I dutifully responded. I knew she didn't really mean the inquiry into my 'cool' response anymore than grandma had meant her inquiry into what had made me get home later than expected. Hence, as I figured, the issue was quickly left alone. It was her attempt at resurrecting the old mom, while the truthful answer would have quickly pulled out one of those dreaded threads that revealed maybe she was tired of the call of duty.

Alright. You, reader, to understand this history – cause it tain't no mere fantasy, you're gonna have to understand the dynamics of my family. Stereotypes of Black families won't cut it, although I promise I'll do my unprofessional best to explain it as briefly as I can, or? Having grown up under the lies of your enemy, you *will* mistakenly try to understand me through those stereotypes about Black Boys that are not one size fits all. Heck, those stereotypes probably don't fit you, either, as they don't fit most of us, in any dimension, Heaven or Hell. See, I, tragedy or not, had been carefully trained to be respectful, automatically. Both my parents had a deep faith that Black Men were not genetic thugs and Black Women were not genetic female dogs if

48

you start them out right before a mother is even pregnant. Once we were born, my sister and I, from infancy onward, by a previously strategized, united parental front were precision reared, with not a belt, strap, or switch ever in sight. Not that I'm putting any particular method of raising children down – I'm just sayin'! Mom had been a stay at home parent whose dedication should have been studied by CEOs of every Fortune 500. Verbal discipline and withholding privileges, (along with other stuff that to learn, you'll have to read one of the parenting books my mom and dad never wrote, to learn more about what they called 'Attachment Parenting – Black Style'...). Marcus and Renee operated like a military unit, to prove, what they told us: mind was superior to brawn.

Thus, I'd had a physically pain-free childhood, y-e-a-h, but? SO WHAT?! When you're having a great time as a child, mom and dad are your source of everything – not the nursery, not the babysitter, not your stuffed animal or pacifier – you don't need none of that – you need them. Therefore, incurring their disapproval is 100% painful for a child. Seeing the disrespectfulness of friends around me to their moms and dads, who'd had more hands off parents or had received corporeal punishment, while I didn't, but I was often the only one who wanted to do the right thing wherever I went because I liked the family harmony that'd been all I knew? That made my parents' strategy nano-particularly accurate as it had won the participation of me and my sister in our own taming, even if that made us hysterically different from everyone around.

How DASTARDLY! And I'll raise my son the same exact way. So, to heck with one stereotype that all Black children get their tails tore up.

No, it didn't make us perfect, as one problem with raising children who know their subatomic worth? We also knew who we wanted to be, even if that wasn't always what our parents preferred.

Okay. Not a historian me, and not a stereotype me had to explain that. There's more to come, but for this page, where was I?

Yes. After washing up in the bathroom, I took my place at the table facing Kyerah, retrieving my homework from my on the floor backpack. Mom, taking a pause from her dishwashing to really notice me, I would imagine while pretending not to notice, turned her head back and looked, where I could see her in my peripheral vision. Her hands, independently, scrubbed and rinsed, scrubbed and rinsed.

"So have you made any new acquaintances?" she asked turning back around, her flow uninterrupted.

Reader, every family has plenty of its own quirks, no matter what the predominant population's 'reputation', as I've said. I won't bother to point out most of ours, but another Jackson way was to use multisyllabic concoctions in our private conversations, where letting go of public preferences for mediocrity was a soothing relief.

Yeah. Exactly.

We weren't putting on airs as being 'smart' for us, like I've already mentioned, was as ordinary as having body parts. We were comfortable with ourselves, yet, we'd never, including my mom, talked like that in front of anyone outside immediate us, because that'd be showing off and we liked people more than words. But, we sure did like words, though. I mean we *really* liked words. No. I don't think you get this.

We really, REALLY like words.

That's why I'm a rotten book writer. I don't compose like the typical reader has been dumbed down to expect, if they read at all. But? HA! Maybe I'm stereotyping YOU!

Family book reading time. That's what got me going, since before I can remember. Well I can't have been part of such a supposedly 'different' Black family and not sit down to share a great book, right? It's what got me this Knowledge Keeper job in the first place, being a member of this quirky family. Looking back on it, that shared time, every evening, this verbal repast of what a fine sentence laced together by finer words could accomplish in the heart, kept us all enduring what at that time felt unendurable after we no longer had the participation of one of our fiercest book loving members of the family.

We, Jacksons, I can say with certainty upon reflection – we lived a pure passion for language that went beyond our own combined knowledge of Western literature, even if we didn't realize it at the time. Unknown to us? This embrace of words wasn't set alight by some 2 dimensional pages authored by a white person or a Black person trained by a white person. Nor was it merely a trivial past-time like some families watch Jeopardy, answering all the questions correctly because those questions have answers. Answering correctly without needing to ask the questions, themselves. Filling in the blanks not because they dared to be unlike everyone else, but because they didn't realize their uniqueness had been scripted beyond themselves – scripted by threads that reached far above, below and outside of the known rules.

What do I mean? Well. This Jackson family passion for what knowledge can do was a long forgotten stereotype of Black People, the world over. It was a gift from our 64 different kidnapped Afrikan ancestors who held on to what made them part of the most creative beings on the planet, even if we didn't recall those ancestors' names. It was an inherent hunger, a magnetically connected search for generational harmony that one of our forgotten great, great grandparents had unlocked in a forbidden volume, and had secretly learned how to read it watching the kidnapper's own child learn what slave he or she was told he wasn't good enough to be taught. He was a mere beast – but you don't enact laws to keep your horses from reading. No. I may have never planned on becoming a writer but this love for knowledge sears deep within every Diasporic Afrikan who has time to notice and defeat his own stereotypes started by outsiders who not only didn't know him, but didn't like him. From coast to coast beyond our tiny family's climb out of the years of bondage, this burn for harmony maintains the intensity it'd always been for all of us. Some families arrive earlier at that blaze than others, but that's the meeting place and it's in everything we Black people do. Even when we swear we want to remain ignorant, that yearn to understand the rhythm of existence thrives in our most undervalued world revitalizing expressions, setting soul to soul alight with undeniable fervor, with a uncheckable surge towards the truth. This kindling inspiration – its evidence is manifest (despite seeming to have been made insignificant by both time and foe) – this kindling genius is 60,000 separate generations old, not a mere 5 or 7; it is, literally, the genetic nagging of a couple billion relatives hundreds of thousands, mayhaps millions of years dead, while their cries flow through our veins like the origin of gravity pulls reality. The planet knows there's something a brewing in the minds, hearts and souls of Black Folks. Only We don't know it, other than a ravenous growl for more 'cause We're no longer fluent in Our father tongue of 'Fire'. We just burn up, from the inside out, like lightening imprisoned in a bottle.

Shufflin' through school books and papers, pondering none of what I wrote above, I an swered my mom's question of having found 'acquaintances' with a distracted, "I don't know."

"What?" my sister looked at me with malevolent amusement from behind her math book. She taunted, "Surely, you've talked to someone? The lunch lady is pretty cute."

She gave a smart aleck's smirk to answer my glaring stare. I didn't bother to tell her that she didn't even go to my school, so how would she know that old Ms. Grimble, the lunch lady, and her looked strikingly the same?

"Well, Kyerah," mom's tone, more than her words, deflected the tease away, "Your brother has some valid reason for saying that. Let's give him a listen."

That was mom, acting or not. Reasonable. Rationale. Positive. Even in the midst of pain, mom did her duty. And she'd always been that way, for as far back as I could remember. Her artwork was the only private individuality I saw her pursue, so content she seemed with caring for me, my sister and my father, when he'd been there. And it wasn't as if I didn't appreciate it. I knew without question that I loved her gentility. In my once simple world, I had been so grateful for her free and easy smile when compared to many of the moms my friends had had to suffer through. Now that's a whole 'nuther awful story, but those stories aren't mine. This was my life and my mom, who, alone, had understood, even if a little – she had believed me after looking out the window at that Kattan house, that I saw something change. Grandma had said nothing helpful, dad had brushed it off and Kyerah had made a week's worth of fun of me. But mom had squatted next to me on a slowly disintegrating checkered sofa, staring out the window at the air – she had understood the light, the color, the change, though she couldn't say it in a child friendly way, sorta like I find it difficult to write down to you beyond the grown man I've become.

Mom had been my safety, my source of kindness, a refuge from the rough truth that I was going to be a man, with no soft edges allowed. I looked forward to manhood because of my dad, but I was more than grateful for the warm haven she provided.

It was just that? Her gentility wasn't fixin' anything, right then. All the patience in the world hadn't changed a father who was there one day, gone the next, in a crash that I had been told by them had been an accident and by the insurance company had been a suicide – but I wasn't sure which. That was THE question I dared not ask about Marcus Jackson, barreling out of the house that night, over a year ago, screaming about bills he could no longer afford, a job that was no longer there, when only a short while back, money had been an extra family member, generously providing for nearly all our desires like it would never cease.

Once dad was gone, money's onetime generosity had only filled our former house with the echo of its mirthful participation. There rippled its former camaraderie in the original paintings and sculptures from other artists that had graced the walls of our sprawling house, so those walls had never been barren. Money used to smile with us as we looked in the mirror at how good well-made clothes looked on our persons. The money had enthusiastically chatted with our family in the designer 'appointments' that filled each room. Furniture with signatures is what 'appointments' were when money was your friend. Stickley this, Frank Lloyd Wright that, and Lalique on that table over there, all tastefully done. The money had applauded in pictures of us that it took on vacation whirlwinds, at least once, or twice a year. And it had laughed with us triumphantly in the 3 luxury vehicles and 1 sports car that were parked in our own circular driveway and stored in the detached triple automatic door garage.

Some echoes are sold for much less than their true value on Ebay, as all that stuff, when the money was gone, was used to pay an overload of bills. Didn't matter that much since only the physical artifact remains once it's been emptied of its original joy.

My hero I called dad had also run out, past this evidence of money's promise to be faithful – he had run out drunk and angry, ignoring the rare time when his wife, my mom, had not been calm, had not been happy and had begged her husband to stay home that night. He'd paid no attention, pushing past her, slamming his wavering body into one of those gifts from our 5th family member, 'Money'. It was the Jaguar F and he'd screeched down the street in it or in any other car for the last and final time. I and my sister had leapt out of our hiding place in the dark corner at the top of the cascading staircase, and running after him, we'd wailed in the street without a sidewalk, with our own pleas, shouting our ample vocabularies, a full half block down the road that no person ever walked along. What had made our father so proud of us, his 'gifted' children, made it impossible for him to not brag about us to his family, friends and colleagues, (embarrassingly for Kyerah and me), what made him burst with the victory of careful fatherhood, at that moment, had proven utterly useless in the most important moment.

Funny, how I now realize what a convenient spectacle we would have made for any white people who love to hate Black people, if they had lived in our neighborhood. Yet? Still what a spectacle, I'm sure, we made for some of our Black neighbors, that night, who'd have had to distance themselves and later did because of what we revealed that day. That on the brink of financial ruin, we Jacksons became only a sorrowful bunch of well spoken 'niggers'.

The call came, ringing through our near mansion house, thick with fear from cavernous room to spacious terrified echo, the next morning that call rang, 6 hours after the public blow-up, though time passed only on the clock on the wall. Inside us, waiting for that phone call felt like glue had stuck all the seconds together so the current moment could never move breezily onto the next. No one had slept. Mr. Jackson storming out drunk was a new horror for this family. And that ring, if it did ring at all, lasted a half jangle before mom, who'd been using that phone all night to make a hundred calls – before she'd picked it up.

I learned right then the difference between a movie and real life, no matter how many 3D moments feel like a MGM blockbuster. See, in a movie, it's all so removed by rows of cushioned seats, safe from the action taking place before the viewer's eyes. The popcorn doesn't have time or motivation to lose its flavor during a 2 hour depiction that you walk away from, leaving the tumult of emotions that the screen just pulled out of you, behind on that seat, intermingled with uneaten kernels destined to grow stale, as if those feelings were of no true importance, no substance meant to last.

Real life feelings don't disappear when the lights come on, and go off again, and on and off in your home, the next day and the day after that. Nothing about this pain seemed destined for the maintenance staff's broom, to be dumped in the parking lot garbage bin. Mine was then a new world that showed up and refused to go away. That was precisely when my mom's almost never wavering warmth had disappeared; although if it had stayed, it still would have ceased to move me. As it had ceased to be my haven after her warmth slowly returned months later. Without my even wanting it to, her gentility had stopped being enough. She could never be dad, though I missed her warmth's realness as one misses the real event of a photograph, but you can never recreate that moment. And maybe? I didn't want the moment back.

"I don't know," I lazily grumbled, finally answering my mom's question about meeting 'acquaintances,' "Maybe, maybe not." I didn't yell, but I wanted to leave little room for further discussion.

She turned at the sharpness of my voice, and patiently replied, "It'll happen, sweetie. You're a wonderful boy to know."

Kyerah, surprisingly, didn't giggle.
"Uh, yeah," I paused, my guilt overriding my kneejerk response to my mom's sappy compliment, "Um, sorry."

I did love her. Just didn't...

"I guess I've got a lot of homework, mom," I interrupted my own thoughts, "I've gotta concentrate."

We all knew that was a flimsy excuse, yet this new family routine of ignoring the obvious was a successful one as no one wanted to challenge my excuse's credibility, despite the glaring fact that my homework was a full year behind what I already knew. Seemed, we were silently determined, all 3 of us, to avoid getting tangled up in those loose threads, especially the ones wrapped tightly

54

around our necks.

My sister focused an eye on me while still turning the pages of her book. The death of our dad, from what I could tell, had initially hit her the hardest. In the first couple months, she had cried, every day, for what seemed like hours at a stretch. The slightest mention and her eyes watered up, before the sound and fury of free flowing tears broke loose. I would walk upstairs to my room, past Kyerah's staccato heaves, shut up in her own room. Regularly. Everyday. And then one day, it was as if she'd drained the last molecule of liquid within, 'cause she'd suddenly stopped.

Sometimes her lips would quiver when a shared memory of our father bounced unchecked into the conversation, as that couldn't always be avoided. But that, too, vanished a few months after the tears dried up. I was a little angry with her for that, though I didn't know why. Maybe, she had been crying for me, also, since I'd never shed a drop. Angry questions tend to dam up tears. It was as if I didn't want the right to.... The right to.... What? I didn't then know exactly how to describe my feelings. Not the deepest ones. So, I didn't wanna risk wandering around a neighborhood in my head that I wasn't sure I could get back out of, let alone trying to understand the minds of a house now filled with only sad women, no matter its bucolic exterior bliss. Kyerah had become more like our mom than me, as our mother had also dried her eyes in time and resumed the business of being comforting. It had all seemed like a betrayal, and impossible to straighten out. A smiling cold hearted abandonment.

I looked up to see mom and Kyerah, subtly, focused on me.

"Would you guys cease and desist with the staring?" I protested, "I'm okay..."

"Well, alright." said mom, "If you say so. Just remember that I'm here for you."
"Alright, yeah, mom."

Silence came, but the usual one that comes between people who are comfortable together. My sister and I began our homework in earnest. Then Kyerah popped her head up with an invisible lightbulb turned on above her.

"Mom? Can I go stay at Aunt Brenda's this summer?" she asked.

"What, hon?" mom returned, carefully stacking dishes on a tiny drying rack, on a tinier counter, so the mountainous pile of 4 people's plates, cups and pots wouldn't tumble down. It was a metal, glass and plastic mountain that rarely was chiseled to nothing due to the kitchen being too tiny for a dishwasher.

"I thought your cousins drove you nuts?"

"Well, they do, but?"

Here came an uncomfortable silence, but not too much. This was maybe a safe topic, depending on what was said next.

"But?" Mom repeated.

Grandma walked in slowly, through the crimson red drapes and squeezed herself, between the chair I was sitting in and the wall, as I moved myself and the chair in, squashing my belly against the table. All this she navigated, without tripping within the inches wide space that led to the refrigerator, opposite the sink. She took her careful time, for very good reason, besides being an elder. Anybody could trip through that gauntlet.

"Well? It's better than staying here," Kyerah hesitantly answered, resuming her schoolwork.

I looked up at my mother, caught up in a full blown uncomfortable moment. I could tell because I was in the midst of my own and we were all tied together. Kyerah gone? For the whole summer? Right now? To go stay with our 2 thoroughly silly, shallow, insipidly dull, TV glued cousins, Rhonda and Veronica? Aunt Brenda was nice, but busy and that lack of time showed itself in her daughters. I mean, I didn't like living in Newark anymore than Kyerah did, but at least we had each other. Or at least we'd had each other. I said nothing out loud, but inside, my heart said, 'Dang.'

"I'll have to think about that," was my mom's answer just as grandma chimed in, at the end of my mom's response with,
"Oh, Tyree…" Her voice was always permanently 10 decibels below the average volume of anybody else's voice I'd ever heard, usually prompting everyone's frustration.

"Huh? Whadcha say, Grandma?"

I asked that, right then, to which she said a little louder, though not much, "Brother Cheikh wants to have a word with you."

Having gotten good at straining my ears, I replied, "Did he say what about?"

While nervously trying to locate an item within the depths of the stainless steel refrigerator, she stopped a moment to think.

"I don't remember it exactly. Sister Makeba called and said the brother needed some help. A job as his assistant, I think."

Pausing further, as if not certain whether she wanted to say more, she added, "He really needs someone to help with that house. Gainde hasn't been by in months, and the doctor's been racing about doing everything over there alone. Lights on all times of night and he's more frantic by the day. Poor man. I see him puttering in the front yard, muttering to himself. Goodness knows what's the trouble. You go on over and help him out."

I sensed some sort of fix, more to help me than Brother Cheikh, but chose not to mention my suspicion.

"What? Right now?" I reluctantly asked, instead – though the prospect did get me excited and nervous at the same time. I loved that house, but my mind went back to the word, 'assistant.' Sounded like work.

"No, no!" both she and my mom speakered out.

Mom added, "After your homework is done, and you have a bite to eat. I made navy bean and red cabbage soup."

"Is there dessert?" I asked.

"Apple pie."

'As good as the Chocolate, Chocolate Cake,' I thought, smiling broadly, with an audible, "Mmmmm." Nothing unneeded about my mom's cooking, and if throwing down in the kitchen is a stereotype of Black moms – bring it on!

Curious as to what lay in store for me, I silently ruminated, absentmindedly doing my English homework. It probably was some drudgery Brother and Sister Kattan wanted done, all in a plan hatched by my mom and Mrs. Kattan to cheer me up. Well, exploring that mansion was better than doing nothing but tripping over cramped furniture and loose threads, no matter how yummy the dessert. I wasn't the type to eat snacks as a replacement for the curiosity of youth...

57

=

"Yes, mom," I heard my mother say on her cellphone, as I and my sister sat, quietly reading in our cathedral ceilinged living room, which was decorated with one large wrought iron inn table, hand welded by mom, in the midst of 4 plush green couches, upon which were, back then, an undulating river of accent pillows, strewn haphazardly, but strategically about. And this time, the furnishings were in perfect proportion to the room's... Room, did I say? Nah. This was the Living AREA, graced with arboreal ferns and tamed potted trees. Appropriately large art graced all the walls and surfaces. The wall framing the back of the open loft style area was covered from floor to ceiling in living greenery. A vertical garden, in front of which stood the statue carved by my mom that my dad had loved so much, he insisted she sell it only to him. For which she'd charged him the whopping price of a kiss.

Yech! Parents!

When completed, he immediately had it shipped from her sculpture studio in an old tanning factory a couple miles away, and spending half the day, he made sure it was carefully forklift trucked and 3 man manipulated into the exact spot (yes, a forklift truck could easily roll into and through the 'Living AREA') – the statue commanded the eyes, like a black magnet, silencing stray thoughts with its herculean domination of the entire space; space that was up to the challenge. It was a gleaming granite Black Man, standing behind the couches, in a corner, his outstretched arm reaching upwards, and nearly touching the skylight, some 20ft above, with his whole 15ft height, from squarely planted feet to grasping fingers. Front and center of his reaching, about 12ft away, hung an enormous chandelier, also sculpted by mom out of forged iron to look like the branches of a sienna baobab tree, turned upside down, small globes attached to each slender limb. It was fully lit, that night, casting spheres of amber light upon the space and us.

It had been about seven months since my dad had driven off, leaving our lives in an apparently permanent upheaval. And although the worst of the grief had passed for both my mom and Kyerah, even my sister was, as of yet, not in the mood for boisterous teasing, and decidedly I was even more taciturn, back then, as we sat quietly reading in the warmly hued room. We had both been

58

indulging in the family's favorite word loving pastime with extra ferociousness these days.

And we surely had the books. Although we didn't have anywhere near the collection the Kattans possessed (more about that in a couple turns of this book's pages) – nonetheless, we Jacksons had an ample supply of what we needed. Kyerah's favorite genre was Science Fiction/Fantasy, while mine was? Well. Everything. Like my friends, though, I'd collected all the 'Diary of a Wimpy Kid' books, and 'Shonen Jump' (though I was tiring of the series about that time), but beyond comic books, history had always been my favorite, with Black History my ultimate weakness.

Reading Black History bordered on an obsession for me, because I was fascinated with what, until seven months prior to that day of my faked fight, I had no intimate experience undergoing. Suffering. Intense suffering. I hadn't ever suffered, not really. Not like I read about, and thus, early on, I had become amazed by the enormity of pain withstood by my immediate ancestors. It was so personal it made me wonder endlessly, what would I have done? Would I have fought against what ensnared and killed millions? How does anything that life shattering happen to so many people, and for so long?

As Kyerah, comfortably laying lengthwise on one couch, was peering through a Piers Anthony book, and I, sprawled out on another couch with a propped open history of Nat Turner, I heard every word my mom was saying, from the moment she started talking, though she was the length of that grand room away, in the kitchen off to the side. It was quiet in the house. It was always very quiet in the suburbs of Sandstone. Most of the time.

She was talking to our grandmother.

"I tried, mom," she said, "I knew sales were down for everybody, but lemme tell you, I was shocked! My work's always sold something, but this is the worst I've ever been through. Folks kept telling me how much they loved it, blah, blah, blah, but they didn't buy anything! And that was it, mom. Our last hope. I can't afford to exhaust our savings. Now the insurance won't pay because they ruled it a 'suicide'. Still, ma. There was a time when I'd sell at least 3 sculptures, a good 10 paintings and then 30, 50 prints. You remember. Yes! You were there last year. Just last year! It was so weird, so striking. How could it change so quickly?"

Silence.

"Yes."

Silence.

"Yes. Thank you, mom. You're our savior right now. It's what we've gotta do as there's no more money left to risk on my pipe dreams of supporting my family with my art. Not in this house. It's going to be mighty cramped but, there's no other way. We'll move in with you as soon as I can liquidate what we don't need."

Kyerah and I looked up from our books, sending each other nearly telepathic thoughts with our hopeless eyes. This possibility of moving to Newark had been raised before, but somehow, hearing mom say it to grandma made its finality sound like an iron door slamming shut.

"Without selling my paintings, at least, with an occasional sculpture, carrying this mortgage is impossible. Marcus' income took care of everything. My money was always extra. Why, I haven't worked in over a decade. What job could I get right now in a matter of weeks? Even if the schools were hiring, who'd want a teacher who hasn't been in front of a classroom in fifteen years? Plus, there's no time! I thought the opening would be the solution. Tide us over," she sighed, deep enough that we could hear. "Darnit. I worked so hard, mom."

More silence.

"Not much. Half the savings went to pay off the bills. Then I was a little too sure the show would work out and probably spent more than I should've fixing up the place in case I still had to sell it. But truly, in this real estate market, I'll be lucky to walk away from the house, cash even! I might wind up owing that thieving bank! Without Marc..." she didn't finish, "Well...", her voice thickened and the silence this time was much longer.

She continued more quietly.

"Yes, mom. No. No. Don't worry. We're okay. Better. And we're all going to be just fine. You remember that, too, huh? Don't you fret. I know how you can get. This'll be difficult for us all, at first, but we'll make it. The roughest time is over, so I'll do what's necessary to take care of Kyerah and Tyree. Even if I have to scrub toilets!" She gave a half-hearted laugh, as if this were a joke. "No, I'm kidding! Well. Not actually, if it comes down to that. But as for moving back to your home, yes. Thank you, ma. Thank you. It'll give me time to regroup and figure out what I'm going to do. Hmmm?"

I imagined mom listening almost as intently as we were.

"No. I didn't consider that!" she blurted. "There's definitely not enough for them to go to a private school! Oh, man. It'll have to be public. I don't believe I could homeschool them entirely, as there won't be enough time while I'm looking for work. I'll have to supplement what they learn. Yes. I know. Boy do I know! But don't worry mom. They'll be fine! They're both great kids and if I work with the teachers, join the PTA, it can't be that awful. Heck I went to public school, remember? And I'm not one of those non-involved type parents. They'll be okay."

But I wasn't okay, already, upon hearing that. And from the look on my sister's face, she wasn't either. We both had closed our books, I having lost all desire to reread my favorite part where Turner delivers his death blows to his slavemasters, that I had read 7 or 8 times before. Shock, and not from that memorized passage, had dropped down into my stomach as a cold lump, draining all the blood from my brain. Every other thought didn't have a chance in my head. I hadn't been sure how to get through each day here in my own town, without my dad, let alone to now manage life in a public school a 100 miles from my friends. A public school in Newark! My sister and I had been in private schools since we'd begun school itself, so I suddenly imagined that going to a public one would be worse than a life sentence in solitary confinement.

Not that I'd ever been in prison, let alone solitary. I just knew I wouldn't like it.

I mean, we two had known about the inevitability of moving, as mom had talked about that openly, including us in the planning, and offering comforting reassurance.

She had warned us, "Gallery sales should make us comfortable, but, more than likely? We may not be able to afford this house anymore."

Alright. We didn't like it, but we'd understood. However, no one had bothered to consider if there was no money for our house, and then no art sales, at all – there'd be not a dime for private school! I had taken for granted we'd be in another 'Well-Accredited Institution of Exceptional Learning for the Black Child with an Emphasis on African American Studies', as my suddenly former school principle, Mr. Merle Kingston, at Medgar Evers Prep repetitively said to visitors, and at the outset of every assembly. Heck, even a private majority white school would have been a tolerable alternative.

I felt a rising sense of betrayal at whom or what I didn't quite know. But, it was red hot insistent, easy target or not. Just how much of my life would be torn and torn again, while I could only submit, powerless to change it. Just how much?

=

It was still a sunlight wealthy April day at 5:11pm when I rang the bell on the front door of the Kattan..., um... estate... Okay. There's another feature about that house I intended to mention, but wasn't quite sure how to fit it in smoothly, quite yet (you didn't forget, I'm not a writer?) – but that said? The mansion wasn't only a quadruple leveled, with dozens of rooms on each story, structure – but as I mentioned, it was, also, the only building on that side of the entire block with corner curb to corner curb to corner curb to? You get the idea – with the expanse of that city block belonging solely to the Kattans. So, technically, that's an estate, even if the full lot outside of the immediate surroundings had never been civilized. It was, most definitely, too expansive for 2 older middle aged people to keep up by themselves - even I knew that at 12. On the left of the mansion, if you stood before it, was a 15ft high white fiberglass fence shielding the property from the world walking along Garvey Avenue. On the right, the greater portion of the property was separated from the house and lawn by a circular driveway that fronted the building. The driveway was black asphalt, same color as the roadway between my side of the street and the mansion. Like a river, it branched up the sides, where the Kattans parked their 2 cars. The first vehicle was a lushly burgundy PT Cruiser belonging to Mrs. Kattan, and the last - an old but mint condition, baby blue Cadillac, El Dorado. That was the Dr.'s. The driveway wound on beyond eyesight into the back, leaving to its right, a drunken wire fence that held back for dear life, an undulating overgrowth of the rest of the property - twisted trees, bacchanalian shrubs, weeds that would have talked my dandelions and their crabgrass rivals into getting plastic surgery if they could talk; and then speckled everywhere were colorful chunks of garbage, left by the occasional passersby and more frequent motorists. The litter's inanimate garishness, fought the browns and greens of that part of the estate, which had never been given a purpose beyond running wild.

That wildness, alone, deeply covering the length and width of the block, even without the perceptible change in color near the house, would have been the source of many a residents' ghostly concerns - especially at night when you couldn't perceive any atmospheric color change over the mansion. The specter of that rampaging growth, conspiring with the house, which as sunlight fled the white wooden paneled structure, reached up against the night sky

63

bedecked in Afrikan warrior regalia on its facade, glowing eerily with a ring of lawn lights that cast looming shadows and startling glares – that otherworldly vision had easily secured, not just the house's but the entire block's reputation as hopelessly spooky. Grandma, herself, who as I think I said earlier – refused to move – had sometimes shared some of her neighbors' tales of nighttime wanderings, where they swore they saw terrifying spirits – which? The force of it all had ironically kept Carson one of the safest places in all of Newark, as it kept the actual danger to the community – the very real muggers and hoodlums – that estate kept them anywhere but here. Well, at least it kept them off of THAT side of the street.

My side? Well, there's even more about that, too, later, if I remember. But then again, how could I forget?

That unhinged expanse lay fallow, except for a large garden and green house I knew to be hidden from view by the high white fiberglass fencing which continued on in the back area. First came the massive grape vine covering the back left half of the house, then came a deep row of vegetables, and one plum, one boysenberry and one apricot tree; and finally a heated green house in which Mrs. Kattan (a degreed botanist and herbologist) – that's where she grew a vast selection of medicinal herbs, aromatic flowers, a lemon, orange, mango and cacao tree, and other warmer climate vegetation. This mini farm stretched clear to the other street, behind, surrounded by the backend of that high white fiberglass fence.

Brother Cheikh and Sister Makeba, grew all their own food as they often stated vigorously, "We don't do poison."

Um? They meant they didn't buy the food sold at the common supermarket. Not even at the healthfood markets. Matter of a fact, they didn't buy, let alone eat anything denatured, artificial, genetically mutated or dead – so much so that they, also, collected and filtered their own rainwater, foreswearing against consuming anything made by anyone or group of persons who said one thing in public about their products, but in their actions proved they hated everything alive.

My family was vegan, too, which means we didn't eat anything with a face or a heartbeat. We abstained for many of the same reasons as the Kattans, though, a whole lot less fervently – meaning We ate mostly greens, fruits, nuts and beans, but you'd never find a day in our house without at least one bag of potato chips around. You couldn't find potato chip crumb ghosts in that mansion. Yep. It wasn't even haunted, inanimately.

We'd converted our diet only recently, probably, because of conversations my dad had had with the older couple. Conversations? Heated discussions between folks too polite to bring out knives. The Kattans' place was so big it begged to be filled up with people and exciting people they were, as who turned down a coveted invitation, although, the food was a bunch of veggies, grains, nuts and beans (weeds and twigs as my Sandstone friends joked) both the Dr. and his wife had cooked. They were still mouth wateringly delicious meals. Mrs. Herbologist Kattan would say, "The flavor is in the seasonings and the seasonings are the plants." Well those tasty plants had convinced countless attendees, lucky enough to be invited, that brussel sprouts might not be a potato chip, but they could sure make you smack your lips in their own savor every bite way.

Never a man to take anyone's word for it, 'cause he loved a juicy steak, my dad had researched veganism in his strategic, scientific way, sure the Kattans were wrong, yet, had concluded in the end, grandma's next door neighbors were 100% correct, however?

There was something about the way the doctor and his wife practiced not only eating, but living that was on a scale that brought you to awe. Why, they seemed to exist in another realm that gifted them with a vitality that shone in their clear piercing eyes, inviting you higher, whether you knew how to stay there or merely visit – the same way the house seemed to enrich the air that encircled it and then, reluctantly, let it go. The Kattans enriched people, whenever those people chose and whenever the people were wise enough to step up to the challenge.

They were extra grown grown-ups, whilst I was still a child, with none of these adult thoughts, I'm having on a decades distant morning when my tea tastes so good. That day, 96 years ago, I prepared my normal human boy mind for any possible tediousness that could last an hour or two, by being grateful it was better than doing nothing. Nothing to do between me and the thread of my thoughts, then, was too unendurable a span.

As for the Kattans? I had learned through those rare gatherings, when a variety of 'movers and shakers', as the doctor called them, were gathered in the home, I had found them to be the most pleasantly serious adults I'd ever met. Oh, they did laugh and smile, and often; but it was with a solidity that let you know, should you be the source of their good time? You had achieved something worth remembering.

I'd waited only a moment after ringing the bell, a sonorous beckoning tinged with possibilities, before the tall, elegantly wrapped in Afrika, Sister Makeba opened the heavy oak door. Her skin was a gold mine of ebony, calming the onlooker, instantly, before she confirmed her beauty with a musical voice that flowed harmoniously, bidding me to enter.

"Welcome! We were expecting you!" she said, her words, even more beautifully dressed in a Senegalese accent.

Her smile appeared, without artifice, lingering a moment to then flow from her lips, resting firmly in her eyes. Those healing eyes, in deep echoing black skin, glistened with a knowing of more than I could imagine, at least at that time in my life. And despite my being aware Sister Makeba wouldn't bother kidding around with me, as some grown folk do in order to entertain children, it suddenly didn't matter in the slightest. That's when I remembered, as usual, I always felt a surge of warmth the moment I saw her and upon stepping inside their home, each and every time. I felt revitalized the moment, the door opened and this tall Afrikan woman whom I knew to be at least as old as my grandmother based on assumption and decidedly not on her youthful looks – I felt alive as she waved her arm to usher me in.

Why it never ceased to amaze me how my skittishness vanished as soon as I entered the house. And it had never failed that upon leaving, I couldn't remember a darn thing about how soothing it had been to be in their presence, here. As if I was the ordinary air across the street made to glow, temporarily, while I was inside that unique abode.

I don't know if the Kattans had the same effect on me outside their home, as I'd only been with them when visiting their estate with my mom, dad, and sister. Grandma always stayed behind in her apartment, too shy to want to participate. This would be the first time I'd come to the house, on my own.

Stepping within, I keenly wanted to pay attention to everything. I smiled, happily at her in return, just as sincerely. I proudly stated the most appropriate of greetings Brother Cheikh had taught me, during our last attendance at one of their dinner gatherings, a better time, one year and a half ago.

"Peace, Sister Makeba!" I said it brightly, as she closed the door behind with its automatic self locking, heavy 'click'.

Sister Makeba, with deliberate ease deadbolted the other 4 locks as I stepped into a tidy, circular foyer, happy photons abundantly piercing through the windows on the sides of the door to reveal burnt copper walls with amber trim, closed doors left and right. A rugged tribal hand carved round table, centered, dominated the room on top of which sat a hematite vase, with an uproar of flowers, like a shout within the brown depth of the room's somber tone. The foyer then ended its impressive introduction with a flat wall into which glass doors were set within a Moorish arched entryway. The Kattans had told me 'Moor' meant 'Black' as in Black us.

Through these 'Black Us' doors, one could see a red hallway beyond, ribbed on the left by a grand staircase; and further down, all the way to the end of the hallway, on the right, stood one large double wooden door and then came other doors, most of which led to various, never seen by me, regions of the house. As typical, all the doors were shut.

"Yes. Yes, indeed. Peace, Brother," she put an arm about my shoulder for a moment when done with the last lock. "Come, sit in the library, while I go get my husband and bring you a cup of rooibos tea."

I walked beside her, in silence, to one of the few places in that house I had been allowed into, where I did manage to remember my fun within, long after leaving it. It was impossible not to remember that room, with all the books. Though, the celebrations took place in other rooms, like the grand gallery or the dining hall, only in the library had Kyerah and I always been granted free reign. And this library would have drawn hushed astonishment from the staff of any public book repository, anywhere. Past the wood framed glass doors, which Sister Makeba swung open on just one side, we walked into the hallway and then into those other wooden double doors on the right.

Reader? I must take an extra moment to describe this library, for the words have to be as startling as the sight. And that tain't easy.

I'll begin with the second most striking feature of the library, behind the first. That was the conservative, yet bold Afrikan motif. Yes, it was in complimentary keeping with the mansion's outer façade, rippling in earthly gradations of browns, highlighted with un-abashed colors that moved the eye from one point to the next, comfortably. At the far southeastern end, which was the outer wall of the house, stood 3 stained glass windows, cathedral sized, done by a Senegalese artist friend of the Kattans. The windows depicted persons from Ancient Kemet, Black as the people of that civilization had painted themselves. By itself, alone, the decor was magisterial.

But the feature that won first place, hands down, was the books. It was their sheer number that brought the entrant to a dumfounded state upon his or her struggling attempt to embrace the all of them. The shelving rose up to snare the victory over one's eyes by engulfing all 3 of the upper floors, which had been removed so the volumes would continue, unimpeded, to the Kente rimmed gold ceiling high above. Then the space continued on to the end sidewall of the house. Nearly 1/5th of the whole mansion was this one room.

So detail numbing were the scenic waves of books filling each corner of the available space, that the onlooker might expect a slight haziness towards the end of the room, like a painting in which the artist tries to convey great distances through mimicking the inevitable interference of the atmosphere. This might have made even the directors of major metropolitan libraries slowly nod, agreeing with the astonishment of their humbler colleagues. For although it wasn't as big as major public libraries, there lie, on both sides of the room, up to the ceiling reached by walkways and rolling attached ladders, books. To beside a bank of small tables and one centered main desk, double rack cases, about 5ft high, of books. To the taller free standing cases, 15 rows deep beyond that, more books. And to below the cathedral windows, the last crescendo of books. With only a dozen gaps in between the lot of each shelved volume, as the Kattans were running out of room to place even more of their never ceasing collection of books.

Here were the histories, fables, essays, remedies, wives tales, dissertations, journals, novels, documentation, charts, maps, biographies, studies, archival films, videos, CDs, DVDs, e-books, records, tapes and even cylindrical phonographs, all focusing on every aspect of Motherland Born Afrikans and their Diasporic Brothers and Sisters, that Dr. Cheikh Kattan and his predecessors (whom I was not yet aware of having had existed, at this point in this history) – here was all they had purchased, inherited, copied, and crawled through the very burning sands of time to procure.

I, however, if unaware of the lengths to which Sister Makeba's husband and our ancestors had gone in gathering this collection, I was more than glancingly acquainted with the some of reading in this room. Although, it would take a dozen lifetimes to get through it all, if not more. See, reader? No library I'd ever entered had books anything like these. These mutely imposing guardians of knowledge came anointed with titles that would cause a revolution from shopping mall guard to first Black President of the United States. These topics were incendiary, and not merely in one's mind. The topics of these books were dangerous in real life.

Yet, I had never been allowed to borrow a single volume and enjoy its combustible contents at home. Not a one. Brother Cheikh, after all that searching, after too many hardships that child me didn't know anything about, had become steadfastly loathed to share his collection. As I stated, at this point, I had no idea that such a hazardous vocation as the Protector of Knowledge that would become mine existed. Not yet. Standing there that day, though, I was more precipitously close to that edge of discovery than I realized.

"Are you looking forward to becoming the doctor's assistant, Tyree?" Sister Kattan inquired as we walked into the library.

"Um." Presented one on one with this possible impending obligation, I fully knew I had no idea what the 'job' was I was expected to fulfill. Although curious, I was contemplating too many possibilities to say anything more and risk sounding like an idiot. Maybe she meant 'assistant' flatteringly, like grown-ups do with the young, while not meaning the full definition of the word – that she, instead, meant I'd be the 'Head Lawn Mower Guy', 'Hedge Trimmer Boy', and 'Take the Garbage Out Dude'. 'Cause, c'mon? I was just a child, afterall. Only problem with that reasoning? Sister Makeba didn't kid children.

"Um," I repeated, "I don't know if I could help him with more, er? Complicated things. I don't know whatever it is Brother Cheikh does. Perhaps he should hire a college student?" The hesitancy of my answer, if that did not reveal my nervousness, was resoundingly assisted by my wide doubtful stare.

But the sister's eyes gleamed guilelessly, reassuring me.

"Oh, don't you fret, Tyree. Brother Cheikh wouldn't want any old college student as we know you, already. You're a very responsible, brilliant young man. Plus, my husband doesn't expect you to take over, just yet..."

My own eyes grew a bit wider upon hearing her, '...just yet...'

Not paying attention to my startled features, she continued uninterrupted, "and your youth will be a benefit to the both..."

She trailed off, abruptly stopping our walking in the midst of the smaller desks.

"You know?" she pondered. "Let's take you right on into his office rather than have you sit out here, imagining the worst. He is expecting you, after all."

"Oh, I don't mind," I said, as I suddenly preferred facing all those books, rather than a challenge I increasingly felt I'd be a disappointment in the doing

69

thereof, "I love it here."

"Of course you do! You always have and that's why you are perfect for the job. Too many would find this library boring. Even disturbing. And as I said, being young is a great benefit, Brother Tyree, as you aren't completely spoiled like... Well," she smiled again, replacing the serious look that had filled her expression when she had initially stopped.

"Don't let me get started. I could go on with that one for hours. Come. This way."

I chose not to ask her to explain what she meant by 'spoiled', but I stung with a slight offense. I didn't see myself as spoiled, or so I had always thought and worked diligently at making sure I wasn't. I didn't get disagreeably upset at not having my way, didn't I? Hadn't my mom and dad so often told me how well mannered I was; that I was a good son? That they were raising me to be a 'conscious' Black man?

Spoiled? Me?!
I knew how to keep my expectations realistic. How to graciously accept whatever I received.

Um? Right?

She took me to the right of the library and we continued to walk its length, beyond the last bank of bookcases and floor to ceiling stacks. Set into the wall, was a single sided closed ornate door in another arched doorway. This one wasn't Morrocan, but straight from an ancient edifice in maybe Timbuktu or Lagos, upon which was painted in large gold leafed letters:

HIPI

Before she opened the door, I, who had never managed to come this far in the library (the books were that good, yes) – I did ask, "What does 'Hipi' mean?"

"Ah!" She answered. 'Hipi' is a Wolof word, from Afrika. It means 'to open one's eyes'. The white man stole it, a little while ago. Turned it into something silly, using tie-dye and daisies, as they do have a long habit of doing with profound Afrikan concepts – with all concepts. But here, this word is home."

What was 'tie-dye' I wondered, but before I could ask, she opened the office door. However, reader, before we all enter this room, it is necessary to explain why this seemingly callous statement made by Sister Makeba – not about 'tie-dye' t-shirts, bangles and drug crazed formerly middle class white teenagers, nor about the word, 'hipi', itself as the origin she described is true, but about the superficial nature of white people's use of things not white – why that comment, unlike the one about me being 'spoiled' (even if a little bit I was) – why that drew not even a change in a single brain cell for me.

The young Mr. Jackson, I, during many of the Kattan gatherings, stretching back further than my memory would go, as I've said, I'd been an occasional guest vis-a-vie my mother (she'd known them since she was a little girl) – I'd been attending their gatherings since I'd been in my swaddling clothes. My mom, unlike her mother, was bold. More like her dad, she'd often told me, whom, as I've said, I don't recall. So as soon as she, a bold teenager with 'ideas' – as soon as she could walk across the street and ask the deep Black man, the doctor, manicuring the shrubbery in front why he, his wife and son lived in a house so big all alone, a decades long connection had begun. Thus, I'd always been included in the get-togethers, but became the silent eavesdropper, along with my sister. As we got old enough to pay attention to start with, all things, other than lewdness and no one ever cussed – all topics never discussed in polite society were the stuff of regular chit chat in that home and we were an enraptured audience. Now, the conversations would have made anyone listen up, even if they had taken place on a battlefield in Beirut if that listener was still alive; yet, somehow as I cannot emphasize enough – that mansion made my little mind focus beyond its usual ability, as my sister and I, though both bright? We weren't robots even way back then, before we all became gods. It had to be the house or the Kattans that enhanced our typically easily bored by adult talk curiosity. That mansion made one sit up and hear what had never previously been worth listening to before.

Ranging from intimate small dinners to 100 person feasts, the gatherings happened randomly throughout the year, with either many well dressed and important guests attending sumptuous events, or regular folks in jeans and t-shirts, whenever an invitation was happily received. But there were no Easter Sunday or New Year's parties here. The Kattans celebrated Senegalese holidays, anniversaries of historic events and birthdays of important figures, while Western observances, like Christmas and Thanksgiving, were never a reason for which the Kattans gave cheer. Instead Tamkharit and Tabaski were observed, with only a begrudgingly modest Kwanzaa dinner given on Imani, that American celebration's final day. Actually, only Mrs. Kattan hosted that last one, whilst the doctor kept a low profile in other parts of the house.

Kyerah and I came to understand his mysterious absences during Kwanzaa,

71

that my own family observed, all at once, one day on our way to the library. We saw the tall, stately doctor ahead of us, talking with his son, Gainde, and decidedly, they were not aware of our presence a mere 10ft behind.

The doctor bluntly commented, "What do I need with a Christmas substitute, as I have no need for the original fakery, either? I've always suspected the motives of that Dr. Karenga."

Hearing Dr. Kattan speak so harshly about a holiday we had been reared to observe and enjoy didn't upset us too much, since, we were the children of Black intellectual parents. They hadn't gotten to be that themselves without encouraging an environment of questioning – and, our parents taught us to love our natural Black selves. Thus, we'd already known the sordid facts about Christmas, before any of our friends from grade school sensed that Santa Claus was a giant commercial gimmick. Seeing most of them oblivious had made us aware that there were many mysterious layers to this adult world we took any opportunity to peal back, one layer at a time – especially in that mansion.

So, my sister and I, suspecting the doctor might know some grownup truths that even our parents were hesitant to share? I had thought, as a conversation later with Kyerah confirmed, she also wondered, 'What about this Kwanzaa? Is it a fake, too?'

We had looked at each other with quizzical eyebrows raised, and each of us putting a finger to his and her own lips, signaling quiet, we had walked extra silently to mayhaps hear the rest of the potentially illuminating 'dirt'.

Gainde had agreed with his father, though with a sigh adding, "True, Doc, but it at least puts the emphasis on healing ourselves."

"Harumph!" Dr. Kattan exclaimed, adding "You, are too forgiving, Gainde," at precisely the moment when, most unfortunately, as always happens when one is trying to be absolutely quiet, that's just when, scrunching your foot into a tip toed position, in not fully broken fancy new shoes, that's when an unforeseen 'squeak' will always occur. This one had come from me and had gone bouncing off the cavernous hallway walls into everyone's startled ears, complete with a hint of a reverberating echo. 5 nanoseconds after, which is basically instantly, the doctor and his son had turned about to spy the source of the noise, synchronized with the moment my child-sized heart stopped dead in its tracks, along with my feet and my sister's. I don't know if her heart, stopped, but I know we both were as motionless as the Black Man statue at home.

It had probably been a much shorter time between their turn around and my stopped heart, and I'm sure it all happened faster than it took to write or read this, however, whether I'd had a watch or not (and I hadn't) I couldn't have confirmed the length of the actual occurrence as it was busy occurring.

Surprisingly, there had been no grave upset on the doctor's part, and oh boy! Could there have been! The rules of the house had been unmistakably explained on many occasions to never go beyond the library or into any other rooms without the Kattans. But, to the delight of our hearts and ourselves, he simply had given us a mockingly stern look, had pointed in the direction of the library doors, now glaringly behind where we stood in mid tiptoe – he perhaps had not felt saying a word was necessary, as he had said none. For him, being caught was enough, for after having dropped our heads demurely, offering apologies to our host, we had racing-ly ridden his echoing laughter into the library, saved by the refuge of all those books. Hearts pounding again, we joined his laughter, quietly, with hand clasped giggles popping out between our small fingers, our embarrassment being all the punishment we'd be getting that time.

Therefore, reader, with even a beloved Diasporic celebration as Kwanzaa under scrutiny, investigation of every assumption was the standard in that place. Investigation that took apart the 'why's and 'how's of each thing Western, Afrikan, and in-between, with even less kindness than was shown by Sister Makeba that moment, or Brother Cheikh that day or any other such conversation was as normal to me as not looking like a nerd. During the gatherings, my sister and I had tennis ball watching eyes, flittering between the volleying topics about the survival of the modern Black struggle given our Black people's habit of twisting the truth to appease white people's fears – with no general agreement reached in any discussion on how to get past that contortion.

There was little said in that house about white people's ways that would have startled me in the least. Not that I agreed with all that was said, but white folks, as in most Black houses worldwide, were a regular subject matter of conversation, and in my home also, if not quite as vehemently as they were dealt with in this one. In defense, here, the discourse had always come with extensive facts to back up the assertions, no matter how startling they might have been or might be to you, the reader. The Kattans, emphatically, never countenanced lies.

Now, about whether I was 'spoiled' or not – indeed, that had caused a small blip on my emotional radar, undoubtedly. But, still, h-e-r-e? In that house? As I said, from store guard to president, this humble abode made one's mind combust in a 'hip' sort of way, hallucinogenic drugs, not required.

And thus we may all now enter, a medium sized office bathed in a springtime glow that was ushered in through three medium clear glass windows on the facing wall. Regular windows. No stained glass. Plus, here there was, once again, a ceiling just above, which topped a room that seem to have attempted to place as many books on every available surface as any moderate sized office was capable of holding. There were prerequisite bookcases on the left and straight ahead. In the middle of the floor were towers of books, piled totteringly in various spots; and many were opened, laid out on the tower or on the desk, as if they were silent but active players in some furious research, the scope of which would cause the greatest minds to hush their babble and think. There were titles such as 'The Crazy House Called America', 'Civilization or Barbarism: An Authentic Anthropology', 'The Destruction of Black Civilization', 'The Theology of Time' and a blurring parade of more than my desire to read them and walk into the room without stumbling on those few on the floor, could absorb. There was a thick sense of something happening in this room. I could have sliced into the air and ate heartily, if you could linger patiently through the cooking process to that first delectable bite. The very smell of old pages, pondered over lovingly, knowledge expertly stirred into the mind, hinted of nothing less than that.

The library was breathtaking, but those were closed books, unread even by the layer of dust that covered their tops. The library's books were a tease, while these open air acts of comprehending were witnesses to the scene of perfecting a human mind.

Brother Cheikh, the human mind in question, however, was nowhere to be seen, perfect or not.

"Hmmm," said Sister Makeba. "I guess I have to go track him down. Why don't you have a seat, dear, while I go get him. Read whatever you like, as long as you put it back." She laughed, "I know this doesn't look very orderly, but the doctor has a system known only to himself and its best left as it is."

She turned to go.

"Oh," she added, facing me, again, "and so I don't have to find you, too, don't wander back out into the library. Stay here. I'll be back in a bit."

"Okay," I said, looking at her as if she had placed me in a toy store.

74

Shoot! With my curiosity revved up? I was thoroughly happy to read right there for hours. This was history that my parents maybe didn't allow! What secrets would be revealed here? I took a seat in the one available chair behind an antique desk, and let go an anticipatory deep breath.

Mrs. Kattan's eyes glinted approvingly, and she left, closing the door behind.

Paging through one volume after another on the desk and checking its contents' page to find the section that might interest me the most, I decided to gorge myself on all the titles; getting up to explore the other piles. Thumbing through texts all about the room, it was after my second tier of stalagmite possibilities that I became fully aware of a door, inset with a window, in the far back corner to the right, hidden by a bookcase and another tower of books. Navigating the educational havoc on the floor, I walked up to it, seeing through its window a large enclosed porch area, starting at this door and running along what must have been a hidden side portion of the mansion, with bamboo shades unfurled so that the area lay dim, though not entirely so. The sunlight outside was too bright and bled through the gaps in the shades.

Looking within, I spied an intriguing space, with more books in similar piles, but also with an assemblage of neglected Afrikan sculptures, haphazardly propped one against the other, and rusted gardening tools amidst bric-a-brac, assembled on a pitted metal picnic table. Further back ran a collection of power equipment – a lawn mower, a step ladder, buckets of paint, excess furniture, cords of rope all over the floor, along with other discarded hardware, garden tools and etc.

But what caught the bulk of my attention was an object, spherical, large, but smaller than a car, bigger than a bicycle, poking out right beyond the first garden table, lawnmower, propped up rolled carpet, and a bunch of thick cord. Try as I might, I couldn't tell what the heck that could have been, as it was draped over with an expansive Afrikan mud clothe.

'What is that?' I thought. What could be that size and that shape? My mind got to ruminating. It looked unerringly round, so it wasn't a crate. Crates had corners. Furniture, if it didn't have corners, had at least one flat surface. I became abuzz with speculations, and all my 12 years of book loving, right then, were proving no help at all.

Was it a medicine ball? Nah! Even medicine balls didn't come that big and why would you cover over something that's meant to get dirty? A boulder? If it was a boulder the Kattans had dug up, why would they keep a giant rock, perfectly formed mind you, sitting on the back porch? They bought sculpture. They hired sculptors, but they weren't sculptors, themselves.

Let me tell you, reader – these questions and the tantalizing tease of the mud clothe? Well, tease has made the minds of grown men revert to infants. And I surely was no grown man, smart or not. This puzzle made my brain's neurons surge from un-ignorable spark to the hand I, without realizing, found twisting open the glass doorknob. Not to be redundant, but AGAIN, let me tell you, reader, to this day I have no memory of the motions, but the burning curiosity made my action from standing safely in a room before a pile of books, to standing, without permission, on a porch deck, slowly lifting the edge of that clothe? Curiosity made it all happen so quickly, that I swear somebody else must have picked me up and deposited me there to discover:

Nothing. Absolutely nothing. Or more aptly, absolute complete nothingness. My eyes met a thorough blackness that would make pitch black feel pale. For when I lifted one corner of the clothe, as doing that was beyond my ability to resist, I uncovered a darkness so complete it seemed like a hole in the space before me that came up just to my chin. Like a hole in the ground, only, this one in thin air.

Side to side it was the width of my outstretched arms, if I'd been capable of moving them at that frozen second. But for this moment, before an inevitable chain of events catapulted everything I'd ever assumed into an unpredictable spiral, into that 'accident' I've oft mentioned already – when I would reach out to touch that incomprehensible black and confirm what my eyes could not believe – for that seized second, Tyree Marcus Jackson, me, Black Boy, stared captured by the most nondescript tease I had or would ever know in my life. Or so far as my life has known, as nondescript teases, go...

The ball, upon up close inspection, wasn't fully spherical, despite the perfect shape the cloth implied was there. I slowly began to see, close up, that it had a flattened bottom, as if from its own invisible weight, upon which it sat. As if it had collapsed from the enormity of itself. I wondered, how I knew it was heavy, as for all the world it was just a hole. But it was like a drawing of a hole that when you view in another way looks like a button. It was one of those Escher artworks where a reasonable scene does something impossible. Like, I didn't know it was heavy, but then again I did. Impossible to understand, but I knew this without trying to pick it up as I knew this object, inside myself, as one knows the ocean after a life spent living in the desert. You hear the sound of the crashing waves deep within and it soothes you, automatically, long after you leave. It's calling to the two thirds of you that's the same as itself.

After a few minutes of blank staring that felt like a blink, when my irises, I guess they had become hypnotically transfixed by the orb so the porch dropped out of my awareness – when they had fully opened to admit all possible light, I became aware of a nearly imperceptible sheen, that rhythmically pulsated around the orb on what should have been its surface. Or at least it seemed to be there, like a minute hand moving across the face of a clock. After becoming certain that it truly existed as a faint iridescent flow from left to right, disappearing and reappearing under the mud clothe that I had only pushed back a touch, for me watching it became a soothing game. Like popping the nodules on a sheet of bubble wrap, one at a time.

'Ah,' I thought, as it came around, again. 'There it is, right on time.'

I had begun counting.

With each passing, (before that chain of events began, and not far off from this moment), the glistening ray, (wasn't it more luminescent than before?), it seemed to increase so slightly that when I was certain it was, indeed, brighter – that's when, in the wake of its passing, fine writing, or lyrical pictograms appeared. They seemed much like the hieroglyphs I had seen in my books about Ancient Kemet. Yet, not quite. These were connected one to the other like a pictogram script, as they faded out of my view in the waning slide of the passing light, as a bulb would dim, one amp at a time. The 'button' became a 'hole' of that unquestionable darkness again.

I had to get as close as possible, so I leaned in to see, my own nose, the button that my mom loved to kiss, almost touching the surface that looked as if it wasn't there. It suddenly bristled with either the proximity of the orb's surface and a static charge, or with a..., with a?

Breeze?!

'Oh, nah!' I thought in shock. 'That can't be!'

It was then that I left ordinary forever behind with ease, chose my lifetime career without any teacher's prompting, and stepped firmly into the inevitable – and it only took my one hand, seeking proof that indeed this was a gaping hole in the fabric of the air before me and that gaping hole came with its own atmosphere. I had meant just to graze the surface lightly, REALLY! Browse the grooves of the letters with the tips of my fingers, maybe, since I was certain I

77

was old enough, and discerning enough to do so without harm. And after all, Sister Makeba hadn't said not to come out here. Had she? I definitely remembered her command to not go back out into the library, but nothing about the porch and this... blackness. And so –

'A *light touch*,' I thought, '*to feel if this thing has its own wind. Maybe it's some weird new kind of air conditioner.*'

There. Up went my ignorant hand, which destiny grabbed a hold of with a startlingly unexpected deep voiced Senegalese accented –

"Tyree! No!" –

That boomed from behind that door I'd just stepped through and onto the porch, having closed behind me. It was a voice which struck me like water out of a fire hose, smacking me with blistering force inside my head. It was Dr. Kattan and, I was caught again. Only this time there was no hint of a calming laugh to follow. Charged up, spontaneously, with Insta-Guilt, the chain reaction set off my straight ahead unstoppable journey into the incredible. Though my hand, obeying the call to stop, remained hovering a hair's width from touching the orb, my head snapped back to the sight of that tall Afrikan man racing at the same underwater rate as when I had thrown out my threats to Howard – as he was opening that porch door, my own body trying to follow my surprised head, in order that its owner, ME, not appear too pathetically guilty, if I was facing him rather than the scene of my crime – as I turned that head? If only my feet had been gifted with a set of sneaker-free eyes, which would have noticed the bundled up, excess mud clothe on the floor, and the cord, as my feet tried to turn with me, all at once, but tripped. Over that rope and tarp they stumbled, propelling both twisted and out of control, complete me backwards, in physical agreement with my tripping dumbfounded shock.

Such a shock, that as the darkness of the orb, which it turned out was a hole after all (that curious cat's question was answered, to my horror) – as the hole enveloped me, like I was a finger dipping into a thick batter – such a shock it was, the strangeness didn't hit my conscious thoughts through my avalanche of emotions. My hysterical subconscious, however, had no problem instantly telling its overly logical twin that as there was no logic currently happening, so shut up! My hysteria took over, telling all of me that this was a good time to ... what? To start freaking out! Since the floor I should have hit right away was nowhere to be felt.

That's how and when I started screaming without trying to!

As I screamed, I continued falling, and falling, despite my certainty that I sure as get out should have hit the floor of the porch, way back. The illogically mad me bravely dared to stop my screaming, for a hot second – though I was still terrified – to chance staring wild eyed about.

"What the? Holy...' I said in fully unrepeatable aghast-ment, "Where the heck am I?!"

For all about me was not only that fully verified breeze, but with my wild tumbling, it had become a back wind blowing g-forcefully up against my descent. And though everywhere was the intensity of that jet blackness, I could see, not stars, but an infinite number of mountainous sized glowing spirals as far as my eyesight could reach. Like Mt. Everest-ian coils of glistening glass, they hung iridescently in the grasping dark like trees in a forest, with no beginning, as they twisted dramatically down for what might have been forever. The glowing colors of each coil flowed into the next rainbow of hues, and on more brightly as I fell. And for each, they reached up from an emanation somewhere below me that I could not discern. I was falling face downwards, within a singular gigantic spiral, as I watched its swirling rising up with every second, and becoming narrower in circumference, ever so gradually as I fell. For a moment it was about the diameter of a large sized public park, and then the next, it had narrowed down to the size of a medium schoolhouse, getting smaller the further down I went.

I closed my eyes again, to get back to petrified screaming, wishing, with more certainty than I had ever felt, that the end of my life could have been something wonderfully ordinary, like old age or cancer. Even a nice old fashioned strike by lightening.

I took a breath, opened my eyes, again, momentarily trying to pretend to be brave, while fervently mumbling 'The Lord's Prayer', hoping the ludicrousness of the situation would somehow give my prayer extra power to reverse the horror I was in, despite my never ending sense of continued falling. But as it remained an endless black expanse with no change?

I shut my eyes, again, more fiercely and really started screaming.

It was during perhaps my seventh round of what had descended into hoarse shrieks, (that was a whole lot of screaming goin' on there!) with my eyes firmly sealed for good, as far as my panicked mind was concerned, that's when I resoundingly hit, with absolutely no sound, no force, no pain whatsoever and

Gratefully – that's when I hit a firm, moist solidity. Just like that, the horror had stopped.

This time, overjoyed, the prospect of living slammed into both halves of my brain, immediately. Fully functional in thought and action, sure this was some trick with mirrors, I threw open my eyes and saw above me, the clearest blue sky I had ever seen. It was so resplendently rich a blue, it seemed like a child's crayon drawing, vibrantly unrealistic. I would have immersed myself in its striking depth had I not been more amazed to be alive, since I was startled that my drop hadn't been accompanied by bone shattering cracks, along with some mind numbing painful agony. I was positive that miraculously, I had managed to survive a plunge that must have been double, quintuple what parachuters took when jumping out of a plane. Only I had had no parachute!

"WHAT THE? *How the dangnamit am I not dead?*" I shouted inside my brain.

And Kattan's porch didn't come with a crayon blue sky. Shoot, no sky I had seen looked like the one above me, now. Exactly where or what had I fallen into the middle of?

Just as I began to prop myself up on my elbows to get a look around, that was when I heard a girl's laughter directly behind me.

Actually it was a twittering and very, very familiar.

I crooked my head about as far as it would go and spied my sister, Kyerah, standing in the green open field, a line of palm trees right behind, in back of me, hand to her very young giggling face. I mean, she was really, really *young*. Younger than she should have been. Younger than me – as her body gently shook with amusement, in her uniquely precocious Kyerah way.

But at the same time, it didn't look like her at all! Just her eyes were unmistakably Kyerah's, like no matter how many surgeries Michael Jackson got, his eyes were always Michael's. The rest of her? Though she still had the same sun infused almond skin, now, as with the too blue sky – it was intensely almond and with not a single blemish. It was what all the skin creams in the world couldn't provide. Perfection. She was, also, more slender, wearing a cream colored clothe tunic, with her hair wrapped, as if she were wearing a Halloween costume of an Egyptian child. Only, not that cheap stiff clothe they make children's costumes from. This looked real. Subtle. Detailed with jewelry that appeared to be genuine gold and that I had never seen before, no matter how rich we had once been.

80

But her name wasn't Kyerah here, I had known that, automatically. Didn't know why I knew. It was a name altogether that I couldn't bring to the front of my brain as it had been a long, long time since I had said it. It was, it was....

"Amenhotep!" she laughed, "My, but brother! You are so ungainly! It is no wonder father leaves you home with us young ones!"

"Sitamen!" I shouted aloud, as I triumphantly remembered her name, and a strange feeling of joy infused me, as if I were seeing her for the first time in...

centuries? And, yes. My name was Amenhotep, same as my father's...

"Yes, brother?" Sitamen answered, interrupting my strange train of thought. Thoughts that could get me committed, as 'That Truly Crazy Tyree'.

She came around fully into my view, with a look of concern, probably brought on by the emotion in my voice.

"Are you alright?" she asked. "Let me help you up."

She knelt down upon the rich crayon green grass that I saw had to have been what had cushioned my fall, but, my fall from where? The sky?

"Sister! From whence did I fall?"

'Sister?' I pondered, instantly, 'From 'whence' did I fall?' I stumbled at the improbable sound of my own words, which rang clear as if I had never been hoarse from recently screaming my head off – as it struck me, I was NO LONGER speaking English, hoarse or not! I didn't know what language it was, but my tongue was performing feats with syllables and syntax that were decidedly not the language I had grown up with, and it wasn't French, either. It was some unknown other tongue that felt unexplainably – comfortable, while I suspected speaking English would feel unnatural. For that matter, I was no longer wearing my own clothes, though I knew the substitutes were still mine, as I mysteriously realized so much about disconnected details of this place. Instead of my favorite Darth Vader t-shirt and khaki pants, and although I still had my sneakers on, I was wearing a sheath of the same kind of clothe my sister wore; only this was covering just my groan and backside. My underwear covered more than this, this? LOINCLOTH. AH! I had a loincloth on in front of my sister!

This is one of those spontaneous embarrassing moments that I don't mind mentioning as it's comical to me today, but then? It splashed in to soak up all my other crammed up emotions, fueling me with an urgency to get up, right away. Like the dire need to go the bathroom. I had to find some real clothes. Maybe there'd be a giant leaf, somewhere, I could cover up with, until I could get something presentable.

But as my sister, who no longer looked like my sister – quite – put her arm supportively on my back, helping my strenuous efforts to reach a sitting position, I found I couldn't rise any further than my upright torso resting upon my inadequately covered behind. My feet, for no apparent reason, refused to budge, as if they were cemented to the very ground, solidifying my legs into useless timber. With each struggling attempt, they remained riveted to their position like they were supposed to be returned to the 'Black Man' statue I had borrowed them from, and the statue had laid claim before I gave them back.

"Can you not rise, my brother?" Sitamen asked, concern filling her young face, "and what do you mean from whence you fell? You tripped, Amen, on nothing at all. Have spirits possessed your faculties?"

Gee. I hadn't considered that, that I might have not actually lost my mind, but was perhaps possessed by 'spirits'. Maybe the mansion *was* haunted. Or, maybe, I was still back in Dr. Kattan's office, having only fallen asleep while reading a book about some ancient place. And I guess my mom was right in saying she'd always been proud of what she called my vivid imagination. Perhaps in my dreaming in that mysterious Kattan home, my dreams also gained a new intensity. But staring perplexedly at this girl who looked like someone I shouldn't know and yet I did, I couldn't help but admit my whole experience was too real, too bizarre to be only a dream, or a hallucination that I had concocted in my head.

Even I knew, I wasn't quite that clever.

"I don't know," I answered and meant it, as I tried to wriggle and flex my legs, uselessly, since they were attached to feet that paid them no attention. I couldn't even pull these sneaker clad statue's feet up from off the grass and dirt upon which they lay. I wondered if they had been paralyzed by the fall, or maybe my sister was right and I wasn't dreaming. I had simply, lost my mind, only unlike back at P.S. 47, it wasn't an act. Didn't schizophrenia happen in one's older years? Didn't some people during psychotic fits experience hallucinatory physical trauma, like sudden blindness, or something to that

82

effect? Since, even more so, if my feet had been broken, wouldn't I have been feeling blinding pain? And wouldn't I be able to at least pull them, shattered bones and all, to the side, if only a bit?

But, they were immovably stuck.

"I cannot move my feet," I cried, "not even to pull them side to side!"

"Why, that is impossible! Even if they are damaged, somehow, they are still yours! Here, let me try moving them."

And she put a slender red brown hand beneath one of my slightly buckled up knees and gently, but firmly, pulled.

Not only did my feet not move one bit, but the grass, itself, directly beneath, was like green rock, impervious to the very idea of moving, as it stirred, not at all.

Sitamin's face registered complete shock. She became determined to solve the mystery of this impossibility; frowned at her lack of progress and placed her hand, instead, on the side of my sneakered foot, without noticing my footwear horribly clashed with my loincloth, and even more gently, she applied steady pressure.

"Does that hurt?" She looked hesitantly back at me.

Woefully I answered, "No." I wished it did.

"I'm going to take off your sandals so I get a better grip."

I didn't have the heart to tell her our mom would be upset to know she'd spent so much money on sandals rather than Nikes, but I said nothing as she shoved more and more forcefully, and my sneakers that looked like sandals to her remained where they were. Frustrated when this effort brought no progress, she checked the solidly frozen state of the grass crushed beneath, trying to move the blades, and yet, got the same petrified result. They wouldn't move.

"What enchantment is this, Amen?!" she called out fearfully.

But her voice had become a muffled whisper as I didn't hear my 'sister' over the sudden wash of queasiness that had begun to overcome me, pooling the focus of my worries from my feet to the rush of warmth that radiated, right then, head to stomach, threatening to empty out of my mouth. I fell backwards, onto the ground, as Sitamen became transfixed by the unresponsive fauna.

And it was just like that, that I was catapulted upwards, by the very feet that had been, up till then, ignoring all my ordinary commands. Now, they were giving the orders, taking me high, feet first and strikingly quickly!

That's when, my reptilian brain took over again and I resumed, what turned out to have been my only temporarily halted screaming, which once more came out as a strained squeak. This time, however, I kept my eyes open, preferring to face this fresh horror by seeing it, and being certain that I was indeed, fully awake, even if insane, or experiencing the most horrifically realistic nightmare I'd ever known.

And I still couldn't feel a toe to my name, though through shrill screams and flailing arms, I tried desperately to wriggle them to gain some kind of upper hand that might get me back to the recognizable grass below – before it was a deadly drop away.

I mean, how long would I be impervious to being flattened like a pancake? Falling unharmed had to have been a fluke, I figured. If my feet ended their strike from high up, letting me fall for real? That time might prove fatal.

Yet, as never ending as the fall downward had seemed, upwards I climbed and climbed. And not up through that crayon colored azure sky, but straight back into the batter of indefinable darkness, as if it had been hovering right above my head, invisible to both me and Sitamin's eyes, as I had lain there in the grass. And what about that girl, who I was certain, I had as much a connection to as I had with my own sister, Kyerah?

'Oh!' I thought, '*Who knew a person could have so many stupid questions pop up when facing imminent death?*' For though my initial drop hadn't broken a bone, how long could crazy luck like that keep up, when nothing else made sense?

And there I was, living the illogical in the opposite direction to how I'd arrived. I was rising just as rapidly – feet FIRST, if I need remind you, back within the open interior of a spiral which I couldn't tell if it was the one I fell through before, or another. It was identical to all the rest that faded out into the millions, beyond, I guessed, filling the dark endlessness into infinity.

And I stopped my squeaks, both because my throat had refused to co-operate anymore and because...

84

the vista was actually, amazingly beautiful. Some truths can't be denied no matter how insane the moment, just like silly thoughts.

Thus, it was with that realization, colliding with another strangely un-hysterical random consideration, (that, what the heck, I might as well enjoy my last moment alive) - which finally and permanently stopped my very attempt to scream. I was, almost as quickly as this horror had started? I was suddenly gifted with an appreciation for the preciousness of Life and wanted to squeeze out my last seconds feeling grateful.

The gratitude, only surprising to 12yr old me, came naturally, as it does in moments like these, an appreciation of life, despite being young - cherishing existence came automatically with the fear of losing it. So sweet it was to suddenly feel that rush of knowing that I had, indeed, enjoyed my time on Earth for the little bit of time I had been there, even with my father gone and my emergency, now, I knew without further concern, a scream was, as Mrs. Kattan had implied by talking about spoiled children, a scream would have been the last refuge of those who couldn't accept that fate was nothing personal.

Turned out, I wasn't spoiled enough not to appreciate truly adventurous wonder.

So I let go. Accepted that nothing could stop this end except accepting it. Then - quite without planning - my need to rant during, the last seconds of my breath that would have taken up too much of what little time I had left, or so far as what I imagined I had left - it disappeared completely. The rant faded away into the nothing surrounding me, and was replaced by my burgeoning ferocious curiosity. I was Tyree, walking across the school courtyard, this time with no regrets. No fear.

That was when I saw it. The magnificence in full. I saw what had been thoroughly hidden by my panic. Later I was to learn for certain, but then? I only guessed that endless place to be an echo of God's work made concrete; though there was no 'designer' signature to be seen. His presence was an undeniable feeling, a whisper, a fingerprint in the scope of that swirling pageant of colors - alive as much as I still was. That feeling of intensified life entered my cortex, stimulating all the centers of my brain, and somehow, I knew it. Without need for interpretation, I knew He, was with me as a witness, as a comfort. He was the reason for that majestic beauty's celebration - as if right there, springtime was eternally blooming for Him. All intertwined with this, I felt I could hear an echo call, though not audibly –

'You've done well, son. I'm proud of you.'

So, filled up with a rush of many emotions, produced in less than one hour, to then find joy in the most lonely and barren of experiences? I had no need for screams, anymore, but I surely couldn't hold back my tears. They flowed unchecked until I wiped them away, half expecting one of my Sandstone Hill crew to call me a 'girlie boy'. Also, let me reassure you, an upside down tear stream, that wasn't being dried fast enough by the downward rush of air, is really ticklish on the upper eyelids. Try crying, one day, upside down.

And that made me laugh, from an unexpected well somewhere deep. A rolling chuckle that coiled around the dancing spirals, without an echo. My laugh was tiny, but nothing else was.

I then could see – still barreling steadily upwards by my feet (I had forgotten about my feet) – when I'd first tripped over the mud clothe and fell into this nothingness, it was only a superficial glance that had made the spirals seem to be all the same. Yes, they were all ascending coils, like when my mom would curl her locs, only without the coils being stacked one on top of another, but instead vastly spaced apart from one to the next. And they glistened more than mere glass. Some sparkled as if constructed from the highest polished, faceted gems. No two were alike. Some were long and stretched out, with thin, elegant bands, while others were thick and compacted. With each one, the living blend of colors was an intoxicatingly unique display, with its own concentration of a certain hue particular to that coil. And the concentration of color, I also noticed, changed dramatically with some, gradually with others, and not at all with just a few.

Then there was that hum. Had it been there before? I guessed it was hard to hear anything over the roar of my own screams. It was a sonic boom that played unknown chords which seemed to sink into my skin, linking hands with my soul. It was musical like, though not soul music, classical, hip-hop, or rock as there was no discernible beat. Kinda. More like a steady pulse. If there's a music that could come close, I'd call that sound, 'jazz', for it was as if the beat was invisible and your expectation filled it in. Now that I had become silent I could detect random chords' low but undeniable roll, as they mixed me, nearly physically, with tones that should not have been music, and yet it was the most harmonious rhythm I had ever – experienced. The word 'heard' could never describe the physicality of the exchange.

86

And so, sound and sight combined into a crescendo that was welcoming me to its celebration. A child, who was receiving a standing ovation, felt on the inside, where it mattered. I might die, I knew, but funny how I felt I had already been rescued.

Fear had been clapped away, plus my perception was suddenly heightened. Thoughts were coming at me faster as if the volume on my brain had been turned way up. I made a quick mental tabulation, besides all my other thoughts, that my ascent was at a gradually tilting angle. About 45 degrees I knew instantly – no need for a protractor, a knowing above and beyond what I would have wildly expected myself to know, as math, like science, had never been my favorite, in case I haven't said that enough. But suddenly I could master the basics, there, as if old dusty brain cells that had barely been activated in class, came to the forefront to answer the imminent question at hand, "How will this end?"

See? I had all my usual youthful distractions such as, *'Am I crazy?' 'Will anybody miss me?' 'Darn! Mom said she was going to make pancakes in the morning.'* – but I could hear them in the background, and still focus on precise calculations.

I bent my head up, even further, to see where this tilt was leading and saw the spiral I was in, and all the rest, at the same far distance way above, had been ensnared by twisting strands slamming into them from directly from the side. Millions, by my conservative guess had ensnared their way into the upper midst, turning the strands into undifferentiated grey dim lines, all their color drained away like the scene of a mass strangulation of light bulbs. Most of the coils lay shattered, as if some explosion had ripped them apart and scattered the shards about, stranded above, hovering in mid blackness, the glow from below revealing them with assorted ghastly twinkles. And the invading twists had no glow of their own, no hue, in the slightest. Just a dimness with no glistening intensity I could see, anywhere I looked. Further up I couldn't see a thing, but what I could discern was a chaotic tumble of ghostly ripped remnants, without focus, or aim. And there would be no music up there, either, I knew.

Something beyond violent was happening to all the coils above. It wasn't a scene of typical violence, with blood and gore, no. It was more. It was the murder of joy so it could never return, even after mourning time was finished.

At my tilted trajectory, I doubtlessly realized, my death would NOT be caused by careening into that mass of frantic tangles. That made me heave a sigh of relief. Thank GOD. I didn't think I could handle going there, let alone dying in that waste. No. I could see where I was headed; where I would get the once in a lifetime chance to answer that final question that no one I'd ever met could, "What's it like to die?"

Yet, my own serenity didn't leave me. I remained ever so resigned, even happy, to pay the full fare for this extraordinary ride. My only slim hope was that my impact not hurt too much. My only regret – that I wouldn't be able to share the AMAZING-NESS of this adventure with my family.

My family. Oh, now there was a sadness that took a central seat in with all my other feelings. I prayed they would eventually be okay. As I had no time to ponder anymore, I braced instead for what I estimated to be the point of collision, and where my too brief introduction to life would end Tyree Jackson, beloved son of Marcus and Renee Jackson – I braced myself for immediate impact and certain death.

I started counting, calmly, as I had at the beginning of this experience. Like a final last minute game.

"One, two, three, four..."

At the resurgence of a bit of fear, I reassured myself with, *'But I'm going so fast, it'll only hurt a second, and maybe not at all. There's such a thing as instant death on impact. I'll be pulverized too fast to notice any pain.'*

My guess was almost correct, if only a little bit, that it didn't hurt at all – the impact, that is. Well, not that much. Except for that three strand twisted manila rigging cord that was tightly coiled around my ankles. Like some of the rope that'd been laying on the porch I found the orb sitting in. It definitely hurt and I wasn't sure how it got there but when I looked at my feet there it was, secured around my ankles with a square knot.

I immediately recognized it as the same type of rigging cord they use on fishing boats, from several boating trips I had taken with my family on some of those money blessed vacations. It was always the same ship, out of Montego, with always the same captain, a deep voiced Black man named Jaffa, who would boom to me and my sister, in a thick Jamaican roll, to,

"Stay clear of tha ropes! Ya get caught in dem an' lose a leg!"

And there it was now, an immense thick braid of scratchy fibers that was, yes, squeezing into my exposed ankles quite painfully. I hoped Jaffa wasn't around to soundly admonish my foolishness, or suggest amputating my feet. I hoped my feet didn't need amputating. But this was definitely a mistake in my calculated guess of how I'd die, as although I was feeling pain, most decidedly, I didn't mind since it confirmed I was still alive.

And that made me, unexpectedly, even more happy, if such a state were possible. Although, I no longer had any doubt – my life was truly going to go on and I suspected that nothing would ever be the same, again. That guess I got 100% right.

=

I had managed, during my hurtling ascent, to keep my eyes open through what I was certain would have been the end of my life; and so I hadn't missed it when what appeared as a solid luminescent wall, ten times my height, when it had – rather than feeling like a high speed train wreck to the body, crushing me feet first – it had, instead, soothingly embraced me, feeling more like a warm rush from out of a heat vent, allowing me to enter, without resistance. That was when my speed spontaneously slowed down, of its own volition, so that as my eyes passed through after all the else of me, those swirling hues, which were indistinguishable clumps from afar, a moment before that, then gelled and coalesced into definitive objects, shapes, and there! Those shapes became the beaming smile of Mrs. Kattan, and a seriously frowning Dr. Kattan, whom, together, were gripping my feet and the rope they were tied up with. I had arrived sitting up, on the porch floor, and that's when I had felt the pain in my ankles, seeing the cord that was causing me the delightful agony – a pain which inside me, screamed louder than my previous audible ones – it screamed, without the scratchy squeak, that I had survived.

I smiled so broadly, it felt as if I would touch my ears with the corners of my lips.

"Wow!" was the extent of my detailed verbal analysis on the schematics of nearly dying.

And, startlingly? My voice was its full forced volume. No hoarseness to be heard.

"Greetings, Amenhotep," Sister Makeba had said to me, a collaborative twinkle in her eye.

I had looked dazedly up at her as she put a bucket right under my chin, while Dr. Kattan's eyes furrowed into a unibrow raised slits. Wondering how she knew my name, I continued smiling brightly as my head wobbled a bit to and fro and then, I promptly threw up. I also wondered how she would have known I'd be in need of the kindly service a bucket would provide. Boy, those Kattans were something else! I had promised myself to thank them both for their considerateness, even the stern doctor, as soon as I woke up.

And that was when everything went black. But this time, only inside my head, not all around. All around me, the world was colorfully wonderful.

Chapter 2

I'd heard the arguing voices for a long while, in the back of my mind, before their volume and intensity had woken me up, so that I then paid full attention. I was lying on a beige couch in the middle of a bluntly turquoise painted room, my bare feet propped up on a throw pillow, my mildly aching ankles covered with cold compresses. There was a currently unused fireplace across from me and the couch, and scarce, simple furniture about the room, as I could see. There was another part behind me I couldn't see in my reclining position, as the high back of the couch was in the way. It was from that area, behind me, that the voices, held low but serious, came to my ears.

The doctor and his wife, not arguing, were in the middle of, nonetheless, an intense exchange, about which – its insistent, politely discussed topic – was gently, though forcefully, about me.

"...disappeared!" Brother Cheikh was in the middle of saying in the same Senegalese infused accent as his wife had – only there was nothing singsong in his voice. I knew he'd repeated that particular word frequently, as although this utterance had been the one to wake me up, 'disappeared' had echoed throughout my slumber.

"The boy could have disappeared just like Mumia!"

"But he did not, my beloved," said Sister Makeba, mildly, but firmly. "The sign is clear," she ended.

"Sign? Sign of what? That we have allowed not only a child, but one of these American brats to bulldoze his way into a matter that demands finesse, patience, obedience?!" His voice rose substantially at the last word. He was pushing the definition of 'not' arguing to its limit.

"Husband, I ask you, consider that it was I who took him to your office. I had no idea you had expanded the Breath, or I would have never taken him there. For that I am most sorry. So, I implore you, don't blame Tyree. He's a sharp one, not a wild boy. But the very traits that make him potentially an excellent assistant would also make such an object irresistible to him. It is a miraculous blessing that you caught his feet when you did, and I was right behind you, and could assist you. The Most High does nothing without a purpose."

Brother Cheikh grunted a reluctant agreement in his characteristic two part exhale which sounded, if one could spell it out, like a 'harrumph' and softly said, "Yes, that it was, but in truth, wife, I didn't expand the sphere."

"You," she hesitated. Her volume raised in surprise with, "You didn't expand it?"

"No. I left it on my work desk in its satchel. I'd have never expanded it to then leave it unattended," came his answer, a moment later, but firmly. Undoubtedly.

"Then beloved, it is a certainty! The orb wanted him to find it! You know how it can be, sometimes, doing what it chooses. And you felt his plummet and arrival, same as I, even if we couldn't see it. He's Akhenaten. Akhenaten! Can you imagine the potential of such a soul?" She laughed a bit.

At that the doctor merely harrumphed, but with disagreement, and correcting his wife he said, "To have potential is to have a window waiting for its glass. All things, good and bad, come flying through until the time it's sealed. Potential turns into nothing, if when the time comes to fulfill its promise, the frame is so battered it'll only fall and break. And America and its residents are nothing if not broken!"

I was used to the doctor's strong opinions, as I stated, even though these opinions were about me, pointedly, this moment. I'd heard him, my father and many others, politely but intensely, dither over the smallest details of all subjects, including the best ways to raise children (while Kyerah and I were sometimes trotted out as my father's proudest sample proofs); but what shocked me most, laying there, not wanting to divulge that I had heard his innermost uncomplimentary opinion about Americans like myself (which I could have suspected, as I now knew, sadly, Sister Makeba shared the same feelings, only in a gentler version) – what shocked me was that I was neither hurt nor angry like I had been when the sister had expressed the same about my countrymen. Or in my case? About my countryboys.

This time I didn't want to protest being spoiled. It didn't feel like a personal attack. I wanted to know, if I was, if we all were spoiled, what might be wrong with us, Americans, that would make Dr. and Mrs. Kattan, such astute people, sound so matter of factly certain? This time I was as willing to accept that my

93

concept of 'normal' might not be what 'normal' should be and even more, I was determined to make it right by accepting the truth, whatever that might be.

Too bad, I didn't know how dangerous truth can feel, once you're willing to hear it, to know what you've never known before, no matter how startling.

"That is so, husband," she continued, confirming her agreement.

Still? Just to mention it – I, the young ALIVE Mr. Jackson, felt much better listening to the soothing imploring of the other half of Brother Cheikh, as what a buttery cadence Sister Makeba possessed. Even when a critique came from her, it was more of a ballad than a funeral dirge. I wondered if her gentility could have the same effect, or even half, on its intended indignant party, as it did with me... Then I'd mayhaps be in the clear.

"That is so," she repeated, "but I am sure they are not all that awful. Why, if you give Tyree a chance, you may have found the relief you said you must have. It's no longer an adventure for you, husband. It's a job that's lasted way past retirement for both of us. The Breath is a precision instrument that requires focused dedication, on top of experience. You said Brother Mumia, when he lost his edge, eventually, he became prone to making mistakes, including and especially his final one. Well, can we afford a single mishap at this critical hour when you have no successor? That is one mistake that, thank Allah, he didn't make as he had you to fulfill the mission. How long before we find someone from another place to entrust such a responsibility upon? Gainde wouldn't accept the secrecy of the duty. He wants to expose the sphere to the world...," she paused before continuing, not saying something that only she was privy to, "So? To what place can we turn where the character of the young men is better than here? Do we have another 50 years to search the world? We already know Tyree from when he was a baby. He and his sister have shown exemplary character while he is young enough to learn all he needs to know, quickly.

"Beloved husband? We not only don't have time, we can't return home, not with the sphere, no matter how well disguised; no matter how many books we pack as a diversion without raising suspicion. Should we become active, searching high and low for a perfect assistant, our enemy will, again, conclude we have possession. They would use any flimsy excuse to tear this house apart in their never ending hunt. They'll surely confiscate, if not destroy the contents of the library and seize the Breath, with glee. My love, not only can we not afford to wait any longer, but Allah's Memories chose the boy."

There was another momentary pause, and Sister Makeba seemed done. The doctor expelled another 'harrumph' and then, with a softened voice, Dr. Kattan replied, "I understand your reasoning, but fear, wife, is a poor light. Not to mention, whether the Breath chose him or not – fear cannot be our motivation. The orb chooses many. It chose Gainde, also, but one must want to answer the call. This country has become a zoo where most have lost confidence in everything, especially tradition and faith. Even the fake European Christianity given our people by their oppressors contains some rudimentary guidance, that our enemy has lured the people to ignore and blindly they follow. There is a reason for honor, for faith, as the sphere is not the latest video game. Tyree should have waited, period. And we must be patient in our search, as well, as it will take as long to locate the new Protector as is needed. No less and no more.

"I will do my personal best to remain careful, but? Queen, it is the Tamahue who barge recklessly along, trying to clean up their mess by pretending it's not there, only making it dirtier. So, to win, we must plan further ahead with mathematical precision, not panic. Not exhaustion. There was a particular quality about that boy's father I admired. He was precise. Now, I understand your...," he reflected a second, "...your insistent focus, but we must plan one day beyond forever. And that young man didn't even think past the second he saw the sphere!"

And like that he was done, along with his softness which was replaced by the same anger with which he'd begun.

I could see, talking with the doctor would require my own concentrated patience that I obviously hadn't been capable of a little earlier. I don't know how I knew that as at that stage in my life, not only wasn't I anymore patient than the average 12yr old, book smart or not, but ordinarily, I'd have been filled with sheer dread at the spectre of such an intimidating man angrily confronting me; however, there was no dread in me, now. Could it have been my experience in the...?

'Breath' as they seemed to call that black nothingness that was something beyond imagining. Breath? It was more like a tornado...

I decided to stop my eavesdropping. Even though I'd begun innocently, continuing, now, felt like proof of the doctor's bad opinion, and I surely didn't want to prove him right, straight off the bat.

I made myself cough, lightly but clearly.

My hosts, I could tell by the sound of their footfalls into the room, had been just outside the door that I could see the top of, over the rise of the couch.

95

They came round the same side of where my rigging free feet were propped up, with the sister exclaiming,

"Brother Tyree," warmly, as she was so skilled at doing.

The doctor, on the other hand, came up somberly next to her, that bold frown looking as frozen as my feet had been a short while ago.

She knelt down beside me, concerned, and holding an earthenware mug in her hand, topped by a matching lid. She lifted the lid, steam emanated upwards and I caught a whiff of something tangy. She held the mug out in front of me.

"Your ankles might bruise a bit, though not seriously, because of the socks you had on, Tyree," she said, checking the wrappings. "But, anchoring you to this realm was life or death critical."

"To this realm?...," I repeated in a daze of wonderings that as yet had no answer, so?

"What is that thing?!" tumbled out of my mouth, not caring about my aching ankles, as I pushed myself to sit up on the couch's thick arm rest, first looking at her and then the stern face of the brother. But with a cautionary head shake, she advised me to hush. I took hold of the cup as she placed one of her elegant hands on my forehead, removing a damp cloth I hadn't even noticed. She motioned me to drink.

It was a spicy ginger tea, mixed with something else, so powerfully brewed, the spice, not the heat, stung my tongue, slightly. I drank it without complaint, knowing it was given to help.

Dr. Kattan remained standing, all impressively 6ft, 2in of him, arms folded, eyes piercingly focused on me; his expression undoubtedly disapproving.

"Hmmmm," he exhaled, forcefully, changing from his usual harrumphs, perhaps because a two syllable grunt would have interrupted the focus of his precise anger at me. "You are not in the position, young man, to be asking questions here."

Sister Makeba pulled over a chair that had been against the bare wall, and setting it off to the side of where I reclined, she rested herself in it, folding her hands delicately on her lap. Her eyes were also trained on me, eagerly, but aglow with kindness. Dr. Kattan remained standing, though there was another matching chair on the other side of the fireplace. His lean muscled arms were crossed over his chest, his eyes aglow with glaring.

As I wrote, under normal circumstances, I would have shrunken into panic, shot out a spew of concocted excuses, rapid fire. I admit it. Why, given all I'd gone through? Another me might have started crying. That's only a 'maybe'. Yet, right then? I knew silence was my best action.

"I don't know if you realize it, but you could have been erased from this life entirely, Brother Tyree. Disappearing without a trace. Leaving your family in more grief and shock than they are today. Now, I know the sphere has a peculiar lure. I know you didn't realize what it was, but?"

I braced myself for a confrontation, whether I was calm or not. The doctor might not be calm, on his part.

"You have not impressed me with your ability to think well, as you did not resist the temptation in the slightest. I remember you and your sister ignoring the rules of this house, once, when you both were younger; but now that you're older, are you still in the habit of going places without permission? You're not an adult, but surely you aren't too young to be left alone for a moment? The sphere was not exposed on top of my desk like a paperweight. What made you think it was your affair to investigate it without knowing anything about it? Did you consider you could have waited for my arrival? Did you consider that I would have maybe shown it to you, anyway?"

I said nothing, knowing that often grown-ups will ask you a question when they'll only get angrier if you actually answer. Or, angrier if you don't. I didn't know the doctor well enough to figure out which side his outrage would fall on, and I accepted I was in the wrong. So, I decided to wait, silently. However, the doctor didn't get angrier. He waited, a bit, himself, till he finally narrowed his stare, even more, and remaining silent, he indicated I was, then, expected to respond. I chose the truth, rather than a flimsy excuse.

"I didn't know, Dr. Kattan, but, I know that doesn't make what I did right. You're right. I was wrong and I'm sorry. If there's some way to make up for it, please, it's the way I can show you I know I was wrong."

The sincerity of my voice surprised me a little less than the sincerity of my feeling.

And it must have surprised the doctor also, because he exhaled a quiet harrumph, looked off for a moment, and then pulled up his own chair. Seated from that angle, looking slightly up towards his no nonsense Afrikan nose, he looked quite youthful for an elderly graying man. His hair was neatly shortcropped, though longer than my buzz cut, and his lean darkness gave his eyes a brevity that could not be brushed aside. If he chose to be heard, you'd be doing some serious listening, if? You were breathing.

Brother Dr. Kattan chose to be heard, and I chose to act better than I had.

"Son," he began, though softly, this time – perhaps deciding to talk to me as if I was still a child, and I appreciated the sudden warmth in his tone, despite the fact, I hadn't been scared when he'd been harsh. Simply didn't look forward to his ire.

"You discovered something truly amazing today, did you not?"

And with that, I let loose an avalanche!

"Oh, My GOD!" I jerked further up, plopping the compresses to the side and nearly spilling the tea – which Mrs. Kattan grabbed a quick hold of, just in time. I apologized, but continued with my torrent. Nothing could hold it back now.

"What was that place, doctor? There were these spirals and they glowed, and Kyerah!!! She was there, too! Only she didn't look like Kyerah! Not completely, that is. And I was talking a whole 'nuther language! I even had these other memories!!! What was the name of that place? Kyerah's clothes looked Egyptian. And I couldn't move my feet! Was that the rope that did that? Even the grass was frozen. Why did that happen?"

Though I was only one person I was talking so quickly it probably sounded like two or three at once. And I went on and on, with what I've already described to you in detail, so no need to rehash the shock of my shock. Dr. Kattan simply sat there, listening to my every word, nodding, so I knew he was hearing me. I would turn to include Sister Makeba in the onslaught, her expressions changing from sympathetic concern, to amusement, to knowing smiles. Laughing when I told her about how I had begun to laugh as I cried.

Once I'd exhausted all that I knew about my experience, her smile remained and was joined, very slowly, by her husband's understanding gleam of acknowledgment. Wow. That was one of those excellent moments when you could make the both of them happy with you, even if it was only a kind of smile for him. Close enough for me after that way too authentic encounter with his anger.

In the answer to my avalanche of glacier sized questions, I learned that sphere, called, 'The Sacred Breath of Allah', was, as much as I could understand, akin to a photo album, only on the scale of one compiled by the Original Creator. The spirals were the physical echo of the birth of the Original Children, radiating out from what modern scientists describe as The Big Bang. It was all existence happening at once. Like the hidden meaning between lines on a page, it was the physical connection between, what for us each, seems so disconnected. And it was only by a split second's lucky catch that the doctor caught hold of my feet before I was possibly lost to tumbling forever in, as he described...

...almost smile fading while his warmed eyes remained, and his tone was still calm but deadly serious, "Eternity. Brother Tyree, you fell into eternity."

For some reason, I already knew that, without comprehending the technical explanation – I knew I had been in the middle of everything happening at once. I nodded my head, with my intuitive understanding.

"But, then," I suddenly concluded in horror, "what's up above. The explosion..."

"I've never entered the sphere without preparation, so, I've never seen what you saw. I've heard tell of the spirals and the collision above. The way you entered, if my wife and I hadn't caught your feet, you'd have been lost for good. One must never enter the sphere, alone, unprepared. As for the collision? I was told by my teacher who was told by his and on back to the beginning, it is the end of our existence."

"Whoa." I fell backwards on the couch arm, the tea cup the sister had given back to me some time ago sailing with me, as a cold grip of fear wiped out my sense of calm. I had drunken most of the tea, sipping in-between my tirade, thus it sloshed but didn't splatter, while a low thud sound clunked out of the thick arm of the couch I'd thwacked with my back.

"We have to warn everybody!" I declared.

"Indeed," agreed Sister Makeba, nodding her head, sincerely, but sadly. "That is what we are trying to figure out how to do."

"We just have to tell them," would have been my reply at the start of my visit to the Kattans, but now? I only replied as I understood what her tone conveyed, "They wouldn't believe us, would they?"

"No," the doctor answered, "they wouldn't. It would be nice if they did, but unfortunately, they'd never believe a word. They'd think we were insane and some? Would be more than happy to alert those who are looking for the sphere."

I looked to the sister and saw the agreement in her eyes.

With an audible sigh, she said, "Taught there is nothing more to this world than this reality created by evil men, none could believe such a fantastical truth, all at once. The doctor and I disseminate some facts, as needed, a bit at a time. Trying both to wake people up and not alert attention to ourselves. To do more would bring our defeat about with certainty."

"Doctor!" I shouted and lurching up, once again, swinging my legs into a completely seated position, despite the slight ache in my ankles, "They are going to find it, aren't they?" having no idea who the heck 'they' were - "That's what the broken mess above means, doesn't it? And those coils coming out from nowhere breaking the others?"

He sighed deeply, began stroking his beardless chin and looked away for another moment.

"As I said, Brother Tyree, I have only heard of the collision apocryphally. Our foes have been searching since their creation for The Breath, which they obviously have yet to find, since if they had? I've been told that would be the true enslavement of our people as the connection with who we are, even if held by only one man, is vital to withstanding the lies woven by our foe. They amuse themselves into believing they have the sphere in what they call 'The Stone of Destiny'," and here he chuckled, ironically. "But that's just some rock with no purpose that any other rock wouldn't have. The orb? It's Allah's memories which are even physically perfect and that's no scrap book for the coffee table, nor trinket for the ignorant.

"The collision need not be inevitable. It only portends a possible future, while the true future remains filled with all potentials, like an open window" he ended, with a knowing nod at his wife.

That one last statement brought a slew of more questions to my mind, but as I couldn't ask them all at once, I was content to relax with his reassurance, exhaling an, "Ah! Okay. Then it's not necessarily going to happen."

"No. I didn't say that. It would actually seem to be unavoidable, right now."

As a creeping fear, much colder than the fear I had felt confronting Howard, though not as intensely acute as I'd experienced falling in Allah's Photo Album – as a new fear filled my veins with its prospect of dooming not only myself, but all those I loved, including those I had yet to meet in a manhood

100

that might not come? Well, it did more than threaten to drown me. It threatened to wipe me and everything else out with its dearth of any solution. Suddenly the danger that had been the focus of my thoughts for the past several months seemed like a toddler crying over his nose being cleaned out.

"How do we stop them from finding the Breath?!" I cried while standing up as if that was the way to get started. Even my ankles agreed, by not hurting at all.

"Sit down, brother." The doctor made a soothing 'sit down' motion with his hand. He continued, "That collision is called, the 'Ankh Udje Saneb' and when it will happen isn't at all clear as only Allah knows the appointed hour and how each of our individual efforts will combine to be the solution or the problem. It's all a guess at this point, though the unavoidability of the orb's theft gets closer incrementally, with each passing generation, as the time between Ankh Udja Saneb and now grows shorter. Mathematical estimation concludes the invasion could happen in another 100 years or any moment as soon as the enemy finds the sphere."

"What would be 'any moment'?" I asked. "Would that include during our time?"

"This minute, possibly, Brother Tyree," Sister Makeba answered. "It is why each moment is essential." She turned gently towards her husband. Subtly, she turned. Very Subtly.

"Indeed," the tall Afrikan man, seeming not to notice, stood and walked to the window on his left, unfurling the wooden blind in a whoosh of matchstick clicks. He then went to the other window on his right, screening it the same way, which draped the whole room in a somber turquoise cloak.

As he did this, he offered, like it was a vital meal, each word said slowly and deliberately, "This has been a 6,000 year war, that it seems is about to come to an end, as has been predicted. But just because its end may be near, young man, doesn't mean the result will be in our favor or against us, as many lazily may wish on either side."

I politely interjected, "Brother Cheikh, Ankh Udje Saneb? It means 'farewell', correct?" not wondering how I understood the words, already.

"Yes. It literally means, 'farewell, with blessings', though the full nuanced meaning is lost in the English translation."

"Uh-huh," I replied, proudly adding, "It's Egyptian," saying 'Egyptian' as a force of habit, at that time in my still uneducated mind.

101

The doctor did not care for that word in the least.

"No, no, NO!" he shouted back, but I could tell it was more from exasperation than any anger directed at me, any longer. Wouldn't have mattered if it had been directed at me as I was set to understand, not feel sorry for myself. Nevertheless, its unexpected volume made my triggered a memory, although I couldn't tell if it was a memory of my parents teaching me the proper name or, if it was because I'd been there...

"No." I repeated, calmly, agreeing as I instantly knew the reason for his irritation. "The land was Kemet. We were the Kemetic people, not 'Egyptians'."

When I said 'we' I meant it in real time, as if time hadn't passed. I didn't mean it historically, now knowing I was, had been, one of those 'we'.

"We didn't speak 'Egyptian'," I corrected myself.

"We," he continued, resolutely with a lowered voice, "not only spoke no such tongue, there is no such language as the original people never called themselves 'Egyptians'. Kemet means 'Land of the Blacks' and/or 'Land of the Gods'. And 'black' meant the people, not the soil, as Caucasians love to say. You name your land after what makes it great, and dirt can't build itself into anything. People do. As for calling it 'Egypt'?" He harrumphed, heartily, continuing, "If the French woke up one day and called their country 'Toyland'? It would be because they'd been overrun by Ken and Barbie dolls. The same with Kemet. It began with us coming from Ethiopia, the direction the Nile flows – not Europe, as white people didn't even exist when that ancient nation was founded, let alone in Ethiopia. We called it Kemet.

"It was the Greeks and the Romans who felt awkward pronouncing that name, like some Asians have difficulty pronouncing l's and r's. The Caucasian preferred their own term. That's why this country is called 'The United States of America' and nothing the original people called it because they were conquered; and judging by what little we know of Ancient Kemet, one day few will remember that the U.S. ever belonged to a people without blue eyes and blonde hair. Only invaders need to change the name of a country to help its natives forget it still belongs to them."

"Does 'Ankh Udje Saneb' mean farewell to everything?"

Sister Makeba answered, "A farewell can mean an end to everything, son, but? With 'blessings' so that can be an infinite number of possible endings. It's greeting, also. A beginning, signaling a clean break with the past, for any end can only be complete when it finalizes all that came before, emptying the path for something unknown."

"But if this is a war then wouldn't there be armies? Some refugees? For that matter," it hit me, "who are the combatants?"

"Hrrrrrmmmmm," the doctor did an exact impersonation of himself. "That is the difficult answer to reveal, though that's an answer I know. Have you ever heard of the 'Tamahue'?"

I recognized that word, also. Hadn't heard it for as long a time as I'd hadn't heard 'Sitamen', but there were too many questions swirling in my mind to ask, so I nodded, saying, "Yes. But what have they to do with a war against us?"

He laughed, gently, for the first time, while Sister Makeba got up, brushing the wrinkles out of her kente gown.

"This will be a long conversation, and I have many tasks that need doing while there's still some light. Excuse me, gentlemen. You both will have to do without me as best you can."

Just as I exchanged goodbyes with her in a handshake, I rose, and without knowing I would do so, gave her an earnest hug.

"Thank you," I said.

Spontaneously hugging me more tightly back, she winked at me, pointed to my socks stuffed in my sneakers on the other side of the couch arm, and left, without another word, emptied mug with its lid, in her hand.

When she'd exited, the doctor took his seat once more, motioned me to take mine on the couch again, and resumed with, "Young man, the Tamahue were and remain the race of people that our ancestors knew to be the most disagreeable of all due to the lack of light within them. 'Tamahue' is the name given to those who have a weak to nonexistent ability to follow the ways of The First Creator. Do you know which people they were referring to?"

It wasn't difficult to remember that.

"They're the barbarians from the north. It's what we called them."

"Yes. And they have been our 6,000 year foe, created to be our natural enemy."

"Created to be our enemy?" In my memory, a memory I had no idea where it had come from, the Tamahue were thoroughly, ineptly insignificant. Wild.

103

Disorganized. Unprofessional. Pitiful, to be most exact. "I don't understand," I responded.

A harrumph ensued. But with sorrow, not frustration. A deep knowing sorrow that I would come to also feel, like I feel hoping you, reader will hear my truth. However, I didn't feel it then. Then? I felt...

confused.

"They are the same people who called Kemet, 'Egypt', conquered it as it became weakened with their seed, and to this day have yet to admit that they never built that first civilization and are still yet to admit to all their other ongoing deceptions."

"White people?!" Those were the Tamahue, afterall – but as all these colliding recollections were new thoughts in my head, even though in age they were my...?

OLD thoughts, they had no place to fit.

Wow. My 'old' thoughts, the thoughts of Amenhotep, were spiraling through my mind like children orphaned by mistake, bouncing around with Tyree's thoughts, everything crystal clear if not connected, faster than the words I could speak or write. It occurred to me I had many sets of awarenesses, operating at the same time, without having formulated them so they worked precisely together. It was like a whole bunch of friends had moved into my head. I knew their names, but hadn't figured out who'd be sleeping where, and/or which shelf in the refrigerator gets assigned to whom.

It hadn't dawned on me, in a mix of old and new me, that the Tamahue were not merely the same white people from this day and time as the white people from these older memories, but that that ragamuffin group could be a threat, let alone capable of destroying existence. But alongside those thought roommates? Was a kneejerk rejection of a thoroughly modern kind. Though I was used to the discussion about the oppression we Black people had experienced under whites, the possibility that they were our natural enemy as a whole people made me feel as if some white person would pop out from behind the couch and accuse me of not being 'nice'.

I became terribly torn. It was one thing to know how awful they'd historically been; how once I had simply known that truth without guilt - with rage, actually - but it was another concept to think of myself as at war with all of them, today. Those days were over, right? And thank God. Those were some galaxy wide awful things they'd put us through. Maybe all Black people's lives weren't great but at least, now, we each had a chance. Plus, there were a couple of white kids at my old school, Medgar Evers Academic Prep. I hadn't known them so well, however? They hadn't seemed like my enemies in the least, let alone that they would know about some gigantic black hole leading to eternity, so they could come steal it and turn us into permanent slaves.

And a Black man had become president. And plenty of other Black men were in jail for crimes they had committed. It wasn't like we Black people were all good or all bad, either.

"I know this is difficult," he began, not directly answering my question – which in case you, reader have forgotten, also, was regarding white people being created, along with a slew of implied questions – he began, "War is difficult to fathom if not impossible. It makes even blood families fight each other on separate sides, who once swore their allegiance to one another without hesitation. This is not about what anyone may wish to happen. This is about what is. It only takes a few highly disagreeable people to start a war and the gullible ignorant who support them. This one has been waged by a people whose leaders can't afford to let truth win and their people who've a subconscious jealousy and fear of us, at worst; are dismissive of our humanity at least, while none can bear to face the facts. Not just a few, in their case, but most of them aren't capable of admitting their failings when it comes to interacting with us in order to move beyond the barbarity of their ancestors by insisting on humane leaders. Thus? Like a serial killer will never cure himself, they can't leave us alone to our own devices out of fear we'll turn out to be not inferior but an amazing people capable of confirming their fears and exacting retribution." He looked at me, pointedly, seeing, I'm sure, more than a bit of discomfort on my face.

"Let me explain, if I can," he continued without a break. "There are many different kinds of dogs, right?"

"Um? Yes?" I answered with my lack of understanding stamped in my voice.

"Are they all the same, in look? In temperament?"

"No," I shook my head. "But those are dogs. We're all human."

"Yes and no. Dogs are all the same species, too; just as cats; just as humans. They can, same as we – interbreed with their own. And yet? Different breeds have very different tendencies. The only distinction between us humans and species bred to have distinct characteristics by human breeders is that the Tamahue have gained control of the history of breeding men and thereby have gained control of the interpretation of that process when applied to us. They

105

bred our ancestors on the plantations and yet no one else a million years before ever conceived of breeding people like them, when we bred cats and dogs before they ever existed? How is that possible?

"They've hijacked all history through treachery, battle and lies to create a myth that they are like everyone else when no one else has visited other continents bringing only destruction. They've burned libraries, stolen children from the knowledge of their parents leaving the world with a false reality that many know is a fake, but none who know the truth have the resources to challenge them because they've stolen all the resources.

"And each year? A new generation of our people is taught to trust and defend their oppressors. You are Afrikan, son, not 'American'. Your citizenry, here, is a farce and integration has been their most effective treachery, getting us close to what our ignorance made us think was superior, while leaving us without real power to change our circumstances, should we disagree. All they've done is hide their evil deeds more secretly in a vote that means nothing, while pretending they're the same as any other people because they've made us believe we're 'free' by slapping the word on the same old persecution.

"And to notice the truth makes it seem you've become like they used to be. A 'racist'. That's what you fear, but, brother? You can't be a racist any more than a woman who defends against rape can be called a 'rapist'. The facts prove, these people haven't changed at all, nor should we expect them to, ever.

"It is not us who destroy everything that's not like us. All we want is to end the obliteration that comes from only them. For consistently, Tyree? We Afrikans, having gone everywhere, centuries before the Tamahue were ever created, we consistently bring peace."

"What?" I exclaimed. "I thought Columbus was the first to sail the globe."

By now, you are well acquainted with the doctor's habit of exhaling in a 'harrumphal' rhythm. This time he gave a sad long one, like a sigh, saying, "What they don't teach you children would take 200 years of extra life for you each to learn, and that's after a 100 years of unlearning all their lies.

"Son? Where do you think all the people on the earth came from and how did they get everywhere? Spontaneous generation? Magic? No. No. The birthplace of the world is Afrika and Afrikans went everywhere, first; never forgetting where they'd traveled and their established settlements. We visited them, as we were them, and often. Statues were erected in honor of the mother people, not because of conquest, but out of gratitude to their parents.

106

"Not to mention, Columbus wouldn't have made it out of his bathtub without both his Afrikan maps, his Afrikan navigator and Columbus' own diluted, though, still Afrikan blood.

"Oh. And the time you fell into was circa 1355BC, Ancient Kemet, where your name was..."

"Amenhotep, same as my father's..." I finished for him, knowing it was true, though strangely stunned. "But I heard Sister Makeba say I was 'Akhenaten'. None of it's clear, but I don't recall that being my name. And how did you know what happened to me? We're you there and I didn't see you?"

As with all conversations so intense, even one's hairs stand on end to hear every point. There'd been almost no pauses in the steady flow of revelation, question, and question, revelation. But here, there was a long gap before he spoke again, during which the doctor looked off to the side, caught up in a private counsel, then looked back at me, eye to eye, without saying a word. He then nodded his head slightly, as if rendering a mental verdict, letting out a deep harrumph, finally speaking with a hushed tone.

"So many truths, son," he said. "So many lies. It's impossible to right the imbalance that favors the lies in such a short time, as I said."

Another pause, and he casually looked at his watch.

"You were, you *are*, the Divine Son of Ra, Akhenaten. Amehotep was your childhood name until some years into your reign as The Supreme Lord of all the civilized world, when you changed it."

"I remember snatches, words. But none of that," I said with a look of shock on my face. I'm quite certain the weight of his words were too much for me to absorb, fully.

"No, of course you wouldn't remember that, nor even most of what happened up to the moment you found yourself back in that time, without the magnetic grounding of the Aandas. The point you intercepted was as Amenhotep, the child."

"The And... what's?"

"Never mind about that for the moment."

He closed his eyes for a second with a heave, shook his head and continued, "This is why before entering the sphere one must first learn how to do it safely and that you can NEVER enter unassisted. Not even me. If Sister Makeba and

I hadn't been there to grab your ankles, hold you with the cord? The vortex of the sphere, even so limited as it was, would have swallowed you whole. Then you'd have remembered being Tyree with as much sketchiness as you recall being Amenhotep, now. After a couple hours? You'd have thought being Tyree no more than a dream."

"Holding my ankles. That's how you saw my fall," I guessed.

"Yes, though not the fall. Just your thoughts in your past life as Amenhotep.

"There is a much more efficient way to enter the orb," he went on. "However? There's too much to explain, now, and," he stood up, "... it's getting late. You were out cold for nearly an hour. You'll have to look the information up for yourself about Ancient Kemet or come back tomorrow at the same time, and I'll explain more. Then I can show you the sphere myself, safely! Put your shoes and socks on."

I couldn't believe it! He was giving me a second chance! Possibly spoiled, not really an American, but definitely Black Boy me! I burst into an unrestrained beaming smile and stood up to grab his hand to shake.

"WOW! That would be so cool, Dr. Kattan!"

I sat down to do as he'd instructed, my hands and body movements fueled by my excitement too much to notice any pain in my ankles, or that there, actually, was none. To see that sphere again, I couldn't think of anything I would have wanted more in the world, except to see my dad, but my dad wasn't on my mind, right then.

"Does this mean I can assist you, sir?" I said upon standing again.

The doctor gave me a searing glare with all the ferocity of the glare he'd given me at the start, and then nodded.

"For the moment, we shall see."

"WOW!" shaking his hand with renewed vigor. "You won't be disappointed, sir!"

He reluctantly smiled, himself, grabbing hold of my hand with both of his, and returning the frantic shake with his firm, assured one.

"Brother, this is never to be a topic of conversation between you and even a blade of not so green grass, do you understand?" He held my hand steady and forcefully, till it almost hurt, raising one black eyebrow, accentuating the whites

108

of his eyes with command. "Sister Makeba has the greatest faith in you, and because of my faith in her, I will allow you to prove her correct."

I dropped my own smile, though it threatened, any minute, to bust loose and run wild over my barely in charge stoic expression. Holding this expression was much more difficult than it had been acting like a bully.

"But!" his voice rumbled, probably sensing he had to speak more intensely than my joy, as the force of it nearly sat me back down on the couch. He'd dropped my hand and folded his arms across his chest. "But! Your brazen lack of judgment today would have been enough to convince me otherwise, so do not think I'm not watching you carefully. This is for no ears, ever, outside yours, mine and Sister Makeba's. Not your mother's, your grandmother's, your sister's or any bosom buddy. If anyone, no matter how intimidating, asks you questions about something in this house, on the point of death, it's all none of their business. Is that understood?"

I shook my head affirmatively, though somberly, all at once honored and determined to prove to him, to myself, that the best was in me, no matter what country I had been born into. Or what era.

As we walked out of the room in silence, my giddiness revolved around the impossible to have anticipated phenomenon that I had literally stumbled upon. Not ghosts, but eternity. Despair flew away as this afternoon's unplanned adventure was leaps and light centuries away from my, just a couple hours ago, gloomy expectations of my future. Why, this was better than Howard running away. This even made my homesickness for Sandstone Hill the only thing that had gotten lost in that eternity of The Breath, 'cause I sure didn't have a remnant of homesickness, now.

Down the hallway, past the library and to the foyer, I caught glimpses of the doctor's stern profile, to be sure he wouldn't burst out in a sudden laugh, saying it had been an elaborate joke, or that he'd changed his mind.

Then, I recalled what I felt was an important unasked question.

"Dr. Cheikh?"

"Yes?"

"I feel, um... different. Kinda like I have an extra brain," I laughed, self consciously. "Ha! Like I grew a new one in the orb. Have I got super powers or anything like that?"

109

Reader, this is one of those parts where you have no idea how hesitant I am to confess that I was once this young, this strikingly simple, this corny – but? I'll try to forgive myself this small failing as I warned you, I'm surely no way perfect. Hopefully you'll forgive my still youthful silliness, also.

He returned my laugh with one of his own, only full and rolling like I'd told him the funniest joke. His eyes disappeared under the fold of bemused eyelids. He then said, "Please, son. You are undoubtedly a well read young man, and that's why we chose you. However, Tyree? No more Harry Potter books from now on. This is not some magical trick bauble which bends to your will with a few hocus pocus words. Eternity, unbeknownst to most, is very, very mechanically precise. More like plumbing than conjuring. With study it's quite understandable, not mysterious. This is science as the Almighty is the most precise mathematical scientist there is. If you are any different, son? It's only that you are more of what you are meant to be. The orb does that. It probably cleaned out a few cobwebs, but I've been into it thousands of time and I'm pretty much the same man as when I started, just a little older, along with a little more tired, so please don't go shopping for a flowing cape and a magic wand."

Ouch! That was a let down. I gave a knowing, while not knowing, "Oh!" cause I still felt like something drastic had changed, just didn't know what. I said no more, figuring I'd asked enough questions for the moment, and didn't want to chance being dis-invited for tomorrow by becoming more annoying than he would tolerate.

And all on my own? I found out the very next day, before I got back to staring wonderingly at that thing that I once thought to be a boulder on a porch – I found out at the end of a very satisfying day in school of enjoying my enhanced abilities, that, in truth, I had no super powers whatsoever. Coming up will be the documentation of my next and bigger imperfection, beyond being nosey, and embarrassed in front of my sister for wearing nothing but a loincloth, and several other silly things I did that I might not recognize I've just written down, until after this history's been published and I'm a permanently documented flawed hueman...

Suffice to say, the next day, I realized that there was nothing magical about me, at the exact moment of my second accident, which as I briefly noted at the beginning of this rendering was to be that right cross I hadn't seen coming, slamming squarely into my very non-super powered face, giving me the first black eye of my life, by the way – it was that second accident which taught me, without a whisper of a shadow of a doubt, I was soooooooooo totally flesh and blood normal. Okay, maybe I was able to think a whole lot better – a w-h-o-l-e

110

lot better by seeing things and people, myself, more vividly, but I was thoroughly still breakable, still clueless modern me.

If I was going to have any super powers? I was going to have to work hard to get them, just like everybody else. Which we all did, eventually, but boy, was it ever a lot of work.

=

It is the forty ninth day of the year, 51574 cubed; and as such, I, the 17,059th Protector of Knowledge? I have a meeting to get to where I'll be one of the honored guests. And it's happening right now!

Well, not this second. It merely feeeeeeeels like its right this second as this assembly meeting is nothing to take lightly, even though I have. It's a gathering of the elder gods, in the capital city of Abjerusalem, from the councils of the various villages of New Eden, Planet Earth. Our governmental structure is not like yours. It's a re-connection with our ancient traditions, for those of you who've been separated too many generations from their original ways, no longer remembering what sanity looks like. And the most ancient traditions, of course, began with our Afrikan ones which seeded all the others because the entire Earth was given to the parents before it was loaned out to their children.

But, unfortunately? Sometimes the elders listen to youngsters like me, and? Sometimes they don't. Especially if the youth haven't got their acts together.

Oh, in case I haven't mentioned it, yet – I'm 131 years old.

So, in attendance, there'll be myself and my assistant sister, Queen Sitamen, who, if you recall is 3 years older than me. The youngest of those considered elders are at least 250.

Gods are long livers. They also have strong LIVERS! Ha!

Whoa. Bad pun. 'Xcuse me.

The pressure must be making me nervous, since this is my first official book (that I haven't finished, yet) – although this won't be my first official meeting. It'll be my second. The first one, just a too quick year ago, I sat, what I thought was incognito within the vast main audience comprised of over 10,000 nearly immortal beings. There I was, quite comfortably hidden in one of the numerous side rows, columns up, way beyond the more important participants, further in (though technically there're no 'cheap' seats as the gathering hall is more cylindrical than conical, plus the speakers levitate up and down, level to level – under their own power, but of course). There I was, feeling so honored – at least, *then* – so lucky to have received an invite to the most august assembly in the existence of man and mankind, and would have continued on so happily, blissfully, if the most important speaker hadn't, in front of that awe inspiring gathering – if he hadn't stopped his hovering directly in front of me (I was humbly surprised as he ascended and halted right before me – I thought he'd simply stopped and not deliberately focused on me in my not so hidden, afterall, seat) – he stopped to highlight my part in our freedom, and then decked me with the task you are now reading in this 'history'. He told me, in that world known soft Southern cadence of his:

"Brother? The Most High has asked me to request you do a recounting of your story."

Whew, it sure felt like it, but that wasn't the punch I've hinted about.

So don't get mad at me for taking you on this whirlwind chronicle. It's not the greatest first impression I can give you, reader, but, I'm doing my best. I know! It's a little choppy, but, get mad at that speaker. His name is The Honorable Elijah Muhammad and I'll include his mailing address at the end of the book. Send your complaints directly there, like so many used to...

I mean, look. I don't want to sound ungrateful or whiny because I love reading. Mighty glad thousands far better than me have left continents of libraries, since I could read every day for the rest of my extended life, however? Well, I've discussed this part of my dilemma plenty, already, and you've stuck around long enough to read the result. Yeah. I'm a regular well read, Huckleberry Finn Black, writing whatever pops into my mind, only there's no more niggers, anywhere, and nobody named 'Jim'. 'Neguses' are plentiful, yes, but that's because the Enemy doesn't command Our plans, anymore, or the words We use...

Note to Reader: Look up the word, 'negus'.

That last gathering happened the year before, and directly after, I spent the first 6 months, sadly, not worried about time's peculiar habit of speeding along – while I looked for 'critical' information throughout history – as that's my job, if you recall, even if I enjoy it – and then the next 3 months were spent puttering in my garden with my wife (gotta get those weeds before they take over, of course) and finally? At that exact minute when I was primed to get to writing (no, really, I was) – about 5 months ago? That's when I found out my Queen was pregnant. Delirious joy tends to take one's mind off of work you don't want to do, and I entirely forgot about the book in the face of the need to pat and talk to my beloved Jepkemboi's tummy for hours at a stretch! Imagine my agony should my boy not recognize his father's energetic soulprint.

113

More about that, soulprints, energetic fields, auras and the like in time. Maybe in the next book.

Next book? Did EYE say that...? Ah! If only I hadn't been singled out, I'd still be putting this history conveniently off...

Forever.

Maybe, if I'd put out a pamphlet before that gathering, I wouldn't have heard my name spoken by?

The Honorable Elijah Muhammad. Yeah, I'm repeating that so you can sense my nervousness as he hovered right in front me, looking me dead in the eye with that unwaveringly calm expression that's like a mirror to your conscious.

Can't ignore that.

Other than my initial, hesitant, "Yes, sir," which left my mouth after reluctantly rising (several brothers around me had to nudge my shoulders to get me to stand up). "Yes sir!" I repeated, again, since the first moment I spoke, the volume of my voice was being strangled by complete shock (even reminded myself of my grandmother's frustrating low timbre). Yes, it was my name he called, and how considerate of the Revered Messenger to include every single last one of my titles as he called on me, in his enigmatic soft spoken timbre, making my refusal utterly impossible in the light of both who he was and that he was also broadcasting telepathically on enhanced frequencies, leaving no doubt to every one of the 10,000 attendees, the 100,000 surrounding the facility and the untold billions watching or listening via broadcast that he meant me.

Gulp.

Despite all those flattering titles and dramatic stadium lighting honed in on my perfectly acting stoic face? I, in no way, felt up to the challenge, and admittedly, still don't. I'm a seeker, not a maker. Up to this writing assignment, I've been having fun roaming existence. Severed limbs, included.

More about that in this volume, I swear. Sooner or later..

Now, no matter how you, personally, may feel about The Messenger, which I don't mind as long as you know we must be free and even in Pre-Heaven, he never called for anything less – understand, in a moment like that, with him hovering questioningly and me cornered with the world watching, defenselessly – no matter who you are or where you're from? Ya DON'T refuse Elijah Muhammad without branding yourself permanently pathetic.

114

So today I'm on my way to the plenaries, which'll last an incredibly brief 2 weeks, and that's all the time left to finish this history. I'm about to exit my bedroom, dressed in casual traveling slacks, a nondescript brown shirt, my suitcase ready to grab, stuffed with toiletries, dress shoes, a spare set of sandals, my Enscriptive Writer (much like a typewriter that I'll explain, in a moment) and my ceremonial robes – though not too ornate as I'm a humble youngster, not looking to appear ostentatious...

Well, truthfully, again, I'm not looking to get noticed at *all*, though I have a feeling it won't work any better than it did the last time. I'll be in the heart of the city doing everything I can to avoid the question, "Brother Akhenaten! How's that book?"

That book, THIS book, is packed in my briefcase as a small rough draft, no bigger than these 107 pages you've already read as it is these 107 pages. And in not too fast a while, it'll be a whopping 108.

I'm sure you agree, extra page or not, I had better lay low.

In the meantime, as I look for little necessities, let me acquaint you with the essential details of our god life here in 'Heaven' – starting inside my own home.

Our house is on the ground, not up in the clouds. BAM! There you have it. Book finished.

The End

Have a nice day!

HA! Wish I could start and end the whole assignment right there, but that'd be the most badly received presentation in the annals of nearly immortal existence. Might get me drummed down to a dimension like the one I've just escaped from. One like your own. No insult to you, but how the heck do you stand it? Well, at least I used up a whole 'nuther page. Hehe....

So, yes, I'm alive, not a ghost and I and my wife live in a house, not the sky. Old misdirecting movies and confused preachers may have taught you Heaven's some fluffy white clouds you have to die to get to, but that's NOT PHYSICALLY POSSIBLE. So, let's dispense with that dribble right away, since, one –

Dead bodies don't move, and two –

Spirits don't need to live anywhere, and three –

Clouds are loosely condensed and thoroughly insubstantial water vapor floating in the more insubstantial troposphere realm of the atmosphere. That region of the planet is not capable of withstanding the weight of walking feet, dead or alive, let alone an entire house with a garden, and our home's furnishings, fancy signature pieces or not – all of it would fall one heavier than water vapor nail after another to be pulverized soon's it hit the ground; after we'd leaned out of the plane trying to construct it, by putting the hardware down on our cloud lawn. How they got over with that story never ceases to amaze most of Us, here. And it's ironic, but when you achieve your own heaven you'll know why living in the sky would not only be impossible, but mind numbingly dull. Seeing an endless vista of white fluffiness every single daggone day is nothing compared to seeing resplendent gardens dotted with flowers, rolling hills, gushing waterways, and a nearby bustling city or two – all far better ways to enjoy The Creator's work, from pillar to post, than watching paint dry, albeit, shaped like clouds. Or would it be clouds that look like paint drying? It wouldn't matter, as you've probably gone stark raving looney, in a matter of one hour spent gazing out your 'heavenly' window, with no intensified anything to bring back your sanity.

Our earthbound dwelling, that said, isn't a typical Western type structure, either, so banish that other Hollywood nonsense from your mind. As if a house shaped like a square box is a sign of what's 'normal' when it's only a sign of limited thinking and easy market turnover. Curves are hard to mass produce if getting rich is your first consideration. Whereas this blissful world is peace driven, not money, and that's why 'heaven' (for REAL) is the best description; though the young folks born here don't call it that. It'd be too corny, and oh?

Young people here are still 'cool'. Just the new cool is living to be 500. Can't do

117

that being a reckless idiot.

Also, on a grand scale, there's no homelessness, let alone poverty stricken ghettos, hunger or starvation. We have plentiful food, along with homes for everyone, rent and/or mortgage free. Each home is fashioned as we each choose and have the individual gumption to maintain. There's no 'eminent domain' where all you've built can be seized by some distant, heartless government because community, here? Is where the individual is sovereign to him/herself, understanding and valuing his effect on his neighbors, even her/his neighbors on the other side of the globe. That means We are really, *really* free. As I said, love put into action is permanent freedom from tyranny.

Not to mention land is plentiful on a whole enormous planet where upon there was never a population problem amongst its butterflies, and never has there been one amongst its people. Except for that enormous overpopulation of those pathologically greedy jerks, the 'Robber Barons'... One of them per galaxy is too many. But they're all gone! GONE!!! The greedy people, that is. The rest of us number in the fruitful and well fed double digit billions.

Mine and my wife's modest house, with room for expansion as our family grows and grows, was Jepkemboi's and my own personal design. We based it on our desire for an Afrikan centered abode that spoke to our soul's passion. There are no dusty corners. Rooms flow one into the other, with their interiors humbly but attentively decorated. On the exterior, since we built the structure with sweeping architectural flourishes, like used in a traditional Timbuktuan dwelling, this house has no cold jutting roofs, but it has plenty of rooftop edible vegetation and fruit trees keeping it temperately comfortable all year round, though we live in the northeastern region. If there's any undulating grass, it's ancient springtime wheatgrass (before half of it grows to stalks of wheat, she juices a good portion to barter with) and it covers the tops of a series of rounded adobe extensions, which fan off the main core of the house, interrupted by our sunken garden. Very Gourounsi. (I don't know what they call it in your dimension, but in the one we left behind, they called it 'googling'. Please do 'google' Gourounsi architecture. Nice, huh? See what happens when you leave Europe behind thee....). The vegetation topped roofs roll into a hill, directly adjacent to more rich edibles.

And our vibrant multi-hued abundance makes that Kentucky grass look comatose in comparison. But, nope. There's still no sidewalk, and definitely not a broken up one. No roads, either, and no need for them. There are plentiful walking paths with plentiful people walking them, any hour they please as there's no one or anything to fear. That sky above will not only never be populated by anyone other than birds and planes (more on Our vehicles, in a sec – be patient – I'm an amateur!) – but, I've been informed, in just a couple decades, it'll achieve that crayon blueness I so vividly recall from my first arrival inside Allah's Sacred Breath. I regularly visit Ancient Kemet and many other pre-industrial ages, now and then, to refresh my memory of a real blue sky's magnificence. Though, our's is pretty royal, already.

We have every electrical amenity we've grown accustomed to, with a twist. Electricity with us is physio-electrical. I'm not going to explain it as I'm no technician, despite the orb having enhanced my thinking skills – it may have also increased my stubborn skills, too. Suffice to say, our electricity is FREE, CLEAN and SELF-SUSTAINING. No electric company bills ever arrive in our mail (yes, we get mail). Free energy could be for you also, and that may be why you're reading this history. To discover you're in Hell and what to do to get OUT.

We reside in one section of Abjerusalem's residential areas; a whole neighborhood with its own distinct Afrikan flavor. In each section people with similar aesthetic tastes gathered to express their visions and create a harmonious community. All the homes, in each area, have a concordant style. There are sections where the residents felt best in the familiar settings of their lifelong memories. Those houses are European, American, Southwestern or Asian in design, although the occupants are all Black. The separate tribes of Man have their own regions. We, Diasporic Black people, offspring of the Terrible Abduction that our enemy called 'The Slave Trade', we live in many territories of the southern continents and the Carribean, but here, Jepkemboi and I live in the city of Abjerusalem, capital of New Afrika. We're a small part of the fallen and dissolved United States. It's only the size of about the original 13 colonies, with all the lands beyond that returned to the original natives.

Other nations' people visit New Afrika and Our other provinces, such as Asians, Nican Tlaca (the original Red people of the Americas, also called Native People), Polynesians, etc., and they surely can live here if they choose, but, like Black us, they each have their own tribe, their own story, in their traditional homeland and they like being themselves. They come for world governing meetings, but mostly as tourists to be warmly welcomed as we are when we visit their countrylands; as it was before confusion gripped the Original Peoples' minds – yet? None of Us, even those of mixed blood who made their allegiances with one tribe or another – none of Us want to return to a reality where one group dominated the other with force and/or mass confusion. Mutual respect of differences is a better glue than treachery.

Some neighborhoods, such as where my mother and grandmother live (yes, my grandmother, when The Ubuntu [have I mentioned that yet?] – when The Ubuntu happened, she was the most enthusiastic to move into a new home, finally) – some homes are purely Afrikan, and some are Afrikan in being nonstop creatively inventive, because We are the original source of humanity's drive to be distinct, in the first place. We, Originals, remember our past, once more, but we acknowledge we've been forged into a new, wiser people. So, my mom, the artist, and a joyous one, now, *had* to live in Western Abjerusalem (called 'Westab') where the bold let their imaginations flow, in harmony with their neighbors. It's quite the tourist destination with its unprecedented release from the shackles of Westernized 'normal'.

The city, itself, where the gathering will be held, is built on the wreckage of the old world the Tamahue, or the 'Yurugu', as some call them, the city that they'd built with the blood money they stole, and which their shoddy civilization destroyed with their nuclear leaks, chemtrails, fluoride, poisoned foods, money driven neglect, and yadda, yadda, yadda. Whew! What a list, right? Allah allowed them sufficient time to teach us that peace must be defended, no matter how pleasant 'looking' the attacker, or how 'nice' some of its members. Those 'nice' members had never been enough to change a daggone thing about the overall psycho-globalcidal whole entity.

Graduated from that furnace, we've built and rebuilt the world's cities with the industrious visions of the Peoples, who no longer require Caucasian approval to be themselves. Or require it from an indoctrinated Designated Special Negro Class, whether Black or Brown, all of whom swore nothing the Originals did could be worthy unless it was a close imitation of our oppressors' ways – even more vehemently than our oppressors ever could have defended themselves.

Abjerusalem, is a living burst of Afrikan centered architecture, mostly – transcending the old wedding cake skyscraper with organic warmth. There are tall buildings, but it's not a hazard course of nothing but sharp angles, leaving the casual viewer feeling like he/she might be chopped to pieces by either the buildings or the culture that would fabricate such harsh structures. The city has sweeping curves, arches, and entire complexes built of life in fully blooming trees, bridges of spanning twists and swirls, towering waterfalls, and many edifices fashioned from the recycled materials of the wastes of the old world. Serenely somber, however – not a chaotic amusement park menagerie - it's alive or what Manhattan would have been without greed as its' building bricks.

And, by the way? It's where Manhattan used to be...

This time, without the ghettos, the filth, and there's no longer instant urine or fecal matter nostril assaults, from humans or dogs as there are clean, safe public toilets everywhere (a heartening detail for those who remember the old Manhattan) and we clean up after our pets. There's still pigeon poop, though. And robin, cardinal, bluebird, lark, swallowtail and yellow-breasted bunting bird poop. Not to mention deer, raccoon and the occasional bobcat, lynx and black bear really big poop, though for the sake of the children, we telepathically keep the predatory animals happily wandering in the more un-populated areas, while every regular citizen will clean up any fetid mess, simply voluntarily. No fighting over who should or who shouldn't keep it clean, like a pristine environment doesn't benefit everyone. All the cities, world over, radiate with such peace, with a little tweeking on Our telepathic part towards the wilder animals, and the worldwide embrace of nature's harmony. Why, I've been greeted, right before I clean it up using conveniently located public cleaning supplies, contained in always a handsome receptacle – my boot or sneaker or sandal has squished into a wide assortment of avian and mammalian salutations; or a couple times, it's been deposited on my hair. Oh, haven't I told you?

Heaven ain't anymore perfect than We gods are.

Okay, this is a lot of info, but skip it if you must. However – I'd be severely remiss not to mention the pyramids. *Of course, there's pyramids*, so dazzling they make you forgive the occasional air borne splat or foot mash. 7 sweep about the perimeter of the city, though miles apart from one another, and 3 within the interior of Abjerusalem. They're all the source of the city's 3 million residents' and 5 million suburban dwellers' abundantly free energy that doesn't harm a hair, a feather, or an amoeba on this healing orb of ours...

New Afrika has lots of pyramids, feeding 23 million citizens with all the sustainable energy required.

There's still, now and then, the Tamahue – about 1 to every 1,500 Black people. They're the reachable ones, who've been judged genuinely good; thus as a result, they weren't damned. Actually, they're not merely good people, truthseekers, but more importantly – they're Truthaccepters, which makes them bona fide great white people. Yes, such do exist and how difficult for them to have resisted the nature of their own, or the normal tendency of all beings to make excuses for the wrongdoing of folks who look like mom, dad and Uncle Richard, or Cousin Helga. It was truly astounding how few of their Pre-Heaven numbers could stand hearing the truth about themselves, preferring arguing nonsense over listening to the cold facts. Incredible. 15% of

121

the world's population and getting fewer each day, having the nerve to tell everyone to be patient with their nonstop disagreeable-ness. Whew, and then those of *us* who loved the Tamahue so much, we denied the facts, also, going down with their hundreds of millions of damned ones.

In this realm, though, as a vastly even smaller group? White people have been entirely stripped of that credibility they once used to cover up their enormous crimes. It's not that we've arbitrarily concluded all white people are evil. No! Of course not! That'd be ludicrous. It's that we know they have too much to learn to believe them any more without checking – like we once trusted them – allowing their doctors to inject our children with poisons they presented as 'cures' that brought nothing but tragedy – we know much, much better, now. Matter of truth? We don't blindly follow us gods, either; although no deity would have the emptiness to knowingly harm a soul.

My, weren't we crazy back then? And to think... the Yurugu were killing their own with those poisons, too! Epic outbreaks of paralysis, autism, cancer while they swore with straight faces they didn't KNOW why this was happening, or that the bereaved parents were 'imagining' the devastation they eyewitnessed. What agony was endured by all. They even had the nerve to admit their globalcidal plans in their monument, the Georgia Guidestones, which they used that aforementioned 'trustworthiness' to minimize. But? What mass murderer would be rich enough to write a list of his future victims in stone and no governmental investigation needs to be launched?

When the radiation took hold, though? That prior carnage was a walk in the park, even with all the carnivorous creatures free to tear you, flesh from bones. Like I said, the enormity of it numbs the mind, and the clock on all life, unaware the world was during my childhood, was ticking...

Many of the Truthseekers of this current time, of real peace, study with whichever of the original tribes will have them, despite their Tamahue-an tendency to be fascinated with the look of a thing, and not its essence – making it a bit difficult to explain spiritual subtleties to them. They wanna know, "What school of thought is that from?...", not, "What wisdom can you share, even if no one's ever heard of you?" Painful truth can feel like a trap, not a freedom, for anyone, me included. But they seek permission to accept it as if they need crowd approval to take in the obvious. I've had some apply to become my assistants, but I'm with Dr. Kattan, who once told me, "It's not an insult to the 2yr old when you don't hand him the keys to your car."

Yet, if each and every one of them were as ready for immortality as the older

122

souled Black and Brown people? If each and every one of them were the kindest, gentlest people on the planet, that still wouldn't make them our rulers. Just like Black Us, they only have the right to be their own rulers, within the measurements The Creator allows, until they can create their own universe that'll somehow thrive on their self-destructive concept of truth. That's exactly what the damned ones needed – their own universe – instead of running around the world telling others who'd gotten along perfectly before they'd arrived – running around telling others what they were doing wrong when it's the Tamahue doing the worst!

In the meantime, till they can create, rather than destroy, the forsaken ones, the majority of the white people, try as we all did to open their eyes, they've been cordoned off not on their own continent, but, this time – in another existence, where they can verify that anti-matter – the exact opposite of everything – they can verify that anti-matter exists as The Lake of Fire. We have nothing against them loving themselves, but, not when it comes to destroying the whole planet, which they almost did...

The Most High says, one day, they'll understand, like We do. In the meantime, they never figured out, while they were here? To love one's self, you have to be loveable.

But, what the heck am I rambling on about when I've got to hurry and get driving before I'm late for the orientation (yes, if we have planes, indeed, we have cars)! But where is my wallet?! I'm looking frantically about! I'm certain I put it on the dresser, an undulating rough hewn expanse of drawers that I am opening fruitlessly searching, hoping I'll find it before I've looked through all 40 drawers. Jepkemboi went clothes bartering one day and the next, this dresser was delivered. It's a magnificent piece when you haven't misplaced something. So I'm opening another drawer, and another, and another. I'm finding nothing.

My queen has just come in, and in the midst of my frenzy, her beauty, haloed by her softly swirling tendrils, calms my frustration, making a portion of my brain contentedly wonder when will her presence cease to soothe me? That's not really a question I expect you to answer, as I don't need an answer, because she is Allah's daughter, guaranteeing my dedication and commitment. Little 'g' gods know better than to undervalue THE God's gifts.

Wish I thought of writing as a gift.

And what a present my beloved is handing me, right now. My wallet! Yes. Gods have wallets, too, for all civilization requires some sort of organization. So? We have rules; but for us, they're maps, not obstacles. We also have literal maps, business cards, photos of loved ones, bits of forgotten crumpled papers filling our wallets, but not driver's licenses or even ID cards. The Divine tend to be the most responsible of drivers, learning the rules of the road because we want to. You don't need a license to walk, although you could accidentally trip somebody. Our minds are free of belief in negativity, enhancing our response time, making high speed driving almost as easy as walking. No need to prove you can drive or walk if you have a working heart. Makes you do what's right, all the time. That's why Heaven is eternal. That's what Hell may have taught you is so impossible, it might as well be up in the clouds.

"You left that in your study, love."

Thank you, Queen!" I am saying, while putting the wallet in my canvas arm satchel. "Are you certain you won't come with me?"
"I'm not the invited guest, you are! I'll have a better view on the TV, plus? You aren't about to get me back in the thick of 10,000 Black and Brown people who love being free so much, they drone on about every little detail..." she's hesitating, with a devilish leer on her face... "sort of like you, love..."

We both are laughing. She's read what I've written so far.

"You know what I mean," she's continuing. "They're so tied up in the minutiae, they're missing the big points. Oh no. Thank you, very much! I prefer to watch our vegetables in the garden grow, trade recipes with our neighbors, and if I need to go to the city? I'll do it at the end of the month when it'll be a lot less crowded!"

"Ha!" I am laughing, again, as I know she's completely right. The excitement over being thoroughly free from a disagreeable treacherous Tamahue has led to an overzealous enjoyment of each and every detail of governance, and okay... maybe me, too, writing about every detail. Skip whatever you choose, but you'll be missing out as there's so much to reveal, with no devil hiding in these details, anymore – and for the Venerated Elders, they obviously adore running our own civilization, once again.

Now, I am asking her in my best official voice, "Before I head off for this historical gathering, my Queen, would you like to say something for the book that chronicles the beginning of Heaven on Earth? Specifically, as you played such a pivotal role in that history?"

"What?!" her face is looking quite convincingly shocked, "You're recording as we speak?!"

Feeling quite efficient, I am adding, "Why yes. I keep the Enscriptive on continuous transmission of my every thought, speech, and the events around me, even when it's packed up. I'll edit it later, but this way, I don't miss a thing, as I don't have much time left." I am quite pleased with my resourcefulness, smiling proudly. But?

She's staring at me, now, with no nonsense indignation. Oops. And her hands just went to her hips.

"Guess not, huh?" I am venturing.

She's responding with an exasperated eyebrow raise, terribly silent this moment, refusing to speak to posterity, though she has such wisdom. Don't blame me, my son. Or my great, great, great to the 100th power grandchildren...

"Can you sever that connection, King?" she is whispering, gently, though the Automatic Writer is so sensitive, it catches the proverbial pin dropping sound, that my god ears can hear, too, these days. The Writer does catch thoughts, but only the thoughts of the person who is operating it.

And that, reader, with a quick telepathic mental nod is what I did. I cut the Enscriptive off as soon as I saw my wife wasn't havin' it. Today we call responding to the wishes of others, beyond one's personal desires, 'thinking', even if I didn't quite do that ahead of discovering she definitely did not want to participate. We gods catch each other's thoughts, also, but person to person mind reading happens only by invitation, as it's a very intimate connection between the closest of friends, family or mates. Thus, I've turned the Writer back on, now, in my briefcase, as, with my sister, Queen Sitamin, I am swiftly driving to the scheduled gathering in the Epidome in the heart of Abjerusalem. However, I asked my sister's agreement, this time, prior to beginning my recording, again. I absorb my lessons.

Told you I've never done this task before.

After turning the Enscriptive off, after Jepkemboi's quiet but insistent request, I'd nodded with a smile and a warm 'thought' to let her know I understood and accepted. Yes. There are many transcendent abilities that we gods do possess, such as bending dimensional space, limited levitation, and voluntary

125

telepathy, but our best ability is our respect for each other and the wisdom to say, "Sorry." After not just you, but your people harness that one great habit, all the 'superpower' stuff comes easily.

Embracing my honestly felt thought, she placed her slender richly black arms around me, giving me a loving physical embrace that I returned. When I met her, she wasn't this hypnotically dark, like a softly enveloping blanket that brings comfort on a cold night; but like all of us, like the sky, she's been strengthened exponentially, inside, out, by eliminating what were the true shackles – those in our minds. It's been the air and the colors that had circulated solely over the Kattan house, now, circulating all over the planet – only the effect is in our bodies and out to our skin. It's confirmed that change I once saw in the air's intensity looking out my grandmother's window was not my imagination. The colors did grow more vibrant because in Our world, as in that house, pure truth healed everything and severed the power of negativity, from our inner organs to the outer ecosystems. We are the Orb, now. It is a process; not magic, as the doctor said, that evening, long ago.

Knowledge looks like magic to the unitiated.

"Beloved," Jepkemboi began, once the Enscriptive was shut off, loosening her arms, voice brimming with love I could sense, "Only should you get the opportunity, please explain the importance of the youth's voice to the Venerated Elders. You know how that can help our future even more, and you, alone of us, have their ear. Some of the elder gods are so stubborn and wounded, they're reluctant to listen to anything but their own counsel. They've forgotten truth can come from unexpected places. None of us can afford to forget, the youth set us free."

She was right and had been since we both started discussing the matter a year ago, after I received the first invitation. With that, being the youngest to ever attend, it seemed a whirlwind compliment, but it was strange that I was the only youth who received such an invite. Trying to correct that discrepancy by bringing it to the elders' attention, neither of us realized the complications of dealing with more intensely very human near immortals, who are certain they know what's right.

And here I just finished talking about the Tamahue, right? Proves to even me that, nope. We're not perfect, either, in any way.

My wife had gone with me then, where we both figured The Council of Venerated Elders would listen to everyone, only to frustratingly discover, as we approached one elder god after another with the idea of, if not an invite – then, at least a separate council for our youngest gods? It became apparent that each one, in turn, with the respectful air of considerate people who didn't want to hurt our feelings, they said they understood but there were designated protocols, routes of authority, codes of conduct, and that's when she and I noticed the conversations went on and on, without going anywhere substantial.

Though, this time, they did invite my sister, as she's my assistant.

Placing my hands upon Jepkemboi's face, looking deeply into her one in a million eyes, I said, soulfully, "Yes, that I will, with no doubt. I know a few others who feel the same. Sitamen, even, and she's so dutiful. It's a matter of convincing those who have, perhaps, too much of a reverence for tradition. However, we must be patient. We can afford patience in this matter, finally," and leaving no breath between words, because I didn't want to give her time to protest, thinking I was acting as immovable as those elders, I continued, "yet, I will still be insistent. During my presentation at the lectern, I'll say, 'No brilliance can be neglected'."

She nodded her head, satisfied, and I then knelt down, putting my hands on her slightly swelling abdomen. Soothingly, I said to my son within, "Your father is working for you, Kanefer. I'm going to help you come out swingin' like the son of a god is supposed to."
Jepkemboi, laughing, reminded me, "As you must go swingin' out that door, or you're guaranteed to be late for the opening plenaries! That'll make quite the youthful impression."

With my harried agreement, a kiss, my rush out said door, to my four seater red hovercraft, a toss of my suitcase in the trunk, more kisses between myself and my queen to help us endure until my return in 2 weeks, I wound up driving with a thought propelled collapsing of the dimensional space beneath my car, operating at maximum speed – I wound up on my way, with my sister, seated next to me whom I picked up at her home, some dozen miles along the way to the city.

I told you we can collapse space with our minds to bend distance to our will? Didn't I? Ah. History books, especially ones about your potential future. So many details...

Although this moment? Onto to the detail of my sister. She's called a Queen, as all goddesses are, though – there are no singular Kings or Queens in actual

127

authority. We need none. But? Even you are going to rule over something or somebody, if it's only tying your own shoelaces. Tie 'em up well, along with reigning well over all else you do, to have the best life possible. Sitamin has been dubbed 'Queen' since she chose to become a healer who's now a legend in Our time. It was difficult for most people to relearn how to live after The End, as they were crippled with addictions to Yurugu poisonous foods, medications, various other narcotics and the overall addicting nature of that entire lifestyle of childish pursuits. Learning her craft from Sister Makeba, she's become one of the prime builders of our renewal, helping everyone who's sought her assistance. That's been 95 years of putting an end to bad habits by teaching healing ones. Being 3 years much older than way younger me, I have no idea why she's not a designated Venerated Elder. She is so ancient...

Oh. Ha! She's glowering at me as I speak. Back to being purely complimentary...

She did all that along with?

Being my Protector Assistant, almost from the start.

Here's something very Afrikan. My Protector duties will fall to my sister's first born, upon my retirement or death. Not my own son. Seeing, though, how I'm enjoying my job, and Sitamen has yet to find her soulmate to have a child with (I'm a nice brother, so I'll refrain from making too easy remarks about what excessive imperfections she has that make her still single) – it'll be a while before I'll have a successor. Traditional custom commands power not remain in one direct bloodline. Of course, The Creator could choose someone else that's not related to either of us, at all, but no matter who? The honor will be bestowed without envy, though it's a unique, bountifully adventurous profession I've come to love and so many others might, too. However? Can't have the whole world traipsing through eternity.

Yet? Living in a world where fruit trees burst on every corner; when you can eat a meal in any restaurant because they can eat at yours for free, jealousy is too costly, and much less valuable than universal friendship.

That reminds me! Most of us were unaware in Pre-Heaven that economic depressions are no accident, as dirt, seeds and water always work, and so do able bodies that till the Earth. The Most High never doles out unemployment checks because His Creation is perpetually sustaining.

All that to say, I'm loving my duties, leaving no danger of me getting lost in another era or dimension due to haphazard actions on my part, to be permanently lost like Protector Mumia Sirius Negus Ra, whom no one has found yet. According to the chronicles written by Dr. Kattan, right before the heady days of The Honorable Marcus Mosiah Garvey, during the 1920s, Brother Mumia made a grievous miscalculation, which Sister Makeba mentioned, so long ago. Probably, it was his extended career, constant lack of sleep, especially in those awful lynching days when he was forced into hiding by those elite white people who were endlessly searching for The Breath – it had led to one careless miscalculation that was miscalculation enough, with such a precision instrument. Acting on their suspicion that Brother Mumia was the caretaker of the Orb, way back then, the elite Tamahue used their police force to frame him for a murder committed by one of their own. Trying to quickly conceal The Breath, Mumia had disappeared when he was accidentally absorbed, whole, by the sphere; while his new assistant, a young and not at all a doctor yet, Cheikh Kattan, witnessed Protector Mumia Ra being swallowed by the unfathomable blackness – while the future physician, holding both Aandas in his palm, watched helplessly from the other side of the room. The authorities had triggered the tragedy when they'd begun breaking down the door, shortly after Brothers Mumia and Cheikh had entered, bolting the door behind them, unaware that they'd been stealthily followed the entire way into the woods to what had been their secret sanctuary, a seemingly abandoned, rundown shack.

The police startled young Cheikh Kattan into immobility and Mumia into hasty action. Since they didn't realize they'd been followed, under the cover of darkness, inside their hideout, they'd expanded the Orb in the one room wooden hovel at its full dimension. Usually, they maintained it shrunken sized as a marble, which can be unnoticeably dropped in a pocket, or in a flower pot. But in a frenzied haste, at the start of the 'authorities' banging on the door, Brother Mumia initiated a sequence of prompts on the Orb to shrink it, without fully verifying what he did, as the first officer cried out on the other side of the locked door, "Open up! This is a raid!"

Pressing on The Sacred Breath, perhaps too forcefully, or incorrectly, altogether, and definitely too quickly, he'd initiated an extra sequence that took his own personal chain reaction destiny to a tragic phase that could have been mine had the doctor not been close enough to grab my ankles, when I'd fallen in. Protector Mumia did reduce the size of the sphere, but as he placed it inside his pocket, collapsed to the diameter of a large marble, it had begun to absorb him up whole, pocket first, in less than a second. The future Dr. Kattan was instantly alone inside a shack that everyone would have called 'tiny' – but right then the gulf between himself and Mumia, inside that rickety cabin, must have been the doctor's first experience with mansions, only far bigger, 'cause the distance between the two was the span between galaxies, too wide to offer the older man rescue. Brother Cheikh looked on in horror at the complete absorption of his venerated teacher, while standing helplessly mute when the door was kicked into shreds, staring at a black marble as it dropped from mid-air to the floor, its tiny ping sound drowned out by the splintering thwacking the police officers made, though the doctor swore he'd heard it. Through the battered apart dry rot pieces of a door hanging off matching rotting hinges, raced several deputies, precisely when agonized Brother Cheikh did have a blink of time to run and kick an unobserved marble sized sphere, laying innocuously on the floor, into a small gap between two old floorboards. He was grabbed, beaten, revealing nothing, then arrested and jailed. Upon his release, 2 years of hard labor later, he retrieved the deeply dust covered Orb from the same crevice, the shack, then, a splintered remnant in a wild open aired forest.

Although, he couldn't retrieve his revered teacher anywhere he traveled in Allah's Memories, he'd never stopped searching, until I took over his duties. I'd search, too, but I didn't know the brother. You have to recognize a person's soul-print.

Even now, there's been too much time between that long ago day and today so that Protector Mumia remains lost in time. You can't pick up the thread of life when it's been stretched so thin, for such an extended period. As always, there's an honorary seat left empty on the dias, of The Gathering, amongst the seats of our other most venerated elders, who were each and every one, well known and not so well known, historical, beloved warriors during their individual manifestations in the midst of our once seemingly endless war. Each one of them, and the rest of the 10,000 are here to guide us young deities further up the road, but their presence is in sync with this age. Perhaps before I pass, Mumia's will be, too.

I'd love to meet him.

It's not difficult to understand why one hesitates questioning the authority of persons like the Magnificent Marcus Garvey, himself, here with Us, even after the whirlwind has abated; and most Beloved Goddess Harriet Tubman; and? Revered and still a genius, El Hajj Malik Shabazz, a.k.a - Malcolm X; the eloquent Patrice Lumumba; erudite Ida B. Wells; and but of course, The Honorable Elijah Muhammad, Messenger of Allah. They are all our teachers for having internalized this near immortality before The End ever happened. To be heard in midst of that greatness, to appeal for the inclusion of the

130

youth? With this likely unfinished book as my introduction?

Oh, boy. This might not only be overwhelmingly difficult, but it may be daggone near impossible to be taken seriously by that crowd – they are *doers!*

Especially The One. The Alpha and The Omega. Our Greatest Ancestor God of All. The Best of Doers. He's Allah, Yahweh. Elohim. As I said, the list of names demands the reverence due, and He'll be there, also, this time. He'd been in Japan during the last session, but, just as Heaven isn't in the mysterious clouds, The Creator is not some ghost, nor a diaphanous colorful blob that changes from this skin pigment, to that in order not to hurt anyone's feelings who isn't *yet* His color. He's simply Black, so you can also dispense with that DaVinci propaganda – DaVinci, who was ordered to paint the Sistine Chapel's version of God in a color even the artist admitted The Almighty had never been painted as being. Nope. God's one color – the most hypnotic Blackness you could never imagine, having created Himself from the most complete darkness that ever was. Triple Blackness. That black was nothing compared to Him, as He fears nothing – especially not the womb of His Self-Birth.

However? Color is not, nor has it ever been His point. And neither is it the point of this history book, as t-r-u-t-h?

Truth...

HAS NO COLOR.

None at all. Never has. Never will. No age, either – as long as you bring the facts and not some foolishness.

With no doubt, Allah sees straight through every single trick, even the tricks played by the Children He Created in His Image.

=

Before the brutal discovery that I surely wasn't a superhero, and that, my own personal hurricane was still nearly 24 hours away – on the evening just prior to that pain, when I'd left the doctor's home, I turned off his forewarning the nanosecond I stepped into a new reality that was a floodlight in a pitch black room. Carson Avenue that had several hours earlier horrified me? Looking at it, now, walking out the Kattan house door? I was pretty darn certain the doctor was, MOST likely, mos' definitely one hundred percent wrong. Not about his information regarding the sphere, or even the war he'd described, but? Maybe, I, excitedly considered... maybe I *was* a candidate for a new Marvel character, after all, as the evidence was not only inside my mind, but literally, the proof was all around me.

It was as if, as soon as Dr. Kattan closed the door behind me, with the long day's light still dominating the world around, it was as if the intensity of the colors that had, priorly, hovered over only that mansion, were now everywhere I looked. Even across at the wreck of my side of the street.

And it wasn't just the colors, mind you, but something about the meaning of things that hit my mind the loudest – including how regular people, walking, sitting, talking all around were put together. I couldn't place my finger on it exactly, anymore than I could see when the air changed from dull to vivid over the house, as this change wasn't wildly different from the way it had been, before. Nobody had grown wings or horns, but, it was as if I had touched down on a whole new planet, or had x-ray vision to see 'inside' everything and everybody. More like I had vision to 'understand' as it didn't feel strange - it felt more intensely *real*; like I saw everything I glanced at in its true self, and knew the truth of it to my core.

That same broken sidewalk I had stepped onto, earlier, grumbling at the 'The Why' – the indignation of living on such a modern day ruin called my home – that same buckling block? Crossing the street, and placing my foot on it, then, was not quite the treacherous mountain climb I had sworn it'd been. The slabs still jutted up at the same angle, but it didn't seem a personal slight. The never before considered conclusion hit me, all at once, that the sidewalk was like that for some reason that could be fixed, no matter how long the fixing would take. It was a matter of determination and even more - of patience.

Then, the raggedy weeds in our front yard seemed to have ceased being engaged in a brutal plant slaughter. I could plainly see, now – that lot had been simply, neglected. Dirt could grow flowers, too, besides just dandelions, I considered. Or vegetables! It had never occurred to me, but it did then – '*I could fix that, if it bothers me so much. Can't be too difficult to plant some seeds.*'

It was a shock to go from hopeless despair to a sense that I could and more importantly, would do for myself. It was such a departure from self-pity to self-assurity? It felt like nothing less than having new..., um... powers? Nah. That's too TV, for what I was feeling and what I was seeing. As I took in the suddenly not quite so dilapidated condition of my new home that could be healed with a few coats of paint – I admit, what I was realizing wasn't exactly magical, but, it was a new enhanced 'seeing' that brought possibilities and conclusions which would have never entered my mind, before. That feeling, brand new to me, the force of it, seemed nothing less than supernatural.

And for lack of a bunch of better words this limited English language can provide, I'll continue using the word, 'power'. If you fear that word, it's because you're comfortable with having none.

Up and down the block, where a few neighbors sat talking, laughing, or enjoying the comfortable day, the arguing neighbors included, who were relaxing peacefully on their porch that minute, which I suddenly realized they did quite often, only I'd never paid attention, before? Looking at them, all, they were a re-born joy to my heart. It's not that I hadn't seen them each throughout my short time living here, and on those occasions when I had visited my grandmother, but? I suddenly wanted to know them, when I hadn't up till then. I realized, too, that I'd been disappointed, angry with them, for being so visibly Black like me while living in the most embarrassing of conditions.

So, pssssssst... Here's one of those weaknesses I don't want to admit, but have to reveal in order to tell the whole truth. All those years I spent yearning fruitlessly for my grandmother to move, despite my own interest in the Kattan house? I mean, I didn't care so much about that house that I needed to endure the 'hood' to see it, 'cause it wasn't our house, afterall. However, without having the innate cruelty to admit it to myself, despite having always enjoyed being Black, I wanted to be Black without Black people. Certain ones. My Black Pride, you see reader, was limited.

And that's how I was struck cold by the shame of my former cowardly thinking. It was nothing but cowardly because I had preferred to cast blame on everyone but me. It cut through my heart like a knife as I felt I should lower my head with the weight of the shame, then and there, while I opened the rusted gate in front of my not such a shack home, afterall. But with that renewed 'seeing', my new enhanced thinking quickly dispensed the self-defeating emotion of shame, as I realized the uselessness of the feeling since being sorry for myself in the Orb had proven a waste of time. If I was ashamed, then doing better would make that shame, just like the weeds on the lawn, the wear and tear that was on the house, no matter how long it would take, my work would make my self-disappointment go away. Granted, there was much more to learn, but for the moment, it all seemed easy.

This X-ray Visioned Black Boy me might have been made of wishful thinking, yet, my thinking was also composed of certainty that something would be done, by me, a factor I'd never considered. So, I took a moment to enjoy the warmth of the day and the greater warmth that exuded from my neighbors' brown faces, quietly. I had to actually wrest my eyes from staring at them, openly, which I wanted to do as their beauty hit me like I was seeing people for the first time after decades of solitary confinement. Rather than continuously gawking, I looked straight ahead, walking very slowly up the path, as if I might be bored and tired in my ambling along. I turned my head, casually side to side, as I moved. Though, truly, I wanted to stroll right up to each of my neighbors and introduce myself.

"Hi! I'm your neighbor and you may have noticed me, sometime or another. I can tell you're an amazing person and I bet you've had some heck of a life! I'd love to be your true friend, if you don't mind or already have too many..."

Uh, yeah, RIGHT.

Well, thank goodness I was thinking clearly and wasn't certifiably that insane Tyree I'd been promoting heavily the last bunch of hours, even if I was guilty of being naïve. Wanting to explore the reason for my neighbor's radiance was a passing desire, while I knew acting like a fool would work like Icarus' waxed wings reaching the Sun, should I behave like somebody'd emptied out Bellevue earlier that afternoon. Deeply, I did want to know where the stories of their shades of brown would lead – did they have common and uncommon hopes like me? Or were they the quintessential poster children for aimless inner city people, but what got them that way? Here I'd been pouring over static history books from the day after I could read, soaking up our harrowing Black triumphs and travails, while the living books of those times were happening in the children of those ancestors. Pre-history, the future before it happened,

134

living right next door to me. How much more riveting could one get?

There, at the house with which ours shared a sheetrock wall, was a middle aged woman with cheeks so animated in good nature, they seemed to have a mind of their own, puffed up in amused exasperation with her 3 of the happiest, carefree little cacao girls I was sure I'd ever seen. Their mother (or their grandmother as it's always hard to tell the age of a Black person) – she was simultaneously in an animated conversation with the aforementioned, but not arguing right then, arguing neighbors. The other combative half had morosely, but saying nothing, he'd joined the ladies, taking a vacant rattan chair, as I'd crossed the glistening asphalt street. I knew I'd seen that grandmother plenty, and her grandchildren, but had never bothered to pay attention. I wondered if it was any of those little running wonders that I'd heard crying, sometimes, through the walls of my family's home till late at night which had always driven me a little crazy. Up close, the children didn't look annoying, or miserable, racing from one quickly reached corner of their house to the next, only momentarily paying heed to their ageless grandmother's warnings to slow down, before they ran once again.

I didn't know their names, those girls, nor those women, or the husband. I'd been comin' to visit my grandma since before I could remember, and if my grandma didn't talk a lot to us, she surely never talked more than politely with them. However, suddenly, I was burning to know, how'd they wound up here, on this forgotten block?

Further houses down, there were some young men, probably all of 16 years, 5 of them, on the stoop, who looked so imposing and one of my favorite words – 'obstreperous', which means 'dangerously malingering; looking up to no good'. Nobody used words like that in those days, but? If they'd had, one of those boys or one from another posse would have been calling himself, 'Ice Obstreperous'. Now, seeing the truth of things, I understood why they were so impressively frightening to the entire planet. These Black young men, winning the dubious honor of having everyone warn everyone to avoid them, I could see, they weren't thugs, nor even obstreperous. They were teenagers. They were, potentially – like the doctor had told his wife an hour earlier – here were potentially the greatest warriors in the world capable of striking fear by merely breathing on their opponents, and I knew maybe because I was going to be one of them – I knew they were angry not because they were born to be the terrors of their community; they were angry because they were meant to build monuments of awe, whether they or the world suspected that or not. I could see that their fearful power on the outside was a reflection of what was inside, even if the inside had been deformed by the world's perception. Nobody called rich white brats, 'thugs'. They were called 'rogues', or suffered from 'affluenza', terms white people defined, no matter who thought differently. Yet, clear to my own? These young men's souls, screaming at them with frustration, wouldn't let them forget who they were, even if they didn't know how to be that themselves. Rich or poor, lack of faith hung like a vacuum nozzle above their heads, on full suction.

And though I fully perceived some of them were drained by the pull, I still saw them. I saw who they were, because they were me.

Overcome by the people's beauty, why, I wanted to thank everyone I covertly spied as I purposely dragged up to my own stoop – I wanted to thank them for still being so daggone genuine. So untainted by devotion to an uptight rich society that'd never innovated anything which inspired billions without bringing an army to shove it down the conquered's throats. But these young men had changed the entire planet, with not a dime. I wanted to thank them from the depths of my soul which felt almost as deep as The Breath, for letting their humanity burst outside the walls of their homes, to share the uniqueness the rest could only copy. It was here, at the bottom of no one's notice, and everyone's contempt, I could see more solutions to what ailed us than anything I had ever seen at the top of Sandstone Hill where none dared walk down the block, let alone be seen relaxing outside on their front lawn, enjoying harmonious heartbeats. In proper monied society? You had to go on a braggable vacation, documented in pictures and keepsake 'appointments', so you could officially enjoy the outdoors, and talk about your expensive 'adventures' that proved you had enough money to afford an incarcerated notion of freedom.

Yup. I wanted to walk right up and introduce no longer suburban Prep me, but Tyree, Freed Black Boy. Even apologize for having been such a jerk. However, let me repeat. My thinking was much, much better. Weird, but definitely, not insane. I had to be patient. I had to develop some plans.

Thus, as I dutifully entered my door, cool and appropriately reserved, putting these new desires to the side of my mind, I was suddenly unexpectedly overcome by another set of emotions that had been hiding beneath the clutter of the entire day's worth of thoughts and reflections. Hiding beneath a year of denial and distractions as it all came upon me innocently pure, without warning, like a dive into a freezing cold pond.

I missed my dad.

Just like that, the blood that had gone through so much intensity that day,

136

stopped flowing and drained from every vein, out every pore, as if it knew what was about to happen. Finding no distraction that not only could, but wanted to challenge this sadness, no rationale to explain the emotion of this truth away to a safer distance, as I opened the first door, I could barely make out the keyhole to the inner one, through my sudden flow of tears. These tears, not tickling my eyelashes, as I was now correctly positioned so gravity pulled them way down my cheeks, came from the same unexpected place that the feeling they were being shed for came – from the realization that I'd never again see the greatest man I had ever known. My tears came from there.

Managing not much else but the second lock and the door, I turned, slamming it closed behind me, and collapsed with gravity's pull on my body, downward, upon the first step, going slowly, as if my body was flowing like one giant tear, I gave in, without resistance, to heaving sobs. I didn't want to cry, but the emotion wasn't listening to me.

And I could feel him, my father, in the wooden banistered stairwell, in the air, standing beside me, around me, within my being and without. Why I didn't even need superpowers to reconstruct him from the molecules that hung in the air I breathed as his presence was more real than the oxygen. It was the meaning, the energy of who he was, resurrected, which when he had lived, I understood I hadn't taken enough time to notice who he had been – what made him unlike anyone I'd ever know.

I yearned to hug him; get his reassurance; hear his peculiar roll of a mildly Georgian accent. No other being, I knew, would ever, ever, sound like him and I knew I'd be listening, fervently praying to hear him, see his unique features in the pieces I could gratefully find in others that would be slightly similar to his. One piece at a time, I'd see him in a way that would never add up to a whole that used to be Marcus Jackson.

The fact that I could sense him so clearly and yet could not touch him congealed with my sorrow, consuming me, like I had fallen into the Orb all over again, and more completely than the first time. For during the worst of my agony in that void, I had been certain that sooner or later it'd be over, even if badly. But at that moment, alone on the stairwell, I was overcome with knowing I couldn't see the end of this sorrow.

I didn't hear our neighbors, nor did I hear our apartment door open, with feet coming down the stairs at the same time that an attractive chubby deep brown woman with her 2 slender children came out of that first apartment to stand above me. But suddenly kind Haitian accented voices, both young and adult,

137

asked if I was okay. I smiled weakly, both attempting to wipe tears away that had their own life, and trying to politely ignore them, as I was sure if I could answer truthfully with a 'No,' I'd have to explain the unexplainable in not easy to explain, nor understandable terms – not because of the difference in languages, but because my ache came without words.

Then my mother's arms were around me, holding me, her cheek rubbing the top of my buzz cut head. She began gently humming an Afrikan lullaby I think she'd made up, but always sung to me so dulcetly when I had fallen on my toddler legs, remarkably finding, like all the most frantic of children (as I was) – an, as yet, unscraped part of my skin. Up till that moment, I guess, I was lucky for having never broken any bones or anything else. Up till that moment.

"Tula, tula,
hush, hush, hush.
Tula, tula,
hush, hush, hush..."

Soothing flooded my being as this tune had been firmly embedded into the DNA of my first born mind. It meant love. And soothing love always meant mommy, even for 12 year old boys. So I laid my head down on her shoulder to cry some more. This was mother and mother either takes away the pain, or makes the stubborn ache not quite as bad as one thought it was.

The downstairs neighbor, whom we'd all only seen enough to wish a friendly 'Good Morning', after she placed a comforting hand on my head, returned into her home, with her young son and daughter, after a gentle reassurance from my mom.

There alone in the stairwell, in the haven of mother's arms, I cried with no need to stop. I relaxed into my grief like a pillow that was no longer suffocating – 'cause pillows can be used as weapons, but they were made to comfort. With my mom, there was no need to end my yearning for dad with polite conversation that'd be a distraction. I didn't have to explain nuthin' to her, since, despite feeling dad everywhere, I knew my searing wish would find no resolution. Momma couldn't fix that part of the pain anymore than her singing could heal my boo-boos. I knew I needed to feel my grief because it'd only been hiding. I'd been hiding it; and now that I had given it room to show itself, I was ready to accept the depth of my love for my father, bravely.

So, as my 700th droplet drained away the last of the fluid from my eyes, as my heaving sobs lessened to staccato whimpers, I found a sad, wrung out,

138

gratitude, that I'd even had a dad I adored so much, that I could feel his very soul after his body had ceased to be. My, quieted by my mother, whimpers, got even quieter, till they faded to little inhaled breaths and then completely, when I was okay with feeling sad, my tears ceased.

"Should we go upstairs, sweet, and get some iced lemonade?" she asked.

I nodded, wanting her kindness more than the lemonade. Though, granted, her lemonade was the best. She added spices to it.

In the kitchen, after filling 4 tall sparkling glasses, mom sat down with us all. The presence of even grandma sitting at the table left no doubt that the sounds of my crying had hit every ear in the house, and how couldn't they? Why, as I walked sheepishly in, like a deflated balloon, with both Kyerah and my grandma getting up to hug me, asking if I was okay - my big sister had been wiping away her own tears.

When mom took a seat, that became the unannounced signal that a family meeting was to begin, minus one member, as I could never help but notice, but I wasn't angry about it, any longer.

She started out, deep concern pooling in her expression, "Did something happen at the doctor's house that hurt you, son?"

Grandma added her own, "Tell us, what happened, Tyree."

Uh oh! Instantly, I knew what they were thinking, the mere suggestion making my skin crawl. My surprised shock went first to my eyes before I sharpened it with a vehement, "Oh, NO!" and "No!"

I looked disbelievingly at grandma, knowing she preferred simple reasons for everything, not understanding she came from a legacy which had not only stifled her joy, it had drained that joy from the minute our ancestors had been kidnapped away from the last sanity any of us would know for hundreds of years till this day, and beyond. Then, I looked at Kyerah, whose eyes I had seen in another younger face. She was content to support me with silence, so I ended with my mom, connecting intently with her, wishing so dreadfully for the easy honesty of just a moment ago's soothing to hang on beyond wordy misunderstandings that I was sure were about to unravel some of those apparently still tightly wound threads. But I didn't know how to keep that soothing going, despite my heightened 'powers'. I didn't know how to get her to understand that everything was finally okay.

139

At the same time, I knew I didn't have the ability to avoid pulling on anyone else's threads. I could 'see' the pain inside of them as clearly as I saw the meaning of the strangers outside. Their pain was my pain, and it was all too detailed stitched in one big lump, that doing nothing was too tiring. There were too many messes that a messed up me was tightly balled up within and I couldn't stand it, any longer. Here's where, maybe, I was a little impatient, 'cause it required too much effort to string together a better plan, that minute. But I was determined not to let my feelings overwhelm me, no matter their intensity. If that sidewalk would take time, I could surely put even more time into my family.

For one, I knew, if I'd told my mom the full truth about my little fall into an endless hole, then into a past life where I'd been the son of a pharaoh (which I remembered from my Amenhotep memories – my father's title was 'nesu', not 'pharoah', as again the Greeks incorrectly used a word for our ruler which meant 'house') – if I'd mentioned a bit of that, I'd probably have been spending every afternoon and the last of our house sale money on a therapist's couch, heavily zonked out on psychotropic drugs, rather than back at that mansion across the street, a world away, where I wanted to be more than anywhere, other than with my dad. The place where life was strengthened, no matter how gloomily it had been before. So it wasn't hard to say,

"Nothing happened." And mean it, concerning that house. What happened to me was another time, another place, another reality. I was cool with this scanty logic, as I'd made a promise to the doctor to think before I tripped.

I gave all their piercing gazes one of equal intensity, "I had a great time." Which I did right after having been scared out of my wits.

"Then what's the matter, son?" Mom didn't use the word, 'son' often, unless she meant it.

I focused down upon the poorly laminated brown kitchen flooring, coming apart at various seams. I thought about how easy that would be to fix with some tack, and put my head back up, languidly.

"I miss dad. That's all." My voice, thick with emotion and thoroughly truthful, this time.

Her eyes, lids and brows, rose a bit, taking my comment in, but not as though she disbelieved me. It was as though she had been expecting that for some time.

"Of course you do sweetheart. Maybe being around Dr. Kattan, I guess. You haven't spent any time with a fatherly figure, since the accident."

She reached across the huge table to stroke my shoulder, making her rise up out of her seat to reach me. Then, jerkily, careful of the glasses of lemonade, she got up to hug me from across the expanse.

"I know. You've been holding the pain inside. I know."

With that, not meaning to be cruel, just honest and honestly tired, I pulled the biggest thread with one tug, all at once like pulling a band-aid that's stuck. Quite stuck.

"Mom," I didn't know my voice would come out so cracked, "did dad commit suicide?"
There was a barely perceptible – but that's what made it undeniable – 'gasp' from grandma, Kyerah's sympathetic smile instantly dropped from her face, like it had been one of those charade masks on a stick, and my mother released me, a bit too suddenly – while probably trying to appear as if that wasn't the case. I could feel that soothingly attached thread between us, as she sat back down, slowly, a bit stunned – that thread stretched out thinly, weakly, and then she looked at the same floor I had.

I wondered if she saw the potential for fixing it.

Silence fell until Grandma filled in the deafening lack of sound in the room, with her nearly echoing, girl toned:

"Now, you know that's not so. Don't even think such a thing."

Grandma had never been the type of Black woman to say, 'Chile', or 'baby' with a southern roll. Her people were from Ohio; Catholics to boot and sounded nothing like my dad's side of my family. Kyerah and I talked like my mom and she talked like her mom which was not the standard portrayal of the typical elderly Black woman. You know how a stereotype will be based on a measure of truth. It's just that, though, she wasn't learned or formally educated beyond high school, my grandma wasn't a stereotype, as I've said, much as our whole family wasn't. She was soft and gentle, not rough and/or loud, as many Black women can be, but more frequently all are portrayed, ad nauseum, by those who not only don't begin to know what we're all really like, they have no reason to find out and expand the narrative.

Bearing that in mind, the family I grew up in didn't use 'made famous by Hollywood as Truly Black' boisterous gesticulations, either – even if we felt them – which you, the reader, might expect and thus already could be imagining us doing, as you read. And not that there was anything wrong with feeling the spirit and showing it. But, great overflowing emotions in my family flooded between us without much fanfare, or enhancement, on purpose, since we came from a long line of taught to be 'proper negroes', from both Cleveland and old monied Jack and Jill debutante cotillion Georgia. Though being born darker than a paper bag for several generations had excommunicated us from what some called 'The Black Bourgeoisie'. Nevertheless, my ancestors had remained stoically reserved, rather than being whatever our Lord had intended for Black Folk to be and whatever the heck that was supposed to have been. Hundreds of years of living with another people's opinion of what's 'proper', people who with a wink determine how much food you had on your table – people like that can change your own feelings about your behavior, public and private. In my family, we sought to piss white people off by being everything they said we couldn't, which was just another kind of shackle since we'd have pissed them off more by not giving a hoot.

All that to say, 3 hours before, I'd have never asked that question, '... did dad commit...', though if I'd had, getting that brief a response from my grandmother or anyone else to a unanswered query so obviously important to me? To us all? I would have become angered, but not visibly enraged. I'd said nothing, got up and sought refuge in the tiny room I shared with my grandma. If it was the designated time, which was a limit of an hour a day, I would have played my video games furiously, as a target for my anger, without ever giving vent to that anger, directly, to the faces of those who might cause me more pain with their not detailed enough versions of truth.

But now, after that accidental fall into the Orb? Even trouble looked preferable, or at least to me, as long as I approached it with proper respect.

So, I answered my gentle grandmother back, gently, "I don't know that, grandma. That's why I'm asking. I want to know. I want to know what kind of dad he really was. I want to know everything about him, even if it's not good," I heaved, feeling frustrated with my effort as every word counted so dearly, yet, I raised my voice ever so impolitely, "I want to miss my real dad, not some illusion."

I turned to my mother, the soother, asking, "Mom, did he?"

Kyerah piped up, "How could you even think that, Tyree?"

I could see disgust on her face.

"No," my mom answered over her, but still gazing at the floor, "It was an accident, no matter what the insurance company said."

"But we were there, that night, and we saw how crazy he was!" With that outburst, I felt the old standby habit of wanting to play video games to ignore my emotions calling hard. I had crossed a line. I had pulled a tightly woven cord, nearly rigging thick, and this one might be the one that didn't save me.

My mom turned. Eyes pleading, intently saying in non-hysterical, un-accented English, "I knew your father. He wasn't perfect but he wouldn't commit suicide, Tyree." Now her voice was thick, too, saying, pleading, "and you must believe that, son. He surely was under a lot of stress. Laid off from LMG, all those bills. He was a proud man, yes, and we were going to have to make a lot of difficult adjustments, so he was upset, but?" She shook her head, wearily, pausing before she continued, "He was made of sterner stuff than that. Sweetheart, put your doubts to rest."

But, I wasn't satisfied.

"How can you be so sure? You weren't there, in the car with him. He went through the side rail straight into that truck. How is that an accident?"

"He was drunk."

Still, superpowered impatient me was not satisfied.

"Ma? Dad didn't even like liquor, so why was he suddenly drinking so much, those last weeks? Then, the truck he crashed into was two lanes over. The collision was right near where his car crashed through the divider. To veer that wildly? That had to be on purpose..." while I thought, 'Drunks swerve haphazardly; they don't aim for trucks.'

Quiet descended again, like a sheet on a dead man, and this time everyone contemplated everything, but each other.

All by myself, I'm sure, I felt an unpredictable bit of relief. Like my

143

unpredictable victory by default over Howard. This was a bit of air, a release. Tense, but still a relief as I had said what I'd only been dreaming of asking since the crash. More accurately, what I had been 'nightmaring' of asking. However, I was swamped with sympathy for the pain I had obviously caused them, and had a keen desire to be part of everybody's relief. So?

"I'm so sorry," I apologized, trying to restitch the snag I'd caused, realizing they weren't ready. They needed to want to be untangled. They needed to know they could be, and I couldn't make that happen – certainly not in one early evening in a very cramped kitchen.

Look, I had never been this brave, nor this profound, reader, not at that age. I was figuring this had to be some weird superhero 'vision', cause daring this much painful truth at 12? That wasn't me. Or, I should say, it didn't used to be.

"I hear what you're saying," I continued. "You want me to have faith, and I do, Mom! I was just wondering," and finding a wide path around the elephant in that tiny breakfast nook to hopefully change the subject, I added, "You're probably right about Dr. Kattan. Yeah. I guess he made me remember dad, that's it."

Eagerly, the three females of my little family, a family which when extended to the breaking point, included an estranged uncle, 2 aunts, and lots of cousins who would have never been anywhere there in devastated Newark, as we Jacksons had fallen so low, even lower than my family's inability to pass the paper bag test; but eagerly, my mother, sister and grandmother all metaphorically squeezed around that gigantic pachyderm to meet up with me, as their half smiles returned with half unsmiling eyes. But at least they were looking in my direction, again.

"Hmmmm, it's okay, Tyree. Don't get me wrong. I surely understand your asking questions. You're a curious, intelligent child and I adore that about both you and your sister. There's nothing wrong with asking questions," she reached across the expanse of the table again, and cupped my hands in hers, "but, yes! You've got to have faith as your father?" Pause, and changing her mind, she said, "Perhaps the Kattans is not a good place for you right now."

That made me nearly panic! "Oh no, Mom!" I cried! If I didn't return to learn more about that sphere? I might insist on the strongest brand of thorazine, myself! So I continued, "They were the best! And the doctor wants me to be his assistant with his research! Not just help him mow the lawn!"

She was impressed by that.

"Wow!" Kyerah gasped, her disappointment in her traitorous brother forgotten.

"Oh, please, Mom?" I added with the last bit of 'still your little boy' cuteness I could squeeze into my pleading eyes, despite my emotional exhaustion.

"Well, I don't know, Tyree. That was quite the moment, there, you all torn up like that. I haven't seen you that way since you were a little boy. I'll have to think about it."

And just as I was going to run down an instantaneous list of at least a hundred reasons why I must go back, Grandma pre-empted me with,

"Renee? Let him go."

That stopped the conversation.

The striking thing about a person who never talks, is when they do they don't have to say much, because, it's so startling? His or her few words hit like a thunderclap, trumping anything that'd been said before. And that's what grandma speaking right then did. BOOM! Why she didn't even have to add, for her what would have been another person's 3 hour lecture, she didn't have to add, but she did –
"That's a healing house. It'll help him through."

BAM! I knew before my mom's face underwent a series of changes, from reluctant to conceding, looking at grandma, then me, then at an even more anxiously supportive Kyerah – I knew the conversation had not merely paused, it was over.

Her, "Well, alright," was just the confetti falling on my already in progress victory parade.

I grabbed her hands, flipping mine out of hers, which she hadn't released, yet, and I squeezed jubilantly.

"Oh thank you, Mom!" Exuberance had replaced my exhaustion, like water on dirt banishes dry earth. "Thank you, grandma!" Then, for the first time in what seemed like forever, I clunked Kyerah on the head, saying, throatily, my tears almost returning, but not quite as I was done with crying, "Thank you, big, really big, big pain in the derriere, sister!"

"Hey!" and across the table she swung a slap, though I ducked her before mom gave us a frown, instantly replaced by an easy smile that revealed her relief to see a bit of our old joy, from both sides, this time. She laughed while warning us, not really meaning it –

"Cease and desist, guys before somebody gets a periorbital hematoma, and it'll be me who does the punching!

"Ooooo, good one, Ma!" Kyerah and I agreed, me asking, "But what's a periorbital hematoma?" I knew the penalty...

"DICTIONARY, SON!!!" my mom and sister spouted out. Which I got later and for your fast information, reader, it's a black eye, that I'd soon learn about, dictionary not required.

We grimaced and laughed, except for my gentle grandmother, who only smiled. Though it was one of those smiles we knew was real.

After finding 'periorbital hemotoma' in the medical dictionary; after that evening's book reading time, "Manchild in The Promiseland", by Claude Brown; after the next day's clothes had been set aside; after I'd brushed my teeth, then looked in the mirror to see if I could notice any superhero changes (none, except I swear I looked a bunch blacker); and before I settled in a double bed next to my grandma, and then Kyerah was about to go into the slightly bigger bedroom (there were only 2 bedrooms in that apartment) that she shared with my mom, while Mom and Grandma, still in the living room were beginning to watch a movie, I asked my sister in our funnel of a hallway, both of us leaning against our separate doorways,

"Kyerah, for real. Can I ask you a question?"

She, locs wrapped around pencil sized pink curlers, lavender and yellow floral pajama wearing, big orange fuzzy slipper wearing her had been about to enter her room to go to bed. Her inner glow which I could sense, her 'aura' – for lack of a better word – was warm, strong and smart, with something more complex I couldn't put my finger on. It's so hard to understand girls at all, but most difficult when they're one's sister. They start out reasonable at the beginning only to descend into girl-ness. Girl-ness to boys seems so unnecessary in general, but when it's your sister? I mean, dude? It's your sister, who doesn't count as a female cause you know her, she knows you, you both know pretty much the same things, whether you can see her soul or not.

She squinted, as if bracing herself for attack.

"This had better not be anymore of that nonsense about dad!" And she gave me a blistering stare.

"No!" I strongly reassured her with a smirk of agreement. "Nah, I said enough about that," *'for the moment...'* I thought, continuing, without pause, "I just want to know," not knowing how to put it, "have you ever felt like you were someone else?"

"What? Someone else? You mean, like multiple personality crazy?"

"No," I shook my head, "like re-incarnated?"

She took a moment to reflect, stroked her chin with a hand, and said, "Come to mention it, I do believe I was a zookeeper once, looking after the cage you were locked up in!" She chortled, more amused with her moderate wittiness than it deserved, in my estimation.

I gave her a droll roll of my eyes, with a contrived guffaw. Very contrived.

"Still failing your 'How to Tell Good Jokes' class I see?" I retorted.

As she was about to launch into more woeful one-liners, I stopped her short, saying, seriously, "No. For real, Kyerah. I want a truthful answer! Have you ever thought you've been here before, in another lifetime?"

Slowing down and looking at me, I could see her with a slightly younger face, browner, leaner (although she would want me to emphasize, here, that she was in no way barely even chubby. Just solid), I could see there was no denying it. She was that same girl, only here, today, pondering the unusual question of her little brother, hair entwined in pink curlers rather than covered by a Kemetic headwrap.

"I don't know," she answered. "I guess I never really thought about it. No, I think."

~ ~ ~ ~ ~ ~ ~ ~ ~ ~ ~ ~ ~ ~

147

Excuse me, readers, but my writing (seems I'm finally putting serious work down) is being interrupted in the middle of my recording this moment, as I drive toward Abjerusalem. It's only an hour since the last time I recorded, which I'd still be doing, but I'm being halted by none other than my older sibling, who is sitting beside me while I project my recollections onto the Automatic Enscriptive Writer.

Yes. I am driving as I write with no danger of crashing. It's that god thing, where unlike driving while talking on a cell phone, which was a deadly distraction in a 3 dimensional universe – not to mention how deadly cellphones were in so many other ways that I can't mention right now, and that our enemy benefitted enormously from not revealing – in this manifestation, we think and exist multi-dimensionally, in many time frames at the same second, with no effort or distraction that can throw us off our focus. Collapsing or expanding these physical planes by coming upon them from other timeframes, which is also how I make my vehicle hover, is no problem. Not to forget there's no carbon emitting gasoline, nor toxic trash bound batteries required.

Did I further mention, there're no longer gravel, asphalt, tar or cement roads and highways? None of any material? Yes, I believe I did.

Ha! Sitamen is glaring at me, but I must share, reader, there are plenty of paths, and causeways for pedestrian strolling, skating or biking, but they amble through forested, meadowed undulations of the ripest greenery because our ability to make anything levitate (including ourselves) eliminates the need for smooth roads. Thus, I'm piloting above the carpeting of the densely green Hai Valley on the Southern end. 'Hai' is Swahili for 'alive'. It was never that when formerly called the Hudson Valley. It was pretty, but now, it's robust as the flora and fauna no longer fear people, and our Solar System has orbited so much closer to our original twin star origin, Sirius B, expanding the life of everything which lives according to what's right. Well, everything's right, today. And let me tell you! There is nothing so invigorating as hovering above the ground, at high speed, over the canopy of magisterial life, with no limitations. You can zoom over glens, zip without disturbing herd populated plains, roll with the windswept sand dunes, and ride pregnant rivers (though water is a bit unpredictable, so, I, like most take the bridge over the Nzuri River). Some, with focused practice, even scale mountain ranges. I'm not about to attempt that one, myself. See, nearly all omnipotent beings? Can still feel all agonizing pain, and kill ourselves making stupid decisions. Even we aren't superheroes, though it sounds like it. Not yet. Maybe not ever if any of Us is still choosing impulsive stupidity over longterm continuity. However, no matter. Complete All Powerful Divinity is not up to us.

There are 7 levels of heaven, with the one you're currently existing inside, being the third.

"Yes, yes. One moment, sister," I am saying.

Seems my sister has some disagreements with my version of the facts and would like to enter her own. Though that may seem rude, to you, and a bit to me? I do agree with her that this history should be as comprehensive as possible, blunt interruptions or not. I have no false bravado. I know I am not the Best of Knowers. I have become a *better* knower as part of a 'We', not an 'I', with which I'm perfectly happy.

So, I present, now, my sister, Queen Sitamen.

=

In the name of Allah, the Beneficent, the Merciful, All Praise is Due to Allah, who mastered the day of Requital; and with this I bid you Greetings, my Diasporic Black Family, still caught in the web of your own enemy's making! Greetings to You, the Mighty, who are about to rise while you are being raised, as foretold by The Greatest Teller. You are the tail about to become the head as the The Best of All Knowers, knows you! Created you! This sojourn has been but necessary schooling for your soul, so you will never forget; because to be so oppressed, more than any other, will only make the most reviled on Earth – the Strongest of Nations that shall not give sway, never devalue its birthright again, to a stranger, garbed in a false and blinding light.

Whew! Chills!

Just had to put a period on that, so you know where you're headed with me, without doubt, without hesitation. My beloved brother is a diplomat, making him probably a better Protector, but? Sometimes war's all ya gonna get. With that said, I'mma briefly step in with my militancy to round out the picture which he has, thus far, rendered so well. Maybe, too well. However, this interruption is not a critique, because I understand his tempered approach to be far more inclusively reaching then my no holds barred blatancy would be able to command. When I was acquainted with the wonder of the sphere? When I realized the totality of what a foe we faced?

Well, I had always been an amateur healer but Theeeee Healer in me woke up on a mission with an internal scream the equivalent to the cries of every newborn ever birthed. I fell to my knees, literally, and cried from the limb stripping beauty of it. Accepting and rising to a challenge is a holy beauty no pageant could every rise high enough to crown.

And to think I had started out defending the devil.

Yes. I'm not a diplomat, though I respect the Peacemakers.

As I stated above, I'm not here to drone on, and that's probably why the Venerable Elders knew better than to assign this task to me, as they obviously discerned Amen's patient nature. Me? A few well placed 'crackers' here and there and I'd have hardened your ear and run you deeper into the hands of the one who would kill, not just your flesh, but, if they could, they'd kill what brings your flesh to life.

Thus, to the point.

It wasn't quite at that moment, when Akhenaten – oh! So sorry. I forgot he was still Tyree then, and I was still Kyerah! It wasn't that long ago, but so much has happened, it feels like a thousand years.

So much horror, so much re-birth...

But I was going to make this short.

When my little brother, Tyree, out of nowhere asked me whether I had ever felt as if I had been re-incarnated? Well, I hadn't f-e-l-t that, yet. So, I didn't put his out of the blue question together with his sudden burst of grief over the death of our father. He'd been tearless from day one, yet I hadn't begun to wonder, that evening, 'What the heck is going on with my li'l brotha?"

See, I love immeasurably, deeply, intensely. When our father died, I thought for certain my internal organs would commit suicide of their own volition, without consulting me, whether my own father had committed suicide or not. I knew he hadn't, though, pulling up a pain so complete, I was sure my brain, heart, liver, stomach, kidneys, even my toes would collaborate to end their suffering by ceasing to function, all at once. And I cried like I would never stop or until those organs ended our mutual suffering, out of kindness.

However, one day I did stop crying, and I was still alive, along with so shocked, I decided it must be I was meant to keep on going.

I love my brother like that, also. Shoot, I love everybody like that, especially since the transformation made my love a mighty action that cures. My love has now become effective. But back then, it was still little powerless me, feeling quite motherly over simply my little brother. I'd been watching his back our whole lives, as it was a dangerous world for Black boys. I'd kidded him when he'd asked me that strange question because I was, as yet, oblivious that something unprecedented was happening in his life that would change everything. Everything. It's beyond words when something changes even yourself. So? Though I had always kept an extra eye on him, the moment he asked me that question, I didn't yet know what I was looking for, let alone that I should be looking for the impossible.

Until he came home the next day, after school, with that bloodied nose and the big shiner right under his eye, insisting that he still go over to the Kattans! What the? That was when I started wondering, 'Did they introduce him to crack cocaine?' Why all the sudden interest in a nice old couple? I mean, really? The Kattans were great. I couldn't help but love them, too, as I'd known them all my life, same as Tyree. But? The boy looked like a wreck that'd make a wreck go, 'Ouch!' Granted he didn't need hospitalization but surely, he could have started up his assistant duties on another day, right? The doctor would have understood. I knew the library was beyond amazing, but even Tyree was never excited enough about books to ignore pain.

Looking at that black eye of his, as he insisted, I asked myself, "What exactly is in that house?' See, I didn't remember the power of that house, either, when I wasn't in it. I never saw the big atmospheric transformation my brother had out our grandma's window and I didn't remember that I, too, came alive stepping inside the mansion's door.

So, next day, Friday afternoon, I followed behind him to the Kattans', without our mother's blessing. She had enough to worry about, without adding more.

~ ~ ~ ~ ~ ~ ~ ~ ~ ~

"Okay. I'm done, brother, That's it."

"That's it? After all that insisting, all you have is 2 pages?"

"More like 2 and a half and yes, that's it. Oh. Except I must emphasize, again, I was not fat, and there's a lot of silly things that boys do, too."

"Well, geez, Sita. I was thinking you were going to pad this out a whole lot more than that. I really could use the extra pages."

"Oh, no! I'm not going to save your behind, Amen. This is your duty to bear. I have my own."

And like that I have switched the writer back to my frequency, with a sigh.

"You're right," I am saying. "And thank you for that addition. Adds a bit more tension to the story. History can be so dry, especially for the young ones."

"Exactly," she is saying, as we are coming to the last stretch of a dwelling dotted hillside beyond which the outline of the city is rising, reaching up before our eyes, against the blue horizon, the nearest pyramids glistening in the waning sunlight. So amazing how freely Afrikan it is, and yet it's a city. That means, it's as inviting to the soul as is our music. How much genius we limited believing a

152

people who hated us.

If I concentrate and hurry, we might only be a few seconds late for the opening orientation, though I dread it more, the closer we get. Good thing I'm not easily distracted, so I can, also, continue where I left off my writing, as I speed to my appointed hour.

=

"No, I don't think so," Kyerah answered, taking a moment to truly ponder my question, her head tilted to the side, top heavy with that helmet of black locs and pink curlers.

"Oh," I responded, "O.K.," not wanting to go further as I might feel overwhelmed by the desire to share my unbelievable adventure with her. With someone. She was and had always been my confidant, especially now in our new reality, without dad. Even if we didn't talk about him, at least she had known him like I had. Feeling the temptation to let go of my secret like an avalanche temporarily stuck at the back of my tongue – the only thing holding it there being my not wanting to prove the doctor right that we Diasporic Afrikan boys couldn't be trusted – that insistence on not being a spoiled brat held back an iceberg the size of Kilamanjaro...

It occurred to me, though... I hadn't told her about my life or death plan to be a bully, either.

So, I let her answer to my question go at that. Well. She wouldn't have believed me, anyway, as that was an inherent problem with revealing anything this...

unbelievable.

"Just wondering," I added.

She looked at me quizzically, as if expecting more.

"That's it?" she asked, "What made you wonder about that? Are you thinking dad will be re-incarnated?"

Hmmmm. That sounded like a good enough excuse to me, and so,

"Yeah. Just.."

"...wondering. Yeah." She finished my sentence, shaking her head. "There's no getting around this. It's gonna be hard and nothing can change that. But we're gonna be okay. Actually? I was happy to hear you finally letting it all go,

154

finally."

I could feel the emotions coming freshly back to the surface, with her reminder, as if they and I had only met each other, a minute ago. I nodded, deeply, closing my eyes, and she hugged me. I returned it, and then pulled away.

"Don't go, please?" I asked.

"What? Don't go to sleep? But tomorrow's a school day."

"No. I mean don't go to Aunt Brenda's."

"And stay in this dump all summer long?" Hands went to the hips. There were some stereotypical behaviors that we Jacksons did practice, I'm happy to admit.

"It's not so bad, really."

She looked at me as if I'd lost my mind. 'Hmmmmm...' I thought, 'maybe I have...'

"Now I know the Kattans must have switched your brain for a slug's if you think Newark is not so bad."

"Technically, slugs don't have brains. They're gastropod invertebrates with primitive neuron clusters that make up a simple nervous system, allowing them to respond defensively to dangerous stimuli, and perform other life maintaining basics of existence." Wow. I shocked myself. How did I remember all that, which I'd casually read in a science textbook I'd studied, what? 2 years ago? Superhero Hall of Fame, you're gonna need another statue...

"Way to ruin a joke, Einstein."

"Someone's got to save you from yourself."

We laughed.

Smiling, she confided, "It wouldn't be for long, Ty. I don't think I *could* handle Rhonda and Melissa for more than a couple weeks. A month tops. But I know if I stay here in Newark, I'm apt to lose my mind."

"What's so awful about it?"

155

"You're kidding right?"

"It's because Aunt Brenda lives in a white neighborhood?"

"What? Are you certifiable? I don't need to be in a white neighborhood. I loved Sandstone, same as you."

I remembered a little differently. I remembered a girl for whom too much Blackness anywhere meant something must be wrong, especially too much of the *wrong* kind of Blackness; but as I didn't want to spoil our comraderie, I 'diplomatically' said, instead (yes, that's a jovial dig at my sister who just pinched my arm as we drive into Abjerusalem) – I said,

"Well this neighborhood is Black, also. Not as rich as the Hill but you never know who you might meet here that'll surprise you."

"I know I'm never going to meet any amazing Black people here. We met them aplenty back home. Shoot a couple of 'em lived down the block from us. And hello? Dad was one, remember? But those kind of people don't do slums and neither do I." She eyed me with a piercing stare. "What the hey? I thought you hated this place, too?"

That's funny, I thought. I did. I mean I *had*, about 3 hours ago. Something had changed, though. Something profound I couldn't explain 'cause I'd promised not to tell. So I told her another truth instead, and I wasn't being merely 'diplomatic'.

"I just don't want you to go. Not this summer."

That hit the spot as her previous indignation was overrun by a kinder face, characteristic of big sisters like her. Good ones – every now and then.

"Aw," she said, "I understand." She gave me a friendly punch in the chest, "I'll think about it, bro. But I'm not making any promises."

"But you'll think about it? Maybe I can convince you, even?"

"I'll think about it," she answered, as if she meant it, adding, "Hey, by the way? What do the Kattans have? A sun lamp in there?"

"Whadda ya mean?"

"You look like you fell asleep on a beach in Brazil, dude. You're so dark!"

Quick thinking made me answer, "Maybe it was crying earlier clearing out toxins from my bloodstream, giving my complexion a ruddier glow."

She looked at me quizzically.

"Well, Einstein, explain the biochemistry to me another day. I'm sleepy. I'm hittin' the sack."

Feeling satisfied, I wished her, "Goodnight, Sitamen."

"What?" she asked, yawning, turning her head back around that had been fixed on going into her room.

Uh-oh.

Recovering awkwardly but smoothly, I said, "Goodnight, see ya in tha mornin'."

"Oh, yeah. Goodnight, Tyree."

Sheesh.

=

At the first hint of the next day, after an uninterrupted sleep, I ricocheted awake with one determination – to get back to that Black sphere. It hit me so consumingly, once I opened my eyes, that the memory of my dream that night almost crept away from the loudness of the desire, to be forgotten like happens to most dreams – despite the fact that it had been the vividest dream I'd ever had in my brief life.

But I sensed the trail of it, nonetheless; and with grandma, already up and out of the room, as was her habit, I took a moment of silence to trudge that trail, before the scent went cold, with no crumbs left to mark where the dream had gone.

My father had come to me as I'd been looking out grandma's window at the Kattan house across the street. I was that current age of 12, staring at how this time, the air was like the intermingling bands of luminous light one sees in the Aurora Borealis. There was nothing subtle about this change as streaks of purple, magenta, chartreuse ignited with fireworked explosive brilliance, streaming above and beyond the house's gabled rooftop. I yearned to touch them.

"You know, you can fly up and reach them," my father had said behind me, his voice rolling like that low familiar thunder complete with his drawling Georgian rumble, satisfying even my sleeping wish to hear him again.

But as it had been my subconscious mind doing the listening, it was as if he'd always been there, would always be there. I hadn't jumped up excitedly, leaving my perch on the couch. I hadn't turned my head around to look at him. I had been only surprised, as he'd always made fun of my fascination with the change over that house that he'd sworn wasn't happening – I had been surprised that he would've not only confirmed seeing it, but that he would've suggested something so thoroughly unscientific as me flying up to touch the multi-hued air.

"I don't have wings, dad!" I protested. "I can't fly!"

"No, Tyree. It's not something magical. Wings are a metaphor. You lean on what makes you the strongest and you will."

"How?"

"Open the window and do."

I did this, pushing the bottom sash as high up as it would go, and then I had lifted the outside screen.

"Like this, dad?" I'd asked, scrunching my body up on the sill ready to spring into the swirling sky above.

"Don't talk, boy! Do!"

It had all been so vibrantly real to the moment, so solid with actual depth and weight, that in the thick of the dream it'd dawned on me that I was dreaming! And with that I'd realized I could command any possibility I desired, with flying being the most desirable. So I did. I bodily reached upwards and lifted out.

And, as simple as that, I was ascending, as opposed to falling, which I'd had enough of that day, most surely! I drove up through the clear lower atmosphere, feeling effortless, light, free. Then higher up, I'd dipped head first into the swirls of dappling colors, like a spoon dipping upwards into glowing ribbons of many flavored ice cream. They condensed and pooled, brushing my face like feathers, cooling my exposed skin not covered by my striped pajamas. Breezy feathery kisses that kept racing on past. They tickled a little with a bracing cold.

I was soaring!

That's why I oughtn't to have looked down. For the ground, now as far below as an aerial photograph, revealed the checkerboard pattern of the landscape from 100s of feet above and it struck me, immediately, I wasn't supposed to be doing what I was doing. So, I forgot exactly how to do it. In too short a time from my other two experiences, falling forever and crying forever, both too shortly over for me to have gotten them fully in the past, even as an echo in a dream, I had begun falling, again. The only difference was in the dream, I didn't fall so fast.

Not so fast at all.

I had had plenty of time, to see my street, angled to the parallel pattern of all the rest of the streets, coming up slowly, till I had made out the jutted tops of

159

the houses and the jumble of trees, and the garden and greenhouse in the back on the Kattan side of the block. Not to mention, as I fell closer, closer – I had had to get closer, like a far sighted person whipping on their reading glasses to read a fine print, because I'd needed to see a commotion in front of my house, the third building on that side of the block. There had been a moving truck, with men out front ambling an unwieldy, yet, familiar object up the steps and under the porch.

It was the herculean statue of a Black man, from my old house. In the dream, forgetting that it was a dream, I wondered what it was doing there as mom had donated it to a museum. Maybe they didn't want it anymore. The moving crew, having only manipulated the statue's outstretched arm into the small front door, that's when I noticed I had already been standing on the sidewalk in front, watching my father tell 8 Black men dressed in Kemetic loincloths and formal Kemetic headdress on the proper way to get the statue set up.

"Uh, dad?" I had offered, "I don't think that's going to fit."

"Nonsense, son!" he'd answered, boldly. His face was ringed in sunlight, masking his distinctive Marcus Jackson features; hands directing the process, as he had mostly focused on instructing the men, shouting, "Gonna have to rip out the doorjams, brothers!"

My father had never called any random fellow Black men, 'brothers' – not to mention the original crew, who'd moved the gargantuan triple the size of life sculpture into our old home – they'd all been white.

"Don't worry about the mess! Let's give this house a skylight!" he boomed.

And with that, the crew had plunged the statue right through the back of the house, without effort, as if the house had only been a paper origami.

"Dad!" I'd screamed over the noise of the breaking wooden planks and ripping plasterboard. "Mom, Kyerah, and grandma are in the house, and the neighbors! Stop!!!"

He had looked at me, his deep eyes smiling, "They're all right behind you, Tyree."

And sure enough, they all had been – downstairs neighbors, all the neighbors on the whole street, paying no attention to me, along with a million more, what'd seemed like a million in the imaginative opinion of my dream – a million other Black people right behind them, jubilantly cheering the progress on.

I had turned back as the crowd's deafening roar crescendo-ed, in harmony – I turned back to see that the reason for their cheer had been the statue, suddenly larger than it had ever been in our old house, 10 times the size, being raised to a standing position; its head fully visible above as its stretched up arm ripped the roof into tatters and splinters, making plenty of room! The outstretched hand reaching up into the swirling lights about, without effort. Suddenly that hand came to life and grabbed hold of the lighted colors with an electrical burst.

And that was when I woke up ready, almost forgetting my exuberant father had put his arm around my shoulder, squeezing, laughing. Looking behind at my family, once more, I saw my grandmother laughing, too, cheering, and fearlessly.

Now, I didn't do dream interpretation, but even to me that seemed to be resounding agreement that something spectacular was happening. It echoed, boomeranged and rippled back my own conclusion that even if I couldn't fly in real life, I was at least a 'superhero' spelled with a lowercase 's'; which might not be emblazoned on the middle of a skintight spandex shirt (and I never liked skintight spandex, anyway) – but more appropriately stitched on as a LaCoste-like label on a nicely loose polo shirt. A little 's' just below the left shoulder. A black shirt, thank you, very much. Black shirt. Red little 's' with maybe a green circular border.

Rushing through breakfast, my glee forthcoming and quick, accompanied by my family's surprise at the generosity of my mood; breezing as a backpack equipped whirlwind out the door, ahead of my sister, who usually was out before me; giving and receiving hastened 'have a great day's' to both my mom and grandma, as my mom then began her full time job search for a full time or anytime job on her laptop in the kitchen, and grandma sat down in her 'spot' in the living room – after all that, I was re-invigorated to verify, upon stepping out that door, that my new perception hadn't diminished one decibel. Truthfully, it had increased.

Hot dang, looked like I was a superhero!

I'd have sworn my extra perception had been there inside my own abode, but it had been so subtle, so similar to simply knowing my family members, along with the objects we owned, that I lost my surety it was truly happening, or had been such a dramatic difference. Or, maybe coming out of that Orb, I was boiling over with excitement, making the sudden daylight that greeted my eyes when I'd left the Kattan house appear as an enhancement. In my own dimly lit home, it was difficult to see colors, period, let alone a spectral explosion. Mom believed in not wasting electricity given our heavily budgeted reality; added to that – our house was angled so it never received the full benefit of direct sunlight, anyway. Perhaps even understanding, or believing I understood my neighbors had been no more than a series of logical conclusions, and not at all – that I was understanding their souls better, seeing them more clearly, or anything else more profoundly. Maybe it had all been my imagination. Maybe it had all been regular me feeling really good for the first time in over a year.

Thus, to step into everything still livingly radiant, was an undeniable joy that made me near want to run rather than walk. But it was the glory of it that slowed my pace, for all the world was an artist's painting that had brushed ordinary existence aside with an ingenious swipe, giving plain canvas new honor as a masterpiece. Every inch was still neglected inner city but everything was fixable, from broken up sidewalk, to sagging house, to neglected storefront, to pure Black us.

Why amazingly, even there; even on the corner, one block from my street, the intensity had flowed into the usual gathering of, of...?

I was thinking... 'of'... what? Alright, not looking back to what my yesterday's mind would have called them, I had no choice but to own this other word, calling them what my father would never have used towards Black people he didn't personally know, admire or deem worthy of notice. Black people like them. To my dad, there were 'African-Americans' like us, and then there were lost people like them. He didn't hate them, but had given up on their rescue in this current reality that we all coincidentally shared. So this word I'd only heard him use in my dream or for real, with people like Dr. Kattan and his wife – the ones he recognized as helping our struggle to prove to white people that we 'African-Americans' were as equal as...?

Well, with thoughts blazing through my brain, still in multiple levels of full inner individual conversations – now, I wondered, "As equal? As equal to what? Is there something inherently wrong with us that only being with white people would fix? How could all this life we contain, full of complexity, be solved by a simple 2 equals 2 equation?"

I decided to call these men on the corner what I could no longer deny – as the light intensified sight of them filled me with a bursting pride, strange as that

162

may seem to anyone else. Like the young men on the stoop, yesterday, only with experience, they shattered everyone's quiet with doubt you could survive an encounter with them. A fact the rest of the world, even non-enhanced like me, could see. Otherwise, why be so terrified of them, especially if you weren't one of them? I knew in time, no matter what profession I chose, I couldn't pretend the world would see me separate from them, no matter how adept I became at what I chose to do. It was a connection so inseparable, the word my father avoided was the only word to use, because the fate of these men would always strengthen or hinder my own, making them, beyond any doubt...

... my 'Brothers'.

A very good word for these men and those boys whose collective destiny was a family matter, each of us sinking or swimming better or worse as one.

The morning's one or two would come together in greater numbers as the fading daylight signaled their time to rise and shine. They'd be standing, leaning, chatting, in increasing force, and commanding the corners with their loomingly maligned solidity that threatened danger should one earn their reputed easy to inflame wrath. Which might have never truly happened, I suddenly realized. In an emergency, these men may have been my only salvation, long before any police arrived, and even moreso, if the police ever did.

Men. Not teenagers. In front of the garishly plastered bodegas, windows slathered with scantily clad posters of pale women drinking beer, or old faded posters of yellowed food that my mother warned me to never eat – these men had frightened me, as closely as the other day, and every day before that, whenever I went strolling by, with family or alone, on my way to doing something – anything, but be perceived as looking like the vulnerability I'd always felt inside.

What were they up to, lingering with unhurried ease, while I rushed to handle my details? Drug dealing? Pimping? Scoping muggable future victims? The usual list of guilty before proven innocent verdicts filled my mind, courtesy of Hollywood and the evening news. Verdicts that assaulted me from time immemorial, while none of these individual men had ever done a thing to me, or anyone else, that I knew with verification.

Still, the forewarned dangers came to mind with each non-encounter, with no proof, no witnesses, as they did that morning. I couldn't stop these assumptions because somebody else had put them in my mind before I realized I had a mind which could think opposite to everything I'd learned. Now, the

163

guilty before charged verdicts came with something that had been there, but I hadn't been taught to pay attention. Hidden behind those dire verdicts, that had pulled a freight train of shame in the possibility they proved Black me guilty, too - condemned by the actions of even a one of these men - now, those condemnations came with a thoughtful pause...

If God, Himself, had lived their lives, I knew, He, might be on that same corner, and the next, and the next, and the next; suffering from, not lack of innate power, but from lack of self-knowledge, incapable of creating any universe due to his lack of believing He could harness His might, no permission needed. 'Cause surely those men radiated the authority of The Creator in a blinding misdirected strength, full grown, a blazing intensity that frightened the world, as an unchecked blaze, an unleashed inferno of moltenous potential that no others had, whether poor or rich.

Dr. Kattan had said it well in regards to them. There was no Harry Potter magic here. No Lord of the Rings, as these men didn't need a trinket or a magic wand to give them power. They were the furnace that forged the trinkets. That full strength could never be wielded by anyone outside lookin' in; anyone who only captured a dim reflection of the illuminated original.

I was seeing what made the 'ring', The Ring.

Lo to those who'd scorned Him when God figured His way back to His smite capable self. I knew, to my core, I was finally on the right side of judgment, and if I wasn't? Then let me be damned. Not that I wanted to join my 'brothers' in their self-immolation. Looking at them, as I passed, I knew if they knew? They wouldn't be able to stop themselves from harnessing their own super powers. Capital 'S', centered, no spandex, just Divinity.

Walking by those men, I knew a superhero saved others to save himself; not just because he's a 'nice' guy, but to amplify his harmony into the community's serene bliss, ensuring a world that had a better chance to maintain, enjoy, and build the best of people. Which of course, would include...

The mighty sisters. Remember, this is a history book, and no history is complete without telling herstory, if only through my heightened perception that remains a male's. Powers on full, seeing my sisters went way past the physical for me that morning. I felt the quaking need, first and foremost, to be sure that each woman I saw, child, young, old and ancient was protected. The men could fend for themselves, even if barely, but?

164

The sense of how much danger Black women were in, welled up in me like a subsonic shockwave. Yes, they were less likely to be targeted by police officers, though less and less as the latest horrifying news had been reporting; but as I politely watched them, on that warming up start of the day, I went from pure gratitude to deepest concern, seeing them wearing more of their flesh as clothing than their clothes, or wearing their clothing so tight, it looked like flesh. I could guess, without effort, they didn't believe in the magnitude of their beauty, or they wouldn't have screamed it out so loudly, as if the entirety of humanity was profoundly deaf. Wouldn't have thrown it about as if it had no effect or that its effect was weaker, the more they threw it around. Fairly knocked down with all this seeing, this feast of flesh was too much; and I was about to burst from over stuffing.

Honestly, I'd never been drawn to white or any other girls but Black ones. Not because of Pro-Black reasons, but because they felt comfortable to a boy who had been raised by Black parents he liked, in a pretty much solidly Black neighborhood, albeit a highbrow one through my parents' careful selection. And yet, that day, as opposed to the one past where I was used to undulations of puckering flesh-ial exposure? I saw and felt that Black women smiled richer (when they did), laughed more heartily (which they did, regularly, even if angry), they moved with more exacting certainty (which was the original siren song); and the reason for their own reputation as the angriest of the fairer sex was because they did anger more believably, same as the men, with only a little less physical strength – but don't push it. Who could not hear the Black Woman who had ears? They meant it, whatever it was they were doing. Why, I could not only defrost frozen fingers and toes near them, but warm up the dead, as well, as they were the reason the heart beats, keeping all our blood flowing like a river down the highest peak.

So, reader, I know you'll understand, then – I was shocked there was so much of that earthquaking beautiful power on display, while I could see the best of their beauty, their majestic souls, were neglected inside! I was being beaten over the head by flowers wielding baseball bats. Hard to think fondly of a Venus Flytrap when you're the fly. And I was almost as helpless. All that exquisiteness was a trap for parts of my maleness that ran on automatic, deployed to convince me all I was? Was a hapless beast, who had wandered into my own mauling at the hands, the bosom, the waist, the buttocks, the legs – the hypnotizing pulchritude of someone who should have been taking me higher. Someone who was telling my little 's' superhero to shut the hell up and be an illiterate brute, instead.

Honestly, I wondered if I would ever be powerful enough to withstand this

165

kryptonite.

Plus, I knew I wouldn't be the only one, nearly crippled, thus. That's why the last shred of my protector self, stitched me back together as best I could since my stronger instinct was to shield each of these women from every manner of animal, be that feathered, scaled, furred, shaving, or...

prepubescent me.

The noise of it, the boom of it, the danger of it, street after street, made me want to go up to a Catholic school girl I saw walking directly in front of me for a few blocks before she disappeared into one of those bad food poster slathered bodegas, wearing her proper Catholic skirt unholy-ly improperly – barely beneath the bottom of her behind, as she bounced cluelessly into the bell jangling store's entrance. Before she was gone forever from my view, I had wanted to catch her, and cover her over-exposure, like I had wanted to cover mine in that other lifetime in front of Sitamen. It would have broken my faith in my 's' to have heard later on that day that a Catholic school girl had been raped by someone unaware of her value, as her display shrieked she was as much undeserving of protection as the bugs we crush without thought.

She was a diamond who thought she was sand. She didn't seem to know someone precious should never be exposed to the greedy part of a man's eyes. I knew from yesterday's me and from hanging out with my Sandstone friends, that though we males controlled our lusts because we didn't want to go to jail or risk the horrific self-loathing brought on by becoming full-out rapists; nevertheless – our lusts flattered our lowest wit by wanting to believe we could trick that little girl, any girl, and eventually any woman, out of the centimeter of plaid that hid the least valuable of her treasures. This made us 'better' males who could excuse ourselves from blame, since "that girl was asking for it". And when we were done? Well, who keeps old used goods around, as if you couldn't attract something new and maybe 'better'? Who wanted last year's model, when you could get showroom fresh?

I knew I'd always have to control that unthinking side, though no woman would ever be in danger of me. It was terribly distracting, indeed, since their beauty was beyond denying. However, I forced myself, and completely, to focus my grateful attention on those sisters who were safer to notice. And? I did that quickly!

With desperate purpose, I discovered there were more than I'd ever paid attention to, before. Probably, because I finally wanted to find them. From my

166

house to the school, there they were – not easy to spot, in the rush hour crowd, but I saw the demur, the bold, the shy, the rooted, the gutsy, and the polite, all with a wholeness I know I'd have ignored less than 24 hours afore. Why there were even 3 more Catholic school girls whose skirts, though still way to exposing, safely went no higher than directly above their knees.

Made me wonder, 'What kind of a 'religious' school has its girls wearing skirts like those?'

There were so many young sisters who weren't focused on their beauty, alone, becoming more exquisite because, they kept me moving and buzzing, Venus Fly Trap free, all the way to...

that school building. Which was a whole 'nuther experience like turning onto Carson Ave., only in the opposite direction. See, the other days, P.S. 47, before acquiring my little 's' profession – had merely been a decided loser to the ivy coated, mini-Oxford grace of Medgar Evers Prep. It, instead of a stately edifice, nestled in rolling greenery, infused with an atmosphere conducive to deliberate study – here creaked a gigantic windowed sarcophagus forged of weary grit stained brick, with a seeming lean to the left, that wasn't altogether a lean, but the finished product of dingy weathering, pronounced on its right side, giving the optical illusion that the building was collapsing under its own hopelessness, under a tilt no one cared to, or knew how to fix. The other day, this school had been the period at the end of the sentence, 'Yes, this is more proof that my life now really sucks'.

But this time? I didn't care about turning this sorry near relic into a showplace, since it wasn't the building that mattered at all. Turns out, this tomb was not, in the slightest, the star of its own story. For no matter what the onlooker gathered from its derelict state, it was the s-c-h-o-o-l that wasn't worthy of its students, not those students who deserved its blight. Maybe. And that understanding alone made P.S. 47's neglected insult impossible to take seriously as the insult was only temporary.

I repeat, lest you think this the tale of a pretend mad boy turned a real one, rather than a historical chronicle about facts, not fantasy – my extraordinarily enhanced visual experience wasn't delusional, nor hallucinogenic, other than colors had a bolder 'after a rainstorm' clarity, like the air around the Kattan house. It was subtle, but it was real. This wasn't some LSD induced 'trip' that interfered with my ability to think straight. Definitely not, and I proudly confess to this day, I've never tried, nor needed an artificially induced 'high' of any sort, as no gods do. Having real power, truthful power, eliminates both the

167

desire and the need for crutches. Nah. Even 12yr old me could tell this wasn't a 'hippie', swirling, coated light show that left me stumbling and mumbling from curb to curb, every thought a fog, onlookers sadly gazing and shaking their heads at the sight of the pathetic child junkie. To put it mildly, it was my perception that was heightened, thinking with multi-layered precision, many thoughts at the same exact time, in full contemplation, as if there were several people talking in my head and they were all me. More of me. It was undeniable, my adventure inside the sphere, and nothing outside of it had lost its intensity. It'd perhaps gotten more intense, but it's hard to tell this history to 3 dimensional you in any other way that makes sense, so I'm tellin' it one layer at a time.

Wait till you claim your own destiny.

Therefore? The students' vibrant triumph over their ill surroundings was more what I 'felt' it to be than what it actually looked like, with the intensified hues of their beings obvious to what could be called a third eye inside me that'd previously been blind. I could feeeeeeeeel people's 'aura', as the more jubilant a passerby, the more radiant was their 'glow'. And everything vibrated with a heightened volume of meaning. The colors were only the numbers on the dial, while I was seeing the inner electric current, as if I could piece apart the why of an air conditioner, without instructions or dissembling it. What made one object gas, liquid, solid, alive, or not – including the school building, all made sense to me. That school, darn literally, told me it hadn't neglected itself. Sad as it had been left to become, if that collapsing structure could have, it would have shown gratitude for the compliment of being filled with such inexhaustible life. More, truthfully, it was ashamed of itself, that it sent the wrong image to the world that it was these children who were unworthy of the building.

Indeed, all the buildings along my 6 block walk, starting with my own home, and ugly and not so ugly, had said the same thing without the need or ability for words, although I heard every single confession.

Truth filled me up, seeing the potential for magnificence, called Black Us, in the raw, unfinished stage. I had no clear premonition of our future transformation into near immortality, at this time, but from gazing at those moving, striding containers of Blacks, and Browns, I could see the pure ingredients within and swam in the cool, flowing elixir that revitalized, within a river of luminescent beings, they being a clearly visible Aurora Borealis. From the jumble and jostle of children streaming into that forlorn building – one by one through the un-sterile metal detectors, past the indifferent uniformed

168

guards – it was the beginning of a birth, mistakenly slated for mass abortion.

With the building being a silent mournful witness to the impending slaughter.

I didn't know if I could stop it, but I knew, something here screamed for fixing and I would spend my whole life doing nothing but, cause this was bigger than me. I also knew, re-born Tyree Jackson, would let nothing stop him. At least that's what I thought right then. Complicating details were getting closer every second...

Perhaps if I could see into the future, I'd have been more humble, but that morning I felt confident, contemplated forming committees, running for class president, printing flyers, as I floated jubilantly into my homeroom class, into my seat, savoring my plans –

to then notice, that my new cohorts, each present, with Reggie entering the room at the same time I did –

"Hey!" I greeted him.

"Yo! Whaz up?" he returned as we passed through the door, me right behind him.

And James, at his front row desk –

"Peace!"
"Peace!"

And Terrence, shoelaces still missing, coming in behind me –

"Mornin'" he said a little groggily.

Then Maxwell, who I'd noticed earlier in the week, was quite the ladies' 'man', with quite the required ladies' man look, was busy talking to Nyisha, who'd not been even narrowly impressed with my version of a tough guy, the other day. I wondered if maybe she was impressed with Maxwell's version of a suave one.

'Why can't girls see through that game?' I silently wondered.

Impromptu, I wanted to interrupt his focused attention with some distraction, like a cough, as his back was turned to me, but I didn't. Nyisha, though, looked up at me, in between his intent words, without expression. I met her cold look with my own stone face, then nonchalantly chose to scan the room.

The whole room was full of the 'all' of who was usually present – 'all' minus the one – Howard.

"Hey," said Terrence, walking past me to his desk, in a voice not meant for just me to hear, "looks like your boy is a no show. Next time we see 'im, betcha he'll be wearin' that skirt!"

A few snickers went round the room, though I didn't want to join the fun which no longer felt as if it was merely at Howard's expense. Now the embarrassment felt like mine's, which meant, no skirt was required to be weak, 'cause I was wearing khakis.

What had I done? Regret washed over me, doused with a filthy mire of disappointment in my actions, along with unexpected concern for Howard. Why, I didn't even know how to check on him, and say sorry. Not that that would work. Tough guys have no regrets.

I sank into my desk, not realizing mortification could be so heavy, even if it's invisible to the eye. Not to mention I was more than a little worn out by these avalanching surprise emotions when they came roaring upon me without invitation, or a helpful phone call to say they were on their way. I was sure I used to be much better at ignoring my feelings, and if this was a part of my new powers? It wasn't making me feel very powerful.

'*Must be a superhero thing I'll have to ask the doctor about,*' I thought, figuring I had definite proof of my comic book status in my enhanced sensitivity to everything, even my homeroom desk. I swear I could sense the other students who'd sat there throughout yesterday. Not specifically, but I knew that wasn't just my butt warmth in that chair, as I discerned I wasn't the first to plop down on it since yesterday at 8am.

Ewwww! Yech!

I figured the doctor must have been underplaying the obviousness of my new abilities for some reason known only to him.

But, ashamed of what I'd done yesterday or not? I was pretty dang sure it wouldn't have been appropriate to reveal it, right then, at that crowded moment. Admitting my regret for having bullied a boy who was likely as frightened as I was, I now assumed, wouldn't fix anything, in the long run. So, I put up a halfhearted smile towards Reggie who was nodding at me with his easy going approval. He was impressed.

I wished I had the power to turn back time, even without the Orb. Oh! Maybe that ability would come later... I couldn't wait to talk to Dr. Kattan.

Reggie grinned back at my own poorly faked grin, utterly believing my lie – only today, my muscles had a lot less reason to co-operate. Choosing to be patient because my enhanced understanding told me somehow I'd fix this mess, too, I pulled my act together, making those muscles, eyes, cheeks and lips, once again, do exactly as told. That's a hollow feeling, lemme tell you, reader, and I don't blame you should you not be admiring me that much right now. Or haven't for a while, probably. I was having a rough time of it about then, myself. But I did say, perfection is not what got me to where I am, today.

Nyisha smacked her lips, without pretending, blanket-ly declaring, "Ya'll don't even know what happened to that boy, but you so ready to look for the worse!"

A few sympathetic "Um-hummmms," went round the room, interspersed with blunted groans, from those here and there who didn't want to be reminded they were wrong. I wished I could have agreed with her, but her truthful words merely increased the weight of my mortification, so that if anyone had supersonic hearing, which, no, I didn't have that power, either – the sound of my crushed dignity would have drowned every 'um-hummmmm', 'sheesh', 'arrrrgggghhh', and 'uh' out.

But that's when my woes were flipped upside down and forgotten as the air in the room became constricted by the arrival of our homeroom teacher, Mr. Lewistein, who entered, with a mumbled, barely audible,

"Good Morning."

Same greeting as he'd uttered the other 4 mornings I'd been there. Only this time was as startling (for me alone, I'm sure) – it was as if he had run into the classroom naked, with his behind on fire. He still, like he had the other days, looked humdrumly normal starting up the television monitor at the head of the classroom to play that day's 'Line One Student News' program. 'LOSN' – give them 5 minutes and they'll give you...

Lies. Whoa. And nuthin' but lies.

171

Excuse me, reader, before I get to the butt on fire Mr. Lewistein, I have to share how I was shocked by this Lying One broadcast almost as much! Yeah. I knew it to be a generic news program played for students in thousands of grade and high school level institutions, where the school budget was then supplemented by the Line One Corporation, while the children were fed a string of commercials laced together with beads of candy news, as revealed by the razzle dazzle of youthful, un-relentingly throw-up happy and teeth rottingly cute reporters.

This sort of hokum had always bored the heck out of me, having had parents who explained the details of a society that worked tirelessly on encouraging useless greed mixed with rampant self-loathing in the young, intended on turning them into lifelong unthinking CONNEDsumers. (I invented that spelling, myself. Feel free to borrow it.)

But, what I was seeing went beyond my parents now encoded into my DNA warning. That day, those digital pulses reassembled on the glass television screen by a low quality number of pixels (it was a cheap monitor) – although my 'vision' of the television was not as clear as with 3 dimensional people – there was no sense of the 'life' within the televised reporters – nonetheless, those pixels reassembled with a deeper meaning as Cathy Brickham, the very blonde buoyantly enthusiastic teen newscaster conveyed to me, beyond doubt, in her subtle muscle movements, that she and her fellow reporters didn't mean a daggone thing they were saying.

Seemed, I didn't need to know the details of the news item. I could see the lie of it in their faces as they tried to do what I had just done toward Reggie.

Tell tremendous WHOPPERS...

with a straight face, but their lagging, protesting muscles were easy for me to spot.

I'm sure this isn't shocking news to you, reader and future near deity, as we all pretty much suspect the news is fake even if we don't know the missing facts. Even through the non-life of that TV screen, I saw their facial muscles being forced to obey commands they themselves did not believe. They were drowning in falsehood.

Even the one Black reporter, Oliver Turnblatt, though he was skilled, I could tell he didn't have a clue as to what he was saying...

Or why he was saying it.

Part of my multi-dimensional thinking, as I was also, simultaneously analyzing both my mortification, and the various school subjects to come throughout the day, all these observations and ponderings were running through my mind in a harmonized flow that kept me synchronized with each train of thought. There was no lost thought, booted out by another, while I tried to recall what I'd been thinking. Nope. I comprehended everything in minute detail, all while human torch Mr. Lewistein had no idea, in his yellow shirted, opened at the collar, blue jeaned clothing that covered a man of average build, with a strongly featured face capped by a balding head bursting out of the lemon shirt's neckline – he had no idea that one of his students knew his secret, which his body language attempted to hide like his flesh was a Halloween costume.

However, for me, that Dr. Jekyll/Mr. Hyde outfit on him was disintegrating on his body as it was blazing.

See, reader, while he casually turned on the TV, calmly sat down at his desk to arrange papers for his incoming math class, Mr. Lewistein was terrified, deep inside, where it counted more than his calm exterior demeanor. Unlike the static figures on the screen, I could visibly see his emotions emanating from his pores, circling the crown of his shiny palate like a dark cloud. I could almost smell it. And maybe, (this I couldn't tell for certain) – but maybe? His fear might have been hidden from him, also.

This grown man was full of intensified functional terror no matter what he did. To be precise, Mr. Lewistein was a-u-t-h-e-n-t-i-c-a-l-l-y stonecold out of his mind, and unlike with me? His insanity was real.

~ ~ ~ ~ ~ ~ ~ ~ ~ ~ ~ ~

Another brief interruption, reader, I have been promised. Queen Sitamen has a few questions she insists on putting on record. Always the bold big sister that she is, I welcome the constructive criticism. Really.

Or at least I like to think I do, since I'm supposed to be darn near perfect, now.

Akhenaten Ra: You have something to offer, sister?

173

Queen Sitamen: Well, not to interrupt again, but, I am curious, Amen. Seeing how we have just walked into the Memnon Dome and are heading for the opening orientation...

(Ah, yes. **Update:** We're now entering the Memnon of Rhodes Civic Dome through the grand arched doubled doors of the outer frosted and handcarved glass facade. About 50ft high, this entrance opens onto a massive rotunda glistening with a black marbled floor, supported by 10 inner statuesque columns of onyx, several stories high which frame the yawning archways of petrified Afrikan cherrywood. Both the doors and frescoed archways that hold them have been hand hewn with a relief timeline of the final battle, called 'The Ascension'. The doorways have been carved with a raised script of exactly the same lyrical hieroglyphs as covered the surface of the Orb, written in the original language of Allah, in the original script. Each onyx column has been chiseled into figures of ancient and not so ancient warriors, and every heroic figure represents a person who has led us to victory. And, no. There is not one of me, as I stumbled upon my role, literally, and these men and women chose their paths. Our people congratulate me often, but they and I know, I'm no Brother Robert Mugabe.

(Hundreds and hundreds of people are walking about, clothed in sweeping robes, of different designs, men, and women. A few wear Western style business suits, or dresses. No woman's form is overtly detectable beneath their outfits, and many women – not all, but most including my sister – have covered their hair with either a hijab, or an Afrikan style headdress. Some have designed ornamental hats as only melanin rich Queens can design, sport and wear so magisterially.

(The overwhelming majority of the passersby are Black, and then there are many who are Brown, many Asian, with a barely perceptible few whites. There are hundreds and hundreds of people in total, entering the main doorways, sitting on various wrought benches, talking, strolling, yet the space is so enormous, the rotunda seems almost deserted. This is the entrance hall for orientation. The Epidome Quaterium is even bigger.).

Queen Sitamen: (continues) ...Well, I see you focusing on the Writer, so intently. It made me wonder (pauses) how far you've gotten, as here at the Memnon? You just could run into someone who wants to know how you're progressing. And Amen? You've had a whole year, already.

Akhenaten Ra: (inhaling, slightly defensive) There won't be so many

174

attendees, here. Not at all like the main meetings. And there's still 2 whole weeks. If I write constantly, almost nonstop, I should have a fair amount done in that time.

Queen: You're going to hafta write in your sleep if all you have is a hundred pages. Good thing I have my own room. All that mumbling while you snore would keep me awake.

Akhenaten Ra: (giving my sister a raised eyebrow smirk) Good thing you're a healer and not a comedian. The planet might still be in a heap of trouble. And for your information, I've finished well over a hundred pages by now. 163 and this one'll make it 164. 200 pages gets closer with every bad joke you tell, so keep 'em rollin'.

Queen: (smirk returned) Hardy, har, har. But for real, little brother. 200 for a history book is still barely the contents page. What's taking so long? You've had a whole year.

Akhenaten Ra: Well, it's taken some time for me to gather all the necessary documentation,

Queen: Documentation...

Akhenaten: (ignoring her) construct an appropriate timeline,

Queen: Timeline, an appropriate one...

Akhenaten: Schedule interviews with eyewitnesses...

Queen: (interrupting) Oh, now that sounds interesting! Who have you spoken with? I do hope you've interviewed Howard, I mean Negus Mansa Musa! What he and the Japanese have accomplished eliminating all that Fukushima radiation from the Japan Islands and the Pacific Ocean is amazing, truly! No one thought it could be done. Matter of a fact we were certain when Allah gave the order to get started, it would be...

Akhenaten: ...impossible. Um. I didn't mean to imply that I've done any interviews, yet. That's coming up in time, sister. I figured this gathering would be the perfect place to connect with the most important entities rather than crisscrossing the planet looking for them.

Queen: (turning to me with a look of disbelief) You are kidding, right?

175

(suddenly looks ahead, calming herself). I apologize, brother but, exactly at what point in this timeline are you? Have you gotten to the punch in the face yet?

Akhenaten: Almost.

Queen: Almost?! (turns to me again, aghast) It's been 10 hours since my little contribution and we've spent most of that time in the hotel having lunch. It's not like the old days when we had to write everything down or even perform one task at a time. You just 'think' your way through the book. What could be easier?

Akhenaten: It's not that I haven't been writing. I have a plan. I have to explain the 'why' behind the history.

Queen: (nodding) I do understand that, but respectfully, (back to looking ahead) not wanting to write your book for you, but? You are writing this for those still stuck in the latter days of Hell. So, characteristically? They've been carefully taught to barely read the ingredients on the foods they eat, let alone read books, and definitely not ones with 'explanations'. Cut to the juicy parts, Amen, as quickly as you can. The grown-ups are most likely too ruined to accept it. Exciting thrills'll make it easier for the children and, it'll get you something more 'explainable' to The Elders, right *now*. You can pad it out later.

Akhenaten: (sigh) You are probably right, however? I have to do it my way, not yours. I love you, Set, but, you can't play big sister this time. See, our people as you said, are not dumb, just addicted to pleasure. Give them a game to play and suddenly they learn every detail. Well, life or death is the most exciting endeavor they'll ever have encountered, especially presented truthfully. I must be deliberate and painstaking, and *careful*. Otherwise, before the history circulates, the Tamahue will tear it apart, accusing it of being 'racist', when race is not the point. The point is two objects cannot exist in the same place at the same time...

Queen: ... without one of those objects being forced to give sway to the other.

Akhenaten: Yes! The Black and Brown People's intelligent love of self is the greatest threat to White Supremacy. We know that, but they don't. I have to explain it gently, completely, lest our people will never even be given a chance to stumble across the book, let alone have it available in the one book store that might have managed to survive in their Black community. Not to mention, there are no coincidences. This is my project for a reason, as you pretty much said yourself, those so long 10 hours ago. And as you said those decades ago. We both believe in our people, in their passion for truth, no matter where they are. No matter what state, as we all saw what happened when we learned the facts.

Queen: Okay, brother. You've got me there, dead to rights. So, where are you, anyway?
Akhenaten: You mean in the book?

(Queen Sitamen nods)

Akhenaten: After finishing up explaining the Tamahue, I'll be in the lunchroom when Nyisha got up from the table as I and the fellas sat down.

Queen: Awwwwww. Smart sister, even then, when we knew so little.

Akhenaten: Yes, she was. But we were ignorant only for a little while longer. And she still is one of the smartest, wisest women I know.

Queen: Yes, that she is. No doubt. And boy! Were we ever so ignorant, but only for a little while longer. Alright, brother, you, as usual, have won my confidence, against my better judgment. Now maybe you can explain that as well to The Revered Minister Farrakhan. He's walking right towards us.

(Just ahead, moving leisurely, without bodyguards, as none are necessary, any longer, The Messenger Elijah Muhammad's Aaron, as many refer to him because he resurrected the Nation of Islam when the Tamahue had thought they'd destroyed it, he's strolling directly towards us, this minute. Radiating youthful vigor, though, even if he hadn't been, he's always mightily imposing. Yet, this era rejuvenates everyone, adding back decades, signs of aging removed, but, not the wizening years of accumulated knowledge. So, although he must be 200 years old, he looks to be in his mid-thirties, fit and moving vigorously, with apparent energetic depth visible in his eyes even at distance of about 20ft from us. I did not see him until my sister just now mentioned him coming towards us. My eyes are wider, a bit, though the rest of me I command to remain nonchalant. I've had much practice maintaining calm in the most difficult situations. Much practice, and still learning.

He has caught my eye, is apparently about to raise his arm in greeting, but oh! At this exact moment another person intercepts him with an exuberant exclaim. The Minister is being drawn into this conversation. I look at my sister and exhale, as we continue, unhindered, to the banks of chairs set up to announce the upcoming events – chairs that are filling up with some of the most powerful people on the planet, the only ones missing being the young, except for my youthful sister and myself.)

I'm guiding Queen Sitamen to the women's section, to then find a spot for myself within the seats farthest in the back and way in the corner of the men's. Farthest from any questions. But from gods? One can't hide for long...

=

Warning, again: This tain't no novel. Why, this is even more than merely a history of my people during a transitional point, who live on a small planet, third from a small star in a far flung leg of a swirling galaxy. This is a history that's not only personal for me, but may one day be your-story, making it personal for the both of us, whether you know that this minute or not. Whether you agree with me or not ever, in this lifetime. Sooner or later there'll be not a soul left in Hell and we'd both agree – the sooner that happens, the better.

However, admittedly – Sitamen is perhaps, maybe? A little correct. I've got to cut to the chase by giving you a quick synopsis of the why behind the actions to come, otherwise? You'll be on a no-name street having missed the main thoroughfare 'cause nobody ever told you there's a thing called a 'map'.

Did you know, even after the brutality of slavery, most former slaves confessed that they missed the security of life under a master, despite the certainty of being terrorized at the hands of one? Incredible, yet? I am The Librarian Keeper and these are sentiments I've not merely read, I've gone back to the days they were shared with me, hearing these confessions straight from the mouths of the supposedly newly 'freed'. Standing there, listening, I felt the sensation of wanting to shake these dead 'former' slaves awake, smack 'em into knowing the magnificence they were meant to be, while in the midst of my reflex twitches, I remained calm because that's what the furnace of adversity did, if you survived. It forged gods, eventually, and gods are by nature, patient. Childhood isn't easy, manhood can be tragic, but Godhood will never be for the faint.

So, taking a cue from my sister, rather than chronicling every single doggone adventure I've had which brought me proof of our predicament, and to make reading and writing this book a sight easier, let me cut to the quick, since you, reader, trained to think you're 'free' are sorely going to require some sort of shake-up for why you're no more free than those slaves missing out on their masters' freebees, no matter how much the freebees cost.

History can never prove the Tamahue, the Kemetic name for Barbarians, or white people – it can never prove they're all bad, because they weren't and

179

aren't! There're many amongst their kind who inspired the world, gave their lives to defend righteousness, fed the hungry, petitioned depraved despots for redress on behalf of the voiceless and are incensed at what their fellow white men do. But? That didn't nor will it ever make us safe with them, as the bad ones are impossible to tell apart from the good and their good are never up to the challenge of fixing the bad, since no matter their good white people number? There's never been enough of them to stop their heartless brethren from destroying whole planets, let alone enough to jump in front of the bullet aimed by a corrupt police officer or vigilante at one of Us. Innocent or guilty, their history gives them no jurisdictional credibility. Despite the good ones, they've brought death and destruction to every place they visit, eventually, by staying on in the lands they then steal, filling it with their own oppressed Caucasians in ever more increasing, ever more numbers, after stomping white Jesus and the falsity of Cave People virtue into the original residents' minds.

The thieves, also, change the country's name, hand the theft to their children and that makes it all okay. Steal for one day and you're a criminal. Steal for generations and it's your 'manifest destiny'. Good white people have never been good enough to dominate that paradigm. Period. Not to mention, if all white folks were nice, it would never give them the right to tell you and me what's 'normal' behavior.

If you have a 'nice' friend, that doesn't mean he or she has a right to tell you how to dress, how to talk, what to learn to determine your success, *especially* if (I repeat) your 'friend' stole everything from you, even your family story. If you are 'free'? You are the owner in charge of what your success and your story will be. Not him who has no idea what being oppressed by him is like. He's never been in the furnace. His people are the ones turning up the heat.

Quick Lesson on Why You Are Not Free, No Matter What You Are Willing To Settle For Because You Think Settling is Easier Than Building a New Pyramid:

1. We are not only not white, we don't need to be. Glorifying our people expresses a love for oneself, not a need to hurt others. That's two separate impulses. To say they are the same is to say a parent, proud of his/her child's winning first place shouldn't be proud because it means he wants to kill all the other children who have the nerve to show up at the starting line. No! Mom and Dad just feel happy for their child.

White people's pride in themselves should have stopped at that, however? Fear of others helped allow their greed to sanction committing the most heinous crime of all history – a crime exponentially multiplied into the millions reaching into the billions of those who would otherwise have been born in a self-determining reality had their parents not been captured and/or slaughtered – a crime with no hint of an apology, leading to the conclusion Black people don't have any humanity worthy of apology and redress. Thus? White people emboldened, feel justified in continuing to commit varying varieties of the same original transgression, because there's no opposition. They've sucked the life out of opposition within us and who couldn't when the tyrant starts with a child ripped from the life-directing wisdom of their forefathers and the abductor, even the abductor's children never end the assault?

They keep the terror going through an assortment of agents and an assortment too numerous to list. Agencies like the KKK, Cointelpro, the Rockefeller Foundation, the Bill and Melinda Gates Foundation, the medical industry, Hollywood, the Bilderberg Group, Monsanto, ALEC, Blackwater, the CIA, the IMF and World Bank, the Prison Industrial Complex, the CDC, and OF COURSE? The Public School System at the top of any list, it being Ground Zero for contagiously cancerous propaganda called an 'education' (to go beg for a job if you are approved of by your oppressor) – all these institutionable institutions make the brief reign of horror exacted upon Jew-ish innocents by the Nazis the equivalent of a blade of grass to the primordial Amazon.

2. Through their brutality, white people gained all the profit needed to take them from the Dark Ages to world domination, for once Rome (and strange, huh, that it was white people right next to Afrikan people who were the first to rise up and not white people further up north surrounded by nuthin' but their pasty selves) – once Rome was kaput, the Byzantine Empire and that thieving Emperor Justinian couldn't resurrect their own poor (80% of Europeans were 'serfs', landless, abused and hungry) – the Byzantine Empire couldn't save them from the constant assault wrought by rich white barbarians – barbarians whom the corrupt Church had to implore to not kill babies and the elderly for sport. For *sport...*

Ponder that.

So oppressed were the masses, in order to keep the landed wealthy gluttonously well fed and jewel encrusted, those serfs were oppressed with torture devices that had never entered the nightmares of any other people (this is just white people hurting other white people, mind you) – they were so oppressed, an Afrikan asked a Portuguese sailor, back then, if the people of Europe were hung for putting their feet on the floor in the morning. Once the meager wealth the despots could steal in Europe had been exhausted, off their leaders sent the murdering troops during the 'Crusades' to the Middle East, which then put them close enough to Afrika to contemplate raping us also – or correction? C-o-n-t-i-n-u-i-n-g the rape, since the Greeks', who'd come back to the Motherland in the 700'sBC, their DNA was swallowed up by Black People, making brown Arabs. But these still purely white Crusaders had begun the perfecting of their hate filled fear of us and further polished it by the time of the Mass Abductions they called 'The Slave Trade'. Columbus, and those after him – demons like Cecil Rhodes and King Leopold – intended to rid the streets of Europe of the 'unwashed masses' by building the white man's success on the backs of the Afrikans, and the backs of all Brown and Yellow Peoples. This strategy, starting with the Crusades, funded the Renaissance. In the Americas, it turned the colonies from a mudpit into the most swiftly created super power in the history of the world. Can you imagine the wealth you'd secure if you had even 1 of the strongest beings in existence at your beck and call, to build whatever you demand – if you had that kind of assistance for next to no money?

Their subjugation of the world was such a completed theft, the Tamahue made evil, itself, the defacto culture. None dare question the supremacy of evil without appearing naïve. Thus 'booty' for a warlord's men became the profit passed on generation after generation. It wasn't ancient history. It was the change granddad gave his grandson, with no apologies, cause if you apologize?...

3. You admit guilt and from then on? You stop the act that damns you as guilty since everybody publicly knows you're no clueless schoolgirl who only made a mistake. The Tamahue have been the best of thieves, ensuring they get away with their deeds by setting themselves up as the teachers and the judges, too, with, seemingly, no one higher to make them own up. Don't bother teaching children that no one in their right mind wanted to come to The 'New' World so that your lie of being a self-made nation sounds like the hollow boast it is. See, the Americas, like Australia, later, was a place to which only sentenced criminals were forced to go. Australia was settled too late for out and out slavery's 'benefit', (though the Aborigines were recruited as 'included with the land' slaves, or they were wholesale slaughtered). But in the Americas, there had been Kidnapped Afrikans to fuel the fire in the furnace that forged their stolen nation. These crimes are not a ghost from – the past. They are the gelatinously bleeding heartbeat of white civilization's foundation. They're the reason immigrants came, constitution or not. Cause the promise of a better life means the promise of gold in the streets, even if the gold is the blood of our Original Ancestors.

Everywhere they've gone, if they aren't bad as a whole group, despite the individual 'good' ones? It wouldn't be the unrelentingly same genocidal story. So, the Tamahue want credibility as nice folks who have risen above their common barbarity? Then apologize and mean it, so they never do it, again.

4. And a very few may be willing to apologize, but no white person anywhere would be willing to give up the very weapons that allow them to continue to abuse the world. They might temporarily share their wealth to lull us into a sitting duck position, as Brother Nelly Fuller brilliantly detailed, but they'd never share their nuclear weapons. They'd each just turn their heads in denial, hoping the carnage of the Black and Brown people would soon be over – a carnage that they hoped would spare them. Yet, radiation doesn't give a damn as it spares no one, and truth isn't the point of white supremacy, sadly, cause when wrong is your leader? There'll never be a dull moment, nor a safe one. For anyone. The Tamahue have made doing evil as inconsequential as turning one's head right or left. That sort of indifference has no way to stop itself. If Allah hadn't come to the ultimate rescue? We'd all be toast, including the Tamahue, but The Creator told them, long ago – your time is limited.

His, however, is not.

He taught Us all, why the Devil's ways are never an option and oh, boy – did we finally GET THAT. That truth is imbedded in our souls, now. Takes a long time to beat a lesson into a soul. Flesh, on the other hand, is here today, gone tomorrow.

The soul is permanent.

There. I'm done. That's saved both of us a good thousand pages (which, really, I planned on writing, no matter how reluctantly). That said, before I learned this, firsthand, it's what I sensed, looking at them, looking at Mr. Lowenstein, that day. I didn't have the facts, yet, and have shared a needle's weight of them with you in this section; but that day, that day? I had the beginning of what I'd been indoctrinated to believe had to be racist – a pure love for my own people and a need for us to be free to be more of ourselves, not less – without some outsider's censorship. That was the glow I saw in my fellow students. I didn't know 'racist' truly means the ability to cause systematic injury to a whole other people because you not only hate them, you fear their success is your annihilation. See, you may hate your neighbor, but you're only a murderer after you kill him.

I had slammed into a fervent dormant wish to delight in what Allah made me. I didn't want to hurt anyone. I am Akhenaten. Bringer of peace in the face of war, and now I know what I hadn't thousands of years ago. I knew the definition of 'my enemy'. So it's not with hatred when I share that that day, upon stepping into every classroom, running into nearly any white person, from the rare ones wandering the streets or the flood of those employed by the school, from Principal Herman Miller, to lunchroom attendant, Janice Prestile, to my homeroom teacher whose pants were in metaphorical flames (a particularly frightened white person, I confess) I could see the hollow echo of fear in all their eyes. I didn't need to know the historical facts to confirm the obvious. Each one of them was feeling the terror of knowing one day, they'd be found out, the trick would be over and they'd brought to justice.

And I could also 'see' they didn't know this about themselves. So explaining it to them, no matter how nicely, would never bring accord, almost to a man. The weight of the truth was beyond their strength to bear; their fear of us too crippling, while hypocritically, their own forefathers had revolted over merely paying taxes; and defended the settlement of the Jews on stolen Palestinian land, for far less than what we Original People suffered, and settled them based on lies that the Ashkenazi Jews told about having originated from the Middle East.

Geez. These lies are enormous and never ending. That's why no one trusts the Tamahue anymore. We learned the facts.

A serious 'but'? Embracing wrongdoing wasn't only on the Tamahue's part. I saw plenty of Black persons, especially the ones with some authority, who hated Black us even more than white people. All visible in their auras scrambled hues of outrage simmered with the insult that the authenticity of their 'success' should be doubted and dulled by the shadow of 'others' failures. Like I had been before realizing my shame, these Black people were vying to be the Designated Special Negro (DSN – cause I don't want to have to think/type that every time in full), believing one would be successful despite being Black, not because. That's a heck of a feat the DSN must struggle against his/her whole life, careful not to get too close to 'those' people, unless it's to patronize them, to assist the DSN's further ascendance. There's whole populations of DSNs, the world over, from meter maid to high governmental officials whose great dislike for their own kind should be an additional credential on their Harvard sheepskin degrees, or their beauty school certificates. A hatred evident in the flippant manner in which they and all the others like them, especially in Sandstone, treat their own kind. Why? They even poison, beat, and shoot their own to maintain that 'special' status. Now, the way I had treated my people had always been 'polite', but nevertheless, who I spent time with was based on who had the largest house, the biggest car, the snazziest vacation photos, the biggest, most eloquently pronounced vocabulary.

Seems, before I'd tripped and fell into the sphere, I'd been no different from my sister. Yet, I never suspected how complete our own DSN self-hatred was until I could see it in real time in others. Like the Black reporter on Line One Student's News. I couldn't hear his thoughts, nor anyone else's at that time, but I could see the results of his thoughts in the pure contempt in his eyes, where before I would have only seen a pleasant but dull smile. I now saw, "Don't expect me to ruin it with my white friends by having too many of you around. I've got a quota of how many of Blacks and which ones I can know..."
My mom and dad had tried to keep our love of being Black alive by moving to 85% Children of Abducted Afrikans Sandstone, but Black Snob Pride isn't Black Pride at all, since being proud is the opposite of being secretively ashamed.
On the otherhand, most of the Black grown-ups I spied that day weren't self loathing, merely exhausted, clueless; while those who understood our struggle ran the gamut from indifferent to frustrated, to so fierce it was a wonder they hadn't won the war single handedly. And some white people, very, very, very few, had beautiful auras, if a little pale. Seems white people may have taught themselves to dance more like us, but they had yet to get around to having souls as vibrant as ours. Too bad they couldn't see the sorry state of their inner realm, with the vast majority, even the seemingly sweetest (such as the female teachers) fairly soaking in terror. But, I repeat, there were a couple openhearted ones. Maybe a dozen genuinely people loving Tamahue – well...

I'm being overly generous, here, because I wish to be gentle. There was truly only one or two. One of the lunch ladies and one white gym teacher I spied turning the corner to the administrative offices. As she walked past me, her aura radiated a humble genuine warmth, extended to everyone, equally. That was Ms. Prestile, and the lunchroom attendant, Mrs. Hanover; two white women at peace who made me wonder why they were so different, but?

It no longer mattered because none of them were our people. Even we weren't thinking on what would propel Black us upwards – that it was a necessity we move on from the insult of this school and a hundred thousand other insults I now recalled, like I'd recalled the anatomy of gastropod invertebrates, the other evening, talking with Kierah.

As she didn't have a clue she was more than what she'd been taught, Black people didn't have a clue who we were, either.

185

And neither did I, speaking 100% honestly. I was still contemplating rallies, sit-ins and marches, 'cause that was the only methods of protest I'd been shown.

As for how we, in general, felt about them – the Tamahue? I didn't pay attention since I really didn't care, being so wrapped up in enjoying us.

Indeed. Life for me was happening explosively, exponentially on so many levels, I tabulated all this and reams more in stride, including my other shame at having humiliated an innocent Black boy, like myself. It was a conference meeting in my head, on each floor of a small office tower whose windows were my eyes. I should have been 4 or 10 Tyrees for the numerous insights I was reaching, and the strength and determination I felt. Determination to fix whatever I was capable of mending, especially fixing the situation with Howard, whenever I saw him, and in whatever way necessary. I felt plain confident I would do just that. As I went about my day, it was impossible not to revel in my newfound powers of perception.
Small superhero uniform store, here I come.

In each classroom, I remembered details about the subject that had lain hidden in my brain's corners like I'd removed dust bunnies covering missing money. Woefully, there'd been no math textbooks in all that dust as you can't find money if it wasn't dropped there in the first place. But all the history, science, English and I was darn good at biology, removing those dust bunnies covering my brain left me rich. Entire passages read while I'd been bored to tears came clearly to mind nearly word for word.

HOWEVER...

I was no fool, in case I haven't emphasized that enough! This is a history of an imperfect being, connecting with other imperfect beings to become better at challenging imperfection; but there's no stonecold idiots in here as major catalysts. Meaning, I kept my recall of facts, in every classroom, my own little secret! 'Cause in the middle of this photogenic onslaught, I calculated the best way to encourage those around me to harness their innate abilities was not by making them feel like crap. I wanted to share this growth, not hoard it and reap all the benefits by myself. Shoot! If only the Tamahue weren't searching for the sphere, I'd have yelled,

"Come on! Follow me! Have I got a pick me up for you!"...

since I was certain we'd change the world overnight if everyone of us could take a tumble in the depths of The Sacred Breath of Allah – while holding

186

onto their feet with probably a far softer rope, although I ain't mad at the doc for saving my life, of course! In the meantime, I knew the best way to help others definitely wouldn't have been to insult these gloriously full of life people and potential new friends by looking like a daggone freak of nature. I was with them, not against. Not anymore. So, we would rise and fall, together, or not at all.

I wasn't planning on failure. That day I was Black Hannibal (and he only came in one color) – I was he with an even longer term plan to enter the gates of Rome, an invincible conqueror. No longer limited by any fear from anyone, I joked and laughed as much as any new guy should, though I felt so at ease I could have laughed far more.

That's when, after getting my own vegan lunch from my locker (as said, my dad had been a nuclear physicist, and after employing his scientific fact finding curiosity about meat, he'd forever curdled mine and our whole family's stomachs with the brutal horrors of eating flesh. Resistant at first, his reasoning won us over, especially sealing my commitment with the first gruesome photos of trichinosis worms wriggling out of the pores of a man's face. Didn't matter if any other dead flesh was pig or not, as from then on, anything that once moved of its own will? Eating it was all zombies eating rotting carcasses to me) – that's when, after getting my delicious (and yes, nutritious) lunch and then heading to the lunchroom....

....experiencing no temptation for what the school served, w-h-a-t-s-o-e-v-e-r, I was stupefied more than Pre-Sacred Breath me upon seeing what was on other people's trays. Trays full of what was supposed to be the tastier alternative to my worm-free roots and twigs. Even at Medgar Evers Prep, seeing my friends' burgers and cheese fingers was like looking at cardboard cutouts, but that afternoon, at P.S. 47? Heck, lemme tell ya, reader. If an inanimate building could give me a sense of its purpose, my heightened perception might as well have envisioned a fully equipped morgue in the cafeteria, set with beige long autopsy tables, surrounded by plastic lividly orange chairs, occupied by the about to be newly deceased students; cause from the minute I walked into the cafeteria, I could feel a mass dissection was taking place, and the science teacher wouldn't be giving a test on it.

Reggie and Terrence called me over as I entered the cavernous room, which was well lit by a row of more barred windows (that's all the school had, on every bare glass opening) and encased in grey brick walls – it couldn't have been more of a morgue if the temperature had been 25 degrees colder, lunch plates brimming with oozing autopsied organs rather than with substances no living beings should be eating. As I sat down with my insulated pack of a quinoa/chickpea burger on homemade raw bread, a lightly steamed broccoli/sundried tomato medley, fruit salad, and – Oh Man! – a slice of apple pie – as I sat down?

Taking the cheap imitation of an imitation Bauhaus chair, that was more orange than my sister's fuzzy slippers, next to Maxwell, across from Reggie, and surrounded by the rest of the crew, including Nyisha and her girlfriends, I nonchalantly hid my funereal mourning, while glancing at their culinary selections and thus confirmed that something was deadly wrong with their food. It looked like something edible, but so do magazine pictures of recipe results. You know not to eat magazine pages. With this stuff, I could tell, everything, even the ketchup was not only less nutritious than eating pictures of tantalizing meals, but the cafeteria lunch was way more toxic than slick pages or maybe even the stuff at the corner store because it was riddled with straight up poison screaming at me for daring to recognize it. Several *kinds* of poison at the same time. The students might as well have been eating fried coffins, seasoned with extra crispy tombstones.

'What the bejeebus is wrong with Terrence's fish sandwich?', I wondered, watching him gobble down a mouthful, as I tried to keep the shock off my face, realizing there was something glowing inside it, something hot, in between all the other the super deadly fake stuff.
Yes. Somebody somewhere was killing my friends.

I began a conversation in my office building mind, on the first floor, about why or who was responsible, while again knowing it best to say nothing. My mom, dad and other grownups had mentioned GMOs, HFCs and other swill like that, all to many yawns on my part, though my sister seemed interested – a bit. However, to see the poisoning up close? Being happily eaten, while the poisoned victims grinned and chatted? Well, it nearly blew my resolve to be patiently cool, although I held back an 'In Yo' Face!' outburst of,

"NoOooOOooOOOOO!!!!!! DON'T EAT THAT!!!!!"

New kid hysteria never works out right and talking about food hadn't been a hit topic at Medgar's either, when I'd had no superhero insight. A child's only question is, "Does it taste good?" Yeah? Well, then you ate it, no more questions necessary. It occurred to me how easy it was to poison the unaware and gullible young.

Damn whoever was responsible, I knew I'd fix them also, but not for their benefit. I was planning longterm effective revenge. I could see the protest banner, now...

But that was the conference topic on the first floor of my brain. The second, third and fourth and fifth floors were taken up with heated discussions about the Orb, like – when I'd satisfy my obsession to see it again, who was Akhenaten, what could have happened to Howard, who would choose grey bricks for a cafeteria, and the essay due next week for English. I'd finished the whole essay, only needed to write it down. I wasn't worried about whether I'd forget it.

That was no longer possible.

Then the sixth floor (that was the height of my personal business building – though there might have been basement levels, hidden like yesterday's agonizing realization that I missed my dad – still did) – but the sixth floor conference was grateful that this day there'd been no threatening gestures or complications from anyone, throughout the school day. Too bad I didn't understand that the wages of any wrong always find you, sooner or later. Just ask the Tamahue, a couple years from this day in the lunchroom...

But back to.... Nyisha, who looked up at me, carefully, as I greeted the guys and opened my pack. She suddenly, rolling her eyes, and dotting her napkin to the corners of her lips as if she were done, rose to leave. Her girlfriends – by now I knew them to be Lisa, large, light skinned girl with a tangle of wavy hair; Kenya, tall and regally brown with glasses and Afrikan braid-ins; and Shantay, even larger than Lisa, deep black with perfect soft skin, and a stunted spurt of straightened hair – in sync, they all got up to leave.

I admired Nyisha, attractive as she was, for not hanging out with only pretty girls, which she easily could have. But then again, her 'aura' (for lack of a better word) was one of the brightest I'd seen on anyone, adult or student.

"Ladies, you leaving, so soon?" asked Maxwell, looking dramatically hurt, his eyes pinned on only Nyisha.

"We're done, eating," Kenya coldly replied, despite their trays being full of uneaten tombstones.

"What?!" protested Reggie, who had a soft spot for Kenya, as I could tell since he'd get extra sheepish in her presence, cracking more jokes per second than he had without her around, "Lunch just started! Look at all that food on your trays that feels neglected."

"We don't have to explain ourselves to you," retorted Shantay, with Lisa's and Kenya's deep Black girl support. Head nods, and pursed lips mumbling,

"Mmmmmhmmmmm."

"Plus," interjected Nyisha, "It's sorry how you guys picked on Howard. We're tired of all this stupid fighting, so we don't wanna sit next to a bunch of thugs!"

The boys instantly took affront.

"What? You sweet on that cream puff, ain't cha?" one boy chortled, that hadn't even been at the 'fight'.

It was obvious, the tale of Howard's shame at my hands, that never touched him nor blocked his blows – the tale had whipped from ear to ear with my little 's' way too tiny to stop the mightier super power of gossip. Maybe I could scale tall buildings, but gossip could scale Olympus Mons on Mars. Look it up. It's tall.

So, I spoke up, right then. Enough was enough.

"They're right," I said, nodding in the direction of the girls.

Silence fell like the night sky during a total eclipse, during which, no one could have possibly not noticed there was nothing else to say. In it, I saw my less than a day old reputation as a bruiser permanently eclipsed by the light of truth.

'Oh well,' I thought, 'Better face the music now, as I'd rather have to fight endlessly than keep feeling like a fake.'

"I didn't have to get so mad at him," I added, "It wasn't that big of a deal."

Looking directly at me, Nyisha glared, "Then why did you pick a fight with him?"

Let's see, now, reader. Exponentially sorting through possible responses and quickly, I imagined if I answered,

'Because I was scared to death of being the new punching bag as yesterday, I believed you guys were wild beasts... Well, not beasts, but brutes, definitely. But today? I can clearly verify by looking at the emanation of your souls that you are Gods in training. If only you could see how powerful, how noble you are. How everyone's light is so uniquely magnificent. And somehow, with that, I can tell, everyone of you responds best to respect. Respect. That's love in action.'

NOT A CHANCE IN HELL for me to say that one. Threw that out, as soon as it sparked that one cell in my too darned logical left side of my brain. One Tyree conference in the basement, that did exist, dared me to say it, but? Every other level vetoed that, their guns drawn.

Instead, calculating, calculating, calculating – though it was instantaneous, I decided it best to edit it all down with an, "I don't know."

Old reliable, 'I don't know.' A steadfast companion of the other old standbys when caught red handed in the act – 'Who me?', 'What mess?', 'What are you talkin' about?', and 'I wasn't even there!'

Reggie grabbed the helm again, (his own vibrant aura revealed a lot more loving of a person than he'd have had the stupidity to let anyone know about) – he said, "Well, that's lunch, ya'll," and sat down, arranging his tray with that cleverly hidden loving care.
A tray full to the brim with that glowing fish sandwich, french fries, pudding and a Diet Death, called a Pepsi. Swoosh! I heard the dirt being tossed out of his gravesite, in preparation for his eminent arrival.

"Yo! I'm starving. You guys figure this morality thing out on your own. There's a 24hr church down the block." he added as he ripped open his packets of ketchup.
Everybody laughed, relieved, even the girls, reluctantly and...

with an, "Oh well," from Shantay –

Nyisha and her friends sat back down.

Someone, looking at my meal, asked where my real food was and I told him, "On my plate. I'm allergic." I'd been through this conversation many times and had come to learn, this answer hurt everybody the least, while also having been true ever since I saw that worms could wriggle from the pores of a man's face.

191

"He's a healthy eater," Lisa defended me, to my silent delight and invisible nod in agreement. "We should all be eatin' like that," she added.

And then the punch came. No, not right at that moment. We had the typical, no longer eventful midday repast, followed by three more classes. It was later, on the way home that moral karma hit me in the face with the pain a good undeflected slug brings. But before that physical kapow, I was socked in my last period during Mrs. Finn's history class.

The rest of the day had turned out very satisfyingly, despite seeing in my new friends' 'auras' that my confession had diminished their awe of me, ever so slightly. Oh well. Maybe that awe had been based on fear, which wasn't even remotely what I wanted, then. I could nevertheless equally see, my easy and confident warmth, far more genuinely real that day than I'd ever shown anyone in my short life, earned their tolerance, if not their full acceptance. People said 'Hey!' as we passed in the halls, or schooled me about the different teachers as we sat down for class (though I could pretty much tell what they were like before any teacher said a word). I replied to my new potential friends openly, but not exuberantly so. As I've said, often, I wasn't trying too hard. I was listening which was no effort because I wanted to hear about somebody besides myself. They were living history I could actually talk with.

I didn't mind that my scheme had revealed a very imperfect me, as I was patient and though I do repeat myself in my chronicling, I never intended to repeat the same acting like a bully ridiculous mistake, again. I had time. I had dedication.

So, when I'd reached the last class of the day, I'd thought that all my complications were done. Yet, standing in front of her class, very visibly missing one student – Howard Warren – when standing before her class at the blackboard upon which she had drawn a diagram of Greek achievement in architecture, philosophy, politics, mathematics, literature, and medicine, with the names of the Greeks who had heralded those achievements underneath, Mrs. Finn made a terrible mistake. I mean it was awful. It was so glaring, it was a personal insult I could not tolerate, even if I'd wanted to. Worn out from not saying all of what was on my mind with everyone else (if I could I would say, 'worn out from the 'whatS' that were on my mind') – worn out from being sensibly sensible, even for newborn modern me, Mrs. Finn was no one I needed to be patient with, especially with a bit of ancient Amenhotep within. That's why I decided to share the bare truth with her.

I mean, why did she say that?! First, how dare she teach a whole class full of Black children so incorrectly! Then, she not only left our people's grandeur out of the lesson, as if the Greeks were the first people on Earth or had been here for longer than a day in the history of men, but then to steal another people's thunder, altogether? Ignore it. Undersize it. Belittle it, but to out and out steeeeeeal it? Whoooo boy. Alright. Okay. She could talk about Ancient Greece and Rome, which she was, *glowingly*, like the glowing fish sandwich served for the school lunch; but to lie, saying Hippocrates originated what Venerated Imohotep said?

I couldn't stand for it, since my first teacher, my very, very first teacher, not in that sad school, Master Menkheperresent, he had made sure I learned all about our greatest healer.

I can still see every movement of her face – the excited pride mixed in with the otherwise dull pastel swirl of her aura, an aura which hadn't been as terrified as Mr. Lewistein's had, no doubt. Mrs. Finn was happy in her job, while up at the blackboard, she used her white chalk like a guided missile, emphasizing with a scratchy residue flourish, dropped with a bombing screech and then slid under the name of each historical figure beneath the appropriate category.

Phidias, under art and architecture.

Plato, under philosophy, though Socrates got a double line beneath his name in the same category.

Pythagoras, under math.
A bunch of others, not the point of this book and?

Hippocrates, under medicine. Triple underline.

Her pastel aura almost pulsated to an anemic scarlet as she droned on into the creation of theatre and literature, but at that point, I wasn't listening. I was busy chasing a peculiar feeling of an old familiar slate of dark stone in my fingers, even though there was nothing in my hand in Mrs. Finn's class except my pencil in one, and the empty air inside of my clenched fist in the other. The memory came so immediately, that I could feel the cool smoothness of the slate with my fingertips and see what I'd inscribed there with my eyes. The name, the birthdate and the date of the demise of Imhotep, The Father of Medicine. The memory wasn't clear. I wasn't even sure whether the writing was in Kemetic or another language. It was all less clear than my morning's dream had been, but the memory was that of waking life, experienced, not slumbering visions, imagined. The zenith heat of the sun at the height of its arc, beaming insistently on my back as I and the other children sat crossed legged, I thought, in my family's garden, listening while Master Menkheperresent quoted Imhotep – it all came back. Same words as Mrs. Finn was saying belonged to a different man, and she said them in a different language. Same class with all Black people, but a lot smaller than this history class and here there were no sun's rays that could ever make it through the sarcophagus walls of that declining building to shine into this teacher's heart. I could tell this was a no win moment.

But sometimes, victory isn't the goal. Honoring who you love is.

She was already two categories along, underlining Parmenides in the discipline of 'science' when I forcefully stated, "You're wrong."

The silence that ensued was the grandfather of silence. There weren't even swooshing butts on the chairs. Just one pencil being put down. Mine.

"You're wrong, Mrs. Finn," I repeated.

Every head turned to lone me.

"Excuse me, young man?" she said as slowly as she slowly turned around, visibly irritated, and not as impressive as Howard had been. "If you have a question about the information, then please raise your hand and I'll call on you. You can't simply speak up any ol' time you please, Tyree."

"I'm sorry, Mrs. Finn, but it's such a huge lie, I couldn't stay quiet."

"That's a huge accusation. Are you calling me a 'liar'?"
Instead of my kneejerk reflex that wanted to reply, "You wrote it, so you own it..." I refrained from being completely rude, grudgingly realizing, she didn't know the truth herself. I could see it.

"The person who taught you that wasn't telling you the truth. That doesn't make you a liar."

"What truth, Tyree? Parmenides didn't first propose the earth is round by looking at its curved shadow on the eclipsing sun?"

Oh she was upset, now. Her voice had clicked into that quicker modulation that women tend to go into when they feel ready to explode, but look as if they're still calm. Men? Slow down. Women speed up. No matter the race.

"Well, Parmenides did do that, although he wasn't the first. But I meant what you said Hippocrates said. 'Let food be your medicine.' He didn't say that. That was Imhotep. He was the father of medicine, not Hippocrates."

All eyes widened, maybe thinking, '*Here's goes that Tyree, again. Hey? He is crazy...*' and some heads shook. If there'd been a volcano in the room, it'd be erupting and incinerating us all, with no interest from anyone. How dare Black boy I question authority? And Mrs. Finn wasn't about to flip the chain of command around to a 12yr old.

"And who exactly told you that, young man? I have a Ph.D. in classical Greco Roman studies."

I wanted to ask her from where, noticing she hadn't mentioned the name of the graduate school, but I figured, both? It didn't matter, and she hadn't mentioned it for a reason that wouldn't make her feel more friendly if forced to reveal the perhaps shoddy origin of her credentials. More to fact, it didn't matter because I was sure all the schools taught the same lie and more. Even Medgar Ever's Prep where Black History began at the onset of slavery and ended at the signing of the Civil Rights Bill.

Unfortunately? I couldn't reveal the origin of my own information! How could I say, my mom and dad told me? But moreso? That I knew firsthand because I'd been the student of a teacher whose direct ancestor had **been** Imhotep, the Mighty Healer. Master Menkheperresent's very great grandfather times 12 or something extra like that, though he'd never talked about it much, but, knowing where we'd come from was essential to knowing where we'd go. I wasn't clear on the exact amount of 'greats' before he was born, but our master of education's lineage was common knowledge in my circle about...
3,000 years ago. Ah. And there's the rub as this was yet another opportunity to spend the rest of my childhood under psychiatric observation. This time recommended by my history teacher, rather than my mom. Black mother vs. white female teacher. Hmmmm... I could see the stretch jacket, now, so?

I chose not to take the red and/or the blue pill. I took the fifth.

~~~~~~~~~~~~

I left that class with an extra report to write about Hippocrates versus Imhotep, due in a week. Boy, was I ever motivated to put in some research. I'd ask Dr. Kattan for help, that afternoon. Maybe he'd let me use the library. I was sure the truth had to be in there which would make my report a politely brutal smack upside Mrs. Finn's buttercup yellow and blanched lime hydrangea aura-ed head.

I had refused to apologize for anything, though, as Mrs. Finn had requested, several times, before offering my apology at least for speaking out of turn. I had done that, but, I couldn't support lying about one of our people; though I'd stopped using the word lying, calling it a 'difference in understanding' instead. Said, I didn't remember what the source of my information had been but I knew it to be absolutely true. To which she shook her head, saying she had heard so much about my abilities, making her thoroughly disappointed in my 'misinformed' outburst. Without my request, 'cause I didn't care if she did, she decided to refrain from calling my mother, long as such a mishap was a one time error, and I satisfactorily wrote the report. She'd then reassured me and the whole class in a lecture which lasted past the ringing bell that a true historian is always open to the facts, but one must follow the rules and bring facts, not wishful thinking.

'Or wishful lies,' I thought silently on the first floor of my office tower mind that was going to remain patient enough to let me prove the truth, later, on paper. Upside her pastel head. That was from my basement. They were pretty funny, if a little bit blunt.

Thus, when I made that end of the day stroll back home, I made it with not only not really fight hungry Reggie, and the other guys, (who it turned out, I could see beyond their auras, in their actions, they were genuinely nice people, themselves, kinda pretending to be tough, like I had) – but I also strolled home with peacemaking Nyisha and her friends.

Right after Mrs. Finn's class, which it so happened, that Nyisha was in, too – right after we were finally relieved of hearing the teacher's reminder to be good little ignorant negroes (she wasn't so blunt, but her aura was), Nyisha, from across the room, turning her head towards me as she headed out the door, gave me a smile and a nodding wink. I didn't know that I liked her yet, but I did. Guess that's why that wink was for me a new way to describe 'Excellent.'

This time, the walk was a whole lot more enjoyable, because of the extra company and because it happened with none of the lying on my part, allowing Mrs. Finn to be the only active bad guy that moment.

196

Strolling, Friday, no school the next day, extra leisurely home, after a moment of silence, after more of Terrence's further sneaker adventures, video game comparisons, and why girls are so soppy for boys who treat them badly, James said, "I got an uncle who talks about that Egyptian stuff, Tyree. Imhotep was Egyptian, right?"

In a kneejerk, quick response, 'cause I was having such a good time, without wondering where my answer came from, I blurted, "That's what the Greeks called us."

"Called you?" said Reggie, "I thought you were from Atlanta!" a couple of the guys laughed, looking at me, comically, a bit like, 'Where you from, dude?' I could see, they were still wondering whether they liked me or not, favoring the 'He's okay' side the most.

Recovering, I emphasized, "Yeah. I'm from Sandstone Hills, Atlanta, but we're all from Africa and Egypt's in Africa, not Europe. We used to call it Kemet, too. K, M, T. We didn't use vowels in our language. It was the Greeks who called it Egypt."

"My uncle said the same thing!" James added. "Said Egypt is in Africa and white people flooded the Nile Basin to hide all the first pyramids farther up the river. I think he called them 'mastabehs' or sumthin'. White folks flooded them all out cause there's no pyramids anywhere in Europe, so that kinda proves we built Egypt. I mean 'Kemet'."

Some of the group were verbally shocked, realizing the truth was so easy to see and yet none of them had considered it.

"Your uncle's pretty smart," said Nyisha.

"Yeah. Too bad nobody in my family talks to him anymore. They think he's nuts with all that Pro-Black stuff."

"Mastabas," I pronounced the word correctly, out loud, but halfway to myself, not wanting to highlight what I knew, from my parents, principally, but most of all from what I remembered of my own other life as the son of Amenhotep III. Recollections came at me, not deliberately, but same as I didn't have to think about walking. I walked.

I was going to leave them with that, looking blankly ahead at the horizon, lost in my own conferencing thoughts, when I noticed everyone was looking at me waiting for anything else I had to share.

"Well, dude?" piped up Reggie, "What else do you know that would piss Mrs. Finn, off? Which, by the way, was pretty cool."

General agreement, there.

Surprised at this approval, that came without planning for it, but feeling on the spot, I shrugged my shoulders, sheepishly saying, not wanting to seem like a know it all, "Not much. I only know a little stuff..."

"Like?" said several all at once in a chorus.

"Well... the Greeks didn't invent theatre. We did, only it wasn't meant to distract you with silly things. It was meant to make you reach higher." Taking pains to speak as if this hadn't happened to me, though my mouth was still doing what was comfortable, speaking as if I had been personally involved, which I had been – I renewed my effort to avoid saying more things such as 'I especially liked...' and instead offered, "The festivals that re-enacted the murder of the god Osiris were the most popular. Even the Nisuts took part."

"Nisuts?" Nyisha asked. "What's a 'nisut'?"

Oh! I realized I was using the real title we had called the 'pharoahs'. I was actually trying not to say, 'my father'. I'd been so busy censoring what I said, I forgot that most people used the Greek word 'pharoah'. We'd never said that, anymore than we'd said 'Egypt'.

"That's another word the Greeks incorrectly used. They called the Nisrut, 'pharaoh' when 'pharoah' was the word for the palace the Nisrut lived in. It'd be like calling the President, the 'White House'."

They laughed.

"There's a whole bunch of stuff they copied or changed and took credit for doing it first."

"Wow," exclaimed Kenya, "the way they teach it, you'd think they'd invented everything."

"Oh heck, no," I continued excitedly, about to share how our people had

198

electricity, had flown to Earth from the binary system called the Dog Star when that left cross slammed into the side of my face without me seeing it on its way before it got there. Cut my moment to spread the truth of who we are and regain the good faith of my friends for something honest, right off.

Was it a cross? Or a hook? Did it come from up, or from under? Left, or right? I had no idea and that must have been the reason that when it knocked me flat to the ground, it came with a side order of organic, pesticide, gmo free pain.

Let me explain, here. Shock? Is not an emotion. It is the cessation of all emotions, if even for a second, resulting in complete confusion, in which you don't have a thought or a plan to your name. Even the ability to walk straight, or get back up, requires a moment to ponder.

Later, I realized that some guy had jumped out of a doorway and slugged me just as my head was turned towards the group of my new friends, when we had come up to a corner. I hadn't seen him, lurking and suddenly lunging, from that crimson recessed entranceway in a small sized brick apartment building – I hadn't seen that single fist before it knocked me clear over, accomplishing the task it was sent to achieve all over my face. But then the attacker was on top of me, pounding my face, proving you never get used to pain once introduced. Each punch came thundering down, as stinging as the first one, but by now my shock was finished, replaced by an automatic drive to GET THIS PIECE OF GARBAGE OFF OF ME!

I was enraged, but he was pinning my arms to the ground with his knees, my backpack, filled with books, throwing off my balance, and he was big and heavy. Plus, I had been so blindsided I didn't have time to think of what specifically to do, only wonder where were my superhero abilities when I actually needed them? Weren't caped heroes invincibly strong?

"You think you bad?" he was screaming, slathering streaks of profanity in between slugs into my face.

I managed to both grab hold of his legs and use all my force to rock him off balance. Gaining a window of leverage, I scrambled to my feet, though, he grabbed onto me more tightly to keep me down. At least the punching had temporarily ended. However, since he was near twice my size, I found getting to a free standing position impossible to do. I awkwardly wrenched up to keep the front of my body from being turned back towards his longer reaching punches.

199

A couple things I realized right then.

This must have been Howard's older brother, which I could tell cause not only did he look near exactly like an older Howard with that magnetic deep blackness, and the no nonsense nose, but he was too young to have been his father, and my victim from yesterday, Howard, who had been a no show in school all day?

Was standing right there cheering his brother, 'Von' on.

"Get him!" he gleefully gloated, putting his whole body into his passionate yearning for my defeat. "Kick his butt, Von!!!"

Then, I also noticed, though the girls and especially, Nyisha, had latched onto Von to force him to stop, my new guy friends had quietly stepped off to the side, observing, grimacing with the excitement of it.

The girls, on the other hand, gripping onto Von's jacket, his arms, whatever was available, they were screaming out randomly, fiercely, in various rants,

"He's just a kid, Von! Leave him alone!"

All while, though I also realized my instant recall of every fight skill my dad had taught me was, indeed, at my command, equally as had been the knowledge from almost every book I'd ever read – block and duck, bob and weave, bringing a punch from way back for maximum power, and proper stance to ensure balance? All at the ready of my request high speed thinking skills, but?

My dad had never given me instructions on what to do in a real street fight where there were no rules and the punches thrown at me hurt! With girls holding on, and me stumbling for footing against a guy who was grabbing with true bruiser ferocity, and serious weight advantage, we all went down, tumbling, shouting until a grown-up came round the corner screaming,

"Break it up, ya'll!"

But it was essentially over a split second before he called out. Von being set on by 3 girls, more out of respect for their pleas, than from being defeated, let go of me and pulled away with his hands up to signify he was done.

Me?

I jumped to my own feet, finally, as we all got to ours. Now I was ready to really fight, even if it was too late. No longer held down, I went straight into my standard boxing stance, all of 4ft, 10in of me, ready to duke it out with a probably 16yr old, dang near 6ft Von. Or at least he seemed like 6ft. More likely, 5ft, 11 and a half, but who was counting?

Superpowers or not, I wasn't thinking about any of that comic book nonsense as the whole office tower me was mad as Hell! I may have made a cowardly threat the other day to Howard, but? At least I made a threat to his face and hadn't snuck him!

"You wanna roll?" I screamed, "You punk! You gonna sneak me? Well try me now!" All 4ft, 10in. of highly beatable me.

Only Von was finished, heaving heavy breaths, ignoring me, and the bystander who came strolling quickly towards us. Howard looked at me with pure satisfied revenge in his eyes, from behind the safety of his brother. Actually he was standing next to him, but it might as well have been behind as Howard was glued to him.

The girls stepped up to me. Shantay gently put her hand on my shoulder.

"It's over, Tyree," she said.

The intervening man shouted, "You children get on home, now. Enuf of this nonsense!"

Catching a glimpse of me, he added, "Why boy, you's a mess!"

I had relaxed my stance.

The stranger turned his attention to Von, questioning, "Did you do this to this little boy?"

Didn't need the reminder of my age as it was directly related to my height challenged size – especially as it was true.

Von paid no more attention to the man then he did to me, other than to say, looking me in the eyes, while he signaled to his brother they were leaving, "Just don't be threatening my brother, EVER, you hear?"

201

At first, I said nothing as I figured? I kinda deserved this trouncing. Angry as I was, the core of me couldn't deny, Von was right. And eye for an eye, a tooth for a tooth was the rule, but, I'd never admit it – right then. Although, not to forget, I figured, sneaking me was nearly as wrong, so my rage targeted that, instead of my guilt, flying easily over my shame.

"Yeah?!" I shouted after them, "Sneak punching someone half your size ain't any better!" I was not in the habit of using the word 'ain't', dear reader, but? This wasn't a cotillion ball. For me, it felt like a do or die situation. A roll up the sleeves time to prove what I had. I wasn't pretending right then, unlike yesterday. I was truly furious and without thinking, I knew this was not the moment for proper language skills.

"You heard me!" he nonchalantly shouted back as he and Howard sauntered victoriously away.

And that's how the punch happened. If I had known what other far more terrifying dangers awaited, I would have run up and thanked Von for the instruction of why I must always remain aware. To this day, I use that lesson, first and foremost. I would give him a call for the sake of reminiscing and laughing at old times, only that's not possible due to mitigating circumstances – but more on that, later. Much later. Next several books, later.

The fellas then came back up, milling hesitantly, with sympathetic comments about how,

"That was so messed up!"

"Dude was huge!" exclaimed Terrence, stretching his hand up and out as a measuring tape, "Yo! I didn't know Howard had a brother, or I'dda warned you, Tyree, for sho!"

"Um, hmmmmm," Nyisha shook her head in disgust, re-fluffing her own disheveled afro puffs. "Guess we girls were too terrified to do anything to stop huge him. Good thing you *men* were here to save us all!"

No groans, but each of the guys looked defensive, and their silence sent a quiet agreement. They'd done nothing but look on.

"Nyisha, now," said Reggie, "you ain't right!"

"Yeah," she slant eyed him, which with her already tilted eyes, was quite effective. "WhatEVER, Reggie Hudson! Now ya'll just wait a minute while we get ourselves back together."

She and her friends, standing there brushing off, became each other's mirror, which surprisingly reflected amongst the four of them, quite lovely young ladies with real clothes on. It's funny how some things one only thinks privately, never revealing inner conversations since it's hard to explain to your friends. But, I'll share with you, reader, as you know more about me in that time than any other living soul.

For me, from that day and onward, it wasn't as if I had developed a distinct allergy to seeing too much of any woman's or young lady's body, though it felt like it as it was an immediate aversion every time a hunk of something best covered hit my eyes; it was more that to have a girl that wouldn't give herself away to just any onlooker, that she might consciously be choosing a special guy? That a girl like that would want to be with me for who I am, not 'cause I was a boy like all the rest with every applicant welcomed by the desperate female?

That would be such an honor as a girl like that was looking for the one who deserved her notice.

Nyisha, Shantay, Lisa and Kenya, all dressed in jeans that didn't resemble blue tourniquets, with varying loosely draped blouses, festooned with matching scarves, coupled with various other girlie bracelets that looked like they had a reason to be on them rather than on my sister – they each carefully made certain they hadn't missed a speck of that foul street dirt.

"Hate to interrupt your boxing corner break, ladies, but are we walkin' or movin' in with the homeless?" snapped Reggie.

Ignoring him, and turning to me, Lisa said, "C'mon Tyree, let's walk you home. You got sneaked but you sure stood up to that punk when you could. That's more than these guys."

Not wanting to alienate the only male friends I was getting to know, for the not so manly substitute of girl power which no matter how pretty didn't make me wanna hang with the ladies like we were all 'girlfriends', I defended the guys with, "Nah, they were cool. They could probably see I was just gettin' my wind. I didn't need any help, but thank you, for what you did."

"Yeah!" each of the boys latched on.

203

"You gotta let a brother fight his own battles, sometimes," said James, stepping into the forefront. "You girls don't get that. You soft!"

"Oh no!" protested Kenya, "Tell me you did not go there! You don't know a thang about girls, so best not talk about what you don't understand, little boy!"
A din of two sides, divided evenly between boys and girls, rose up in volume, with vehement dithering over the superiority of one sex versus the other.

Neither was winning when Nyisha, raising her voice even higher, authoritatively interjected, "This is not even the point, ya'll, so just quit it! I know Von!" and here she lowered her voice as she had earned all our attention. "He's my sister's boyfriend and I don't know what she sees in him, cause he's a little nutty, you understand? Knowing him? I wouldn't trust him to let it be over. I don't think we should let you go home on your own, Tyree. You are just a kid."

Ouch! That hurt almost as much as the punch!

However, this overrode the disagreement quickly, with a few simmering glares that relaxed into resolution, then nods. And whether out of guilt, actual concern, or a need for company on the way home, our walk continued.

At first we progressed slowly, quietly, as if in a slow motion time delay, running over our separate feelings privately. I couldn't read minds, at least not then, and not now, unless the person wants me to, but I imagine each was replaying the fight, separately. An awkward moment in which every detail, accompanied by my full blown embarrassment, ran through my mind, too. Thus, for the length of the walk, I remained silent, though in the mix I offered a slight head shake here, sincere listening there, when the conversation resumed. At the start, however, amongst everyone, at the end of this real fight, there were no jokes about anybody wearing anything inappropriate for their gender. No references to me or any other boy wearing a 'skirt' while running all the way home.

It wouldn't have been funny, in the least.

Then, hesitantly, humbly, talk sprang up about fights that had happened in their own past. Remembered punches brought out shared groans as if the impact could still be felt, even if the punch hadn't happened to the storyteller. Comments arose about the increasing swelling around my eye, which I could

204

only feel in a stinging tightness. And man, more truth about getting punched, which for real? You don't feel the true pain, until the fight is over. Then? You feel the 'pain'.

"Yo, good thing tomorrow's Saturday," said Terrence.

"Yeah," we all nodded, everyone looking at my face.

Maybe the weekend would be enough time so by Monday, I silently hoped, I could open my eye, cause at that moment? My eyelid was too painful to consider trying to move it, even slighty, and my lip felt like it was havin' a baby. This time my face was giving the commands, while I had to do as told.
"All this fighting is so stupid," Nyisha interjected, woefully shaking her head. "If we were such a great people, we better learn how to do that again, cause this mess ain't workin'!"

This day's farewells came with sisterly pecks on my cheek – my other cheek that I had forgotten to offer to Von to pummel also – leaving only Nyisha continuing with me as the rest veered off upon reaching their particular blocks.

"You don't have to walk me the rest of the way, you know," I told her.

"I know. I just want to. You really don't know Von."

I laughed, stiffly through my battered face, "I sure know his fist!"

She joined me with her own giggle, followed by an, "Awwww!" upon seeing my wince.

"You better put some ice on that as soon as you get home!"

"Yeah," I said.

It felt good to have her care about my condition, while it also felt like I had to somehow prove that I wasn't a little boy who needed her protection. My dad had always taught me that a man protects his community, starting with his woman. Although, I knew Nyisha was at least 2 years my senior, I wish I could show her the best of me, since so far?

She'd seen my all time worst.

"Why'd you pick a fight with Howard in the first place?" she asked.

Uh, oh. But as no one else was there? I decided my best me was honest.

"Cause I'm new, and not 14. I didn't want anybody else bothering me, so I started a fight hoping that'd be enough to make everybody else leave me alone."

Free advice, reader. Honesty truly does work, if you use it at the right moments. Gotta watch out and choose those moments carefully, as the consequences can backfire on ya, big time. That's the difference between 'The Brutal Truth' and 'The Honest to Goodness Truth'. You can't just spit it out like nuclear bombs, not thinking. Gotta let it rain down like sunshine, not radioactive fallout.

Turned out I was sunshine and Nyisha's own radiance wasn't lying, either. She preferred truth. She was composed of truth.

"Ah!" she blurted, "Yeah. That makes sense. Guess they put you in this grade cause you're some kind of brainy kid, huh?"

I grumbled an affirmative, not wanting to linger on that point, deflecting with, "My mom's a teacher. It's her fault."

"Oh. Well," moving on, "...too bad you didn't know about Howard's big brother. Come to think of it, I could kinda tell with Von that you're not really a fighter. I mean he's a big guy, but? You were a sittin' duck."

Seeing me look embarrassedly away, she corrected her comment with, "I mean, you've got plenty of heart, though! More than those guys I would say for sure. Even Maxwell!" she looked at me intently with that, to which I said nothing, not feeling it my place to comment against another guy who was not only a whole lot better looking than me, but leaps taller, too.

"Yeah," she went on, "It's that everybody knows them, so, unless it's a personal beef, nobody bothers 'em. They'd be sittin' duck fighters, too, I bet."

"Wow. I hadn't considered that." No, really, I hadn't! In my pre-move days of panic, it never occurred to me that the boys in a Newark Public School would be young folk, like me. That they'd quake in the heat of the moment. Still, I defended them with, "I don't think they were cowards back there, for real. They were sizing me up, most likely. Angry, even."

206

"Angry?"

"Yeah," realizing I'd stumbled on more truth. "At me for pretending to be a tough guy. They probably wanted to see what I was made of, or see me pay the price for trying too hard." Maybe, this was too much honesty, but the

"Wow," she emitted, now, while nodding with her head....

told me I was doing the right thing, choosing to be frank. My icing on the cake came when she said, "So, you are pretty smart," but then she added without this pause I've just included,

"...for a young kid."
'Ouch,' again, I thought, both complimented and whacked over the head at the same time. Bring back Von. Him I had a hope of defeating, more than the reality of my height challenge in the pretty eyes of a girl, I think I was starting to...

She continued, "You should join a gym."

"A gym?"

"Yes!" She stopped, in a Mrs. Kattan re-enactment, as we were just about to turn the corner onto Carson Blvd. I felt a sudden impulse to say I lived in one of the houses on this perpendicular side of the block we still stood on, safely, unembarrassingly away from 876.

"That's your best chance! None of these guys really knows how to fight. Not even Von. So if you learned, with your heart?"

Remaining at a halt, looking insistently, as she goaded me on to reach her conclusion for her, with hands opening and waving before me like it was her attempt to pull a rabbit out of the top of my head. Or pull me, 'Presto!' out of my brain.

It was then, I concluded in another one of those un-utterable thoughts that make you sound crazy if you mention them out loud (the fourth floor of my mind began to calculate the reason behind that, along with finishing off the last bit of my biology homework – I had glanced at the assigned page before leaving the classroom) it occurred to me looking at this deep mocha young lady, in her maroon ruffled collared blouse, with beaded earrings dangling, wooden brightly hued bangles tinkling and clunking on her waving brown arms, it was crystal clear that she wasn't some dimestore thug novel strumpet simply because she lived in Black Newark, anymore than Reggie or James or Maxwell or Terrence were supposed to be future felons. She, it was then obvious to me, she wasn't an 'In Yo' Face' ghetto stereotype in the least. She was a regular girl with regular ideas, probably regular dreams and an incredibly radiant aura. Dang, hers was better than most others' I'd seen the entire day. As each person had some sort of an aura, from a tragically sad tattered remnant to a glow that near made me squint, I'd seen so many, within hours, that I had stopped paying attention. And I had seen some auras like hers – even brighter; but there was something particularly special about Nyisha's inner fire that spoke directly to me.

"I could keep myself safe?" I answered hesitantly in a question, not knowing if this was the answer she had been seeking.

"Yes!"

Whew. A moment of triumph, even if I didn't think it meant she saw me as anybody but a 'kid'. 'Kid'. A word my family didn't use as my folks had said it described small baby goats, not human children. So to hear her say it, made me feel extra forgettable, on top of not knowing if I could ever make her see me as someone she felt protected by and not someone who needed her protecting. My little 's' cracked and flaked right off my invisible Lacoste oxford, which wasn't 'Lacoste' after all – just one of those knock-off companies, called 'Ya-lost'. Their motto – Our Shirts Guaranteed to Fall Apart After the First Washing.

Wanting to give up on my growing wish that she see me in a different light, I decided there was no reputation worth safeguarding, anymore. Might as well bite the bullet, I decided, by walking with her, all the way around the corner to the gate in front of the horror of what was my thoroughly un-Sandstone home, so I continued our slow pace once more...

Upon turning to the left, I saw Kyerah coming from way on the far side of Carson, heading towards us. Thinking of my face, I inwardly gulped.

"There's this one gym, downtown," Nyisha continued, pondering, oblivious of the surrounding, not knowing my sister was approaching, as she didn't know my sister, "Actually, It's a boys club but more, where they teach all kinds of stuff, including self-defense. Downtown. It's called, 'ASCEND'. Stands for something, but I forgot what. They're very Afrikan, but cool, ya know? Went to their Kwanzaa celebration last year 'cause my little brother joined. It's for boys

208

of every age. Really sharp, too. They teach them not just how to box but how to conduct themselves out here in real time. A man named Xolani runs it. Here. Give me your number and I'll call you tomorrow with their number. Lemme get a pen and a piece of paper."

I don't think she noticed that we had stopped in front of that house which suddenly felt embarrassing all over again, after I had seemed to make peace with it yesterday. However at that time, I'd felt certain I could fix it up, but I knew I couldn't do that in one second, before she had fished out her pen, notebook and scribbled her number on a page inside, ripped it out, handed it to me still unawares, asked for mine – and then? I couldn't have done a doggone thing to fix that hovel she now noticed was where our walk had finally ended.

In a second that would have been barely perceptible for mostly everyone, and me only yesterday, she took in block, burnt houses, sidewalk, Kattan house across the street and my little nearly a shack abode which was way below a humble home. Probably even took in my sister, coming ever so closer, waving.
I waved back, halfheartedly. More accurately, half of halfheartedly. Quarterheartedly.

'Man!' I thought, 'Why can't I have actually useful superpowers? Like flying, turning invisible or walking through walls? What the heck use is understanding how stuff is put together if I can't make it do anything, instantly?'

By the way, I had tried walking through a door – not a wall (didn't try flying as that would have been just superiorly dumb!) – but, during the afternoon from inside one of the school's bathroom stalls, just on a dare with myself. Tried pushing my fingers through the closed door, first, and when that didn't work, had attempted to forcefully crash through it. Nobody was there to notice, nor hear the whomp, except for that one guy with the puzzled look who had come in while I was testing the superpowers I should have noticed I didn't have. I gave him an embarrassed smirk, as I opened the stall the way instructions would have indicated, if they'd been glued to the door's inside, and if there were people too idiotic to know how to open one themselves, or a boy wondering silly stuff like if he had super powers.

Well, turned out, metal doors have nothing in common with pillows, and my shoulder had achingly suffered from the impact. Until my face to fist meeting with Von had given my body something to take its mind off the pain in my shoulder, I'd been aching.

"My sister," I told Nyisha, as she, not missing a step in her flow after taking in the scenery on Carson, she handed me her pen and notebook, requesting,

"Here, give me your number."

Not smiling, not frowning, simply giving up on someone I had not been given any permission to have feelings for, I wrote it down without expectation.

"This is your house?" she asked casually while I jotted.

"Yeah."

She moved right along, saying nothing about my home to instead blurt out, "Whoa. You live across the street from the haunted house."
"Nah. It's not haunted." I handed her back her book.

"Well, I know some people who say they've seen some pretty scary sights in that lot, alone. And how do you know? Have you been inside?" She looked slightly nervous.

"Yeah." I wasn't relishing it, but I couldn't help but notice, now, I was soothing her, even though this was no big deal to me as I truly did understand, although the house wasn't ordinary, it definitely wasn't un-ordinary with anything as simple as ghosts. So I answered without bragging, non-chalantly, "I've been in the Kattan house a bunch, since I was little."

"Kattans? You k-n-o-w the owners?!" her eyes grew wide, Asian flare still undiminished.

Shrugging my shoulders, "Yeah. They're really nice people. The Kattans. And it's amazing inside! Why, they've got this library that's almost half the house. I wish you could see it for yourself."

"Oh, no! No thank you! I've heard way too many stories!"

Inside my head, I had to agree with her. Not about the scary part, but about that house being full of the unexpected. However, I said,

"Nah. No ghosts, anywhere."

"Well, I'll take your word for it, but this is as close as I'm gettin' to that place." she said, zipping up her backpack, just as Kyerah arrived with an on the

210

ground jaw, shocked as she took in my swollen bruised face.

"What the?!" she exclaimed, looking wild eyed at me, and then to Nyisha and back to me, "What happened?!!"

"I'm so sorry," Nyisha answered, "I walked your brother home just in case."

"In case?" Kyerah eyed Nyisha protectively as if she might somehow be responsible.

"It's bad, isn't it? This guy jumped your brother and cause he's a little nutty – the guy, not your brother," she included quickly spotting my sister's suspicious look at me, "...so, I thought it best not to let him walk home alone."

"Jumped Tyree? What nutty guy?!" my sister exclaimed, turning to me, "Did you do something?"

"I didn't do anything; at least not directly!" I protested, saying the last part of that sentence, after the semi-colon, a little less forcefully than the beginning part.

Kyerah heard both parts though, narrowing her eyes as if they could x-ray vision their way into my private thoughts. But I knew she wasn't anymore X-men material than I was.

"It was nothing that Tyree did," Nyisha threw out, revealing no more about my role in the cause of my own whooping, despite knowing more than anyone, other than me.

She introduced herself, with a wave of her bangled wrist, "My name's Nyisha", adding, "I guess your brother can explain the rest 'cause I'd better be getting home. Don't want to get into any trouble getting back too late, and..." looking at me, she continued, "your face will be as big as that house across the street, and almost as scary if you don't put some ice on that eye, soon."

Kyerah, still in shock, had been hometrained well enough to introduce herself, along with thanking my 'protector', and then, before Nyisha had barely turned to walk home, proceeded pummeling me with questions, almost as incessantly as Von's fist, yet, none of which I heard, as I was too busy watching Nyisha heading back the way she and I had come.

She yelled out behind her, "Talk to you tomorrow! Ice!"

211

My basement added, *'Obstreperous'*. Hardee, har!

The tumult of my sister's questions, somewhere included, "Tyree, do you hear me?"...

then, faded into the background noise of the whoosh of a passing car, and those same carefree gallivanting girls ignoring their yelling puffy checked grandma. Through this racket, which included my ranting sister, I watched the retreating strongly built, but slender figure of the girl with the slanted eyes and even more splendid aura as she reached the corner, maroon shirt and jeans then disappearing from my view. She was classily covered, but still? I was seeing more of her than I could handle 'cause she was more magnetic than a million scantily clad girls could ever be, as unlike them, she wasn't available for the asking of merely anyone.

Which included little kid me.

That's how I finally accepted, Dr. Kattan was right, despite my obviously increased capacity to think. I did need to stop reading so many books about magic and superheroes. Strictly history from now on, which would be more reliable than dreamin' about instant solutions to complex problems, as if sprinklin' some fairy dust would fix the sidewalk, or believing that bottomless black holes could make me all powerful.

Chapter

3

We never have two family meetings in a row, unless it's a 'Let's Plan a Vacation' meeting (we'd had plenty of those), or the other reasons – weddings, family reunions or funerals. Each occasion took several noisy round the dining room table sit downs. However, the last and strangely quiet family meeting had been a personal funeral, after my father's 'so-called' suicide. A tumult of emotional confusion had swirled in my heart, then, so looming it'd threatened to drown me, no air bubbles possible, floating or sinking – leaving no choice but to deny my pain's existence. The other day I'd been a bit cloudy, again, with a million feelings coming at me in one island sized tsunami, including, at long last – grief. This day after, I still felt the absence of my dad, but the feeling wasn't washing over me. I accepted it, and the grief was grateful to be welcomed; thus, this afternoon, I was as clear as the pre-industrial Earthly sky, which I knew from eyewitness experience to have been a bright crayon blue. This was a non-funeral meeting, and I felt no confusion, no pain – no intention of remaining silent. I was certain of what must be done, even in the face of 2 grown-ups and one teenaged sister staring at me with their mouths a little slack with astonishment and shaking their shocked heads. My determination was nitrogen freeze-dried concentrated, just with a purpled face and a rather swollen shut right eye. This time, unlike the others, I had embraced my grown-up mind and partnered up with clarity, to make things happen, despite the odds, by using long-term planning, faith, patience, daring, and?

Desperation. Precise desperation, if there is such a thing. And that afternoon there was, for I knew, I might not be a superhero, but, I would convince my mom, as I sat surrounded by my aghast tiny family in that car interior sized kitchen (which looked as if it might stunt my growth a few inches) – I would convince her, while smothering my face with an Icy Blue Blast Pack from the freezer wrapped in a cotton facecloth decorated with hearts – I'd convince her that there was some rational reason to do what on all sides, to her, sounded insane. I didn't need magical skills if I was determined to think.

That's why I was going to go over to the Kattan house to understand what had and what was happening to me, even if I wasn't some cartoon superhero –

213

something drastic had changed, and I wanted answers. The questions inside my mind were so ready to burst, a few of them were threatening to pop out and go on over without me, covered with exploded bits of brain matter and dripping gore. At least it felt like that; thus, 'No, Tyree, you can't go...' was unacceptable.

Understand, initially, I had no idea how I was going to achieve this goal, short of sneaking out the window – which I think I might have – snuck out, that is, if, as I held the icepack to my frozen stinging face, if my insistence hadn't suddenly made me recall one of my family's nearly genetically encoded sources of pride.

I remembered – the Jacksons were fanatically reliable. I mean F-A-N-A-T-I-C-A-L-L-Y. Why, I could have slapped myself on the forehead in front of my mom, sister and grandma right there, as both sides of my family, on my father's side and the Leonards on my mother's, had a badge of honor both would brag about in their family tales of how we'd 'Never Been Late', period. Not for assignments; not for appointments, gatherings, premiers, parties, even paying taxes. Many a larger family get-together conversation was revived by the shared trait of being on time, to the minute.

It was among the first qualities that had attracted my mom and dad to each other, despite the fact, on the surface they seemed to have nothing else in common. She, the free-spirited artist, who nonetheless, craved structure (as was evidenced in always being impulsively on time in a group of carefree creative friends who never were); while he, the exacting scientist, who craved the hint of wildness from her imaginative openness – both found comfort in each other's secure dependability. Dad, before he'd met mom, had almost given up on his preference for a smart, reliable woman, cause the ones he'd met had bored the heck outta him. He needed a free spirit in his world of nerds. For mom? Her relief was to find someone who adored her unorthodox ways without increasing the danger of being an artist by being with an artist, too. In Marcus Jackson, she'd found her 'not too stuffy' but rock solid steady Black man. And she'd have never believed he could be anything but steady, no matter what some insurance company man had said.

When Kyerah and I were old enough to understand, my parents glowingly told the story of what brought them together. They'd both shown up at the campus coffee house for their first date, ready to give up on love, only to arrive on time for that and the many other dates that followed; because on that first one, they'd shown up on time. The rest of their matching polar opposite ways fit nicely, too, but to start with? They'd never been late.

214

'Bingo!' I could've yelled out amidst a crowd of church ladies, picturing myself filling in that last square with the winning chip.

However, before I realized the above, I had endured the following...

"Are you crazy, Tyree?!"

"Look at your face!"

"You look like you were in a train wreck!"

"Did this happen at school?"

"Who was the boy who did this?"

"Do you know him?"

"I'm callin' that school first thing Monday!"

"We should call the police!"

"What the blazes happened?!"

"You want to go over to the Kattans'? Oh, you are crazy!"

I'm putting a synopsis of the questions together for you, reader, at one time, as I don't want you to get a false impression that achieving my objective had been easy. Plus, I'm saving you all that ministering to my face, the 'tsk, tsk, tsks', the 'Oh, Lord, Oh Lords' and the looks of horror like Kyerah's that faded gradually to disbelief when I calmly insisted on going, immediately over to the doctor's house.

And that I was fine.

Oh, and about 2 or 3 times, they'd let me know, he wasn't a medical doctor, to which I answered,

"Sister Makeba is a roots woman. She can treat my face. And besides? You don't trust doctors, anyway."

Ah, the joy of thinking with precision, as grandma had always been suspicious

215

of medical doctors. And mom, too. She believed in nothing but nature's medicines. Hadn't even had me or my sister vaccinated; not to mention there wasn't an aspirin in the house. Plenty of willow bark tea for my pain, though, that I was drinking as I sat there at the table with them shaking their heads.

So, I won't belabor the point, any further. I surely did get over to that 'haunted' house, that afternoon. But, before the knockout punch, this time from me and not at me, I answered my mom, respectfully, one question at a time, calmly as possible, without appearing smug. Or in any physical pain. Which I was the latter. Lots of pain, though the tea and the ice did help. But, as you, reader, have learned and I had learned, turns out I'm a real good actor – with a newly added addition of superhero powers. Ha! Don't worry. I knew my lowercase 's' was inscribed on a grain of rice, encased in a see through box equipped with a magnifying glass. Sitting at that table, I sincerely doubted I had any ability that added up to much more than what would happen if I'd eaten some extra vegetables and had drunk some green juice.

"Mom, I'm fine, really. It doesn't hurt that much, and Sister Makeba will know what to do. For real, it's not a broken leg or something."

"You could have a concussion!" grandma added a new obstacle of concern, in her teeny tiny little girl volume.

"He wasn't a professional boxer, grandma. Just a boy, like me. And it happened a couple blocks from school." I knew my mom must have been truly concerned as she neglected to correct my poor use of syntax.

Instead, she said, "The children today are a lot more violent with all those video games."

Uh-oh, I thought. She's on to the video games, thing. Next she'll be restricting the already too restricted time she allows me to play, which would shoot to smithereens the fact that I only recently got her to agree to slightly more brutal games. That's the moment that coincidentally my brain seized upon our family timely habit, and I suddenly fell in love with a monotonous moment that'd always made me cringe when hearing my paternal Grandpa Delmar, and Grandmas Ethel-Mae and sometimes Ruby (when she felt up to saying something) – and then, mom and dad or any combination of my family saying together in unison, "Never been late!" Except for Grandma Ruby, they were all passed on now, with Grandpa John gone before I knew his face beyond the photos, the black and white ones on the kitchen wall. But back then, the gathering never happened wherein someone wouldn't start the family motto up and everyone else wouldn't chime in. Well, the power of repetition propelled my brain and me out of our own hidden doorway with the best punch of,

"But it's my first day of my very first job, mom," giving her a doleful look from my one functioning eyeball. Very effective to still be her little boy even if unbeknownst to her, inside I was a whole lot older – *a whole lot older.*

~ ~ ~ ~ ~ ~ ~ ~ ~ ~

Which brings me here and brought me there, on time – resolve, dedication, determination and a pathetically sorrowful look only a mother could fall for and did. Desperate Precision got me, a late April afternoon, one day after the first one, a day which was, now, a little cloudy, a little chilly, so I had donned my beige hoodie – got me standing in front of the Kattan's gigantic ornate green door again, ringing that melodic doorbell, and trying not to ring it more than once from sheer excitement.

I was smiling. Well more like grimacing through my pain, which I couldn't help as I was feeling so proud – I couldn't stop smiling, while still holding the icy pack up against my bruises.

First came Sister Makeba and her, "Oh, goodness heavens!" upon opening the door, and standing stalwart beside her as the door flung further back was Dr. Kattan. He was smiling, too, until he noticed the decoration on my face.

"Boy, I told you, you're not a superhero! What were you up to? Using your face as landing gear trying to fly?"

"No. Haven't tried that yet, sir." I answered, grimacing, joyfully.

"Well, I wouldn't recommend trying to smile, either. Not yet. Hope the guy who did that to you isn't looking pretty, himself."

"He was a lot bigger than me, sir, so no, he looks the same way he did when he snuck me."

"A bully, huh?"

"It was kinda my fault, sir."

"My. You need to learn how to fight, and hopefully this has been a

217

humanitarian lesson in what you mustn't do, ever, if you were the cause of this." He used his hand to indicate my damage that looking in the mirror in my home showed me to be highly apparent.

I put my head down, accepting the resultant shame, with a "Yes, sir."

"Come in, Tyree," the sister said, "Your mother just called and told us everything. I've put the kettle on to fix you some chamomile, lobelia, and wintergreen tea with a drop of coriander oil and vinegar. That'll take care of your pain along with some of the swelling. And we'll get that ice pack off to keep you from getting frostbite."

Pondering to herself as I entered, she went on, "I'll give you a comfrey, cabbage leaf and mugwort pack for a bit, till the doctor gets you right as rain."

I didn't understand a word, especially the last part as I knew the doctor wasn't a medical one. But off to the kitchen we went while Brother Cheik said he needed to get some books from his office and would meet us there. We went through the door on the left, while he went straight ahead past the double doored archway towards the stairwell, and the other back rooms, heading for the library.

With me following after Mrs. Kattan, we walked past the large reception room in which the memory of fiery discussions that I only half understood, despite my trying so hard to comprehend them beyond how I'd have tried anywhere else – those debates flipped vividly through my mind, now, with some of their meanings a bit clearer. Then we went to the right through the long formal dining room into a smaller more intimate eating area that led straight ahead to a swinging door opening into the kitchen. I had never been in there.

It was no Kattan library, but it was nonetheless enormous, and sunlight bright, with sweeping back windows that looked directly onto the enclosed backyard garden. It was much larger than our old Sandstone Hill kitchen, having obviously been constructed to prepare meals for a moderate sized school. However, unlike the library, it was mostly unfinished, with cabinets half completed, drawer cavities empty. Most of the doors and countertops, including the near 15ft long island table, were missing a variety of parts, and surfaces. There were large empty spaces between the cabinets where I figured restaurant sized kitchen appliances like stoves, sinks, dishwashers and extra capacity refrigerators should have been, but only the sound of large emptiness echoed in the lonely clack of Mrs. Kattan's shoes thwacking loudly on the red slate floor, the cavernous span bouncing the sharp noise around the room as we entered, like a billiard table.

In the one corner nearest the door was a finished kitchen nook with all the normal residential sized countertops, cabinets and electrical accessories necessary, present and working for a family or a couple that enjoyed entertaining. There was a moderate circular table, topped with a bright floral cloth where she motioned me to take a seat.

The kettle was simmering and she poured the steaming water into a waiting mug, saying, while facing the stove, "These remedies will ease your pain, but the Orb will cure you, fully."

"It'll do what?" I asked, despite believing her since after that fall, I knew anything was possible, except me being Superman. But, coming from a world where miracles were smothered inside holy books I'd never read and children's bedtime stories about Santa Claus, I somewhat incredulously wondered out loud, "It can do that?"

She turned, face unreadable, placing the steaming cup on the table before me, indicating I should wait to drink, and reached for a heavily worn wooden bowl on the counter. Then taking several large containers, that were merely common glass jars purchased from supermarkets, the labels steamed off and re-cycled when the original contents had been used up – taking several of them from shelves in the corner stocked with 30 to 35 more similar jars, of various sizes, all filled with what I could see were a curio shop assortment of powders, leaves, brambles, branches and glistening stones, each jar holding something different – she tossed some of the contents of those she'd put on the table into the bowl and proceeded to crunch and grind it to bits with a wooden pestle. It sounded like walking on fresh new snow. Adding some of the steaming water from the kettle, she mixed the contents with a practiced swoosh of a wooden spoon, then dolloped heaps of the resultant muddy glop onto a square strip of clothe laid out on the table. She folded the edges leaving the inside goo exposed.

"Yes, yes brother, it will," she calmly answered my question while in the midst of her orchestrations. "Put that icepack into the freezer behind you, bring me the red cabbage from out of the crisper bin at the bottom of the fridge, and then I'll apply it with the poultice."

"Yes, ma'am."

Sitting back down after doing as instructed she ripped a leaf from the cabbage

219

I handed her, tearing it into small bits, and then gently but assuredly placed the moist pack and cabbage shreds against the right side of my face. She proceeded to wrap gauze around my head, securing the poultice to the much abused spot that still ached, though only remotely now. The goo was wet and warm against my swollen face. She worked while humming ever so softly and ever so attentively, tending to my injury with light, delicate hands that made me almost forget all my questions. The gentle silence, filled with her humming swayed my curiosity to rest silently in her soothing care. But, I didn't forget my questions completely. I couldn't. They had only felt confident they'd be answered soon enough and so they took a break from hounding me relentlessly inside the various floors of my head.

I did ask, humbly, quietly, when she was done, my head swathed in the warm mushy goo and she'd began clearing up her root healer 'instruments', "Sister Makeba, excuse me, but how will the Orb cure me?"

"How?" she laughed good naturedly. "If I knew that, dear Tyree, we'd have no need for the orb or your assistance. Everything and everyone would have been cured by me, even white people." She shook her head, regretfully. "If only. No, the doctor might be able to answer your question, a bit better. I've never been inside the Orb, myself, at least not physically," she paused, looking at me warmly, "Only he and his predecessors. I can say I've been curious, but..."

Not paying attention to what she might have said, after her 'but', I asked about the, "Predecessors?"

I'd never considered that there had been others in possession of the Orb – that it had existed before I fell into it the other day. I'd never contemplated that the memories of God must go back forever. Every question, every answer opened a college lecture of more to reveal. There was much I needed to know, but the beginning squeak of my next question was overtaken by the thundering noise of the doctor entering the kitchen thlunking a large metal bookcart (yes, I know 'thlunking' is not a word, but that's what the cart was doing) – with extra metal-ly loud wheels that clanked (now, yes, that's a 'real' word, but I couldn't use 'thlunking' twice in the same paragraph – ah, writing sure can suck....) – it clanked onto the stone flooring assaulting the cavern of a kitchen and the ears with nearly equal in volume echoes. Without hesitation, Dr. Kattan rolled it, to the table. The cart was stocked to near collapsing with what it was supposed to be used for – books; and if that cart had had a mouth and power over its own destiny, it would have gone on strike, refusing to be pushed around any longer.

The doctor was smiling. Actually, he was beaming. I had, though rarely, seen him smile, even laugh, though more often, I'd seen him smirk, rage, smug, indifferent, but? I'd never, ever seen him beaming. And there was no mistaking it for any other kind of expression, as when he sat down, one escapee book thumping onto the floor, to which he paid no heed, he was beaming directly at me, and approvingly shaking his head.

"Son," he began, "it's true."

Now, I joined his reverie with my own ear to ear uplifted corners of my lips disbelief, which was easier with my pain dulled by Sister Makeba's natural nursing. My pain was nearly gone so much, it couldn't stop me from reveling in what I knew was his answer to my biggest question of all.
WOW. It was incredibly true!

"So, I am a superhero?!" I asked and exclaimed simultaneously.

His expression turned to one eyed bemusement.

"Now, I didn't say that, young man. What I mean to say is that the Orb has chosen you to be its Protector."

Its Protector? What the? That sounded dull. Sounded lonely and unsung, involved and committed. Sounded like a job, but? Superheroes didn't have jobs. Yeah, I'd wanted to heal my family, fix up our house, the community, and maybe soar in the sky without need of an airplane, (maybe also lift up boulders, defeat bad guys, like Howard's brother – stuff like that would be helpful and get me loads of congratulations, and the confidence of a particular girl) – I even wanted to keep the Ankh Udja Saneb from happening, but I thought that meant adventure and not protecting some hole in the air that nobody can know about.

That was work. If I had known, back then? It sounded like writing...

'Hmmmm, a lot of superheroes do remain anonymous.' I figured. 'Isn't doing good better if you do it incognito?' But that was a conversation on the third floor. The first floor wanted...

... to win the girl at the end of the story with the greatest of ease. I knew there was a way to correct everything, but this 'protector' bit over something concealed and as unfathomable as the Orb, well, it didn't sound like fun.

"Uh, Brother Cheik, what is a 'protector'?"

221

"Ah. The one who safe keeps Allah's Memories, and only it chooses the safekeeper. The orb, without doubt, has chosen you. I thought it was a temporary glitch, your falling in, but I should have known better. There are no mistakes with His plan. Plus, it won't allow me or my queen to enter, any longer. Not for extended periods."

"Chosen me?!! What do you mean it won't allow you to enter? But you guys are the grown-ups! I'm a kid! I mean, child!" I was confused as I knew, enhanced thinking or not, I was only a boy who'd very recently memorized the names of about half the countries of the world and 1/3rd of the world's capital cities. That didn't make me ready to commit to protecting any parts of that world at various times in its existence, no less. Gifted, superpowered or not, I knew I wasn't up to the challenge of protecting theeeeeeee memories of GOD all by myself! I wanted to use my enhanced insight to help those around me to help each other, but, Good GOD. Even Superman, Batman, Spiderman didn't dare try to help the Supreme Being. Comic books didn't even mention God! Superheroes were there for the good mortal citizens of Gotham, ya betcha; but as for The ALMIGHTY or anything that was His? And me being just a boy? Though the poultice was soothing, and I'd begun drinking the tea, my face began to sting, yet again.

"Oh, don't concern yourself, at all. I can still enter, on my own, but not as the The Memories of Allah's champion; not as its Protector. Only the Protector has the heightened ability to separate the pull of the memory he's stepped into from his current reality for a protracted length of time. Your second, who grounds the Protector to this reality, can enter the Orb, too, in his or her personal life frame, but for a much shorter time span. The Librarian can remain for several months, even up to a year to travel anywhere, observe, collect, document anything he'd have never experienced in that actual memory. And once he returns to the true time, all that he stretched out of sequence resumes as it had been, completely uninterrupted."

"Meaning, if you look through the history books?..."

He nodded, "It's as if you were never there. Now, your assistant, your second, will be lost in a wave of forgetfulness in a matter of hours, maybe minutes, swept up in history exactly the way The Creator remembers it. His memory is so precise, down to the very atomic structure of everything He's wrought, that there's no difference from the real and the perceived, for us. For all we know? We, right here, could be reliving a timeframe either of us fell within. And no one lost in his history, unless chosen by Allah, Himself, can return. So, if I want to go back into the Orb, as your second, I can more than any common intruder, but I won't accomplish much, fighting the force of the memory's timeline without permission. I'd risk, with any number of probabilities, never coming back out, again."

"But I almost didn't come back out, so how am I the new Protector?"

His expression grew pensive and he heaved a thoughtful sigh, continuing, "Protectors can get lost in the sphere, too, as I said, retaining their own memories for a time before he forgets who he was and becomes," he laughed, "who he was. They can bend an ancient memory beyond its original parameters, until their previous lifetime's memory, or let's clarify – until God's memories overcomes their mortal minds and they cease to be themselves, resuming a repetition of another time, with no recollection of where they'd come from."

"Is that what would have happened to me?"

"Most certainly, in a week or two, even, as you'd have not been aware of how to defend against forgetting, you'd have ceased to be 'Tyree' more swiftly than an aware Protector. But if you hadn't been the Proctector; say merely the second, having no knowledge of what had happened when you fell? In a matter of an hour you wouldn't remember a thing, except as if this," his hand swept the scope of the kitchen, "had been no more than a dream. See, only the Librarian has permission to enter The Sacred Breath with authority, with Allah's permission. And for him or her, the assistant is the anchor to the time the Protector has left behind. Almost anyone can be an assistant, but only one at a time, and without an assistant, there is no anchor to help the protector return. The second is like the wall socket that the Librarian needs to stay grounded to to get back to this reality. And only one being at a time can be The Librarian, whose duty is to collect firsthand knowledge, preserve it for posterity on the day when we shall be reconnected with all that we are, which is through Self-Knowledge. That especially includes knowledge of who we were.

He lowered his eyebrows, still staring at me in a serious glare and said in a low register, "I repeat. You must never enter the sphere alone, Tyree. It is not a toy, not a game, but a supreme responsibility." The doctor more considerately (for a man such as him, getting more serious was always possible) – he went on, "and I was quite skeptical myself, after you went home that the sphere should choose someone so young."

"And so 'American'", Mrs. Kattan, who'd been silent but intent, added,

223

sarcastically.

The doctor and she laughed.

"What's so funny?" I asked, not amused.

"No child of a kidnapped Afrikan can be an American, equal under the law, Tyree," she explained. "It's like starting monopoly in the middle of a game with other players who already own all the best property and then trying to catch up."

"Oh." That made sense, if all the rest still seemed too much to grasp, especially that weird possibility we could be stuck in a memory, already. Several floors of my mind were wrestling with that one.
"I planned on testing you out before your fall, at the request of Sister Makeba, to get a measure of your worth. I'd have made you organize the books in my office, handle the mail, sweep – common chores. But when I tried to enter the sphere yesterday evening, out of curiosity, the feel was all wrong. The pull was too strong for one who is the designated Knowledge Keeper. That's when I told the sister to pull me out and I started searching in my library for a precedent. Going over the Librarians' ancient tomes..."

"Tombs?!!" I interjected. Exactly what had I stumbled into?

At that he laughed, once more, leaning back relaxed in his chair.

"Oh, no, no! I said the word, 'tomEs', not 'tomBs'! No, Tyree, this is about life, not death. Purified, exponential life! Whew," and he exhaled, without the usual accompanying 'harrumph', "So much for you to learn."

I'm sure my own expression was one of purified confusion, to which he, more seriously, answered, "Listen carefully, son. When Allah chooses you, it's for a reason that you or even I may not be aware of, but have no doubt. There is something particular about you that He has in mind for Him to have placed such an honor upon your shoulders."

"But Brother Cheikh," I sorrowfully said, "because of me you can't get back into the sphere without being in danger. I never wanted that to happen."

"Ha!" he and Sister Makeba smiled at one another as they each took sips of tea. She had prepared two cups for them both.

224

"Ha!" he continued, "Son, but I can enter the sphere as a visitor, for a bit, if I desire. After all this time of working with it day after day, year after year, decade after decade, and this my duty, alone, whether I am weary or not?" He leaned in close, looking me fixedly in the eye, "The sphere calls you to do your duty, and after all this time, for me?" He sat back up in his chair, "That's enough! I've been rattling around in that thing for longer than you'd believe. How old do you think I am?"

"I don't know. Sixty?"

He chuckled, "Not even close. As I said, the Orb is pure life which is shared with its caretaker and the caretaker's assistant, but trust this son. I'm ready to move on."

"Whew!" exhaled Mrs. Kattan, too, adding, "So am I! It's been a long crazy journey!"

"That it has, queen. That it has." He put his hand on top of hers for a moment. Then turning back to me, leaning forward once more, he said, "Now, let me explain as best I can. I went over the most ancient text, even read what I could of the inscription on the Orb, and both Sister Makeba and I can find no precedent for what happened to you."
"Good," I said, "then maybe it's a mistake that can be fixed."

"Oh, as I said, there's no mistake, brother. Allah is the best of planners and the Orb is purely His domain. I couldn't find a precedent but I did find prophecy."

"Prophecy?" You know what reader? Everybody, in his own way, feels extra special, somehow – 'cause they are. Even if it's only special in being an extra screwed up loser. Nobody's a loser quite like them. But when words like 'prophecy' get thrown around that's where you'd rather be as special as any one of a trillion identical ants in a mound deep in an insect infested jungle. That moment, upon hearing that word, I was envying an ant.

"Indeed. The prophecy proclaims our victory shall be assured when the chosen have awoken through the efforts of the one, who'll be brought out from that captive many by seeming happenstance, not by instruction in the ways of Allah's Memories first."

I snapped out it.

225

"Okay. Doctor, did that prophecy say anything about that punch in my face? About how my brain can hold 5 separate full conversations with itself at the same time? 'Cause I don't mean to question prophecy, or be rude or anything, but if it's not going to tell me about things like that, then I don't see what use it's got to offer. So, before I don't know which way is up or down, I gotta say, something incredible happened to the way I..." searching for a word that the doctor found, quickly and voiced,

"See."

"Yes! I can see into people. No!" I shook my head and body, so overcome with a passion to literally explain what was happening, "it's not their insides, like their hearts and livers – not like that. It's their..."

"Souls."

"Yeah! I mean it's not like I can see it, the aura I guess. Or their souls. It's more like I can feel it so loudly it's become a visual reality. An echo! And not just with people, but with everything. How old a building is, if a tree is sickly, if a lawn has been sprayed with pesticide. Why, the food people eat, I can tell if it's actually good for them. I think I can even sense what happened in a space after the people have left it. And I can remember stuff I've read from months and months ago. Oh! And I can remember pieces from that other life like I lived it yesterday. What the heck is that?!!! I mean isn't that a kind of superpower? I know that sounds corny, cause I don't think I can fly or anything, but? What's happened to me? Did this same thing happen to you when you first went into the sphere?" I added that last question with a hint of desperation. If the doctor didn't know then nobody would and I was alone. I didn't know having that little, electron sized 's' could be so isolating.

Come to think of it, looking at the both of them, there was no aura surrounding either at all, just a certainty of their warmth and genuine concern. A certainty that I knew to my core. And for the whole mansion, I'd been so hurried to come over, I hadn't taken notice that for the first time as I crossed the street? The aura that used to be around the house looked like what the ordinary world have looked like over 24hrs before. Why stepping inside hadn't been a rush, or a recollection of how different the place made me feel because I'd forgotten. It all just felt normal. The only 'normal' place I'd been in since I'd left it the other day.

Calmly, the doctor replied, "Look, here."

He stood, and took a number of smaller volumes, old and worn, from atop the oldest and most worn of all. And that one the others had been sitting on was the largest, it being the height of a small footstool. This was the definition of a 'tome' by which all the other tomes, everywhere, must probably be measured, I thought. Opening it up slowly, he motioned for me to stand beside him, while his wife sat quietly sipping her cup of tea, enjoying her husband's renewed enthusiasm for his work, as she would tell me one day, many experiences later.

"I hadn't seen him that exuberant for 6 or 7 decades," she would say. "It was an unexpected joy."

The pages Brother Dr. Kattan turned were thick and coarse, like fabric. The text was antiquely inscribed with ornate flourishes, precise and yet, written with personal human skill, not a typeset machine. You could see the thickness and thinness of the dried ink, as opposed to the uniform flatness of ribbon or laser sprayed ink. Everything written in a language I couldn't understand beyond the periods at the end of the sentences. As Dr. Kattan gingerly scrolled through, expertly lifting the very edge of each semi glossy, heavy leaf, I, having assumed this would be some ancient book written by a cloistered monk in a medieval Italian monastery, I was surprised to see, in the hand painted diagrams and drawings, nothing but Black men, Black women, Black children in an assortment of garments, from loin clothes to ceremonial vestments, engaged in a variety of activities. Not a one of those activities was basketball, nor anyone who appeared to be rapping. They were at work with various implements, building, reading, standing guard, tilling the soil and worshipping with their families, children at hand.
"Here it is," Dr. Kattan said, stopping on a page a couple hundred past the beginning, which showed a black circle, festooned with multi-colored...

"The Spirals!" I gasped.

"Yes. It's your spirals, as described, it says here, by Allah, Himself. No one besides you has ever seen them. I searched half the night for a recording of their existence, as my teacher, Mumia Sirius Negus Ra, like his teacher told him – well, he told me. But I couldn't be satisfied with what could be a mere myth. I'd almost given up, then, I remembered this book deep in the vault. I haven't opened it in decades. "The Netjer Tebeqa" it's called, copied in the hidden libraries of Ancient Ghana, from the original papyrus scrolls, under the command of King Tenkamenin. If it hadn't been secretly secured, the Tamahue would have burned it with the rest, in the late 1500s. It's the earliest history of the first protectors as passed down through more than a million years. Saved by Knowledge Protector Ekow Nzeogwu, though he gave his life to keep it un-incinerated. He baited the invading barbarians with a forgery. They burned him with that blank book and went home, satisfied. For them that means, satisfied for a week or two before they came back, theiving. You'll want to study this, even if you don't know the language."

He grew quiet and then laughed, finding, like I did looking wide eyed at that footstool high book, the prospect of studying that to be quite the daunting suggestion. I laughed in answer, but hesitantly. I suspected he was right that I should study it, so a large part of me agreed with him.

He continued, "...but for now, this one page is what I looked for to confirm your experience beyond the apocryphal, including that vortex you saw above. The Ankh Udje Saneb. It succinctly describes the outer vista beyond the individual life coils."

"Is that what the spirals are, a 'life coil'?"

"Yes. They are the physical path your existence has taken from one lifetime to the next, all connected seamlessly," offered Mrs. Kattan. "That's why you didn't fall into any old coil, you fell into your own as your soul is magnetically drawn to your story.."

"Indeed," the doctor continued, "and one cannot travel through anyone else's but their own when entering the Orb. The magnetic pull is too powerful to step beyond."

"But I fell into a black void. That wasn't a coil I was in. I was in freefall, through that!"

And I pointed, carefully not to damage the book, at the blackened circle on the thick leaf.
"You mean to tell me this has never happened before to anyone for a MILLION YEARS?"

"More than a million, Tyree. And no, it hasn't, per se. So that they've come back to tell about it."

He grew silent, seemingly pondering the text, and I noted Mrs. Kattan looked down at her own cup of tea, pensively. Then he looked up at my anxiously puzzled face and began again in a deeper tone.

"It has happened for various reasons, someone enters the Orb without

228

preparation, or a foe is tossed inside, unawares. But you are the only one who was rescued and brought back to tell the tale. The Orb does offer both the Protector and his/her assistant some decided benefits, but with you falling in the depth of it, there's no knowing what extra-sensory perceptions you've been gifted with, if they are permanent, temporary, or will expand since you're the first to return. Seeing the 'souls' of shall we say, all 'existence' might be a glimpse you've gotten of the way the Creator sees everything."

I felt a bit woozy, with an urgent need to sit. So I did. The doctor began silently reading from the book, while I was taken by the idea that if an army of warrior ferrets came into the kitchen that moment, claiming Newark for the King of Ferretland, I'd have said, "That figures."

"I do believe we should consult the Orb itself," he said, closing the book. "I can observe your response more accurately discerning the truth clearly and it's as close to the truth as we can get."

I looked up, a bit concerned, saying, "Is that a good idea, doctor?" All that prophecy talk had dampened my enthusiasm.

He harrumphed, shaking his head while replying, "Son, first off, if you're the Protector, it'll heal your face right up. Second place? I think you yourself know what must be done."

Daggonit. As always, the doctor didn't need to waste words. He'd nailed it. This Orb was, maybe, all my great plans to repair the damage I was surrounded by – as I had promised myself since yesterday afternoon I would do – it was all my great plans put to the test. It contained facts that could give my childish wishes the necessary details I could then share with those being taught by the Mrs. Finns of the world. I could share with those being neglected by the Mr. Levinsteins, too, and doomed for failure under the influence of the even worse. Dr. Kattan was right. I knew what I had to do because I refused to be merely another 'American' Black Boy who liked to talk about doing something big, but when it came to getting it done, I'd settle for some useless Bling Bling door prize rather than attempting and then mayhaps accomplishing something life changing. World changing... And though in my momentary zeal to walk through bathroom stall doors, I had forgotten the urgency, I accepted, if the Orb wasn't protected (and I had been an eyewitness to the coming collapse) – I had to admit, if it was discovered by our enemy, whoever that was? Then one day there'd be no broken sidewalk to fix, no neighbors to get to know, no Howard to apologize to, no Nyisha to sigh over, since there'd be nothing left at all. I'd finally be an equal to everybody else Black or white since everyone with

229

nothing is equal.

Corpses never conduct protest marches for better accommodations.

I didn't hesitate a moment longer than my thought, which completed its reasoning in what seemed, spontaneously. I stood up, ready to follow the honorable doctor to his office and the patio, through the recesses of the library, but he motioned me to remain seated while reaching into his pocket. Pulling out a blood red velvet satchel, he emptied the contents into the palm of his other hand. It was as if he had shot a silent hole through his own flesh with a soundless bullet, for there was a rounded nothingness, strikingly reminiscent of that uninterrupted by the bastardization of light – total blackness that had mesmerized me just 24hrs ago. I'd forgotten.

Only this time, the hole was a whole lot smaller. A whole lot smaller. It was the size of a child's marble, if the marble hadn't been there. Just that hypnotic blackness that defied reality. Again, I felt drawn to touch it, despite its tiny size. I had to understand the magnitude of something so absolute. That was it. The Orb required nothing added to it, nothing that could be taken away. It was probably the one thing in existence that was finished. Complete.

He placed it upon the velvet pouch on the table in front of me. No words were exchanged. My wide eyes were a loud enough question as to if I could pick it up. I was shocked when his bemused look, full of empathy, nodded, a wordless 'yes'.
"But don't pinch it, or rub it roughly as that will make it expand and possibly absorb you up instantly, with no time to grab even a finger."

Wanting no mishaps this time, I replayed his warning over in my head on each floor of my conference building mind to ensure every Tyree heard and obeyed by shutting the heck up. Then with my thumb and index fingers I ever so gently gripped what appeared to be a bullet hole in the surrounding red velvet. It was solid to my touch, despite looking as if I could put the tip of my pinky finger inside it. I picked it up, looking at my hosts to make thoroughly certain I wasn't doing something wrong. Mrs. Kattan's eyes gleamed supportively, and Mr. Kattan nodded assuredly.
I placed it on my own palm and felt a tingling cool sensation as that part of my hand seemed to disappear, though without a view of the table underneath. It was surprisingly heavy for something so small, and I wasn't in the least bit surprised, though. I heaved my hand to feel the full weight of it which was about the same as a billiard cube, despite being the size of that child's marble; while the doctor took a folded up cloth from the bottom rack of the bookcart

and laid it out on the stone floor. It was the same mudclothe that had barely concealed it on the porch.

"Here, Tyree. Place it in the center of this and then watch me, carefully."

I eagerly did as told, and carefully.

Expecting a few magical hocus pocus words once it was near exactly in the center of the clothe, I was surprised that the Kattans, with Sister Makeba joining in, standing – I was surprised when the Brother – instructing me to face his same direction, along with his Queen, arms slightly bent, out before us, palms face up – I was surprised when he began a simple prayer.

Now, reader. I don't want to share this moment with you since I know most likely you've been taught to avoid 'entertainment' that dares to mention our Creator, let alone any book or movie that would have the nerve to include a PRAYER! But, don't worry. This is not a history for one particular religious faith. I don't care if you are Christian, Muslim, Hindu, or don't profess allegiance to any religious doctrine in the slightest. If you know there is a Creator, then I'm sure if you met Him, you'd instantly submit and pray for His mercy. Let's say, by chance, you're an atheist reading this? If you, too, met The All Powerful, then you, without hesitation, probably faster than everyone else, you'd submit to greater wisdom, unless you're a complete fool; in which case you wouldn't be reading this book or any other that'd enlighten you.

Well, I wasn't into praying myself at that age, nor was any member of my family. We didn't go to church. Why if God was mentioned in my house? It would've been by accident or on holidays. So, forgive me if you come from a world with nonchalant to non-existent regard for the man responsible for your very breath, but if you're about to, not merely view, but enter his photo album? You, too, wouldn't mind showing some deep, deep respect. And submission.

Which I did.

We – the Kattans and I – paid homage to the maker of everything, facing east, standing with our arms stretched out to receive His blessing, as Brother Cheik informed me.
He began –

"In the name of Allah, the Beneficent, the Merciful.
Surely You have given us an abundance of good.
So we pray to thee Lord and sacrifice.

Surely Your enemy is cut off from good."

And that was it. I know! Betcha you, reading this, and EYE, standing there that day, were expecting something torturously long. But no magical words and nothing anymore complicated than a simple 'Thank You for a great dinner, Ma!' Or 'Great job, co-worker!' Only, we gave thanks to the Creator. Admittedly, that sort of praise does seem like magic as it automatically brings happiness to the giver and the receiver – the giver of thanks reminding himself how he appreciates what made him grateful, and the receiver having one's hard work noticed and appreciated. I didn't expect it to be over so quickly, and at the time, little 12 year old, brought up under the domination of an unthankful culture that I had no sayso over? 12yr old me?..

Well, I was delighted and relieved it was a short prayer! I wanted to get to that Orb, not have a church service!

"Oh," said Mrs. Kattan, "I almost forgot these!" Taking a mid-thick gold chain from around her neck, upon which hung another black marble as a pendant, but not the same profound blackness as the orb laying on the clothe, she draped it around my neck. She still wore an exact duplicate around hers, which she also took off and handed to the doctor who firmly gripped it in his hand.

"These are the Aanda. When you arrive, yours will not be visible, but you can signal the doctor by touching the spot where it touches your chest."
"They are the plug and the wall socket," the doctor answered what I had already assumed.

"They keep us in touch so you can retrieve me, right? Without havin' to hold my ankles."
"Right!" they said in unison.

He continued, "But you don't need to attract undo attention by talking aloud to me, like this is some kind of cellphone. Your thoughts and mine will be connected. We couldn't communicate holding onto your ankles, although we could sense what happened to you."

"You couldn't see it, then?" I was a bit disappointed. I thought they had.

"No. The Sphere generates a magnetic force field that only the correct frequency can bend, like a key, allowing transmission of energetic connections, both ways. Thoughts are energy and as rocks don't think..."

232

"Neither do ankles," I smiled.

"Exactly. Neither do ankles. But hearts do feel. The Aanda receives and transmits your heart's Chakra energy as love is the best fuel of any living magnetic force. So our connection to you with these anchors will stay constant. With your ankles?" He shrugged his shoulders, "With great difficulty. We could hurtle our consciousness in with yours, but the pull of our own connection within our lifecoils would not allow yours to reach back out to us in a pure wave. Lucky we did grab your ankles, hence we used the rope to reel you back out. But, your connection to us was nearly non-existent, except for not being able to move your feet. On our end, we could glean a little of what'd became of you. The basics. These pendants allow for a more flexible bending of the orb's g-force field so I can see what you see, you can direct information back to me and can hear what instructions I have to share with you."

"That's a comfort."

"I'm sure it is."

"And the library? Is that how you got all those books? You can bring things back?"

"All those books? Goodness no, that wasn't me alone who acquired all of those. And you can't bring back anything as the memory, or coil, is fixed in its place. It's a memory, not a real time event. Nothing from another time can be brought back here, except for..." and he looked me deep in the eyes.

Nodding up and down, I answered, "...me. And my memory."

"Bingo, so-called American child. The books in the library are a ruse that Keeper Ekow Nzeogwu would have approved. A collection bought over the millennia by all the Librarians in their time, during their own lives. The real treasury of books is those," he pointed to the stacks on the now silent bookcart. "I keep those in the vault, below in the basement. The memoirs of every single Librarian and of what he witnessed. Together, we've compiled a chronology of most of time, limited though it is."

"Limited?" Guessing I added, "I can't I go into the future, huh?"

"Ha!" He and Sister Makeba laughed together again.

233

"No, Tyree," she replied. "If we could do that, there'd be no problem since we could change the current course of time, all by ourselves."

It suddenly occurred to me, "Can I go back in the past and change things from that end? Maybe so the Tamahue would never do what they do?"

"Harrumph. You'd have to change the Tamahue's souls. You'd have to age them a good million years all at once, which would be impossible. No. Each of us, everywhere, is part author of the fate the entire Earth earns. What is, is, and only patience will get us through. Other than that, boy? You can't change the past. These memories are perfect in every minute detail, down to the very subatomic quark in its 3 dimensions. So coils always lead right up to whatever's the current reality for the soul entwined within. What he or she would have experienced as if he'd never left, should he or she be lost. Could take a few thousand lifetimes for them to catch up, but they'll eventually get where they need to be. In the meantime, only the future is ours to fiddle with and the Creator has given us the freedom to choose. But what's happened already? As the Protector, you can bend the memory, go places that past incarnation of you never went, have experiences he never had, talk to people he never would have, but stick around for too long in that timeframe and all that apparently changed will revert to the destiny you already chose way back before, with as I said, no memory of who you were in this, the present time."

"But this time? What happens to this time? How can a lost soul catch up if he has to start at the beginning?"

"You have the false sense that all time is linear, a straight line ahead, when multi-dimensional time, as is God's memory, happens in a spiral, not a line."

"Permitting all times to happen at the same time!" It made, of course, perfect sense.

"Yes, son. This is mathematics, not magic. You are Amenhotep, right now, this minute, and everyone you've ever been, only you don't have access to that manifestion of yourself."

"Whoa."

The doctor and his wife smiled again, making this day the singularly most smile embellished one I'd ever spent in their company. They may have had more smiles in private, some other time, but I know right then, they were pleased with me. It occurred to me that perhaps they'd had to keep this object

234

a secret from the whole world, maybe even their son, Gainde. It was probably a little lonely, being the sole caretakers of something so monumental; thus to be able to pass it on, finally, after...

"Exactly, how old are you, doctor?" I knew it'd be impolite to address the question to Sister Makeba.

"I was wondering when you'd ask that." He paused, before answering, "126."

"And I am not a day over 40, if time would have stood still sixty years ago," the sister answered anyway, adding, "But you both, please get to it, as we must have talked for an hour now. This is no 'The Lion, the Witch and the Wardrode.' Your time in there is the same amount of time out here, principally. Perhaps a little faster, but, dimension is bendable. Not time."

Though I had fifty thousand more questions to ask, and a whole dissertation about how they both looked only a couple years older than my mother was, and yes, my dad had been, there was only one more question that gripped my mind, though I hadn't paid it direct attention until now.

"Can I see my dad?" I paused at the consoling look in his eyes, adding, "I guess I can't I save him?"

"Ah," Dr. Kattan shook his head mournfully. "Your lifecoil is your own and no one else's, with so many lifetimes you've led that you could enter the sphere 3 thousand times before you'd ever run into this lifecoil's father. In other emanations, you might recognize him, but he may be your uncle, your brother, your friend. There is no set format for our current relationships as you may not run into him at all. Each life, we come and go at unique times." He put his hand on my shoulder, "And woefully, as I said, the timeline is set. These are memories, not living occurrences. If you encountered him, you can't stop his fate, or his decisions ultimately. I'm so sorry, son."

They looked at me with a mixture of kindness and helplessness. I wondered if they, knowing the circumstances of the crash, thought, like the insurance investigators, and even me (maybe), that my dad had taken his own life. I guess I paused a long while caught up in my multi-layered reasoning on how I could possibly convince them, convince myself, that that was not true.

"Harrumph!" The doctor interrupted the silence. "Brother! So many questions. So much for you to learn in too short a time, making firsthand experience the very best teacher. Here."

235

We had already been facing the sphere, but he stood more at attention before the Orb (I should really call it the 'marble' but it seems disrespectful) and he motioned me to do the same. Sister Makeba moved off to the side.

"Mrs. Kattan won't be joining us?" I asked.

"You only need 2. Best to keep things simple," the doctor replied, and bent down to the sphere, which he pressed upon with his full palm before rising again. "You must use the same pressure as you would if you were pressing against your eyeball without wanting to squash it or cause yourself discomfort. Just once will do. Anymore, or any harder and the Orb would expand too far. Possibly uncontrollably consuming everything in its path. I have no idea as I have never made that error. The Orb is scientific art, not a button. It can have a mind of its own."

"Like it did, yesterday."

"Indeed."

In the time it took the doctor to say, 'indeed', I don't know if I blinked or what, cause I swear, one minute the sphere could be stepped on and the next it could have rolled over me. Like a silent black predator, it had leapt to bigger than it had been the other day, instantly towering above my head and blocking the view of most of the back of the kitchen with a gigantic 'hole'.

Another 'whoa' involuntarily escaped my lips. The doctor had his 'harrumph' and I seemed to have developed my own exclamation.

"Yes, it can be startling like that. It's as if it'd already been there, you just didn't notice."
And again, here was that deep, cell to cell cry in my very bones to get closer to the Orb to fathom, what the heck could be so complete? If the good Brother Cheikh's hand hadn't gripped my shoulder, my already in progress self, which without thought was, just like the other day, hypnotically stepping towards the Orb? I'd have been, yet again, on my way back into that void, tumbling without a paddle or rigging rope.

"No, son. Not like that," he cautioned, waving his finger, admonishingly. "Time will make resisting the lure easier, trust me as I remember the first time I saw it. This is where an instructor provides the necessary discipline with a thinking mind that knows how to exercise the very greatest caution. This is no toy for the merely curious, and why for the foreseeable future, I, or Sister

236

Makeba must always be your assistants, till you find another. The danger is too easy to forget."

He passed his hand over the Orb's non-existent surface, but without touching what I knew wasn't there. Suddenly, what for me, the other fateful day, had been a barely discernible moving glow, across the 'surface' of the orb, shot forth in a bright arc of white light, stadium capacity. I had to squint till I could see the inscribed hieroglyphs which were crystal clear, now, no guesswork in the doctor's results. And the slight breeze that had once doomed my curiosity, became a pronounced and steady gust, but this time blowing from behind us, into the sphere, not outward. It didn't knock me over, though, as the wind wasn't that powerful, however, I thought about the air coming to life as it surrounded the mansion and wondered if the sphere was the source of its exuberance.

"That's how you activate the full magnetic force." Raising the volume of his voice, slightly, to speak louder than the rushing wind, the doctor continued, with, "A clean sweep of the hand. It's a knack you get the feel of the more you practice. Just one sweep. I don't know what would happen with more than that. Next time, you activate it, for practice. And after a while? You'll get a feel for the script, though no one knows the exact meaning. You'll have a sense of when to enter based on familiarity with where you've been. Until then, we can't know what time you'll be returning to."

"Can I enter another person's coil?" I'd raised my voice, also.

"The magnetic draw is too powerful to go anywhere but to your own. That's where we Protectors are limited."

"Oh."

"We'll do 2 short trips. First one to get you a feel of it, second just cause one won't be enough. Well, son. Step inside. The field is secure."

I glowingly looked to him for only a half second, because I needed no further invitation...

=

I knew it was near midday, the Sun not at its zenith, having risen only just above my head, behind me. It was hot, but I didn't mind, sitting alone on a mound of sparsely grassed dirt, my back against the base of a cluster of enormous Molalla trees. Nobody told me what the trees were called, but I already knew as I knew this spot. Knew the most accommodating trunks to rest upon and gaze at the serene waters of the bay, a short drop below. There were other clusters of Molallas. Plenty to choose from, but I knew this group had the perfect sized crook for me to lean cozily within – that the two nestled trunks were separated enough and not too much, whilst my back was shielded by the other 3 trees directly behind, hiding my presence from prying eyes.

And evidently, I had more of me to hide, for my body was too big, all of a sudden. And too old, with thin red black limbs stretching out onto the ground before me, the dark skin, my dark skin, pulled like an old dried out garden hose over well used muscles and sturdy bones. I wasn't weak. I was strong. And I wasn't alone in the world. My people were a short way from the coast, down in the valley. A rich powerful people amongst whom I was their eldest member and I was adored.

All the elders were respected, revered, but not many were adored as I was. I wasn't trying to be, tried to be downright cranky so I could get some peace and quiet from all the questions, but nonetheless, seemed the crankier I got, the more I was admired – cause?

I could never be cranky for real. Just liked having a little privacy, now and then.

Like the rolling waters washing gently over the narrow strip of sand and cliff, which began its rise where I sat, here against the trees – who I was now, came gently washing into my mind, and principally came the reality, that here, I was thoroughly content. Thoroughly.
There was no concern in every ounce of me. What the? I had never felt thorough contentment, before. It was like the perfect temperature shower, only inside your brain, knowing you'd never be dirty again because you were immune to dirt. Darn. It felt great.

And there was that crayon blue sky again, way above and vast, mirrored by strikingly azure waters, below. And there was teeming, darting life, I could actually see, swimming abundantly in both the waves, as multiple hued fish, and in the currents of air, as soaring fish of the sky, more popularly called 'birds', who were dipping down on occasion to catch their breakfast with skilled beaks. And there, suddenly, was Dr. Kattan's voice – was that his voice, or did I just sense the sound of his voice so clearly it was as if he was talking right next to me?

"Tyree."

I reflexively started, snapping my head and body to my right, expecting to see him grinning at me from the side of the tree.

"Doctor?!" I shouted to no one there.

He laughed, answering, *"Remember, there's no need to shout. No need to talk at all. I'm not there. I'm in your thoughts."*

"Oh," I said, as if this were perfectly natural, looking around, impending embarrassment ready to take over my contentment should anyone have been near enough to see me talking to an invisible person. The brother's voice hadn't been inside my head, but distinctly from right to my side. Yet, there was no one I could see next to me, nor in the gradually ascending rise behind. I had deliberately come to this spot knowing I'd find silent privacy, which was convenient for my first 'official' time inside the Sphere, to have come across this pleasant memory of myself exactly when I needed to get used to this fantastical experience.

And thinking of 'privacy', I asked, "You can read my thoughts? All of them?"

"Don't worry son. I can read only what your conscious and unconscious mind wants me to read, which are those thoughts you project towards me and your immediate observations and senses that your mind is presently absorbing, without censorship. For instance, like a picture in my own head, I can see the landscape you're in through your eyes; even sense the grit of the trees you're sitting against. It's a standard courtesy, though, between the Librarian and his assistant to keep the connection between them mostly silent, once he's mastered the experience, so he can do his job without constantly being watched. That can get quite annoying for both parties as you, too, can sense my observations. Here. Close your eyes and feel for the image. And you don't have to talk out loud."

I, involuntarily grimaced, realizing I was still speaking at full volume.

239

Determined not to make that mistake, again, I did as he instructed, plunging my visual awareness, at first, into the usual dark vista behind one's eyelids, though mine were dotted with the bleeding in radiance of the bright daylight. That was all there was, at first, until I felt the growing awareness of another space surrounding my perception. A space I recognized, though it wasn't an exact photo image – a space I knew was the kitchen. Like getting one's eyes used to being plunged in the dark after being in stark light, I saw the small table before me, and Mrs. Kattan sitting directly across. It was like a memory – hazy. Only firm. Beyond question.

"*Peace, Sister Makeba!*" I said, this time to myself, in my thoughts. A strange feeling, talking in your head, where no one but you are supposed to be.

"*She can't hear you, Tyree.*"

"*Oh,*" I sadly replied since the sister's presence was such a comfort.

As my mind adjusted to the imagery inside it, I could perceive her and the room more clearly, and I watched her get up from her chair, as she told the doctor she was going outside to tend the garden. I could hear her clearly.

It occurred to me, "*Whoa. This is incredible!*"

"*Indeed. This is the strengthening of the connection with the Aanda. Last time we weren't using all the Spheres, the Orb, itself, the marble I'm holding against my chest, right now and the one you can no longer see against yours.*"

I looked and touched my chest to verify he was right. There was nothing there but smooth black skin beneath my robes.

"*With the Aanda,*" he continued with no interruption, "*I can retrieve you, instantly, or simply check in to make certain you're well. I can do that no matter how far I am from the actual orb, or how far you travel from the location where you arrived.*"

I became aware of the feeling of the matt surface of his marble, picturing its uninterrupted midnight finish, which was confirmed as the doctor's eyes, which I was sharing, pivoted onto his long, textured black hand, rolling the Aanda through his fingers, near his green button shirt, right below his chin.

"*I simply put it down, so I'm no longer touching it, and your experiences become solely your own. Pick it back up and the connection is restored as long as I'm in direct contact*

240

with it. Near my own heart's Chakra, the magnetic link is strongest, like magnets, pivoted properly. Sister Makeba usually wore it on a necklace, but I'll have to get a longer chain to fit around my neck. See, when you fell in, it took the two of us to pull you back out and that touch became the weaker Aanda. Like I said, our vision of you was sketchy, at best. More like a loud echo rather than a full visual, but that's how we both saw where you fell. Through your emotional reactions. You have to enter the Sphere with the proper connection or you're on the wrong frequencies for good, since you have to wear the other Aanda."

"Oh. So you 'saw' me as Amen because I realized I was and you read my mind, but you didn't see the void because the connection wasn't powerful, enough, in motion? Did you sense my fear during my trip through the void? I was freaking out big time." I didn't want to admit to it, but, I needed his guidance.

I could sense him shrugging his shoulders, though I couldn't 'see' him as I was in his mind.

"Yes and no. I'm not sure of why or how, but I theorize..."

"Humble pardons, most esteemed father," a male voice startled my eyes open and made me jump, taking my concentration off the doctor's answer and the full cafeteria sized kitchen in my head.

There in front of me but a bit off to the side, as the edge of the cliff was where my feet overhung, a young man stood, dressed in clothing similar to my own, dyed with an unknown African motif. Mine was a full body wrap, while his was a skirt.

Only not a skirt, like a woman would wear or like Terrance had joked that Howard must'a wore running home. This was like a warrior would wear, which the young man was. I knew with his training, he could have as easily killed me as he had greeted me.

His coloring was blue black skin so dark it seemed more like purple, glistening over taunt muscles - though lean, not bunchy as if he worked out at the local gym. I knew there wasn't a gym anywhere, let alone a local one, on that day's Earth and I knew he was a warrior because he was my grandson, Kayikuuzi. I had overseen his training. One of the best of our forces, this young man, loin of my loin, had proven to be.

My name was Ccwa. Pronounced 'Swah', with no break inbetween.

241

"So sorry, father," he said at my startlement, continuing, "I didn't mean to surprise you. I came to inform you that our vessel has returned to port. The passengers await your blessing and permission to re-enter Manyikeni."

Manyikeni? Manyikeni? My mind was instantly flooded with images of glistening rose coral edifices, grand sweeping heights of many painstakingly decorated exteriors and interiors, thousands of them dotting the shoreline, and even more houses dotting inbetween and behind them. Pristine paved streets, market places teeming with vendors and shoppers. The valley setting that poorly educated Tyree had first assumed upon arriving was merely a village of straw huts, was where Ccwa's people, my people lived in a bustling city. One of the most properous gateway ports from which we had peopled the globe and traded our goods with our many far flung children. Manyikeni! Manyikeni! Beautiful, ornate, magnificent, seafaring, world traversing Manyikeni and its equally magnificent, beautiful, ornate, and all the etceteras, etceteras included, people. My people. And this was only one of our cities that dotted the shore of this land and many others. Now I understood why I felt so marvelously at peace...

We studied war as a precaution to keep the Western tribes at bay, but not as a necessity, as they were a nuisance, only, due to their preference for the steady stream of profitable goods we imported. They only occasionally became belligerent to jockey for more of the profit. They always lost. Kayikuuzi, and a thousand warriors like him was the reason.

There was something strangely missing from this reality that I couldn't place my finger on, but full out war was unfathomable to my heart and mind as Ccwa. All the world was inhabited with our progeny, whom we visited often to share knowledge, wisdom, goods, stories and love with from the motherland of us all. But it wasn't the land that mattered as the whole world was ours, without question. It was the people. We had to see our people, no matter where they reached. Ships sailed from the shores of Manyikeni with the trade winds going and the trade winds to return. Kayikuuzi had come to tell me, one of those ships had come home, captained by my first born, Kintu.

It had been five years since I last saw my favorite son. But don't tell his siblings that, and I had never told anyone, either – at least as I could remember from that moment sitting watching the bay. I, afterall, was a wise man who knew I was part of a greater whole which was stronger by supporting everyone...

"Shall I find Elder Matayo in your stead?" he tentatively asked, while waiting for my reply. Kayikuuzi had always been a good reader of my desire for privacy.

242

Kintu's seed was as richly bearing as I'd suspected it'd be.

'Whoa', the Tyree mind in me contemplated. '*I could stay here forever. If only I weren't so old, I'd never leave.*'

"No, no." I answered him, with a much deeper, older voice of a man who knew instantly all the whos involved and what was expected. Elder Matayo was a good man but drat the proof of time had cursed me with a reputation as more often correct than not, and amusing to boot in my delivery of that correctness. Elder Matayo was a bit dry, ever so doddering – I'd warned him seasons ago to eat more greenery and a few less dried fruits. And he could err on the side of pomposity, rather than insight, and insight favors truth over the individual man, even me.

But while I might crave solitude, doing what was the most supportive of my people was my ultimate desire. Thus I insisted on being the one to bless our people's return as the passengers would be honored to be granted permission to step onto the land from the elders, through elder me. It had been 5 full cycles, after all. And quietly, where no one would know, I, myself, would be so strengthened to see my son again after such a long time.

"No, my son of my son," I continued, a bit gruffly in tone, speaking melodically in no language that sounded remotely like English, but felt like the tongue I should speak as un-self-consciously as I spoke the language I knew as 'Tyree' – I continued a bit gruffly which was my 'way', here. I was always testing those around to drag them, if need be, kicking and screaming into thinking beyond the wish for what's easy or what they saw directly in front of their faces.

"Go on ahead to tell the council I'm on my way. The sailing party has endured their journey well enough, I suppose, and waiting a bit longer on me won't trouble them more."

Oh, yes it would, I knew, but only the shortsighted ones, as all our vessels were over abundantly well provisioned on both ends of the venture. Not to forget to mention, word of their status and that of every seaward, landward journey was continuously brought back by others returning; and now that they were here, all further needs would be attended. They would want for nothing. Now, truthfully, I wouldn't tarry too excessively long against my tree, however? Long enough to test their dedication to our people as opposed to their dedication to individual concerns.

Kayikuuzi nodded with an understanding glint in his piercingly white, clear eyes, with irises nearly as black as his skin, and turned to make the walk back to the city port. A vast port, full of those vessels that came and went with the winds. There would be many captains, many sons, and a legion of sons of sons.

I leaned back into my spot. I was in no hurry. The greatest pleasures should be contemplated, savored. Not attacked. In that quiet moment, that's when I, Tyree, realized how easy it would have been for me to forget who I was. Or who I was supposed to be, because it didn't seem so pressing, right then, to be a twelve year old boy. Here, I had wives...

Not wanting to recall all my Ccwa memories, lest the doctor become privy to matters that weren't his to know, "*Doctor?*" I called on him in my mind, as if I had a mouth in my brain which none could hear outside my skull. Closing my eyes again, adjusting to the change of perception, brought the kitchen into view but it was empty as far as my vantage point could see. Sister Makeba I figured was still in the garden, and Brother Cheikh didn't respond. I thought I was seeing from within his mind, but the view was frozen, static, as if I was seeing from something stationary, not a blinking, mobile human being.

"*Doctor?*" I asked internally, once more. Silence was my initial answer, which was met in my heart by an instantaneous dread. What if something had gone wrong? Funny how dread, fear or any negative emotion can rise up from nothing, but once there it insists on being felt. I put my fingers to the spot where I guessed the Aanda should have been.

"*Right here son,*" the doctor's voice came sonorously pushing aside my foolish worry. The worry of a child, I thought, disappointed in myself, when here I had been a wise old man.

As if I had suddenly grown legs inside my mind's view of the kitchen and stood up, the view was lifted higher all at once, now clearly emanating from a pair of blinking eyes that I wasn't telling when to blink. I assumed I was again connected with my new, far more fascinating that any other, ever, teacher.

"*What happened?*" I asked, not able to completely dismiss the retreating dread except with the relief one feels when a parent rescues you from a dark room after a bad dream. The child feels better but cannot forget the talons of his fear. I was a little annoyed, too, or was that Ccwa being cranky?

'Funny,' I thought. '*I, Ccwa, have just been tested.*' The old man that was me laughed out loud to nobody but the birds, the fish, the too blue sky and the undulating waters of the bay, at the ironic justice of it all.

244

I guessed irony was lost in telepathy because the doctor only responded with, "*Sorry about that, Tyree. Thought I heard a noise outside. Well, time to bring you home. That'll do for today.*"

I'd intended my full vehement protest to be something like, '*What?! But I only barely got here! I haven't even seen the city! I haven't seen Kintu!*' But after I felt no more than a hint of a shuddering wave throughout my body, with no catapulting upwards into a black void this time, and before I could launch into my protest beyond more than a chopped off, "Wha..." I was stumbling out of the Orb to a short halt in front of Dr. Kattan, everything changing in faster than any blink, from secret scenic seaside resting nook to enormous incomplete kitchen, without need for my agreement.
I wondered if I was going to hurl again, but I didn't feel as if I would, which was convenient since Brother Cheikh didn't have a bucket in hand. I wondered if my son had arrived okay, way back then, thinking it strange to be a boy knowing what it's like to have a son, along with wiveS. I wondered what the doctor was looking at because he was rather distractedly looking above me at something else, as though I wasn't there at all. Didn't he know this was the most astounding experience I'd ever had? Hadn't all this once been brand new to him and didn't he remember?

"Is something wrong, sir?"

He harrumphed in a wordless question I couldn't answer for him, and after peering intently at the large windows behind me, brought his still distracted attention to me.

"In this advocation, one never knows not if there is something wrong, but when there will be something wrong. For the moment, I don't believe there is."

Forgetting my disappointing too soon return in exchange for concern, I asked, "Where's Sister Makeba?"

"Tending the garden, son. And she's fine," he smiled, soothingly, and then finally noticing me, he said, "Well, quite a good visit you've had, wouldn't you say?" He took a seat at the table, continuing, "Most times entering the orb, before you know how to target where you wish to specifically go, you're most likely going to travel to places like Manyikeni. We've been in direct if undeclared war with the enemy for only 6,000 years. That's one heartbeat in the entire life's worth of beats for, say? An elephant. With a miniscule 4 to 5 generations oppressed here in these stolen lands, yet, we are the original people, here since the minute our Father created us, which as it was trillions of years, ago? We've been in existence for several hundred millions of generations. Most likely, more. We Protectors are only still documenting it, with the earliest account going back 2.5 million years, on other planets, even, just as the Venerated Dogon tribe remembers. Why, most of our time here on this planet has been one of sheer peace, coast to coast, with not a white person in or out of sight."

He said what I had suspected sitting so blissfully against my favorite tree as a respected elder. Or should I say, I realized that was why I had been sitting so blissfully against that tree, as I can never adequately describe to you, reader. It was right then I understood, if you've been hunted so endlessly much it seems normal, you don't begin to know what that does to one's sense of safety. To your perception of what's possible. You don't even wonder that your reality of trying to withstand doubts created by another is not natural to being alive. If the antelope expected no hope but to be eaten by the lion, that there was no other outcome but his demise, he'd never run away with fleet footed bounds. He'd serve himself up with a side of gizelle's liver. It's faith that pushes his strides to escape. And if the lion looked like the antelope, yet with all the motivation and intention of the predator...?

"Yes," I answered, almost to myself, "I realized that after a moment."

He motioned for me to take a chair, but I wanted to remain standing.

You know reader, it's funny when one's a child, even one whose brain has probably, decidedly, been enhanced in some regard – it is funny because one absolutely remains a child seeing how you aren't in charge; and if you're a child who's learned that complaining defeats achieving your desires faster than never having had those desires at all, then when you're looking in the eyes of the person who is in charge, and you want something really, really, really badly?

You get ever so humble and do a lot of praying that luck and self control are on your side. Ccwa would have argued, maybe even gotten unreasonably loud, then reasonably calmed down having measured the complexities of Brother Cheikh and fine tuned the sound logic of his method. But Ccwa, venerated elder who would have been listened to seriously had died a happy man, most likely, many dozens of thousands of years ago and I had to carry on as the boy I actually was. The child who was not in charge here, and so, couldn't – best not – start ranting and raving.

246

Well, truth be told, at least I was alive with lots more life to come if I kept my eyes open.

Softly I reminded the doctor, with intent eyes which caught his and refused to look away, "You said one time wouldn't be enough, and you were right. Please, sir. May I return once more and I won't ask again."

I figured curt requests were best with him.

His face, unreadable to start with, offered no clue to his thoughts, but the glint in his own eyes seemed to sparkle. He smiled.

"Take the mudpack off, son," he instructed.

My hand went immediately to my face, having altogether forgotten the wrapping that encircled my head, several times, and the pummeled cranium muscles underneath. I hadn't felt it, nor remembered it during my visit to venerated elder me of Manykeni. Finding the small metal fastener, I unhooked it, began unraveling the guaze, careful not to let the contents lop out as I pulled away the inner poultice and placed it on the table. I then felt where my bruised eye and lip...

should have been, only they weren't. Okay, both my eye and lip were there, of course, however, there was not only no pain, there was no tightness as I scrunched my face to search for it. My skin felt thoroughly healed as if it had never been wounded. Jubilant, but without a mirror to be certain I should be joyous, I smiled tentatively, expecting maybe an echo of pain. There wasn't even a memory of it.

"Today," the doctor said, seemingly out of the blue, handing me a dampened facecloth, which hung on the side of the wooden bowl that was still sitting on the table.

I looked at him, as I took the cloth answering, "Huh?" to his one word comment.

"You won't ask again, today," he detailed, adding, with continued lack of emotion in his expression as he looked unwaveringly into my eyes. "Wipe your face. There's cabbage leaves and mugwort stuck to it. Not that you have to look your handsome best going into the sphere, but as you never know what may greet you on the way back out, best to maintain neatness. Exiting can almost be as surprising as entering."

247

"Yes, sir!" I joyously snapped back, saying no more as the doctor stood, one last time beside me, at the ever present complete black hole, which remained the same size but without the moving stadium floodlights and gusting air intake system that I had no idea how that worked – after I laid the washcloth down, face clean and clear, had turned to face the orb, he joined me and with a gesture, a nod, and no words, either, with his hand he indicated that I should sweep my hand over the surface of complete nothingness as he had done, what seemed days ago, but had only been 20 minutes prior.

I ignored my reflex to hesitate because I didn't want to act ignorant as I had been paying attention on every floor of my growing multi-storied mind when he had powered Allah's Breath to life, before. So, precisely as he had done, I brought my hand to a hair's width above that missing surface, watching its floodlights glare to life as brightly as they had with his command and felt the wind once more push at my back. The doctor nodded his head, approvingly, as I stepped into...

~ ~ ~ ~ ~ ~ ~ ~ ~ ~ ~

... a hail of bullets!

Now bullets are serious as death, but to this day I don't know which pierced my attention first – that hail of bullets, the adrenaline that this me from another time was riddled with, or, the searing pain screaming from my right thigh where I knew I had been hit by one of those bullets, a second before I'd arrived. Or all of it at once, most likely, as this triple barrage came at me in the awareness of a man named Cletus Walker. And it came at me fast. I knew him completely, without thinking about it, in less than a second's second, seeing how Cletus was me.

This time I was the warrior in the middle of the war. Every noise, the way the wind blew, the angle of the sun, the distance between clusters of bushes, the short but deadly span of open grass before and between me and the safety of a thicket of dry cypress trees slightly to my right, their bottom heavy trunks offering desperately needed protection from bullets aimed at me – every molecule of this timeframe, I understood, instantly. I was alone, out here in the open, hiding in the midst of bushes and one thin young cypress, drawing our enemy nearer to my fellow warriors who lay in wait, deep within a waterless swamp – it all swept through my senses with hyper clarity.

248

There'd be no peace in this era. The Tamahue ruled, now.

I had to make that line of twisted gnarled trees, and bring my brothers a little gift, agonizing pain in my bleeding thigh or not. See, this wasn't about Cletus, like I was a paying visitor to a wax museum. This was about me. I knew the extra kink of my hair that resisted all grooming, so I shaved it bald whenever I could find a straight razor and a strop to sharpen the razor's edge. I knew Hoppin' John was my favorite food, with or without a slab of bacon - but it had to have lots of onions. I even knew why I was here, risking death in the dried out swamps to serve under the leadership of Commander John Horse. Truthfully? I knew what had made me a warrior who could move beyond the pain of wounds or fears. Just had to get beyond those bullets to keep on fighting.

The smell. It was that smell which never fully left my nostrils, as if I could sniff it out in the dry air, itself, a decade later. It was an acrid, yet horrifically sweet odor that felt as if, should I look around too carefully, I'd again see those flames leaping, dancing over what looked like cords of wood. Cords of wood that had been people, family, enjoying both kinship and friendship just the night past. I guess, lucky for me, though I wasn't sure about that luck at the time, it had been a bonfire of horror I'd seen from the distant safety of another thicket I had been dragged to by young John Horse, crack of dawn amid a frantic commotion of hooves, screams and white men's uniformed commands, and ghoulish laughter.
I hadn't known what was happening, as he'd covered my mouth with his only barely larger hand than my own. He dragged me up from my straw bedroll, out of a sound sleep in the darkness of my family's cabin, strenuously whispering that we had to run. And now.

We'd scrambled behind the rest of the cabins that his dad and mine had built 2 years before. They'd built them with the other men, some of whom were born free, most escaped. They'd thought this little encampment they named 'New Mose' was secure enough to occasionally attack the encroaching white settlers and their soldiers along with the slavery their permanent occupation would inevitably enforce - the men of New Mose thought the village was deep in Florida territory enough, secure enough, hidden enough to keep the women and children safe during the men's strategic attacks to dissuade our foes, however?

That morning, during my child years, when the men were on a raid, a troop of soldiers had found New Mose and that's why John and I ran, mostly crawled with panic into the yawning cover of the trees, as the commotion turned to shouts, the shouts to screams of agony, like nothing I'd ever heard cause I'd never been a slave. I'd been born free, like him in the Gullah, thus I didn't know there were those who wouldn't hesitate to kill the young and defenseless to increase the size of other men's profits.

We hid till there was no more sound from anything human. But to me the quiet that came wasn't interrupted with the usual morning birds' first chirping, either. Maybe they were singing their songs but I didn't remember as my nose took charge of my entire awareness, assaulted by that sickly sweet smell I could feel brushing the very hairs inside my nose with every breath I didn't want to take. You can never forget the sweetness of burning human flesh, especially when you knew that flesh had once been alive. You so much don't want anyone you love smelling remotely like what momma fixes for breakfast. You want it to smell like the horror it is. Like the horror you feel.

It was a wonder I could smell anything, after a mere whiff of that.

My mind, property of a man who'd been fighting back every day with no furlough, giving him massive hands on expertise – this mind was so full of spontaneous calculation, it instantly informed Tyree me to lay low or otherwise I'd have made some deadly error trying to crawl off. Well. The pain in my right upper thigh, with all the plentiful bloodflow one would expect, seeping through my thin black cotton pants leg into the muddy ground I was lying upon, that might have kept me still, safely hidden by the bushes, or it might have made me panic even more, scrambling into the open ground in the midst of real bullets that didn't sound anything like the bullets in movies I'd seen. Here, to my ears, gunshots sounded so tiny.
But not to Cletus. He'd never seen a movie and thus knew what or whatnot to do. And being he wasn't scared, neither was I, cause...

I was him.

Dear Lord! I hadn't wanted to leave them, but John had made me. Standing at the smoldering remains, after I could hear the birds singing again, as if nothing had ever happened, I couldn't get it in my little boy's head that they were gone. All of them. Everyone I'd known and loved. Burnt to a crisp before they could say 'Good Mornin'. Even lay in an unrecognizable pile of what were then to be called corpses, but just a moment ago had been all the people I'd known in life. There was my mother and all her sweetness that I couldn't recognize in the smoking remains. And there was Sarah. I recognized her. I recognized that my perfect chance to tell her how I loved her was laying twisted in that heap.

Sounds strange for a boy of 13 to feel true love, but? Little boys knew their minds back then, while Modern Black Boy me knew this because, as I said, it had been me standing at that smoking heap. I could see the wide contrast between my life in Newark and my life then. A child back then didn't have a choice but to study day to day details as we had lived before entertaining distractions got in the way of paying attention to life and –

to that small patch of Sarah's yellow shift dress that had evaded the flames... That patch that made me recognize, this body-like charcoal stillness was her. I pulled a small piece off easily from the rest of the charred embers. After carrying it in my pocket for a year or more, I'd placed it in a leather satchel, stringing that on a cotton cord which I never removed from around my neck. It hung there, now, while the bullets flew.

It was 1830, or something, as I didn't know what year it was cause I didn't know how to read and didn't really care about such things given the necessity of knowing other stuff – like how to build new cabins, deeper in the swampland and how to tease a whole regiment of soldiers, coupled with then running, bit by bit so they and their slavery would follow me to their mutual doom in an ambush, bullet or no bullet in the side of my leg, as paying attention to life had made me perfect at defending that life, under the leadership of John who went from being my rescuer to a rescuer and commander of men.

John Horse had been born in Florida, like me, a free man. Could have gone about his life as most did, but he'd never taken kindly to being told his were born to belong to any man but their own selves. Working from a small parcel of land he'd gotten from his father, we'd toiled diligently, growing that parcel into a fullscale sugar plantation. Sugar may be brutal work, but? It was sweet gold in the pocket.
In less than a decade we'd become rich enough to put that wealth into funding a war against the United States of America with Spain aiding our efforts. He was a battle strategy genius with a natural gift for inspiring men and his campaign, complete with armaments and soldiers' uniforms for the near thousand runaway Black men and the Native peoples assisting us, he was was highly successful; and having never had a defeat? We kept those white men from ever sleeping peacefully in Gullah Land.

We'd been burning down the sugar plantations across the border in Georgia, one by one, with an army of the righteously incensed former 'slaves' who knew

251

they weren't property, because tables and chairs don't smell sweet as they burn, and they don't complain when they don't like what's being served. After all, things not only can't run away, they can't fight to protect their right to live free.

Stupid fools, the U.S. Army! They wore these glaringly blue uniforms and always attacked in formation. We, Gullahs (that's what we called ourselves, while the white folks called us 'Black Seminoles', but we were no Indians) – we, Gullahs, had learned our lesson on tactics at The Negro Fort the British had built decades ago, which they gave us at the end of their battle with the colonists, rather than carry through on their promise to take us to England. Seemed white men everywhere were white men, everywhere.

Problem with that fort? Our people didn't realize that they were in a big ol' soup pot. When my father and the men had built New Mose on the Suwanee River, they stuck it deep in the swamps, not out in the open, but Negro Fort? It was a fort, for goodness sakes. Trees cleared from around it all the way to the shore of the Atlantic, from whence a U.S. Gunship blasted it to incinerated memory, back in 1816, and since that day, a date I remember? Slavery was still going strong and 'cause we didn't like what was being served, so were we. More and more, everyday, were running away from enslavement to join us, here. Why, the tale was more were coming to Florida than were going north, especially the 'I'm Not Furniture' fightin' kind.

We'd simply adopted the native people's fighting methods, picking the enemy off one at a time, which in tangled, slippery vegetation and, by the way? The jutting roots of the marshlands? Spelled 'doom' perfectly, for those blue feathered sitting ducks, even for me, whose expertise wasn't with the written word.

And I couldn't have been more educated, as I sure was equally skilled at fishing. Today's haul was a small contingent of bright but stupid blue uniformed soldiers, about a quarter of a mile back. They'd stopped firing, and that only meant they'd sent a scout up ahead. I knew the pattern, which never varied, and that's what I counted on as I couldn't linger behind this tree forever, as this wasn't Manyikeni (though Cletus didn't know anything about that). I continued the actions he had been in the midst of, without hesitation – tearing the sleeve off my white shirt, the handsome black private's jacket still hung half off on my left arm as my pride in it made me loathe to discard it. My empty rifle (I'd killed at least 3 of their men, I was sure) – my rifle was propped slightly up on the tree. I tore the sleeve into strips, linking them together, quickly, and tied the lengthened strand around my upper thigh. Then I tightened the bandage viciously, going past the self-torture (and trust me, like the difference between movie gunshot sounds and real ones? There is nothing that can prepare you for the totality of genuine pain that makes a punch in the face feel like a love tap. If not for Cletus' expertise, I'd have fainted from the agony) – I went past the level of red hot poker searing into my own flesh pain as I used a stick to twist and twist the tourniquet tight enough to stem the growing pool of my blood in the mud beneath me. There wasn't mud anywhere else but under my leg. I managed all this while not screaming, as I was Cletus and he knew a scream meant more than my death. It meant my failure, and the possible slaughter of my brothers.

As I did what I had to do, I wondered when the doctor would interrupt my ministrations to again yank me out from this brutal reality before I was ready to go. See, I didn't want to leave, insane as that sounds to you, reader, who's been with me through so much. I had a duty to perform that went easily past the duty I had to my flesh. Wrenching that tourniquet to halt the life that was flowing out of me, I was capable of enduring the torment only because, as a warrior, here, I had gone through worse, emotional and physical. I knew I had to reach my fellow warriors, if only to keep them from wandering into a reverse ambush that would turn them once more into tables and chairs, or worse, yet, cinders. Plus? There were many of our settlements, miles further within the swamp, full of the new innocently vulnerable young and old.

There were no excuses for me.

Short of bleeding to death or getting hit by several more bullets in un-tourniquet-able places, or an unwanted inquiry from the doctor, nothing would stop me. That's why I didn't mind not hearing a familiar, 'harrumph' as I twisted the stick I'd found at the base of the tree, examining my wound to ensure the gushing swirl of blood had slowed enough to make it the couple dozen yards into the swamp without collapsing from blood loss. And I'd have to get to those trees fast!

After securing that, I looked around for a length of branch, long enough this time to serve as a cane and facilitate my race to the scene of what I'd planned on being the enemy's ambush. That's when I heard the expected crack of dry fallen branches being stepped upon.

I, also, heard my heart pick up its beating, while Cletus' familiarity with man to man confrontation, thanks to his 14 years of experience, guided me to turn my eyes before my head and body, so as not to make the same noisy mistake this intruder had made. That they all made.

253

I could see his shoddy black boots right to the left of my covering, with a hole in them where the tip of a crusted sock poked through. Those boots were thinner than my own, and were all the view of him I could take in, as they crept slowly through the crunchiest part of the bramble, their owner not having learned how to pick the softest places for footfalls, how to be patient when scouting in order to live to scout again. I guess he thought he was looking for no more than a credenza or even less – a foot stool.

To my great advantage. If he had snuck up on me, silently, trodding on the sparser vegetation while I lay within a barely complete cover of bushes and behind a narrow years old tree, as close as he was, I'd have been dead in between twists of the tourniquet.

I wondered if I died here, would I be dead in Tyree's world, also?

No time for relaxing thoughts. Alerted, as he stepped one stride closer, I slipped the branch I had been seeking to use as a cane, and had gratefully found – I slipped it up between his next step and felt the weight of his body tumble, heard the sound of his outcry as he went down. He was heavy, reflexively attempting to jump back up, but not fast enough to escape my assault since I had planned my attack, and he'd been looking for a breakfast table. Propelling myself out of my sparse cover, I was on him, leg pain no match for my will to live and succeed.

Seems I was not only a huge, strong man, but my boxing skills were 1+1=2 accurate. That was more than simple enough mathematics for me. This soldier, this white man I found myself decking with a crushing right to the chin, whose name I didn't want to know as whatever he was called, for me, his name meant 'enslaver' – this man was out cold with that one punch. Whoa. Tyree me was quite impressed with the power in my fist. I saw why it can be tempting to become a bully once you've felt the surge of easy victory.

But not quite so easy since I still had to get out of there, and it was possible other scouts were nearby who'd heard this one's cry. As I always did before starting what seemed impossible, I touched the worn leather pouch tied about my neck, as a reminder of why I couldn't stop. Then, powerful me, by pulling myself up on the branch, grabbing the unconscious soldier's gun, and hooking it and mine onto my belt loop, I hoisted him by the collar, dragging him up like a sack of wet sugar, and draped him, hanging down over my back. A short stretch ahead would take me straight into the line of cypress as I counted on my enemy seeing that U.S. soldier's near turquoise blue jacket on top of my back, and thus not shooting their comrade. Without him, I knew, Cletus and I, we'd never make it. Into the breach I stepped, leaning on my branch with one arm and lugging my blue jacket wearing ransom note with the other.

I made it to the start of the yawning twisting tree line, and for a while so did my still breathing human shield, but? Although Cletus had calmly suspected the outcome, while I only woefully learned in a moment? There is no honor, no respect possible from those who can't see the difference between a work bench and a man. The troops opened fire. Several sickening dull thuds that nearly made me fall with the impact, but didn't cause me any pain, hit the soldier I was lugging. As soon as I made the depth of the canopy, standing cautiously behind those enormous tree trunks, I dropped my now lifeless cargo where it would never rise from, again. Funny how I could tell, even when one wasn't moving, a man was intended to be a man.

And to this day? To this after The Event, that We call 'Ubuntu', when we became unconditionally free? I found out what happened to Commander John Horse. He won. He and his men defeated the United States of America in the only successful slave rebellion in this country that the U.S. made daggone sure no one ever heard about. They made laws against mentioning his name in any classroom. But, I have yet to find out whatever became of that determined warrior, Cletus, because as he, as I headed on to join my brothers, bringing my gift of a big stupid fish, dressed in gloriously blue uniforms, I was pulled out of that timeframe and haven't managed to locate it since. Though seconds before my forced exit back into my Tyree world, it wasn't the doctor's voice, screaming, maximum volume in my mind, right then. I heard, instead, my sister Kyerah's piercing cry of...

"OH MY GOD, TYREE!!!! YOU'RE BLEEDING!!!!"

Geez. It was such a screech, you would have thought it was her who'd been shot!

255

=

"It's alright, dear!" Mrs. Kattan was saying as I saw the colors of Cletus' realm dissolved instantly into the world of the old me. Well, old, considering how much time I'd spent being Tyree, and that a couple days ago, this world had been all I knew.

"There's your brother, safe and sound."

And lo and behold, but there was my sister, Kyerah, sobbing, gripping some item in her clenched fist as the gold chain of what I knew belonged to the Aanda flowed out between her almond brown fingers. Actually, her fingers were slightly darker than her face as I note happens, sometimes, with us melanin rich folks.

But let me not waste time with unnecessary details as everything up close is more detailed than from afar. Use your own imagination. Think of your own life and its subtle uniqueness. My uniqueness is, I gotta finish this book, quick time...

My sister ran out of Sister Makeba's embrace to grip me, the moment I exited, almost tumbling us both backwards with the impact of her unbalanced weight, into the windsweeping vortex of the Orb. I could feel gravity taking charge of the top half of my body, abandoning my lower half that was responsible for me staying firmly where I was. I knew she didn't fully grasp there was a gaping hole right behind us.

'Not again!' I thought! "WHOA!" I cried!

Had Dr. and wife not been there to stop us, both, there'd have been another nail biting tale and a third accident to add onto this history, of sister and brother falling into Allah's More Than a Photo Album, with the Aandas, our only round trip tickets back out, going with us!

"Whoa!" I chimed, again, incredibly relieved, as their arms encircled us, together, stopping our wobble one weeble before we fell in.

Kyerah's eyes, previously stuck on grief, suddenly opened wide with the proximity of danger to her own self, now. The couple walked us to the kitchen table, their arms draped around our shoulders and we sat down without protest. That's when Kyerah, mute from the near fall, suddenly shouted at me, pointing down at my bluejeans clad leg,

"Hey! Your leg! Tyree! But you were wearing black pants. I saw them, and you were bleeding!" She turned a sharp glare at the Kattans, one after the other while only Sister Makeba sat down at the table same as we did.

Not wanting to be the kowtowed little brother as she had interrupted my duty as Cletus, the definition of a full grown non-kowtowed man, plus? I had some things of my own to say, with "There's no bullet wound now. I'm fine," and I snapped my retort out, sharply.

"Bullet wound?!" She asked, horrified, while I was still talking, as she stared at my leg, once more. Obviously she hadn't known why I had been bleeding while I was Cletus, let alone that my leg was whole, once more.

"What are you doing here, Kyerah? That's what I want to know!"

"Yes," The doctor agreed, looking quite stern, "I'd like to know that myself." He went over to the Orb, still expanded, still its own gust chamber of apparent nothingness, where he waved his hand and fingers with that detailed precision over its surface like a dance.

Sister Makeba nodded her head, in concord with what the doctor and I had said, looking equally gravely at my sister.

"Are you in the habit, Kyerah, of trespassing on other people's property?" she asked, point blank.

Caught in her own wrong, a wrong which I was surprised to hear she'd committed since she almost never did anything outside the rules that would then require her to be contrite – and boy, was she expertly contrite that minute – her plain as the guilt on her face silent confession made my own eyes widen with the newness of it, while Kyerah's shocked features had suddenly softened to a guilty as charged look. Her eyes went downward to gaze at the red slate floor. There were no cracks in that floor.

"I'm so sorry about that," she said. "I didn't mean for you to find me and cause a problem."

"Child," the doctor said with his deep Senegalese flare, as the gigantic hole he had been sweeping his hands about without touching, shrank instantly to a little hole in the sienna colored mud cover it sat upon, silencing the blustering air flow about the room with a soothing 'whoop' sound. "The problem began the moment you thought about doing such a thing. Does your mother know you're here?"

I don't think my big sister was listening. Who could in the midst of the fantastical come to life?

"What is that thing?!" she asked, hypnotized, same as I had been the other day.

"Something your brother will now have to explain, later, along with the strict need for secrecy," he answered, placing The Breath into its pouch. "But, I need your explanation about what you did, now."

He came back to the table, placing his hand, palm up, between us. It took a moment for me to realize what he meant.

"Oh!" I said, reaching around my neck and unhooking the bauble still hanging there by its gold chain, almost expecting the dirty leather pouch with Sarah's bit of torn shift inside to be there, instead. I nodded my head towards Kyerah, who was clenching the Aanda's partner as tightly as ever in her fist, understanding dawning in her eyes, so she then placed her gem with mine in the doctor's open hand. He put them both in their own separate pouch, and placed them and the Orb's pouch into that.

"Yes, Kyerah?" The doctor took a seat, expectantly, and my sister 'explained' how she'd been worried about me, prompting her to come snooping at the back windows where she'd tripped over an unseen rake. That made the racket that alerted Mrs. Kattan, who then alerted the doctor. This was why my communication with Dr. Kattan had been interrupted when I was Ccwa and had later gone completely silent while I was Cletus. During that first investigation, they had found nothing apparently amiss since my sister had scrunched deep down behind a set of rain cisterns. The doctor returned to the Orb to assist me out of Ccwa's timeframe and Sister Makeba got back to transplanting some tomatoes; but then Kyerah made the same mistake that soldier had, crunching on a few twigs underfoot, barely hidden within a 6ft high cluster of hydrangea bushes next to the barrels. Stretching upward in an attempt to get a clear look through one of the kitchen windows is how she saw me disappear before her eyes into a huge black hole on my second entry. She gasped, leaving no doubt for Mrs. Kattan that there was an intruder in her garden. The hydrangeas were pushed aside by the livid Sister, who was soon joined by the doctor, whom she'd called again, upon discovering Kyerah.

Apparently, my sister, making such a noisy spy, hadn't understood much other than what she described to us, but? I have to admit, I wasn't that angry any longer. I was flattered that my usually dutiful sister had pretty much skirted the edge of criminality to discover (as you already knew she had planned, reader, but was news to the Kattans and myself) – she had trespassed to discover why I had vehemently insisted on coming to my new 'job', despite my injuries...

my injuries... oh, yeah.

"Hey!" she interjected, staring aghast at my smooth, unbruised face. "What the heck?"

She pointed at my leg, again, too.

"What is this?" she questioned, grabbing my face, firmly but not painfully, by the chin to closely peer at my eye and lip as if this were a trick of the lighting, although the daylight was still streaming in the banks of the windows. I relaxed through her amateur exam, without protest, admitting to myself, anybody would be astounded. Annoying as she could be at times, here, I agreed with her shock. *What is this?* my thoughts repeated, exactly.

"I'm not sure, either, Kyerah," I said, "but whatever it is, it's wonderful, not bad."

"And whatever it is," the doctor added, "must never be shared with anyone outside this kitchen. So, young lady, I repeat. Does your mother know you're here? For that matter, you don't have any other friends lurking about the lilac bush?"

"Uh?" she responded startled, not expecting his jovial ribbing. "Oh, NO! Brother Doctor, my mom thinks I'm at the store getting garbage bags and light bulbs. Really, it's not like you might believe. I'm not stalking you or that... that thing." Shocked realization took over her face, once more, as she shouted, "That thing that almost killed my brother!"

"Ah," he nodded. "I don't know what happened but I guarantee, it was a human being who almost killed another manifestation of Tyree; not this object. The Orb doesn't kill anybody. It can't. It's merely a recording. A sort of book. But it especially wouldn't kill him. He's its Protector. The Protector can't die in The Breath."

259

"He's its what?" she asked as my multilevel brain noted the answer to one of my million questions. "And he can't die in the... the...," she continued in a sputter. "...the Breath? Maybe you didn't see it, but I did! He was bleeding in there! Heavily!"

"And as you now see, daughter, he's not bleeding out here. There's not even the bruises he went into the Orb with."

She did a quick look back at me, then returned to stare mutely at Dr. Kattan as he'd hushed her up effectively with that one, while the ensuing silence amplified the buzzing of a fly near Kyerah's open mouth. She brushed it aside before it flew in, as the doctor went on...

"The Protector is the only being the Orb...? Let's say, 'respects'. Or even better? Notices. You? If you fell in? In sight of 5 minutes, you wouldn't even remember this life. Wouldn't remember your own name. Oh, yes. You, now, can surely die, should you find yourself inside it. For that matter, my wife or even I could die in there, now; though I've traveled through its realms hundreds of thousands of times. But I'm no longer its 'Protector', Tyree is."

I was worried that fly would happen upon Kyerah's sudden new habit of keeping her mouth hanging open like that. Luckily he'd flown off to some other locale in the kitchen.

"It's okay, Kyerah," I exclaimed. "I wasn't even scared. I wanted to fight Cletus' battle. I was Cletus! Only, I still remembered who I am. But he was amazing! Did you see me deck that soldier with one punch?! POW!" I recalled that power packed moment and demonstrated, at the table, with my fist.

My effort, sadly, was unconvincingly weak. I mean, though my dad had taught me the basics, admittedly? He should have stuck with science, not 'fisticuffs'. Anyone could have seen, if I'd have defended myself from that soldier with that amateur punch, Cletus would have been killed by a really ticked off, deadly white guy in a shabby bright blue uniform.

"What the?" I gasped.

Sister Makeba's husband, put his head down, shaking it woefully as it went slowly. His wife smiled, shaking her head side to side, more gently.

"Oh, Tyree," she began. "I'm sorry I missed your stunning punch. I'm sure it

260

was something to have taken out a mortal foe trained to fight, but any skill a previous incarnation of you had?" She harrumphed! "Your muscles have memory. These muscles you have now, I mean. They have no memory of being anyone but Tyree. Any skills another timeframe of you had acquired? Unless you perfected, here, what they learned same as they did, there? Perhaps undergoing decades of instruction? Your present muscles don't have a clue how to perform the same tasks. Having seen the doctor gain hundreds of different skills, instantly – he remembers the details, but not the expertise."

The doctor looked up, with a pretty accurate repetition of the exhausted look he'd had the other day. His muscles were getting plenty of practice at being frustrated with American children.

"Son," he said, "Whatever you do, don't go around thinking you're Cletus, now, chasing after that guy who decorated your face with those bruises you had." Concerned he added, "You die in the Orb? You pop back out here, straight away. However, get yourself killed here, and it's over. Go. Sign up for that boxing class, karate, Afrikan defense. Learn how to protect yourself, here."

"What is that thing," my sister asked again, her voice drained of anger, replaced with the wonder of it all, "Is this magic, only for real?"

The doctor smiled, saying, "Magic for real. Charming. And Gainde wondered why we're so secretive," – saying this almost to himself. To us, he stated, "Again, as I told your brother, yesterday? Dear girl, there is no such thing as 'magic'. There is only Allah and if one of us had been stuck in nothingness like He was, for seeming eternity, we just might have figured out how to create the science He has, most of which we still don't understand. What you don't understand can seem magical, especially the more advanced it is; but, maybe we'd have been able to birth ourselves, eventually, like Him. Maybe. And then, maybe I shouldn't have let you back in the Orb so quickly, Tyree, with so much to teach you about its peculiarities. But, I was so enthused..."

"Peculiarities?" I broke in.

"Of course. We're talking about the memories of a Man, not a computer. There's always more to learn whenever you attempt to get know a person, or this greater lesson we are all going through would be done and obviously, it's not."

Not understanding what he meant, "What?" both I and my sister said in unison. If this hadn't been such a fantastical moment, I'd have turned on her

261

jokingly shouting, "You owe me a coke!" That's a little game our 3D realm played during our un-godly days. It wasn't an un-godly game, but just as grown-ups have a hard time explaining details to children, and since I am trying to keep this more brief, I, also, won't try to explain the minutiae of my childhood games. It's those details I don't have time for and you probably don't need to know.

Though? There's a detail here that you'll understand towards the end of my chronicle (if I remember to mention it in my hurry to enscript this tale). Years after insisting we all go vegan, my dad began including strange additions to our diet, such as green drinks with chlorella and somethin' he called 'Liposomal Vitamin C', while heavily processed anything, like cereals, sugary snacks and sodas were outlawed in favor of homemade and homebrewed. We ate the occasional potato chips and vegan pizzas, but he had to okay it first. Kyerah and I continued to play the 'You owe me a soda!' game, out of habit, like you say, "God Bless You,' after a sneeze, long after the reason why the world started the habit has been discredited.

But I recall in those last sensitized days, walking on pins, dad had spent much of his jobless time in his office and 'poisoned food' being shipped to our Black community had become his preferred topic of conversation.

Almost an obsession. Proof he had been going crazy, it'd seemed to me at the time.

But brief, Akhenaten. Gotta keep it brief. I think I see Brother Patrice Lumumba heading my way, so more on this, as I said, if I remember. If not then, it'll be in the next book as it's critical...

"Nothing I have time to explain, children," the doctor said, standing up, placing the pouch in his white linen pants pocket. "Kyerah, I have great faith that your brother understands the enormity of our situation, why knowledge of the Orb is not for idle gossip. He can give you the rudiments so that, if you like, with our guidance, you can assist him in exploring the Orb."

My sister, burst at the seams, saying with anticipation, "I still don't understand, but okay!"

Mrs. Kattan grabbed her hand and squeezed it, warmly. "You will understand, Beloved. You will."

"Brother Cheikh, I have one question," I chanced. "If I can't take the skills

262

from past lives into this one, can I take the skills from this one into them, in turn?"

"Oh! That's a good question! Well, it's a struggle as that memory is set to do as it did in real past time, but, as Protector, you take all that you now are into that manifestation. It's like the saying, 'Hindsight is 20/20'; only in the Orb, Hind-Existence is everything. Learn more here and you can do more there."

"Wow," I said. "So if I learn to fight here, say I run across a me that couldn't?"

"He'd be able to kick butt," Mrs. Kattan stated, one eyebrow knitted.

Giggling, my sister added, "That'd be great if you can keep your own behind from being kicked, since whatever that Orb thing is, it won't be fighting for you, out here!"

I shyly smiled. "Well, a friend told me about a defense class. Guess I'll check it out."

The doctor, involved in his private task of reloading the rebellious bookcart with those monstrous volumes, seemed in a hurry to move on to some other unrevealed task he had to do. He halted, mid moderate sized book to cart, immediately upon hearing his wife respond...

"Why Gainde teaches just such a class downtown. He's quite the champion fighter. He can teach you!"

A huge "HARRUMPH!" issued from the doctor like what rightly terrified the citizens of Ancient Pompeii from Mt Vesuvius, almost as much as it would have terrified me if I wasn't so calm. Startled my sister, though.

"Excuse me, dear wife" he gently spoke while grimacing, "but may I speak with you?"

They went to the first island kitchen counter and began to whisper quietly between each other. My sister and I stood up from the table, sauntering to the swinging door, wanting to get a polite distance from the exchange, and knowing it was time to leave. With nothing to look at in particular since we couldn't exactly stare at them, we looked around, halfheartedly, feigning no interest while their whispering went from barely audible to still too low to discern what was spoken, but was nonetheless intensely grumbled.

263

More shortly than it seemed, Mrs. Kattan, a sweep of grace as serene as morning sunlight, returned to us, Mr. Kattan directly behind, hands clasped, militaristically behind his back.

"I am so sorry, Brother Tyree," the sister said, looking resolved, yet sympathetic. "Truthfully, recommending Gainde has proven too problematic."

I was curious to know the reason, but with so much else on my dolby stereo mind, I diplomatically answered, "Oh, that's okay. I'll check out the place my friend mentioned."

"A fine plan," the doctor announced, slapping me firmly on the back of my shoulder in a way that told me, mine and my sister's visit was done.

"Thank you, sir."

"Um," probably picking up on the same silent signals, herself, as I was, Kyerah said, "We'd better go. Shouldn't take this long to buy lightbulbs."

"Guess it depends on the type of light needed," the doctor's wife commented, looking wistfully away, adding, "Yes. She might be worried about you, by now. Best be on your way."

"But be sure to get those items," Brother Cheikh advised. "...or she'll wonder even more where you'd gone. I don't like this situation one bit as it's wrong to lie to your mother, to anyone, but, Tyree will explain so you understand the enormity of the situation." He looked at Kyerah intently, "And why you must agree you came here to pick him up, and lingered longer than you should have without mentioning what you saw. The Orb is not family dinner table conversation."

Kyerah looked strangely at me, then, and for the first time I'd ever seen in this lifetime at least, it was a look full of both respect and something else I detected, ever so faintly. I think it was the tiniest bit of envy. Very, very tiny. Nah! I must have been wrong. Must have been her own spiraling emotions.

I'd do my best to clear up any questions she might have. Just couldn't do anything to address her answers.

~ ~ ~ ~ ~ ~ ~ ~ ~ ~

And I had been right the night before. She'd have never believed a word I would have said if she hadn't seen the Orb for herself. Even then, she mightn't have believed if she hadn't, also, seen what it did through my own eyes, since she in turn told me that when the Kattans found her on her tiptoes, peeking into their kitchen window about to faint - to reassure her that I was okay after disappearing before her eyes, they'd taken her inside and handed her the Aanda - if she hadn't seen through my perception that I was someone else altogether, named Cletus, for real? Then she'd have proven my prediction that she'd have found me 'crazy' and would of had me committed. As it stood, knowing I was telling the truth, she only wanted me doped up on Ritalin, not smashed out on Thorazine - which I would have recommended to myself, yesterday.

But, for me? That was only if I hadn't been able to go over to the Kattans. Now that that cat was satisfied, I was fine. Shoot. I was better than fine. I was Akhenaten, Ccwa, Cletus and I'd had wives.

Okay, she didn't exactly say she wanted me on meds, but I could tell by the way she blurted out, "You're crazy, Tyree!" after I tried to explain my adventure, that she'd have broken open her glass piggy bank to pay for the prescription.

Funny, how I'd wanted that to be my reputation - 'Don't Mess With That Crazy Tyree', but after all I'd come to realize through the lives I'd lived before and this one wherein the volume of my comprehension had been turned way up, it frustrated me, now, hearing it from her when everything I was saying made such perfect sense...

But all this came after leaving that mansion, as we headed to the store and back home, with me going over the whole incredible experience, from tripping over my feet, falling through nothingness, to her as a velvet skinned Sitamen, to my new perception, to the other past lives, and oh. To that little detail about a war. A 6,000 year old one, at that. My big sister didn't care for the details of that part, whether near or far - not one bit. And I'll get to our conversation that we had, after what came once we said our goodbyes to Dr. and Mrs. Kattan. Stepping out the closing door to head to the discount store, my head had turned forward to see....

Von.

Across and only slightly up the street. He was standing on a porch of a particularly anemic green house, with that same 'Can't Hang Out on the Corner 'Cause Those are Real Men There, So Let's Hang Out on the Front Porch, Instead', group of teenagers I had been amazed by the truth of, the other day. Today's truth?

Well, the sound of Dinah Washington's 'What a Difference a Day Makes' was suddenly played in the basement of my office tower mind. Those Tyrees were proclaimed the comedians of the building. Hardee-har-har-har.

Kyerah noticed my minute hesitation.

"What?" she asked, almost sounding like her past self from another time. "Something wrong?"

I'd hoped he hadn't seen me, but exactly when I recognized him, his eyes were focused in my direction. He nodded his head at me, slowly, but this time, boxing skills or not, Cletus was me. I wasn't scared.

"Come on," I said smoothly, gently pushing her to walk to our right, down the circular driveway. It was a choice based on calculation, not on fear.

"Wait! The store's the other way!"
"They shut down those streets."

"They shut down all those...? Wait a minute!" and she stopped, turning to me, "What's going on, Tyree?"

'Geez,' having no idea what lay ahead in the future for We, Gods – I thought, 'wouldn't telepathy be great to have right now?'

"I'll tell you as we walk," I said, terribly audibly. "But we have to go and this way. Trust me, alright?"

It must have been something in my voice, that made my big sister say, "Okay," with no hesitation. Telepathy Lesson #1: Ya gotta feeeeeeeel whatchu say.

"That was the guy who decked you?!" she exclaimed as we circled an extra block around, in the wrong direction, soon as I told her who saw us coming out of the Kattan's.

"Do you think he was waiting for you?" she asked.

I distinctly sensed Von was as surprised as I was, and like me, he was a good actor.

266

"No." I answered. "That's his friend's house. He hangs out there all the time."

"What? Do you know him?"

"In a way, but not really."

"Huh?"

And that's when the long explanation of the Magically Not Magical at All Accidental Adventure got going. You can re-read pages 54 thru this page in case you missed anything. Probably scan pages 6 to 14, for total clarity, but I don't have time to repeat all that. This is a history book, so that means - Pay Attention. And study as many real history books as you can find. You'll find yourself in them, so it doesn't matter if I have no idea how to write this one in a more marketable style, that would make it an easier read.

Hmmm. Isn't this interesting? Seems like I'm getting a bit more brusque as this is the time to complete this work or, oops! Is that Sister Ida B. Wells I see smiling at me from across the aisle with Sister Assata Shakur? I am waving and they're returning it. Okay. Now, they're looking back at the podium. Whew!!! Now, where was I?

Oh, getting to the part where my big sis said I was nuts. It was when I'd finished the basics and got to describing The Ankh Udje Saneb to Sitamen - oh! I mean, when I got to describing it to Kyerah, that's the time I had to mention white people's role in a war against Black and Brown people, and thus? Not being able to fault her for not realizing there was a war, that's where we get to her exclamation of...

"You're crazy Tyree!"

She shouted this in the 'Family Savings Galore' store, as we looked for the aisle with the light bulbs, and then she promptly lowered her tone, although I hadn't asked her to speak more quietly and I didn't lower mine's. I wasn't shouting, though - simply talking in a normal volume that anybody near could hear, if they Paid Attention. I didn't mind speaking in a normal tone as I wasn't talking about the Orb. I'd finished with that part.

Again, she repeated the diagnosis of my mental state according to her, in a forced whisper, leaning towards me, professionally adding,

"How can that be true? All white people aren't bad!"

"I didn't say that," I replied. And, once more, reader, I was extremely calm, talking to her. I had no need to shout or whisper as I was certain of my conclusion, at peace with the truth of it. My body language reflected that, which strangely made my sister calm down herself.

"I didn't say they're all bad, as that's impossible," I continued. "When nations go to war, it's not about the regular individuals, it's about the systems that're run by the powerful individuals."

She paused for a moment, contemplating what I'd said. Buoyed by a sudden defense, she retorted, "But Black people aren't a 'system'. We don't have a nation in the United States. It's one country. Plus, it's a democracy. We can vote for change."

I grabbed a couple boxes of bulbs, not even looking at her, answering, "How has that turned out?" Thank Goodness, I thought, Kyerah was a reader, coming from reading parents and thus was well acquainted with all the recent tragic disappointments we Black people were facing; otherwise her 15yrs of life would have doomed her to not know what I was talking about and she'd have been defending the ignorance a book-less life would have made certain. That'd have been a much longer conversation, and The Ubuntu was merely days away, even if we didn't know. Everything wouldn't have happened the tragic way it happened, so quickly, and this history book would hafta be as big as the one the doctor wheeled into the kitchen that day...

Without losing a breath, she answered, "It's turned out a lot better than going up against the United States Army with a bunch of pitchforks would have turn out."

I placed 3 boxes of bulbs in the basket she held.

"Because you're scared, that's a reason to accept a broken system that never changes no matter who's in office? That's a reason to tolerate injustice? To tolerate another Trayvon?"

"You're twisting what I'm saying! I'm not scared. I'm realistic. We're all one human race, Tyree. And look how many Black people have made it! Have you forgotten where we used to live?!" Her voice went up almost to the level her diagnosis of me had been.

"Oh. Yeah. We were free. Tell, me, then. Have you ever heard of Manykeni?"

"Many-what?"

"Exactly. Here upper middle class Black us went to Black schools run by Black people and they never taught us anything about ourselves before The Slave Trade. Before they kidnapped... no! They abducted us 'cause if you kidnap somebody, you hold them for a ransom you get from their family and then you're supposed to return them. You get the money, or you kill 'em. You don't keep them and their children for 400 years, building whole institutions based on keeping them ignorant, poor and on lockdown. Why, they don't teach us about any of our pre-abduction history, like we never existed before they, ahem! 'Found' us swingin' from trees. They don't even teach about John Horse..."

"Look, I don't know what that Many-something is, or who's John Horse, but I know to make it in this world, you need the education that's going to open doors. Spoutin' some obscure trivia during job interviews will slam the door on your face."

But I wasn't listening, or at least most of my mind wasn't paying direct attention. I'd heard her. However, I was looking at the bulbs in the basket. It was the same CFL brand we always buy, but horrified by what those bulbs told me, I started taking them out, and putting them back on the shelves.
"Yo, dude? What the heck are you doing?" Kyerah protested. "We're here to get bulbs, remember, not re-arrange the shelves."

"No. Not those bulbs." I searched and located the incandescent ones, down on the last shelf, only a few packages available. "There's something wrong with those. These are safer." I placed all the boxes I could locate, about 5, in the basket. There were dozens and dozens of CFL boxes on the shelf, in contrast.

"What the?", she asked. "Whatever. I hope this experience hasn't turned you into some kind of weirdo."

"Define 'weirdo'?"

We went to the garbage aisle. I mean – the plastic packaging section.

"Weirdo! Where you're not like most people. Where you become a freak loner."

Ooo. That changed my calm state a small degree, as I truly didn't want to be all

269

by myself, sorta like the Kattans, though, that's what I felt had been happening, lately, despite the incredible discovery of the Orb. Good thing, the 4th floor came to my rescue. Not just for the sake of the debate, but for the sake of my own worries.

"Then dad was a weirdo, also."

She brought out that forced whisper again, and this time, I guessed, she was at least attempting to mask the depth of her affront.

"How can you say that? Dad was brilliant!"

"Exactly, Kyerah. Dad did what he knew was right, not what was popular. We live in a world where thinking outside the norm is suspect. Who do you know who was like him? Who has the courage to change when the cold facts are staring at them? Who does that in this world you wanna study so carefully? That's not a good system when being brilliant is abnormal."

"So, what? Not everybody can be Einstein. Plus? Have you got a substitute for this 'system'? Or better yet, you think white people," she started whispering, softly, again. "You think white people are just gonna give us a chunk of their country and say, 'Thanks for all the memories, pal! Here's Nevada, Colorado and Arizona...'?"

I looked at her, with all my concentration, and? That's a whole lot of concentrating. We were standing in the checkout line, without a single white person inside the store, (or outside, for that matter) - except for one extra pink guy whom I took to the be owner, since he rushed in, looking very self-governing, telling his Black employees what shipments were being delivered the next morning.

I didn't need it to, but that white man's aura glaringly confirmed my analysis that only a plantation owner's aura would have been more smug. He was frightened but he felt triumphant as what he feared was wholly subservient to him. He was the proud hunter with the trophy heads of those he'd slaughtered, not splattering his living room walls but doing check-out and restocking his store's shelves. This white man was happy, and if the plantation owners weren't buried in their graves, I was pretty sure their auras would have radiated the same story.

Staring intently, now, at my sister's aura (which until then, still hadn't been as clear to me as everyone else's I'd observed outside my home) - despite the

270

warmth of her glow I could see she was as frightened as, if not this triumphant white businessman, here, whose terrors were, so far as he was concerned, under his control – she had a lesser kind of the same on fire fear that Mr. Lewistein had. See? Both felt their fears controlled them. The difference? He was terrified of losing everything, which gave him no hope; while she was afraid she'd never get not what she wanted, but what she needed. She'd substitute with trivial stuff in the meantime, obviously, as she not only didn't know what she needed, she didn't know that she needed it, terribly, like a hunger of the soul. And though in contrast to my big sis, darn near all the white people's fears were their core, occasionally flecked with hard won happiness, her fears suffocated her joy that was her bedrock. Fear was the poor soil thrown on top of her denatured harvest. It was starving, forming a well of emptiness within that should I stare deep into her eyes, would have consumed me entirely in a desperate attempt to fill itself. I could obviously tell, between both Kyerah and Mr. Lewistein? Neither one knew they had fears at all.

Making both crazy as Hell, only for real. Everybody around me, I could see, was a little insane. I just didn't love, nor respect Mr. Lewistein's mental disability.

Maybe seeing my sister, then, as I knew her personally, became a key to understanding everyone around me, better, because whereas I'd been overwhelmed by the warmth of their auras, earlier – right then I could sense the same hunger from each Black person in that store, even the most at peace ones. Even the most clueless. Each place I roamed from thenceforth, I could hear their deep insides grumbling a ravenous ache for the sustenance their existence craved because fake food is no substitute for nutrition, no matter if it's not one's body that's malnourished, but the spirit, that propels the body to love. Everyone was starving off of meals of fake life.

I was quiet as my sister handed the cashier our mother's scant money, wanting so much to say,

"The white man's going to give us back the whole planet, one day" but, I couldn't as I didn't have any proof. I didn't even feel that, completely myself, since I couldn't guarantee any future with the Ankh Udje Saneb up ahead and knowing no way to fix it, quickly. I felt no fear, however, honestly? I couldn't see my own aura, at all, right then, to confirm my authority to proclaim my faith in our certain victory was 100%. Maybe there was nothing to hope for, given the harsh soil of this world's reality. Thus, responding to Kyerah's comment, I said –

"I don't know."

"There!" she retorted with no worries about being overheard, now.

She grabbed the handles of the bag, brusquely, that the cashier, dressed in a brown hijab head wrap, handed her. That was out of character for her usual politeness. Or her politeness to everyone, back in Sandstone. This sister, didn't appear to notice, but I spied the fraction of a second her aura was insulted, and its smooth recovery as she continued her duties with the next patron in line. She'd gotten used to rude customers, like my blood sister, stereotypically, demonstrated quite well, that moment.

I smiled, at her, trying to make up for the rudeness, but the woman paid me no heed, in turn. Together, Kyerah and I left, to a still well lit daytime, walking the extended way home where Von had been hoping we'd return, because he'd been waiting for us, and I could see his own confused stereotypical plans screaming out in that silent desperate language of the famished soul.

=

"I am Sophonisba, unwitting owner of a face that is my hapless undoing. A face which has brought me into the awareness of men and beasts who have used it like a play piece in a children's game. A face others call the most beautiful in the world for its incomprehensible blackness – its full lipped delicate balance. A marvel for me to look upon, also. But I have found it, in usage, to be a face that is my curse, for the rapture it causes has brought death to thousands in wars waged for the right to marry me, its victim. Or worse, some desire nothing less than to rip me apart, no matter that I am not the maker of what causes others ceaseless yearning. Though, initially, as a younger child, I found all this flattering – especially when I was still protected by my people; but now, with my enemy's victory assured, those Roman Barbarians certain to drag me naked through their streets, past their sun starved till they're blanched and sickly to look upon – past their gathered masses, who'd be jeering, lusting, loathing because they can never be us – I want none of the agony having such beauty has brought. I only wish to live a good and virtuous life as my father taught me, however, instead? Even he pawned me off to the highest bidder and nothing I call me, even this cursed face, do I truly own. Only my mortal fragility remains firmly within my grip.

And that grip is eternal, for I am Sophonisba of the Sun Drenched Lands, the Land of the Gods. Therefore, I choose if today will be the day I close my eyes on this face for the final time. Let it live in the hearts of kings, the loins of dogs, but let me kill the body, willingly, with one word from my new husband, Massinissa, son of Gala, King of Massylia, with whom, our nuptials may have lasted longer than the few euphoric days which ushered hence, if but for this dangerous visage I wear as flesh. He has proven to be the one and only man I can and must trust. I can and must trust him to tell me if I, daughter of General Hasdrubal of Carthage, if I, this day, shall use my own hands to staunch this beautiful affliction which refuses to stem its pitiless perdition upon the poor woman who endures its curse."

=

After more arguments back and forth between my sister and myself, quietly in her and mom's room while the matriarchs watched a movie up front – arguments that went like:

Me: God will save us.

Her: God? And exactly where is this 'god', huh?

Me: You saw the Orb. Imagine what He's like if those are His memories.

Her: I saw a... what did you call it? A PHOTO ALBUM, Tyree. It was definitely amazing, but, it doesn't do anything, so that's not God.

Me: It's evidence.

Her: Of what? That He's on permanent vacation and every now and then He pastes up some snapshots? I've got a Facebook account with a photo section, too, but those photos won't save the world.

After our on and on tug of theological war, with me no closer to convincing her than when I'd first mentioned this thousands of years old real war, we were too tired to care anymore, and I'd attempted to end the simpler tussle with an exhausted 'goodnight', when, her tone sounding more agreeable, almost like Sister Makeba's, like Nyisha's, she took advantage of the pause to ask,

"Tyree? Was the Orb the real reason you'd ask me, yesterday, if I'd ever felt like I'd been alive before?"

"Yes. You'd have figured I'd really gone insane if I'd told you the truth," I answered, a little tired of our verbal volleying and not wanting to go wherever she was planning to take this random question. I knew it had to go somewhere, but had no energy left to go there with her, enthusiastically.

"You got that right. I'd have sewn you a straight jacket that night. But, you said you were wondering whether Dad would be re-incarnated?"

"Yes." Hopefully he will, in a nice less argumentative family, my worn out

274

basement mind proposed.

"Well? Why should we wait for some distant time in the future to meet him again? We won't even remember this lifetime. Why not enter the Orb and warn him before the accident?"

I sighed, almost harrumphed – so much did I wish that were possible, that my fourth floor commenced with the calculations.

"The doctor said it won't work," I exhaled. "Each life coil is a magnetic force of its own, and shortly after the Protector does anything that interferes with that force, the sequence will go right back to where it was predetermined to go, anyway. If I were to meet him in the Orb, it wouldn't be the actual him."

"Oh." She looked down at her Tropicana colored sasquatch slippers. I was sitting in one of those high back dining room chairs (we'd had 10, but now only the 5), set up against the wall, while she sat on the edge of her and my mom's medium sized bed. Same size as the one my grandma and I shared, only, to get around, you didn't have to squeeze between it and the dressers, here, in my mom's and sister's room.

Her head popped back up, "Well, maybe if only to see him again? 'Cause if you see him, so do I with the Aanda."

"That'd be great, sis, but? The Orb is... complicated. It's not like some H.G. Wells, 'The Time Machine' kinda thing with dials you can set. The doctor says after a while I'll get a better understanding of picking the destination, but for now?"

"It's hit or miss?" She answered my question, looking off as if accepting that somebody had, indeed, stolen her lollipop away.

"We could try, though, until we get it right," I offered. I didn't want to see that thread pulled loose, worried that it held back a torrent of her tears I remembered more clearly than I remembered the amount of time since they'd stopped.

"Yeah. That'd be great." She turned back to me, lollipop gone for good, but dry eyed, like a baby beyond its years. "Look, I'm not going to accept all this war with white folks talk, or the 'All Praises to Allah' stuff, either, but, if I can see dad, again? I'll spend every summer in this godforsaken place till the day I die. Okay?"

275

I should have been excited, but I only felt strangely disheartened.

"Okay."

I slept on the couch that night, after mom and grandma had finished their movie and gone to bed. Neither questioned my impromptu desire to spend the night in the cramped living room because truly the couch was enormously cozy, making sense it'd be far more comfortable than sleeping next to my gently snoring grandma.

Mom brought out some sheets, a real pillow which she fluffed after setting the other ornate ones on the other 2 seater couch, and sat with me for a moment, not saying anything. It was a little awkward, but I knew it was what she needed, though I didn't. I wasn't the same son she'd said 'Good Morning' to at the start of 2 days ago.

I broke the silence.

"How's the job search going?"

She sighed, saying, "It's only just started. I'm sure I'll find something."

'Something' I knew meant 'Not so good', but she couldn't say that as 'Head Mom in Charge'.

"You'll find one, soon," I reassured her.

"Yeah."

The silence interrupted us, again.

"So," she broke it, this time, after a few nervous smiles between us both, "...it went okay with Dr. Kattan?"

Not knowing what would qualify as 'okay' or not, and wanting to minimize the time I would have to talk about my visit without talking about my visit, I answered, "It was great, mom," without too much exuberance; without sounding like I was giving her the brush-off.

It was pretty funny how she answered, "You're giving me the brush-off, aren't you?" She squinted her eyes at me, crumpling her Afrikan nose at the same

276

moment in a signature Renee Jackson expression. It occurred to me she'd always had superpower perception of my feelings, without needing to trip into any of God's photo albums.

"Uh? Maybe?"

We broke into a case of the chuckles.

"Well, Tyree," and she almost put her arm around me, but then decided not. Brushing the wrinkles out of her exclusive 'we used to have lots of money' satin robe, she stood up, continuing, "...your dad and I had you to be a free person."

She smiled inwardly, continuing, "I used to tell people I was raising you and your sister to be 'free range humans' and that means, as long as I see you behaving maturely, as long I know where you are, whom you're with, I've talked with their guardians and that you'll be back within a reasonable time, and will call in case of emergencies..."

'That's some list,' I thought, but she'd explained all this to me a hundred times.

"...then you're a wonderful boy whom I have no reason not to trust."

Admittedly, older or not, that felt pretty good, so I said, "Thanks, mom," and I meant it. It was a trust I intended to honor as she'd been someone I'd always admired. She'd only been mourning my dad's death, while she was no unpredictable, baby momma – no drama queen. Mrs. Jackson, along with her husband, had made quite the stalwart impression on me; and that's why it felt so awful that I couldn't tell her all that'd happened in the last 36 hours. A year ago, I'd have not hesitated, but on top of my promise to the doctor, it was like the distance between us had become a necessary habit. Maybe it was part of the business of growing up to be a man.

"Hey, mom," it occurred to me. "Why don't we ever pray?"

"Hmmmm. That's a good question. I don't really know, but your dad and I sort of considered ourselves spiritual people, not religious."

"Does that mean you guys didn't believe in God?"

"No, we believed. I believe in God. We just didn't..." she paused. "I don't believe in rules about how to be faithful. Why? Would you like to pray?"

I don't know why I'd asked the question to start with, but my answer was true.

"Sometimes. Yes."

"Right now?"

Perhaps it's the first step to becoming telepathic, to activating that dormant DNA which boosts reception of mere thoughts – thoughts which bend frequencies too quickly for the ordinary mind to catch, but not for the mind of a god – perhaps it's the beginning of awakening when one realizes amongst friends and family...

... it's okay not to pull out all the threads, at one time.

"No, no," I reassuringly replied. "I didn't mean now, but maybe sometime in the future. It'd be nice, maybe."

She answered, "Yes, that sounds like a good idea."

I couldn't tell if she meant it or not. I could read her aura, but I had yet to read her mind.

I stood and for the first time since dad had died, I hugged her. She seemed startled but then after an almost imperceptible hesitation, she hugged me back.

"Goodnight, son."

"Goodnight, mom."

I couldn't see for certain, but I believe, as she disappeared into the drapes that hid the kitchen, she wiped back a tear with a whoosh of her sweeping satin sleeve...

~ ~ ~ ~ ~ ~ ~ ~ ~

I didn't go to sleep right away, but turned the light off and sat in the dark room staring out the window at the Kattan's.

A wafting breeze shuffled in through the screen as I drank in the blue world outside, with only struggling yellow street lights every 20 yards on my other

278

side. Then, the front windows of the house were black, but the Kattan's lawn lights were casting leaping beams that bathed the masks with startling ferocity, throwing larger leaping shadows admist the peaks of the gabled rooftop. In the darkness, it was all too obvious why its specter made the hearts of grown men skip many beats if they dared walk next to that abode once the sun abandoned the sky. Waning daytime was the signal to steer clear, and some, if they wandered unknowingly onto Carson, to the man and woman, each preferred to scale the buckling sidewalk on this side of the street. I saw not a soul so much as park a car over there, let alone chance running full speed past the famous 'haunted' mansion. Funny, I thought, 'Bet the ghosts would be too scared of the mansion, too.'

I'd hadn't bothered to look closely at it, during the night before, out of habit, because, when I was little my bedtime was early, like it is for all small children. Super early. Didn't matter really as it'd always been the intensified daytime air which interested me the most and I couldn't see that in the darkness, let alone, after my fall into the Orb, anymore in the daytime as the rest of the world looked like what that Afrikan shout of a mansion used to seem. Knowing it wasn't haunted, at night it looked like any other big house, no difference between any other. I'd seen those in Sandstone by the hundreds.

That moment, I stared for what seemed hours until the calm, quiet gloom, interrupted occasionally at first by my prolifically profane neighbors, and the grunts or laughs of buckling sidewalk climbing passersby, until even that commotion was replaced by soothing cricket chirps, the distant whoosh of cars on the main street or a far away whining siren. Until the grandness of this bit of a momentarily sunless side of Earth convinced my brain, I, also, needed rest.

But, oh?! I apologize! You're probably wondering what happened between myself and Von, I bet. Frankly? Nothing happened. Nothing at all.

I haven't mentioned it because I don't need to give it any importance, like it was something tremendous. Why should I make it more than it was when I felt no fear, seeing him as dusk descended, leaning up against that fence, staring directly across at the mansion, hanging with his friends. I was so much more than that Tyree he'd snuck earlier. Same as I said earlier, I would have thanked him, if I'd known his punch would be my first motivation to learn how to fight for real. However, especially after seeing through the eyes of men who were free because of their willingness to defend freedom to the death, even if Von could have killed me in this timeframe, the threat he presented meant nothing to me but a momentary interference in the greater work I had to do. He was no more

279

than the buckling sidewalk, which would be addressed and fixed, in due course. Being God's assistant, however?

Now there was a challenge that made me nervous.

That's why once I'd risen early that next morning, took care of my chores, did my homework on paper (it was already done in my head), made a mental note to call Dr. Kattan to see if I could research about Imhotep in the doctor's library (I'd forgotten to ask him for that favor, the day before, given the pressing intensity of all my other questions and because writing has never been an imperative with me, o-b-v-i-o-u-s-l-y) – after I'd gotten permission from my mom to go check out the defense class but get back home in a timely manner like she'd told me, again, I called Nyisha to get the address to that program she'd tipped me about and I caught the Dover 31 bus downtown, late afternoon.

I have a confession to make here. That morning, all was not balloons and confetti with me. Plainly? Same as I'd spied in my sister's aura, I was feeling downright hopeless, despite my nonstop activities, despite my 'superpowers' which included my increasing ability to understand the meaning of everything. What did that matter, though, if 'Non-Magical Not Harry Potter, Easy to Beat Up Lowercase 's' Me' couldn't get Kyerah to accept the truth' – what did any semblance of superpowers matter if I was overwhelmed by the difficulty of convincing a soul beyond my own multi-plex brain? Or worse yet?

What if Kyerah was right? What if there was no way to save the world?

So, I was working frenetically because I had to try something, even if nothing I did solved anything. See, my doubts had been confirmed by the somewhat distant 'Good Morning' my sister gave me at the breakfast table – a stingy 'Good Morning' further supported by the enormity of the problems I no longer had to imagine faced us, since I could seeeeeee the problems, one aura at a time. As I stood waiting for the Downtown 31 bus – all this made me realize, I'd rather be plain old ordinary just another ant Black Boy me.

I know I've talked about my ability to see the good side of Black people, but that day? Dang. Their problems greeted me with every blink I took as I sat down in my seat. Apparently, rather than unraveling our family threads, alone, I'd discovered fields of spools outside, like a river that doesn't drown you, yet, strangled the life out of everyone.

Not to mention, but I always do – here in my real time – I've got an appointment with Allah. Yep. Reader, I kid you not. I'm scheduled to meet the One and Only in 4 days 18hrs and 37mins. I've been ducking everyone rather well, from orientation to elaborate dinners. Been writing steadily without drawing attention to myself, but this invitation came directly to my hotel room via messenger, with a startled me there to receive it. As we gods don't lie, so I would never say I hadn't gotten it, even if I hadn't been there to have an ornate paper thin leaf of solid gold placed in the open palm of my hand – that didn't tremble because I willed it not to? Acting skills or not, there's no ducking The Origin of Existence, The Best of All Knowers, no matter how incognito or calm you hope you are. I'd assumed Allah contacted anyone He wished to speak with telepathically, but maybe that's too ordinary.

And here I am with chapters yet to enscript. I may dislike writing books, but as a top spelling bee champion, I can not only spell, but can painstakingly define words like 'Yikes!'

Guess that's why I remember my mood that day as it's similar to how trapped I'm feeling right now. Though, Von wasn't a big concern, not at all, back then. My slumping mood had nothing to do with him in the slightest. Kyerah's resistance started it, indeed, but it kept rolling on upon seeing all those other spools of thread that were strangling everyone to death.

'Cause?

Walking down the block there was Fatness.

Waiting at the bus stop there was Fatness.

As I took my seat, in poorly designed chairs for that fat age and time, there was Fatness.

Everywhere.

So what? You can see that for yourself in your current realm, too, I'm sure, and you don't hafta trip over or into nuthin'. Plus, lots of fat people can be drop dead gorgeous, so if even you, yourself, are fat? This is not an insult. It wasn't how people looked that made me doubtful, as we'd all seen increasingly plus sized folks for decades. It was that I could see the drop dead death brewing inside them, where they, themselves, had no idea it existed.

HOWEVER?

The skinny people were dying, too. They only *thought* they were healthier, when, nope. Their bodies were swimming in a hundred times their weight of the same toxins that were drowning their larger sized comrades.

Maybe it was my sour mood, I don't know, but? Whereas the morning before I'd gloried in exponential life, today I saw Kyerah's dark yawning abyss times everyone – in more ways than, given my impending appointment, I dare take time to describe. Everybody was not only crippled by unmet soul deep needs, but they were also being killed, as surely as that soldier I as Cletus had lugged across the breach – as surely as he had died from being riddled with that hail of bullets. Only the people I saw, Black, white, Asian, Hispanic, they were dying slower, so each was blissful to the degree of their clichéd ignorance. Their hail of bullets ricocheted in cellphones stuck up against heads, pinging in shopping shooting spree grocery bags, slaughter slathered personal care products – even in their make-up and the off-gassing fumes I saw emanating from the clothes they wore. Then? There was another other affliction I sensed. I couldn't specifically identify it back in that day, nor any of the other poisons I only sensed and have briefly, very briefly mentioned, but its aura was redhot, super red hot, and tiny. I'd seen it before in Terrence's fish sandwich. Tinier than the rest of the toxins, yet – far worse than anything bigger and these itsy bitsy killers were everywhere as invisible bullets hotter than the Sun. What the hell was this stuff?

Plus, the pets, the squirrels, the birds and the ants weren't spared that super nova deadly glow. There was no safe place, including being another species to hide from this incinerating attack.

Dang. The Naziis couldn't have built a gas chamber this big. This was gas chambered Earth! Why, I could smell the burning heat of dying cells that were still being lugged around inside bodies alive merely by the grace of God. I was Cletus, resurrected, walking through burnt corpses that didn't know they were being fricasseed, or that you didn't need ovens to burn people like logs in the fireplace. You didn't even need a big ol' bonfire.

On the bus ride, I passed the entrance to the graveyard and it wasn't the one with the gravediggers and headstones. It was the one way entrance that guaranteed the gravediggers steady business. The hospital. The building told me there was very little healing going on in there. Looking at it, the crowded bus grumbling and grunting heavily past its majestic cream facaded several rectangular buildings site, the most prominent building christened with a somber blood red 'New Jersey Multi-Faith Hospital' marquee up top, the movie 'Aliens' could have never prayed to duplicate this true life ghoulish scene of blood soaked horror. Neat, well credentialed, highly educated, trusted blood soaked horror. Oh what that hospital's aura revealed would keep you awake and trembling for the rest of your life.

I vowed to never joke about taking any medications, ever again. I vowed I'd never have to take any...

Okay. That was a Hell of an afternoon, but rushing right along through these details that grabbed my heart that morning, understandably dragging 12yr old not too impressive a superhero me into despair? No wonder Von couldn't begin to compete. Oh, he was on my mind, in one of my brain's multiple levels. Probably in the 3rd floor cleaning supply closet, but before my eyes was a 3D Zombie Movie in Triangulated Dolby Surround Sound.

Made worse cause I loved zombies movies. Still do, but these zombies were historical reality...

I wasn't thinking about how my sister and I had come back from the store, either – to find Howard Branch's confused older brother and friends leaning on the Acme wire fence in front of our house. He was looking dead at us while we crossed the street to our home. My sister had slowed her step a touch, but I'd gently placed my hand on her arm (she was much taller than I was, at that time), to urge her forward.

"That's that guy!" she heavy whispered, again.

"Yup," I nonchalantly replied.

She looked at me, glaring slightly. "Don't forget what Dr. Kattan said, Tyree. You're not Cletus. You can get hurt out here."

"I know that. Von doesn't want to fight me, though. I can see it all over him."

"Oh."

She moved on ahead without slowing.

"You know those people who live in that creep house?" Von asked me, directly fixing me with his eyes, as Kyerah and I navigated up onto the sidewalk. Starred at me just like his brother had done the other day. It was essentially the same face, only different ages.

"That's none of your business," I said, matter of factly, walking after Kyerah who'd opened our rusted gate door.

He grabbed my shoulder.

"Who the heck do you think you're talking to?"

And reader, of course you know his language was from a place that Von had no idea he was not meant to linger.

I snapped my body about, escaping his grip, (my dad had taught me that much), ready to continue our earlier confrontation, if necessary, best as I was able. However, as I could sense, Von wasn't in the mood to fight. Not that he didn't posture like he was ready, but before a young girl who'd been leaning on his own shoulder and got knocked off when he grabbed mine, before she told him,

"Hey! He's just a kid. Let him be,"...

before she'd uttered her protest, I had correctly seen he was focused on other teenage thoughts to which I was a momentary distraction. He quickly resumed his lean with one foot propped up on the creaky fence as if the whole world was a distraction.

The teenaged girl resumed her own lean on his shoulder and I wondered if she was Nyisha's older sister that Nyisha'd said was his girlfriend. Since there was no resemblance I could identify, I couldn't tell, and I wasn't exactly a mind reader...

not yet.

"He's the tough guy," Von answered, though not addressing the girl, as if she wasn't there at all.

To his leaning or standing buddies around him, he said, "Better watch out for that one. His baby smooth face may not look like it, but it'll wear out your knuckles..."

The group that I'd been certain I'd understood so well yesterday burst into hearty laughter, at what they thought was my expense. Too bad for them, I didn't care in the least. But let me tell you, reader. It's hard to like folks who don't like you, even though I had to admit, once again, hearing him, Von had been right. My face didn't show a trace of his earlier handiwork.

I was glad he hadn't seen the full bruising his battery of punches had caused, or? The distraction of my existence might have gained his interest when he realized I no longer had a mark on my 'baby smooth' face. So rather than going upstairs to do that verbal wrestling with my sister I've mentioned, I might have walked in our apartment door with fresh bruises in whole other places to replace the ones that had 'disappeared'.

Oh yeah. My mom and grandma had been initially shocked by the extent of my 'cure', when I got upstairs, but Mrs. Kattan had called them earlier as she had said she would, extoling the healing power of mugwort wraps.

"Hmmmmmm...", my mom had commented, looking at me with disbelief, holding my chin in her brown fingers, turning my head side to side, but least her son was healed, right?

"Well," she added, "I'mma stock up on some mugwort. Whatever that is, it's amazing!"

And that was my surprise encounter with Von Branch. Like I said at the outset, it'd been nothing at all, and I'd planned on keeping it that way, no matter what he'd had in mind. I couldn't read his mind, exactly, but I didn't like the smell of what was cookin' inside it.

It wasn't a hotter than the Sun kind of heat, but it was nonetheless too close to the wrong temperature...

285

CHAPTER
4

Now this? This was the happiest building in Newark.

Standing in front of it, wanting to be positive I'd arrived at the right place, I checked the directions I'd written down according to Nyisha. The WISOMMM Cultural Center, 34 Washington Street. Yep. This was the place.

"What's the building look like, so I'll recognize it?" I asked her, during our morning telephone talk.

Expecting it'd be some ugly sweaty gym on an abandoned of all hope block in the heart of Newark, I was surprised when she had said,

"Oh, it's the WISOMMM Cultural Center and it sooooo beautiful. It's right near The Newark Museum and The Public Library. In the historic part of downtown."

"This is an Afrikan organization?"

"Yes."

"In the historic part of the N-e-w-a-r-k, owned and run by Black people?"

"Uh-duh, smart guy! Those are the Afrikans. And it's run by Black women. WISOMMM stands for 'Women in Support of the Million Man March. But the program is run by brothers. A.S.C.E.N.D. stands for Afrikan Sons Co-operate to Enact a New Destiny."

I thought, *'Must be living in Newark has lowered her expectations of what constituted 'beautiful', poor girl. It may be historic, but it's gotta be severely neglected. It is a Black city, afterall. She's throwing praise around cause this is the best city she has. Maybe it's the best she's even seen, besides in pictures. I know how inner city youth don't get a chance to travel. The museum and library probably look like sweaty gyms, too.'*

But, standing out front, after having walked the several blocks from where the
286

bus had left me off, I wasn't doing exactly an imitation of my sister with a fly buzzing near my open mouth, but looking at the WISOMMM Center, I certainly could empathize with Kyerah. And I could hear an Afrikan Goddess somewhere snickering at my expense.

Or was that my comedic basement having its good ol' time reminding me to open my eyes and see...

beyond the regions that I'd assumed had been abandoned and neglected, no doubt, beyond cheap and crass store after store, crammed with credit card rich Black and Brown people; after I had left that area, walking from the bus stop into empty block after block, where white folks suddenly appeared out of nowhere, walking these streets of thoughtfully constructed, lovingly maintained architecture, both residential, commercial and public, like The Newark Museum that was quite elegant – beyond the first disappointment of what Black Newark should look like and sadly, it did, came this surprise that we owned an amazing structure, like we should own more, just the same. It was a lone chapel, one of the most magnificent buildings in the area that cried out sheer and utter joy from its towering ashlar masonry walls, supported by stacked rectangular columns, to the meaning of its heart which was more beautiful than Nyisha would have known existed, unless she had some hidden superpowers she was keeping to herself, same as I.

My extra-sensory insight was bathing in a glow of spitfired will and determination. The aura from WISOMMM was, I would have to say, my first glimpse of Heaven, on the ground, were it mattered, whether I knew that's where Heaven was or not, and I didn't know. I felt it. But I could also feel it was in trouble. Big trouble. I had to get inside that building, now.

The entrance to the program was around the corner from the arched doorway to the chapel, on James St. A humble wooden door which gave way to my push, after passing another gently rounded entryway before it. It opened onto a nondescript beige hallway with a stairwell on the immediate right, going up one flight. At the top I stepped up into a massive open auditorium, with polished wooden floors – though they'd hadn't been polished in a bit of time – and a vaulted high ceiling, supported by walls decorated with Afrikan regalia and masks that made me feel right at home here in a Heaven I didn't know I needed so badly.

And there were the sons of the Motherland, no matter how many greats removed from their original grandparents. Dozens of them, Black boys like me, all ages, seated at a couple large metal fold out tables, which despite the tables'

287

sizes, were no match for the volume of space within the auditorium. Not caring that their mass was outnumbered, the young men huddled attentively over their composition books while someone I recognized, instantly, instructed them to write down what he was sharing with a thundering voice, so familiar. I didn't know what he was teaching but I knew I wanted to learn from him.

If only Dr. Kattan could have seen his son leading the future so well, he'd have forgiven Brother Gainde for whatever it was that made the doctor believe that Gainde shouldn't teach me how to defend myself against all threats, physical, emotional and spiritual, which was exactly what my soul needed to grow.

~ ~ ~ ~ ~ ~ ~ ~ ~ ~ ~

You know, Awakened Gods need sleep. Lots of it, as our constitutions are intensively energetic. We take in enormous ranges of frequencies combined with ambient waves of complete spectral light, resonating inside our entire bodily frames at higher radiantly pulsating charges which result in critical fluctuations that can...

Ahem. 'Xcuuuuuse me............

I'm rambling, again, aren't I? THAT'S BECAUSE I'M FRIGGIN' EXHAUSTED!!!! Look, dude and dude-esses, I've been up for 48 straight hours, owing to the appointment I have with not just my maker, but OUR ONLY REASON FOR EXISTENCE. Excuse me, but,

%@#$.

It's not that I haven't 'seen' Allah before, from a great distance as part of a flowing crowd. That was more than a decade after The Ubuntu, right before He came to teach Us, directly. Just as He'd said, each and every head was bowed and not because we were frightened, but because We finally understood. We were ever so grateful that we'd graduated from Hell, and having not been turned into cows, We knew We'd never allow Hell to emerge again.

Some were, though. I mean turned into cows. Or ferrets. Or bats. Or maggots.

HA! Nay!!! I'm kidding, a-g-a-i-n!!!! That didn't happen, but? Had you fooled, there, right?

Oh, guess I didn't. Okay, you're too 'hipi' for that, at this point, so... moving right along...

Dr. Kattan was correct. Allah is no hocus pocus magician. No magical wands, despite the fact, standing there that day, in the desert, He called out from the sand itself, and fresh water and manna for the gathering millions, coming from every point of the globe, appeared. We stood in the desert, thinking with the desert Our Enemies had made of Our minds. From the dry wreckage of Our spirits, We were filled with the thoroughly satiating nutritive sustenance of His Forgiveness.

In other words? We all brought food and drink, shared amongst the multitude so that none went thirsty or hungry that day nor any other since. The open plains of the former U.S. were simply a large enough space to accommodate the masses. No fairy dust, but loads of dry Earth kicked up into the air by thousands of buses, still fueled by gasoline, and millions of pairs of feet led by all who could verify, Allah didn't need a wand. Despite our numbers reaching out for miles, His voice rang clear through each of our souls, although He wasn't shouting. It was the first genuine telepathic exchange such an enormous crowd had ever had, with no assistance.

Yet, He wasn't larger than life, either, except He felt larger, standing firmly and slightly elevated on a solitary red monolith, dressed in flowing white robes that the winds seemed to gain a mind to flap about only with Him, much more forcefully than with all the others dressed similarly. I couldn't see the details of His features, but He had our complete, undivided attention, so even if He'd only spoken in a traditional verbal manner, each would have heard every single word. It was that hushed. We were desperate to hear every word, and every breath in between – we craved His guidance so fervently that Our silence made the sweeping expanse of the desert seem cozy. And once His too brief declaration was done, not a single person asked, "What did God say?"

Nor, even, "What did God mean?..."

Plus, He'd never asked us to bow, we just did. A magnificent sea of finally wizened Hue-manity, stretching the span of an entire former state who didn't mind not noticing the hours slip by listening to their True Better,

Theeeeeeee True Better, with whom very accidental me has an appointment before I've actually finished the book that HE requested.

Oh, boy.
Since the notice came 2 days ago, I've been hermited in my hotel room (nice one too, with a balcony overlooking Olantunji, the largest pyramid in the city, composed of multi-colored glittering fragments randomly welded together like faceted jewels in the largest pendant in existence) – I've been here, writing furiously. Why I must have written all of... (just a moment, while I check...)

A full furious

t
e
n

pages. Oh, great.

Well, alright. I guess I was reading, watching a little more TV than necessary, staring at Olantuji and meditating while organizing and re-organizing my thoughts. I think I must have been doing that a lot. Organizing. Definitely not writing.

Did have dinner sent up, telling Sitamen I needed solitude, which she understood, though I moreso needed a break from our nonstop comedy routine. Okay, I admit that she can be quite funny, but it wouldn't be helpful right now. Panic has a terrible sense of humor.

And I hadn't wanted to admit to my dread over the phone, but when my beloved Jepkemboi called, I was obviously grateful. By the way, in Heaven, we use landwire phones since, as I've said, cellphone technology is slow death, and unnecessary, today, as we have telepathy. However, over long distances, unless heightened by an emotion packed emergency, it tends to become a transmission mostly of non-specific sensations, which is about as effective as emailing a friend during the heat of an argument in order to reach a compromise. Somebody is bound to misinterpret your drift as they can't see your facial expressions.

Oh, yes, yes. We have computers. Um? Reader, please? Can we get on with this?

"Peace, Queen," I began our conversation, my voice warmed by relief upon

291

viewing her number on the handset's LCD display and her face on the hotel's console, when I'd accepted the call. I carried the handset and console, attached to a long wire, out to the spacious terrace, the evening's sunsetting sky reflected in swirling cotton candy intensity on the faceted pyramid.

"Peace, King," she responded. "How's it going?"

In her voice I could hear she knew something was amiss and that she knew, I knew it. But gods are gentle, careful not to intrude on another's right to privacy, especially in a marriage. At least in ours. Heaven ain't perfect or I wouldn't have been kinda panicking...

but, I don't pretend with Jem.

"Not well, Beloved."

"I could feel that. What's happened?"

"Allah has requested my presence."

"You're kidding?!" She sounded thrilled.

"Well, there can be two answers for that. If I had finished the book, I'd say, 'No Doubt!' But as I haven't, I have to say, 'I wish I was kidding.'"

"Uh-oh." I could feeeeeeel her concern, outside of the line connection.

"Yep. I should have started a long time ago," I confessed to her, but didn't say that I knew it was too late for a leisurely execution of my task.

"I'm not trying to make excuses for you, but? You're more an adventurer than a historian."

"Don't I know it."

"What have you got so far?"

"Plenty, actually. Just no ending, yet. And what I have is choppy, reflective, and thoroughly unprofessional."

"So you say, love. But I'm sure it's phenomenal. How long do you have till you finish and then when's the appointment?"

292

"I have 2 days till my appointed hour, and who knows when I'll get to the ending. I've got dozens of scenes yet to go and I have to contemplate what I'm writing first…"

"Yes. I'm still finding post-it notes all over the house. There was one in the refrigerator."
"No! Did I leave one in the fridge?"

"Just kidding!"

She and I both laughed from sheer relief. Ah. Her sense of humor embedded with support was just the tonic. Even though I was doomed, there's nothing better than laughing when one's forecast is extra grim.

When our chuckling subsided, I said, "Well, I sure hope The Creator has a sense of humor, too," letting our moment of fun brighten my outlook.

"Hey? You never know. That day in the desert is all I've ever seen of Him, and although we were pretty far back in the crowd, He looked like the most kindest man, ever."

We both remained silent. She absorbed in recollection, me – trying to see if I remembered in His features, that I couldn't see that day – if they hinted of the Person within. That's when it struck me…

"That's IT!" I shouted.

"That's what, beloved?"

"I don't have time to explain, my dearest, most fabulous goddess! First, I've scheduled an interview with Brother Mansa Musa this afternoon and then? It's back to work, and pronto. I'll call you before the interview!"

"With Mansa Musa?"

"Oh! No, with Allah."

"Okay, and if you say you've got it, then I won't worry about you, anymore. But I'll still send positive thoughts your way, even if you don't need them."

"Oh, I always need your positive energy. It's my B12 shot."

293

She giggled while I smiled, we said our goodbyes, I hung up and went back inside to get my notes and questions for my brother. I'd hadn't thought to tell my wife that I didn't even know where the appointment would take place...

You know. The one with Our Maker. I wouldn't need notes to meet with Him. You arrive ready or you don't arrive at all.

=

It is not true what some of my handmaidens say, that when Massinissa stormed the palace, before we had even courted, that I did not know him. Yes, I did proclaim directly to him and no other, "Thy courage and thy fortune have given thee victory and power over us. If it is permitted that a captive embrace the knees and touch the hand of a conqueror, I pray thee, with the royal majesty which we ourselves were invested but yesterday, not to hand me over to the caprice of the cruel Romans. Dispose of me thyself."

The maidens chattered about my distrust of the handsome victor, but how could I have known who he was, in character, even if his bold, black features remained the same I'd recognize anywhere? He had entered our city not only after defeating every one of our warriors, but he'd won his victory in league with our avowed tormentors, those very same cruel Romans, with their heartless Scipio as their goat herding general. How was I to know that this powerful, imposing in stature, bravery and skills above all men, Massinissa, who has never lost a battle except he lost my once promised matrimonial to him – a matrimonial promise which was traded to another aspiring conqueror – Syphax – how could I have known this was indeed the same man, within? The man no one could have not heard the legends surrounding, as my entire childhood was replete with tales of his unrivaled skills – barring perhaps those of my Uncle Hannibal. His successes are relived in words, songs and hushed awe throughout all the kingdoms, both noteworthy ballads and doggerals. Who could not know Massinissa if they were even one minute from either birth or death?

But, how could I have been sure he hadn't been changed, from that kind, quietly rumbling voiced young man, who'd so long ago hesitantly spoke of his eternal love for me – only within a heavily monitored moment in the royal gardens, as the light clothed itself in the scurrying waters of that sanctuary's fountain, my father's plentifully vigilant guards as quiet as the still air? Who could have been certain of who Massinissa had become, since not many of our people, but some – the weakest ones – have succumbed to the twisted tastes of the barbarians, taking on habits too vile to reveal, even inside my mind. Habits that all persons with sense know – ways that are the tastes of beasts and demons. How ever could I have surmised he had not been corrupted by the debaucheries of these convincingly brutish people?

Hadn't he joined their side to fight against my father, after all, and contact with contagion is the surest method to achieve infection? Hadn't he snatched his initial victory over Syphax using treachery, though he later erased part of that shame with expert prowess, winning battle after battle until he, with that morning's earliest greeting, dragged my once betrothed, King Syphax of Numidia, before our city's front gates, hobbled in chains?

Army defeated, our people opened the width and breadth of our fortress to him and his men. They hadn't razed our structures nor ravaged our women as the Romans are infamous for doing, but the anticipation of horror does not abate simply because the horror takes its time. If anything, that pause grows one's fear to the greatest heights.

Then there, in front of my childhood home arrived my own potential personal horror in a man as dark as the depths of one's imagination and I thought, looking at this mountain of a conqueror, if I am to die, please let it be by him. Let it be by a comfort I know rather than a pale terror told about in the soulless eyes of escaped victims of Rome. Hundreds of the dead stares of men, women and even children I'd grown up seeing all my life.

Thus, I shared my desperate desire to die with dignity with a man whose own brutality might at least come to my person with a familiar face.

That's when he dismounted his black steed, as I could hear in his clanking weaponry, for my head was bowed down to the red earth and I could not see. I had upon his arrival, kneeled till no air could pass through any joint of my limbs, and he fell down upon the ground beside my prostate form, covering me with his mantle of sinew rippling arms, draped over with a vast silken cloak. His bejeweled swords that he did not unsheathe were cold against my back covered only by silk, and thus his sheathed sword startled me, yet, caused me not the slightest cut.

"Dearest of brave hearted beings," he said in that familiar voice which must make the deeper layers of ground envious, "who could have imagined thy inner brightness outshines the most luminous of faces? Stand my queen, for I come to fulfill the original promise made with the sincerest love, never intended for cruelty."

He lifted my arms and shoulders, gently, guiding me to stand, but out of my blinding fear not of him, but of them – I resisted, replying, "I love better to depend on a Numidian than a Roman. I prefer those born as I, under the skies of Alkebulan. Let death take me rather than a Roman." I wasn't trembling but

I don't know how I wasn't.

He took a moment, perhaps reflecting, I thought. Later he told me he could not devise a response to the firmness of my request, as he'd been so overcome with joyful certainty that our woes were permanently laid low. Instead, wordlessly he insisted, with his firm but gentle grasp, lifting me up to walk beside him into the royal main entryway. Wherein through the tenderest, most lengthy and involved of conversations I've ever been a willing captive of, I discovered his youthful vow to love me till he died had never ebbed in its devoted kindness. We were married that very day, as he convinced me this would ensure his ability to protect me, and my heart convinced me this man was meant to be my King.

After that it was days of the sweet relief of laughter, realized love and thus pure bliss. And this barren moment, less than a full moon later, when my new husband has gone to speak with his demonic allies, this in a terrible contrast with our brief splendor, has become a night of ravenous death, confirmed by his letter, sent by his servant which reads,

"I would have been happy to keep my first promise but a superior force has made the achievement of my desire impossible. Now the only thing left to me is keeping my second promise not to let you fall into the hands of the Romans. May the remembrance of your father, the illustrious general, and the thoughts of your country dictate your conduct."

With this missive came a curiously small, unadorned glass vial, wrapped in plain oiled chamois. Removing the stopper, I calmly poured its crimson palored contents into the remains inside my goblet. A mere dram of now permanently numbing wine only the hopeless would find comforting, and yet this thimble of liquid was wider than the span of the Mediterranean that did nothing to keep the devil from my doorstep. With a steady, soft touch, Massinissa's servant, a noble commoner of silent bearing, had placed my beloved's gift upon the dark mahogany table where I had until then been absentmindedly pushing morsels of uneaten food upon my silver platter. A sumptuous selection, which I had no appetite to even taste. Then he'd handed me my Beloved's note. The meal, the platter, the repast, and my attendants, all have disappeared as if dropped into the draining hue of that protective wine.

Now, looking at it, and at no one else, for no one is here but me and this tonic, leaving my mind with no room for any other vision, I see it will be an Alkebulanian Preventative for calumnies that shall surely be inflicted upon my flesh and then, worse? Calumnies inflicted into my spirit; a spirit that instead chooses to defend my true beauty. No man, except my sweet Massinissa, will ever know that face.

It is an easy choice I make, today.

"Tell him," I am commanding this man who has most assuredly seen fields of blood soaked gore, but I would guarantee, none so voluntary as my violence this moment, "... tell him that I accept the wedding present without regret, if it be true that my husband can do no more for his wife. Tell him that I would have died even more willingly if greater time had elapsed between the wedding and the funeral."

Having poured the contents of my 'gift' into my chalice, I embrace my salvation, bringing eternal sleep to these blackest of my people's black lips...

=

By the way. I never wrote that report for Mrs. Finn and I didn't care 'cause neither I nor any of my new crew or a single member of the entire population that went through those abortion clinic metal detectors ever went back to P.S. 47 in a way that mattered to those who were each day filling our brains with lies. Wound up, none of us had to tolerate the intolerable, any longer. But first? My interview.

With the Revered Mansa Musa! Yes, You know him! Richest man this planet has ever known and unlike the Tamahue, in his ancient timeframe, he gave away more than he kept...

~ ~ ~ ~ ~ ~ ~ ~ ~ ~ ~ ~

Testing, testing...

Ahem! Greetings Beloved Readers and Viewers. I'm in the humble but regal home of one of Our most cherished brethren, here in the heart of the city of Abjerusalem. Handily this Brother is one of New Eden's most celebrated citizens. Other than my sister, there is not a one from our age range who is more recognizable.

Those who reside in this time, from my small introduction, alone, are probably already beside themselves with anticipation as this honored guest, who has so generously conceded to be interviewed for my history book, 'This Black', is a modest god who prefers work to applause. And resounding applause it would be, indeed. I, of course, am referring to the world famous, world loved, reknowned Particle Physicist, King Mansa Musa, whom I mentioned earlier in this chronicle under his former, not well known at all slave name – Howard. Howard Branch. I am quite fortunate that Queen Sitamen secured this interview, the first of what I hope will be many more interviews with all the parties involved in the initial awakening of our people, whether they facilitated our triumph from up close or from a distance. Truth must be recorded to continue unimpeded.

Starting with the man whose reputation outshines any introduction I might attempt. So, without further delay, let us begin.

<u>DOCUMENT</u>: Interview 1

GUEST: Negus Mansa Musa of the Mali Empire, First Restorer of the Ring of Fire Lands and Purifier of the Oceans

INTERVIEWER: Negus Akhenaten Ra, 17,059th Protector of The Sacred Breath of Allah's Memories

DATE: 51574 Cubed, 3rd day of The Renewing, 2nd Aquarian Season of The Solar System's Rotation, 10 days to The Gathering of The Ascended

<u>BEGIN</u> -

Interviewer (IN): As Salaam Alaikum, Negus Mansa Musa. It is an honor for us, all, that you have agreed to record, for posterity, clarification of your role in the awakening of our people.

Negus Mansa Musa (MM): Walaikum Salaam, Negus Akhenaten. It is I who am honored that you'd consider my small part worthy of recording with what you set into motion. That was an august introduction, but you, too, must be part of any discussion about New Eden's most celebrated young citizens.

IN: (laughing) Well, that will be for others to determine, and anyone who knows the tale, which is not enough people, would definitely not call your role 'small'. If I neglect revealing your side of what happened, which I was not aware of at the time it happened? The universe will think you were a coward and a bully, when nothing of the sort was true.

MM: (nodding, appreciatively) Gratefully, this is a different time, where, even if I had been a cowardly bully - (taking on a mirthful grin) which I might have been - documenting the truth is paramount to our stability. Yes. Thank You, brother.

IN: First, let me congratulate you on the rescue of the Pacific Region and clean up of the rest of the planet.

MM: On behalf of all those who made the rebirth possible, I appreciate your congratulations. I couldn't have managed it, alone. The radiation from Fukushima nearly left that part of the planet uninhabitable for millions of years and the other parts only seconds behind that one in toxicity. Together, we normalized everything in under 50 years using simple sound waves, and orgon technology magnified with our united melanated resonance, combined in activated prayer. Yes, We had to dig deep into the mantle of the planet but who knew it'd be that easy? Sadly, half the population of Japan had already succumbed to the radioactive contamination before we'd begun. We couldn't save the dead, but? Ultimately, the scale of healing we accomplished would have never been possible without directions from the Man who created existence in the first place, and He, alone, fortified our melanin, specifically, during the onslaught. The activation was the key, while we merely co-operated, joyfully. It's what The Ubuntu brought to us – the necessity of co-operating with His plan, whether we have our own interpretation of it, or not.

IN: What was it like working directly with The Creator?

MM: (looking surprised) You've never worked with Him? In all your years of service?

IN: (shaking my head) No, but this is your testimony, not mine. I have a whole book about which I've been told I've said too much, already.

MM: (laughing) Well, I can't wait to read it, Brother. Hmmmm. Working with The Alpha? It's not easy to capsulize. He's? Well, He's *God*, for goodness sake. The Original Creator of The Original Peoples. Before you even meet Him, you're sure it's going to be the worst day of your life, since He knows every rotten thing you've ever done. Even your physical dad doesn't know all of that! But He's your perfect Father because He not only knows that rotten stuff, He knows good stuff about you that you don't know. He's also surprisingly funny, and warm. He's the most comforting being I've ever met.

I mean, He's more easy going than your pre-assumptions could imagine, but He's no clown. He gives you the answer you know you needed, which is usually not the answer you hoped for, though. Yet, He makes truth so plain, so obvious – it makes you wonder that We ever accepted the rule of such a contrary people for even a day, although in the grand scale of existence, Hell didn't last very long.

IN: (bowing my head) Indeed. 6,000 years of rule by the Yurugu is a short time when measured against the trillions of years We've been here. They burned out like a short match in an inferno.

MM: Yes. You can't build anything permanent on top of lies. Not even your DNA. With or without consciously acknowledging Allah, every soul yearns for truth, with emotions as a vague road map. How is it not logical, then, that our very flesh yearns for truth, as well, like the plant yearns for sunlight? It's not that The Creator rescued Us while we resisted. It's that He gave Us a choice and We accepted the rescue He'd always been.

MM: Ameen, my Brother. And in keeping with the truth, Negus Mansa, what really happened so long ago, when my ignorance made me single you out as my foe rather than my friend?

MM: (sighing) The most difficult time for everyone, no doubt, as we had no idea the battlefield was inside our minds. We were in a funnel with all the God given ability to withstand gravity, but instead chose to do nothing, as if destruction was a menu option [shaking his head, pausing].

I suffered from asthma. Pretty bad asthma. Had since I could remember back in those sickly times that had darn near everybody overcome with something. My childhood was loaded with late night trips to the hospital to keep me alive. If I had fought you that day? It could have been my last.

IN: Is that why you were a loner, of sorts?

MM: Probably. There were other reasons, but not being able to run around with the other guys I'm sure didn't help. My brother, Von, shouldered a lot of the father role, when he didn't know anything about being a dad anymore than I did. He did what he knew, although it led him down a dark path.

IN: Yes. Sadly. It's too bad The Ubuntu happened too late for him to accept, as you said. I know losing him must have been very hard on you.

MM: Yes, that it was. We'd been very close, but? None knew it was the time, save Elohim. None realized from whence they'd truly come, so that going back to divinity would feel more natural than remaining insane.

IN: 'From whence they'd come...' Funny. I said something similar to Queen Sitamen, at the very beginning of The Ubuntu. 'From whence did I fall, sister?' It makes me think, you were the mighty Mansa Musa who single handedly reduced the value of gold throughout the Eastern lands for 10 straight years. You were the richest man ever in all the history of Pre-Heaven, yet? You were humble, while swift to demand unquestionable justice. So, during that final time in the lifespan of Howard Branch?

MM: I fell through the funnel, like everyone else. Like my brother. Like you.

302

IN: Why do you think that was?

MM: Sometimes I think I know and most times I have to admit, I'm not sure. But my foremost belief is that We were teenaged souls before Yacub created our challengers. We'd been around since dirt, with Our Father guiding Us, step by step, while We didn't know what He had to do to keep a roof over Our heads anymore than any child understands what mommy or daddy does to pay the bills. The Devil kept perfecting his Hell and We had no power to remember all Our manifestations like We do now, because We must master the next dimension before graduating to that new level. Then on top of that, We looked like grown-ups, on the outside – sure. Built nations like grown-ups, but We were children building with blocks; whereas, He built with living tissue and He remembered everything. We couldn't possibly comprehend what He did, let alone why. Our little successes made Us cocky, arrogant, while We couldn't understand the complete depth of maintaining Heaven, like it invisibly maintained itself. We were teenagers who believe, when they start driving, accidents happen to other people. Assuming life'll be a peace of cake, you never think about the work involved. And then there young souled Us went, opening the door to a strange people who promptly robbed childish us blind.

IN: Deaf and Dumb, too. But here you are restoring, rebuilding the ruined cities, once more. That's far beyond what Mansa you did collapsing the gold market for a decade.

MM: (laughing) No doubt, Brother! Getting used to creating, to making things stronger, for the longterm, for everyone, building is the finest wine of godly thinking that ages over several millenia. Any devil can rip a thing apart. But to build? Now that's immortality.

~ ~ ~ ~ ~ ~ ~ ~ ~ ~ ~ ~

Another interruption, readers, but for this time it's me interrupting myself. I know, I know I said I mustn't do that but? I admit it. Time's a-wasting, as I attend the orientation at the Gathering of The Ascended. It's taking place in The Hall of Atonement, here at the Epidome and it's jammed packed. No levitation, mind you, as this isn't the much not anticipated by me final gathering. This is only the last in a series of plenary sessions with just folding chairs (plush ones), set out in that cavernous hall of sunlit black granite flooring and gold imbedded marble columns that Sita and I had walked through when it was far more emptier than now – all before a black granite

303

raised podium on a wooden stage that's been visited by speaker after speaker. Um.... since this morning, and it's heading into mid-afternoon.

My sister is seated off to my right with the other women.

Luminaries. Each and every presenter and they've all been sharing vital information, no question. However, seeing how I have less than 3 days to finish this text and here I am, barely past the middle of the book and too far into the middle of this last orientation day to not realize it might go on forever, with long winded speaker after speaker as Jepkemboi predicted? That said, while, one, too many times I've been stopped (politely, of course) and asked about my progress, which was followed by gentle surprised nods when I revealed that my book was "No, not finished, yet"...

Seeing that and how I have an appointment with The Almighty, Himself? Let's cut to the chase. In a future unabridged volume, I'll print the full interview I conducted with Brother Mansa Musa and the others I've done since, including with Negus Lokman (slave name – Reggie Turner), and Negist Hatshepsut (slave name, Renee Jackson). I'm even praying (literally) to get interviews with those who ascended before The Ubuntu. Those who laid the map for us, when we were children and reached the destination – the end of their 'his'story. Until that safer than now time, I'm busy writing, here, in my seat, while appearing focused on the events. I don't think anyone in the hall will notice, since I can both listen attentively (remember my multi-leveled office tower thinking? Yup. It's not a superhero thing, anymore; it's a god thing. Everybody can do it) – no one will know if I'm extra silent, as I concentrate on the Writer, continuing to chronicle the moment I learned, with my Brothers' help, how to build Heaven....

The color transformation that took place about the mansion could actually be seen in the dark of night, once one realized the house pulled in colors so completely, the whole night air on the entire block was blacker than it was over every other street. The effect wasn't due to a lack of street light as there were many lampless streets that had been brighter than my block and mine had the same amount of lamps as average. Maybe it was my enhanced ability to see, although? During the daytime the Kattan estate now appeared to me as normal as what the rest of the world once had been. Thinking about and seeing how, on Carson in particular, the casual passersby thinned out to almost not a soul, and certainly not a ghost I'd ever seen – though all the other residential areas were well populated (with people that is – not ghosts) – it made me wonder if the magnetism of the Orb was more powerful on each person's awareness during the dark half of the 24hr day, no matter what level of superhero he or she was, 'cause everybody avoided that one block of Carson every night of every year. Apparently? Everyone's perception was heightened when the Sun and all it appeared to illuminate – when the color-full noise of the world was no longer a frenetic distraction.

No, the night depth didn't tell me where it was going, as I watched from the window inside Brother Gainde's used Audi, zooming us through artificially glistening Newark. I simply knew, before he turned that fateful corner, as the deepening became thicker with each mile left behind. Seems from inside my grandma's home, I'd been looking at the mansion the wrong way, expecting less black and not looking for more. Granted, I'd only been getting that small view outside the window, but supposedly smart guy me should have remembered when colors come together, it never gets whiter. Plus, having never seen Newark at night with eyes that wanted to see through the gloom, I noted the difference between every shade of black, all degrees deepening as they reached the edifice that drew each color contained within the darkened sky to the doorstep of The Sacred Breath.

Makes me further wonder what existence, itself, does to reach The Original Man who had lived all those memories of everything He'd created.

Um. If that makes sense....

However, getting back to this history? That day with A.S.C.E.N.D., I'd begun

305

to learn to fight – for real. Or, let's say, I was better prepared after being taught a few handy tricks by brothers such as Gainde, who told me,

"Never stand still for your opponent. Keep it moving, and bend those knees!"

I got put right in the ring, immediately – though it was just an open auditorium – with a brother about 2 years younger than me, named Kenneth, who proved might has nothing to do with size, as Kenneth, 4 inches shorter than me, handed me my butt, gift wrapped with one punch to the jaw.

Stars in the sky are lovely. Stars in your mind are not quite.

"You okay, man?" Kenneth had been kind enough to ask, which I'd heard about a second after I'd heard him say, "You okay, man?" He'd only said it once, though.

"Oh, yeah." I hadn't gone down, but, I shook off the feeling of losing touch with time and space, shaking my head and bouncing around a bit to regain my sense of pride, which wasn't that hurt cause these brothers were cool. Since entering the door, there was nothing but support, not a hint of 'In Yo' Face' threats, here. I felt like Cletus probably had upon reaching his fellow soldiers in that tangle of cypress trees, and I knew I would have sensed the same sincere greetings from each young man and the 5 older group leaders whether or not I'd had the ability to 'see' their genuine acceptance in their auras. Which I did, but it wasn't necessary, is all I'm sayin'.

That's why I wasn't mad at Kenneth as I knew he was sincerely worried he'd hurt me. And he surely had, physically – although if he could have seen the exuberance of my aura, he wouldn't have bothered asking.

I was ready to get back to sparring, but the head of Ascend, Brother Xolani, said:

"You've got heart, son, but let's give your skills some time to catch up."

Cletus, Ccwa, my office tower mind and I were disappointed, defensively replying, "I'm okay!" I could have said, "We're okay," but I hadn't been knocked senseless, just dazed.

Brother Xolani, a medium skin toned, thickly muscled man, who looked like the long lost twin of Muhammad Ali, only with a voice like Barry White, shook his head, saying, "ASCEND's been meeting every Sunday for the last 15

306

years with no plans of stopping. You don't have to learn everything in one night."

Sensing my enthusiasm might be a bit much upon hearing the other members laugh, (for which they were firmly corrected by the leaders so they immediately stopped on cue, as if they'd rehearsed) – accepting my own correction without hesitation I conceded, too, with a head nod.

And that had been only the beginning of the session that was mostly about learning to fight with my Black Mind, economically and spiritually. Unlike using this telepathic Enscriptor, we used pencils for that training, however? Like in Heaven, we learned fists aren't the most important lesson in what makes you powerful.

Initially, Gainde had asked, "So, whacha think, brother?", after he and I had been driving through the dimly lit residential streets of Newark for a few minutes once we'd left the WISOMMM Center. He was built like his father, only with a more sinew-ed solidity. Just as dark, too, but there was no Senegalese accent. He spoke straight Black man in the U.S.-ish. It was strange, being so used to the Kattans, to see a reflection of their faces speaking with the flat nasal tones of a regular American.

Especially since Gainde was as far from being American as East is from West, and he was so much more than my little 's' powers could conceive.

"It was great!"

"Guess that means you'll be back."

I dropped an un-doubtable, "Definitely."

"Well, I'll give you my number to call as by next week we'll be meeting at another location, crosstown."

"Why?"

"Ah, the owner's being evicted." He was silent a moment, continuing, "Things get complicated in life, but Ascend goes on."

"Why don't you hold it at your dad's house?"

The silence lasted a little longer, ending with:

307

"That sure would be great, Tyree." And he said no more.

After a few turns round blocks I remember seeing since I was a child in the family car, watching places go by that we never stopped to check out, he and I continued our chat about dismissible details of my life, such as how it felt to move to Newark and go to a new school; but our conversation truly got started after he turned onto Carson from up the block. I noticed a change in his energy (yes, I could 'see' or best said – I could 'feel' a person's aura in the dark, it turned out) – but I detected a distinctive change in the easy going flow of his...?

Fire. It was more than a hint of light. It was light.

Brother Gainde was luminous, internally and thus externally, with the most radiant aura I'd seen out of thousands that day and the last. I'd discuss its particular intense frequency more, but I'm runnin' outta time to finish this history, and I think you've got the idea, already.

Anyway, as I was saying – (in the middle of this way too long orientation here in the Epidome, but no one seems aware of it) – as the Audi turned onto my block, and my heart didn't drop while he neared my ramshackle home this time cause Gainde not only wasn't a pretty girl I wanted to impress (remember and never forget – NO HOMO in Heaven, nor amongst those who didn't know they were building it) – but, he knew where I lived, and on top of that, I also felt thoroughly revived, thoroughly supported so much? Conference room level 3 sent out a memo to the other floors that Tyree had not a daggone thing to be ashamed of. Matter of fact, Level 3 added to the memo, "Tell 'em, Ccwa said so.

HA! I'm kidding, ya'll. But then again....

Maybe I'm not...

As I was enscripting ....

I couldn't help but notice, not a dimming, but a recalibration of his aura, just as his hand and arm coolly turned the steering wheel – like a hunter cat would tense up to attack if he'd heard or caught a whiff of, not a possible meal, but of a possible combatant lurking close by, in his territory.

'Wow,' I thought, '*He and his dad must truly be at each other's throats.*'

308

"Oh," I said, a pang of guilt forcing my honesty, "I'm gonna be helping your dad with his work."

He mumbled a brief acknowledgment, appearing more impressed by an indistinct plain white van that was parked directly in front of my usually arguing next door neighbors' row house. The house was quiet now and there were 2 passengers in the front cab of the van, but I wasn't paying attention. Sort of like I hadn't paid attention to that sneak punch the other day.

I repeated myself, figuring he hadn't quite heard, or that his thoughts were trained on some past disagreement with his father.

Gainde suddenly turned to me, calmly announcing, "He's shown you the Orb."

For some reason unknown to me, the guys in the basement started playing Talib Kweli's 'I Try', which accompanied my silent head nod of confession, since the brother's knitted brow gaze at me was as piercing as his dad's, but I could see Gainde's aura.

I knew lying to him wouldn't work.

"I understand," he said, rather casually, looking behind as he pulled in front of my house and backed up to the van. "It's not your fault Tyree."

He cut off the engine, and it sputtered out.

"I mean you're just a boy, for goodness sake. It's not fair for him to place this responsibility on your shoulders when he should be sharing knowledge of the Orb with grown folks who can help."

"There are people who can help with the Orb?" I had been convinced they weren't.

"Of course there are!" he answered matter of factly, continuing, "The doctor is under the impression that he and his wife are all alone in this struggle, but no victory in history after Allah birthed Himself has been won by only 2 people. They believe no one can comprehend the spiritual dimension of this war, but there are powerful, aware beings walking this Earth who submit to God's Law and aren't afraid of the repercussions from flouting the white man's tyrannical bastardization of divine rule."

It was such a relief that this authoritative brother didn't need any convincing from me about what was at stake, but I asked, "Brother Kattan is afraid?" hesitantly, shocked by the mere suggestion.

"Hmmmm. I misspoke there. He's not afraid. Sittin' in that huge building the whole community could use, while the Enemy keeps shuttin' down our programs. He's not afraid. He's too damned proud."

It was like the day Kyerah and I had overheard son and father discussing other realities we'd never been told existed. My mind, every level, wanted to know more, and I didn't need to be in the Kattan house to be able to pay close attention.

"What do you mean?"

But the brother wasn't explainin'.

"I'm sorry, Tyree. I've said too much. He should have never told you to begin with as I know he had to have sworn you to secrecy..."

"He didn't tell me because he wanted to. He had to. I stumbled into Allah's Breath."

"You what?!"

"The doctor didn't mean to tell me anything until I'd proven myself. I tripped over some rope and..." I put my hands up, body language conveying my ineptitude on that afternoon.

He was looking at me with 100% disbelieve, while knowing I was telling the truth.

He shook his head, saying, "Ah, man..."

"...I fell in the Orb. If the doctor hadn't caught my feet with the same rope I tripped over, I'd have never gotten back out. How did you know I'd even seen it?"

"Dude, it's all over your face. You think I didn't live with that hole in the air every day? I've seen the way it intensifies everything near it. When you walked into the Ascend session, it's like you were a 30yr old boy. No nervousness, no hesitation. What child does that?! Probably why Brother Xolani put you up to

310

spare straight away. He thought it was cockiness."

"Does he know about the Orb?"

"Brother X? Nah, nah. Nobody but us, four."

"Five."

"Five?"

"My sister, Kyerah knows, too."

He bubbled out an ironic laugh, with a puff of air – not a harrumph, but darn near close.

"I ain't even gonna ask how that happened, cause the more who know, the more may get to know and then we can do the real fighting. But I knew sumthin' was up with you the minute I saw you, 'cause I know, the Doc needs an assistant with a pliable mind, to take over for him. No offense, intended..."

I didn't take offense. It wasn't that kind of conversation. I 'pliably' nodded my head in agreement with the plain truth, feeling relief at the same time that I was saddened I'd broken my vow to the doctor.

"I just put 2 and 2 together."

"I promised your dad not to tell anyone."

"Aw, dude! That's not your burden. What are you? 11?"

"12. I'll be 13 in December."

"Geez! Tyree, look," he took on that intense American – no, correction – he took on that intense Diasporic Afrikan man's flow, bringing his hand up to cup his beardless chin, "That's not your burden, to keep such an enormous secret from the whole world for who knows how long. That's not your job, brother! The doctor (he didn't call him 'dad' or 'pops', just 'Doc' or 'the doctor') – he keeps that thing and himself prisoner in that house waiting for who knows what to come along and fix everything. In the meantime? We're dyin' out here."

He chuckled to himself.

I wondered what could be funny about us dying, when he added, "Though, I guess, this is no easy time for any Black child, no matter what side of the street you're on, or what you're told. Reality is brutal enough."

I weakly smiled, thinking of the buckling sidewalk and the collapsing porch. I remained certain I could fix all that, but I was wrapped up in the proof that I was still a child, but at least this time? It felt good to realize that's what I was meant to be. That I didn't know everything. That I still needed guidance 'cause it's okay if there were men like my father. Men like Gainde and even the doctor to be the map.

"You said there are people who can help. Who are they?"

"Oh, plenty. Legions of folks are realizing these are the Last Days."

I nodded my head. I'd seen proof of the Last Days for myself.

"Most important of all, The Honorable Minister Farrakhan. I know the Doc's brand of Islam thinks the Minister is some kind of con artist, at best, a murderer at worst, but? The facts say different and he's the only man out here, in the public, who's independently sharing all the truth with every man, woman, child and all the governments that're holding their people hostage. These are the Last Days, but if we're replacing the Devil's Rule, we have to have something better to replace it with. We all need the Orb to put to good use – if it has a use.

"There's no army of only generals," he added, "and that's what the doctor is unwilling to accept. He just may be merely a foot soldier, when the war is won or lost on the frontlines. There's legions of us foot soldiers who've been fighting for decades, without whom? The Ankh Udja Saneb..."

I turned to him, my expression steady, only my eyes registering my fear...

"... will happen for our Enemy's sole benefit."

"You know."

"Brother, of course I do. I was supposed to be the next Protector, but I refused. My victory? Is out here, workin' with our people." He motioned with his right arm sweeping beyond the windshield, but I don't think he meant to include the white man who seemed to instantly appear as if out of nowhere, stopping on the left side of the Audi, standing between us in the car and the Kattans' out of no place abode.

He rapped his knuckles outside on the driver's window.

Gainde rolled it automatically down, and just as automated, my fear welled up. Despite my new mind's ability to think dispassionately and logically, it wasn't as fast as every single headline I recalled, telling the stories of multiple bad endings for other Black persons who'd begun their personal last days exactly like this, with a cop casually walking up to their car window. My Insta-Fear kept humming after the buzzing window sound silenced itself, the glass barrier disappearing into the door's recess.

The younger not a doctor Kattan effortlessly said, "Good evening, Officer Tereshchenko. You're out early."

"Ah, Gainde," Officer Tereshchenko pleasantly returned in some sorta lightly tinged Eastern European accent I couldn't place, "I haven't seen you at the folks' house in quite a while. Where've you been hiding?"

My Inst-Fear clicked off, now, replaced by pop up new and improved Insta-Distrust.

"You *know* him?" I asked under my breath.

He hushed me with a wave of his right hand. Not missing a beat, he answered the very white, hard faced, 'bout 30ish policeman, "Keepin' roof over head, sir. How's the beat treatin' you?"

"Well, it is what it is. This is always the quietest street around. Should be soothing, but it gives me the creeps."

"Hmm," was all the lean Black man said.

One of those awkward pauses got started right here, which Gainde didn't bother interrupting. Officer Teresh-something did.

"Well, remember to give me a call if you see anything unusual." He tipped his hat.

"That I will, Officer. You have a good evening."

313

"Good evening."

I could see him walking around us, back up Carson, getting into the white van before I'd repeated my question, distrust filling every word.

"You know him?"

"Oh course I do, son. Him and a dozen others on a first name basis. You've only visited your grandma during summer vacation. This block, this city, our people have been my life. And right here, it'd be impossible not to know them. Cops keep the school on 24/7 survelliance."

He meant the Kattan house.

"That's why Dr. Kattan was so jumpy."

"He has a right to be jumpy as he's not kidding when he says the Tamahue want that Orb, even though they'd have less success with it then the doctor would all by himself."

"Then why don't they go in and take it?"

"Cause the doctor is a prideful man, but he's no fool. He lives a clean life while the police need probable cause to search a well-connected Black intellectual's home. Were he a common man, the Orb wouldda been snatched up in a heartbeat, but? Staying well connected, that's what the Doc does. Hosts events and researches for darn near every Black History scholar there is. Writes some of their books that they take credit for, also, but he's respected 'cause he knows his stuff, and he's well paid for it. That with finding hidden, overlooked treasures using the Orb? He's got both learned back-up and he's got money. Cops can't mess with that. Not easily."

"He uses the Orb to find treasure?!!" My mind glowed with dreams of hidden troves, which easily trumped distrust of Brother Gainde's familiarity with the police.

That's when my mom gave me a start, knocking on the driver's side window that had since been rolled back up, eclipsing getting an answer from Dr. Kattan's son.

"Oh, hey!" she heartily greeted Gainde, like the old friends they were.

314

He and I, both, got out of the car. They hugged, and began general chatting. That's when, as I stretched my body out of that cramped small car crunched-up position to stand, I saw the unmistakable Von, leaning into the passenger side window of the white van behind us, talking to Officer Tere-I'm Not Gonna Try and Pronounce That Name Again and the other cop in the driver's seat. They weren't talking loudly, or my mom and Gainde would have heard them.

Or?

I would have heard them, but woefully, my supersonic hearing was still on order at the non-existent superhero store. I didn't need it, though, because my soul could hear, if it couldn't translate the exact words – it could hear the wrongdoing being planned. And boy, I didn't know what it was, but was it ever so wrong! Unfortunately, before I could alert Gainde, stepping up to the buckling sidewalk, I had to wait till he and my mom finished reminiscing, said their goodnights, along without taking a breath that I could interrupt, and then she said to me,

"Let's get upstairs,Tyree. It's rather late."

"But, mom! I've gotta tell Brother Gainde something!"

Now reader, I know you're thinking I should have piped up my suspicions about that conversation at the white van, without concern for being a dutiful son, but, here's the problem with that.

1. What the heck could I have said, really? That I *suspected* something rotten was goin' on in Denmark? I mean, on Carson, in tha hood? Yeah. I see you see my point.

2. Unfortunately, one of the strong Black Mind lessons of that Ascend's session, was respecting one's mother. Or, oops, I meant to say 'fortunately', although it was quite unfortunate for me at that moment, as the brother injected,

"Step up, young man. You can tell me another time. Remember to respect your mom's commands."

And finally?

3. I was in the habit of obeying my mom, remember? Call me a woose if you want to, but I was going with the faith that even if I didn't agree

with the grown-ups, maybe somehow, someway, this time? They'd prove my concern that they were acting like idiots wrong.

Now, that's harsh, but that's what I felt then, knowing sumthin' –

did I say 'awful' enough, already? –

knowing sumthin' AWFUL was on the way. Yet, rather than complain, given all the points I made directly above, I just said,

"But…"

"But nothin'," Gainde went on. "Is there anyone about to die right this minute?"
My mom was quietly impressed with her old friend's intervention. I was not, but, frustrated, I conciliated, "No, sir."

'At least not today,' I thought, and my office tower, including the basement, wasn't joking.

"Alright then." He reached in his pocket and pulled out a business card he handed to me. I could see 'A.S.C.E.N.D.' embossed upon it, with their logo of a man walking up a flight of stairs and his full name in smaller print above a telephone number.

"Call me, tomorrow, if that's okay with your mother…"

With a warm satisfaction, she nodded her head.

"… and we can discuss this further."

Yeah, reader. You know how my next day went without me wasting your or my time describing it in detail. It was full of auras, extra-sensory perceptions and?

COMPLETE ANXIOUSNESS AS ALL GET OUT, 'cause I knew something

awful, a-w-F-U-L-L

was coming. Didn't know exactly when, didn't know exactly what, as like Dr. Kattan said, we can't tell the future, but I sure had a feeling something preventably terrible was going down that very Sunday, and only I could stop it, if? If, before it happened, I could figure out what I had to do to stop it. Oh,

316

man.

However, this present minute, now, waking up in my hotel room after recording more of this history (my apology that I forgot to inform you that I'd left the plenary session, yesterday evening – have you met me? The brand new writer) – writing when my thoughts are freshest – first thing in the morning seems to be my most productive time – however, before I skip to the juicy bits? I've got an appointment with The Original of The Originals.

Whoa.

I'm sure you understand if I don't tell you what happened all those decades ago for another page or two. Or 3..... or.....

gulp.

=

It wasn't that He had eyes I feared would begin disarming my soul the instant I looked into them, me breaking that gaze to look down even more quickly. It wasn't that He'd just gotten back from His morning run, dripping with sweat which He wiped away with a plain white towel a disciple, standing by, had handed Him. It wasn't any of that which shocked me. It wasn't even that He left me to wait for His return, after stating, "...Gonna hit the can, Brother, take a quick shower, and then We'll talk..." speaking normally, and yet authoritatively, like?

Any down home rich voiced Black man...

No, the depth of His eyes may not shock anyone; and while it could shock 3 dimensional you, dear reader – even horrify some others – that Allah has a body with all the functions thereof, but, none of that shocked me. See, wise men naturally have the power to hold the aware with just a look and for the rest of my unexpected encounter with The Creator this morning, including his very human lavatory needs? Well, I've heard The Honorable Minister Louis Farrakhan speak on how human the prophets are, despite our desire they be magical, complete with fairy dust and sound effects, so? Of course I was fully expecting Him to be The Wisest, while I wasn't surprised The Original is more Man than the men He created, as He's the measure of everyone He's made. What did stump me was that I knew Him the minute I saw Him, only?

I couldn't quite place His face.

When I saw Him before that tumultuous gathering, He'd been too far away to see, and there'd been no 50ft screen projectors, as His presence didn't need amplification. We'd all heard every word in Our hearts, minds and souls. So, I never saw His exact features, but here, in His direct presence? It's like encountering something, someONE, that your deeper mind recalls instantly, and yet your subconscious mind decides conscious you don't deserve to be brought in on the secret. Either because you haven't been eating correctly enough to empower inter-cellular communication between brain neurons, or because you're a jerk who never thinks of anyone you can't use, so you forget anybody one second after you discover they've got nothing you want. Or? Because, like me, who's enhanced capacity for thought didn't suffer from the above mentioned nutritional deficiency, nor is anyone in Heaven a selfish jerk,

318

anymore – you know Allah at first glance, and yet, you don't know Him due to His having created you and not the other way around.

What do I mean? Well, as a baby knows his momma, like I'd felt drawn to the Orb before I'd even seen it, that blackness the pull of the ocean's waves upon the magnetic equivalent in your being – that's what standing that brief moment before Him was like, only far more magnetic, as HE?

Is what pulls the tide and everything else. He is the destination of the planets and the stars. He is the source of magnetism, itself. With one momentary glance, and then dropping down upon my knees before Him without hesitation, kissing the hem of His running pants, which fell with their NBA-like gym satiny gleam (black, with red piping) – they draped down upon the tops of His running shoes –

[Side Note: His sneakers were a no name brand as I've hinted, everything made today is no name top of the line manufactured for passion, not profit. Our craftsmen don't need to brag since they and everyone else produces because people need shoes, clothes, furniture, toothpicks – so you make 'em shoes or whatever, and that's how your passion is answered. If that ain't enough, then you better find out what excites you, besides bragging, since with the whole Earth free – no one has to beg or prostitute himself for money, 'cause you can eat and live pretty much wherever you roam.]...

But, excuse me – as I was enscripting – when I'd dropped prostate before Him, the First Man leaned over, placing one dry hand upon the back of my bowed head, and with one more lowered glance upward so I would only peripherally connect with those piercing eyes, I knew He is what all existence celebrates.

The destination of everyone's journey is Allah.

He'll be back out in twenty minutes or so, His disciple just warmly told me, and like gods in training, like sneaker makers who are content covering people's feet, please be joyfully patient, reader, and have a seat with me, since it's not about me and it's not about you – it's about Us, together, reaching Him...

I arrived crack of dawn this morning, hours ahead of my appointed time, and yet, He'd been expecting me, the end of His 5 mile jog timed to greet me the minute I'd stepped out of my car. I'd parked along the roadway that turned into His estate, and happy to encounter what I'd thought were two of The Creator's disciples, I was utterly floored to realize one of them was Him. I admit I'd expected a formalized introduction; not something so?

Regular....

Ordinary, even.

Overwhelmed, I'd dropped without artifice, down upon my knees. Good thing We were on one of those grassy sidewalks like from my old Sandstone Hill neighborhood, and not standing on the black tar driveway alongside, or my knees would have felt the force of my 9/11 nano-thermite free fall pancake collapse. Calmly requesting I stand up, He explained what He had to do next, and put my comfort in the care of one of His assistants, whom I was told and I see, this one and dozens of others are always within arm's length of His presence. But, Eye equally see, they w-a-n-t to be within His presence because they need Him, and not the other way around. I mean, Allah is never in danger, anywhere He roams. Anywhere. Any dimension.

Oh!

To inform you, should you have been wondering – I don't see such a contrast in auras here in Heaven as I did in Hell, as everything's radiance is the same level of intensity due to the liberation of reality, itself. I think I had mentioned it at the start of this history – evil is a negative force destroying down to the atomic structure of matter, weakening the vibrant connection that thinking beings not only gather from light, but as nascent gods in training? We were sources of light from within, dimmed by Our Enemy's grip over Our melanated electrical pulse. I theorize the liberation inside Allah's Sacred Breath is what allowed my light within to reinforce my connection to existence as it healed the pathways within my body through which my light could travel and I could receive faint signals and restore their meaning inside my sensitized brain. All so complex, I know, so suffice to say, in His presence? Even here in Heaven? Never have I seen such color, and I've seen a lot in my decades.

No wonder He didn't need to ask for helpers. I'd been told by others attending the gathering, way back at the Epidome, wherever He is, you were bound to see His disciples either somber, or cheerful, or laughing, or crying, or debating, or simply living their life near Him for whatever reason they had, while busying themselves with the matters necessary to keep up the home of The Creator. Tain't no lazy people hanging with Theeeee God, along with no crowds of mere gawkers and hangers' on. We, every last man, woman and child – We ALL respect the process and only seek His direct guidance when We need Him, specifically – because He accepts all seekers. And when it's time to go?

Yo.

Ya bounce.

Also, for your other question, reader? Yes, His attendants are Black, Brown, Red and a few are the so-called 'Yellow' People (they look light brown to me, only with those tweeked eyes, like my Jepkemboi). Not a one is white because His vibrancy is beyond their physical capacity. I know some are angry to hear that, but think of their limited tolerance for the one inanimate Sun in the sky. Here's what fuels the Sun, so standing near Him is certain death only for them. However, percentage wise, His disciples are nearly all Black, but, none of them are anywhere near as Black as He.

Nothing in reality is as Black as that Man. Not even the Orb.

Now, I'm out here, where I'd been ushered to wait for Him, taking a seat on a living Baobab tree bench, at least 30ft wide, the trunk of which was pruned and coaxed from germination to sapling to full grown cozy resting nook, shaped along each stage and continuing its flattened 60 foot height up the side of where a covered porch used to be attached to a very familiar house, or should I say? A very familiar mansion in a very familiar region outside Abjerusalem, as it's the self-same house whose air I had once stared at from the living room window across the street, only, today? There's a yellow field of dandelions before me, in front of further crops where a tangled lot used to be. And there's no across the street, only an apricot orchard where my better than Detroit shack once clung to its nail and rotted boards for dear life, along with all the shacks that'd had been next to it. Then beyond that lies the dirt road I'd bumped into Allah upon this morning. In the midst of the orchard?

Stands a 70ft recreation of my mother's original sculpture of that determined Black man reaching for the sky – re-carved by my mom, as her gift to Theeee original, Original Man.

Now, mom's not the most famous of Our artists, but she's had a lot of time to perfect her creativity. We all have. All Praise Due to Allah that We finally brought the Heavens down to Earth for each to luxuriate within, peace and serenity abundant, but not a distraction, so We don't get to work. You know those futuristic movies depicting a perfect world where ¼ way through you find the bliss of some is the horror of others? Nah. Not here. With The Ubuntu, same as with my dream, We'd come back to life to re-build the ruined cities and while We were at it...

the ruined countryside. Why, We started with that untamed wild tangle of fallow land next to the Kattan estate that lays before me, pristinely resplendent, as I wait. Along with thousands and thousands of acres of renewed and de-pesticide, de-gmoed farming territory, the lot was long ago chopped down, cleaned up, tilled and sown into an open plot of edible greenery, ready to be picked by anyone hungry. As we'd all planned for it, some 93 years ago...

Actually, every rotted, careworn structure of old Newark unto old America, had one by one been torn down, along with sidewalks, buckling or not, every span, removed and rebirthed – each soul numbing strip mall, parking lot and abandoned structure – each had been reclaimed in the name of humanity's need for beauty. Neglected land was reseeded and refurbished land was cultivated. Wild land was de-poisoned for actual wild life to thrive within, not remain endangered, whilst We picked up the trash from latitude to longitude. We'd started here in old Newark, but by the time we'd collectively purchased our houses to tear down, re-cycling the debris into fewer but grander residences for the entire community, the truth of who We are had reached from pillar to post, so there was little trash left, anywhere, by the time We came to the next neighborhood to extend Our expanding Heaven. All that was left for Us to do was applaud as others built their new cities, new villages, new towns, new farms from the purple mountains majesty to back here in New Manykeni (I suggested that name for old Newark). Pretty cool, if I must say so, myself.

Abundance sweeps over the hills, nestles in the valleys. But no crowds, though Our bounty could handle it, as sadly most of us from that End Time?

Well? Hell is far more crowded than Heaven, for the present – not because the damned are trapped, but because? They don't wanna leave the addictions of perdition! See, there's more food than several planets worth of beings can eat, but? Tain't no MacDonald's any place We've healed, and We've healed it all. No Wendy's. No Chipotle's. There's mansions for everyone, but no White Castle's from sea to shining finally non-radioactive sea. No clubs or bars, either, to get your drink on. No corner dealers as there's no cornered by the hardships of life users.

However, once again, I'm getting ahead of myself, and I think I hear The Almighty laughing in Dr. Kattan's former office, directly behind me.

I've been told He laughs a lot, however? I'm too nervous to turn around, so lemme keep on enscripting...

Okay. What does this feel like, waiting for Theeeeeee God of The Universe, knowing He's the reason for my ability to breathe? Hmmmm. I don't know if I can describe it as my first sensation is to maybe pass out 'cause I have far tooooooooo many sensations right now. After these 97 years of service, although my brain has only gotten more multi-layered, more skyscraper-ish, surpassing its former commercial office tower height, and I've gone through more harrowing moments than I can fit in this book – after all that, as I process this, the greatest avalanche of feelings I've ever felt, I can understand the stories about how when you die you see your whole life blazing before you. That's what's happening to me right now, like a vivid replay of my every deed and misdeed, when I have multiple lifetimes worth.

Good thing I'm more alive in this reality than I'd have ever been back when Carson Avenue had been Carson Avenue. I'dda been dead in an instant, being in the undoubtable presence of The Most High, which explains a lot of what happened to one of those recessive gened people, that next evening after Gainde dropped me home...

But as I was saying...

Some may find it hard to sympathize with my fear, thinking you'd handle meeting The Almighty more calmly. Some may be thinking – dude? You're a god and yet you're still goofy. To that I say...

'Yeah, and so?'

I told you We, Gods, are more human, not less. We laugh more, We love more, We can be angered more disastrously, but We know how to protect Our humanity long before Our peace is threatened, after thousands of years of reaping what We used to sow! That's why We, now, defend peace so it's everlasting. Yeah, listen up, tough dude who's drowning in a sea of Devil-made confusion. Reaching higher was always that easy. This has always been Our-story, not some momentary ruler of lies and tricknology's 'his'story.

Eliminating all devilishness? Tell me, what's there not to rejoice about? What's there not to feel a little goofy over? I'm back in Manykeni, with more understanding of how to keep it safe, and my house is about 10 miles up the road. Only have one wife, though. Oh, well, here? That's finally enough.

By, the way, reader? Have I introduced you to The One and The Only?...

'Cause He's standing right in front of Us.......

323

He's walked up to me and I can't help but feel compelled to drop back down to my knees and kiss the hem of his white linen garment – the traditional garb as worn by The Ancients – an unadorned robe draped about his entire frame, tied around the waist by a simple hemp rope. Ah, and dropping to my knees, again, is what I've attempted after rising halfway up to fall down. However, He's gently, without doubt, grabbing my left shoulder to stop me.

"Asalaam Alaikum, Heavenly Maker!" I say, instead bowing my head, reverentially.

He nods, but He's not laughing or smiling, and yet, with no harshness, he says, "Walaikum Salaam, brother. Come. Walk with me..."

We're leisurely heading in the direction of the orchard, winding through trellised strawberry patches, covering the once asphalted street. It's a short stroll, but it seems so much longer in the grip of Our silence. I'm breaking it first, getting straight to the point.

"I'm not finished with the book, Sir."

"Yes. You aren't. I know, son."

"Oh. You don't sound angry."

Allah is laughing, again, as I'm shocked, once more – not due to his laugh, but because I'm realizing – this isn't my imagination. I know exactly who this Man is, as I've worked hand in hand with Him during my early years as Knowledge Protector.

Omg. I had been working with The Beneficent, The Most Merciful, The All Knowing right up in my face and I had had no idea! This explains so much I sensed, but didn't understand back then.

Nodding at a passing elder sister disciple, in between His chuckles, He's saying, "Ah! Brother, you don't want to see me angry! And for this small imperfection, I have no reason for ire, but? You knew that, already, didn't you? You know much, Amenhotep, have no doubt."

"Yes," I'm shaking my head, while I continue, "Shortly after I received Your invitation, I realized You'd have always known my trouble completing this assignment. Not even the formation of a child in the womb do You miss. Plus,

324

You know me."

He's turned to me, catching my eyes with His, looking slightly down from his exceptional, but not unusual height. He must be about 6ft 2, while I'm 5ft 11. His hair is woolen white, now, not the jet black as I remember it, decades ago. Its shimmering brightness a stark contrast to the absolute depth of His skin, the blackest I've ever seen on any man, showing no age greater than, say? A man in his early 40s would show if he'd never eaten a toxic thing in his life – the flawless sheen of His skin stands as an irrefutable witness to His purity. His chin is a chiseled compliment to His physique which is broad, not slender, nor rotund. His cheeks are pronouncedly striated, but not wrinkled, muscles fortified from perhaps centuries of good use smiling, laughing talking, making His expressions accented as if with exclamation points. And His eyes?

I've turned away because His eyes are not one lone orb sitting inanimately on a side porch, but two orbs intensified with the mind of The Greatest Thinker. Eyes which enter into my soul, not the other way around. He didn't use to have such a magnetic gaze, but, He didn't use to be so Black.

Well, he was my guide back then. Someone I looked up to and had enjoyed plenty of father/son good fun with, but, now? Shoot! He's THEEEEE GOD, for goodness sakes, and that's why, stunned, I'm continuing to address HIM with the total formal humility due to the Creator of my very breath, admitting without daring to acknowledge I could ever know HIM, I'm now saying, "Who could really know You, Sir? But Your memories starting from before the beginning of time are precise down to the atom. You know me from not only when I was Tyree, but from when I was Ccwa, Akhenaten and more timespans than I've run across myself. How could You be anything but aware of the totality of everything?"

"Precisely to the neutrino, son, but as you said? You'll leave the science to the Protector of Science. Until it's your time to understand that, too."

That's hit me for a loop. I'm not looking at Him, but the concern comes out in my voice, unhindered as if I was talking to Him as I once knew lower case 'h' him, saying, "Will I have to know science, too, when merely writing this history is more than I feel I'm capable of, even now?" Recovering my sanity, I'm quickly tacking on, "Beloved Allah?" I feel the impertinence of my outburst.

Cold with fear that I've gone too far, He's answering, yet His face shows no indignation...

325

"Hmm. You are still connected to the physical impact of having lived as Tyree, and you believe having never finished their limited schooling your abilities are hampered. Yes, you've discovered multiple transformations of your energy through time, a soul without flesh is as powerless as useless lightening in an open field. I know Satan taught all My People to be bored by not only the building and maintenance of civilization, but by the very methods I used to create life, itself. As if they can't do the same. But in the time only I know, your duty is to do as is your original nature. Which is as your Creator's. Your nature is My own, for there is no realm that is not but another room in My mansion."

We've taken many more paces into the gaps between apricot trees, heavy with ripe fruit, which span randomly wide in dozens and dozens of trunks and more dozens deep. I'm noticing the return of silence between Us, as I spy the base of The Original Man statue, between the trees and clearly visible over their low tops. I understand the shortness of the apricot trees watching how easy it is for the various disciples, scattered throughout the orchard, harvesting – it's obviously easy for them to pick the bounty, from any angle.

The Creator is reaching down, lifting up an empty basket on the grass, among the several lying about. He's handing it to me, getting another for Himself.

"Let's gather Our breakfast, Amenhotep."

I'm nodding and reaching out, twisting one velvety apricot easily off the branch which gifted them with sustenance, the quiet between me and my Maker a comfort now. Natural. I've dropped the fruit into my basket, as The Creator does the same with His. We continue picking, looking for the ripest pick.

"Brother, what college degree do you think I have that taught me where that 490th atom in that apricot will go in your very body when you nourish yourself with its flesh? Which professor instructed me on how to formulate one of the most poisonous substances known – cyanide – into the flesh of the kernel within the fruit's pit, so when eaten it only kills cancer cells and not you..."

I must confess, inwardly, I hadn't considered that.

"You don't have any degree, Holy Maker."

He's continuing, "I have all the degrees, Beloved. Especially those they don't

326

give out, as will you. Only the degrees are a spiral, not a sphere since time itself is an echo of the Original Birth that gives reality the chance to always do better. And if you look well enough into any phenomena, you'll always find Me and My guidance forward."

"Will that help me finish my task, Sir?"

"That, Brother, will help you create your own universe. Your faith this day is almost the size of the mustard seed and thus you say, 'Move mountain..' only you do the moving, although unencumbered, about the mountain, while it stands still. One day, your faith, alone, will move whole continents, and then planets. As this tree was once a sprout that had no map for its plan, so shall you succeed in all My realms, until you succeed in all the realms of your own."
"I don't understand, Holy Creator."

"Pick a few more apricots and ponder, Brother, the skill it takes to perform what for the look, seems an easy task. But there are creatures who employ a host of other methods to do what you take for granted, and to do what they accomplish would be impossible for you, but? They don't have My nature, which is free, giving Me, giving you, the ability to screw up, but then the ability to learn from your mistakes and move on. It is your nature to have ease after hardship not because the hardship disappears, but because your strength is greater having overcome it."

"But what if my sense of myself is something else? Something Self-generated? Must I become what I don't feel is me?" Despite my reluctance to admit it, I find myself growing angry with Allah's answers, disappointed that I must still finish what's not been comfortable for me. Picking apricots is no work compared to writing this narrative. Compared to understanding what He means. I'm worn out.

I've looked down, angry with myself for not being the dutiful disciple I was certain I'd be. This isn't the way I pictured myself behaving. Dang! How could I be so rebellious?

The Creator is silent, still picking His apricot meal. I can't tell if He's angry or indifferent, His stern, wizen face, unreadable. I best continue pulling fruit, too.

He's saying, suddenly, startling me from my task, "Why is this assignment difficult, Brother? Don't you already know?" He's put his hand upon my shoulder, and just like that? His forgiveness feeds my ability to forgive myself,

327

and think better.

"Because I don't think I can accomplish it. Because I doubt myself."

"Hmmmm," he sighs. "So your confidence is being guided by a contrary people's directions, when what you've written so far? It's all that's necessary to begin the climb. View yourself beyond the limits of a cage forced upon you and leaving the cage becomes easy, as you'll explode it. You don't believe in your destined triumph because your mustard seed of faith, in what only EYE gave you, grows in the doing, not the hiding."

He spoke quietly, authoritatively, only emphasizing what I've enscripted in capitals, as my heart receiving the intensity behind the words.

I'm chancing looking into His eyes, knowing I fear what they're now revealing to me of who I am. I see a young boy told he was gifted because he so skillfully excelled at what white people told his kidnapped ancestors who then told every generation up to the birth of me, what would make me successful. I see me taking sustenance from the wrong fruit growing on the wrong branch of the wrong tree, making me spiritually nutrient deficient. I see a man who must determine his own limits according to my Maker, who has none. I see this and more than I can say with not one second of this insight being anything magical, as the speed of thought is faster than the speed of light. No sparkling fairy dust twinkling around Allah's eyes necessary. No special effects holly tree wand swirling light beams anymore than I ever saw hallucinogenic auras. I saw the real beauty of regular people, if they'd only believed in who made them. I'm seeing just me and The Original Man picking apricots, as common brown sparrows chirp their staccato chirps and the air is filled with the scent of true success.

I see what my Maker's led me to see within myself.

The Creator turns, his hand on my shoulder guiding me to follow. He says, "You knew all this better back at The Beginning, which for some was 'The End', but you've forgotten, like the adult forgets his childhood. The adult is further away from His connection to what I began. Our People are here, abundantly alive because they've learned enough of who the Devil is to survive the gift of a long life. Otherwise by the time they'd reach half your age, they'd be ready to sell it all out, again, for 40 pieces of gold. So finish your story in the method you desire. You have everything you need. And plenty of years to do more. Now!" He's clapped his hands, happily, contentment exclamated instantly in His smile. "There are some friends here who'd love to see you,

Brother. Bring your basket! We'll go harvest some berries and pick some dandelion greens and get to preparing Our meal. And turn that enscriptor thing off."

"Humbly, Sir, may I ask You one question with it still rolling?"

Without looking directly at me, He's saying, "Yes."

"You were there the whole time, living with Dr. and Mrs. Kattan. No wonder You never called them Your mother or father, but? Did they know who You were?"

As We begin leaving the orchard, after a moment He answers, "No one ever recognized Me, except for my Messenger, Elijah. He knew. But I'm back to my old self, and now everybody can tell."

A moment is passing as we walk, quietly. The Sun is shining in a lightly clouded sky, rich in that vivid blue.

"You have another question you've forgotten, my son. And because the answer is yes, some secrets are best left secret? Turn that thing off and only You and I will really talk."

Contented, I'm now shutting down the Enscriptor....

=

The next day, all Hell broke loose for the last time.

Um? I mean the next day in the limited, negatively charged dimension We used to suffer through – the one I was having one heck of a week within as a 12yr old, modern Black Boy in a modernity that was collapsing as we each breathed. Seems all Hell had been breaking loose and apart for thousands of years as there's no place in Theeeee God's universe for falsehood, but that day? The day after bumping into Allah, Himself, at Ascend? Only I'd had no idea who He was, and wouldn't for all these decades till meeting The Creator up close this morning – OMG! – so as a grown man I've verified that indeed, He is the man I used to call, 'Gainde'? That day, All Hell was doomed to become some Hell, until it became – no Hell at all.

The clock was ticking....

I mean on my grandma's nightstand. It was one of those old analog clocks made with a real wood oversized casing, with a huge telescopic glass covered face that magnified the iridescently green numbers, making them clearly visible in the dark of night. Her partial dentures were in a clear glass next to them, which was disturbing to my child's mind, but I was happy, again. I'd found myself awake, staring at the clock, being soothed by its soft ticking long before I'd wanted to be soothed and wondering how I was gonna get my grandma to part with it as the green glowing paint was slightly radioactive. I could sense the same energetic particles like it had been in the school fish sandwiches. In the grocery bags, in the people – only the clock's radiation was nowhere near as frantically active as what I finally recognized was pinging everywhere – what had to be a radioactive deluge. My 4th floor nerd section gets all the credit.

I concluded, the white man had figured ways to bring not one Trojan Horse gift, but numerous invisible Trojan Horses, carried into every household in the world, making everywhere the biggest battlefield there'd ever been...

"Oh, well. I'm just a child, so one step at a time..." I thought, early rising light interrupting the gloom through the one shaded window, casting a sword shaped beam upon my sleeping grandma, who lay next to me, gently snoring. Yeah. Guess I wasn't spoiled, afterall, as there I was, dealing with a situation no 12yr old would easily agree to – sharing a room with a 75 year old woman,

330

after having luxuriated in my own room, for all my known life (at that time) – my room that had been about half the size of our whole Carson apartment.

Well, I'd been epically disappointed with this arrangement, however? Like I said, what would have been the point of complaining? Yet, for reasons you can guess, reader, the last few mornings, it no longer bothered me, foremostly. As with everything else, from grandma's clock to the Ankh Udja Saneb, I didn't know what would change, but I knew I was 'gwoine' to change sumthin' for the better, even if it I did it slowly, cause being a child without all the answers was okay, *'Thank You, Gainde!'*

Now, in the back of my thoughts, I still had suspicions about Gainde, and dire suspicions about Von, the latter that I regretted having not voiced when I'd had the chance. But, a night of sleep had washed my cares away, maybe – as with my suspicions about Gainde – the ones about Von had been more intent on,

A
C
T
I
N
G

like a superhero. Maybe I had been reading an SOS into what didn't need my rescue. That humanizing talk with the younger Kattan, made me happy to do my part as a littler part of a whole. It was okay to be a boy. No need to be a man, this minute, let alone one who could leap over giant buildings, when I could more reasonably research how to fix a buckling sidewalk for everyone to walk on, googling it right off the internet. Maybe sell some newspapers or lemonade to get the money. No more need for a little 's' shirt, not because it didn't fit, but because it wasn't important. What 12yr old me wanted was to have friends, hang out, play video games, get good grades, and not care that my big sister was so mad at me.

If a war was coming, it'd come or go no matter what I did, so? Whatever, dude...

But, speaking of good grades? My forgotten school paper?!!! Dang! Well, you can verify how I have a bit of a history of procrastinating writing assignments, though I didn't mind writing short reports. You can use your smarts to write papers overnight. History books, on the otherhand?

Whew.

So, I'd forgotten to call the doctor, but I'd use my mom's laptop for some web research. Who could miss an opportunity to shut bold faced ignorance up, and so handily? That? Well, unlike how I began this history nearly drowning in my own bad choices, this was something I could do a double back flip, half gainer dive into.

But let's have some breakfast, with Allah, first!

~ ~ ~ ~ ~ ~ ~ ~ ~ ~ ~

Oh, you best believe I was feelin' so renewed by my conversation with The Maker of Reality, same as I'd felt upon standing in front of the Wisommm Center, decades ago - as He put my soul at ease, helping me realize that the key to civilization is thinking and planning waaaaay ahead, knowing Our impact falls not only on oneself, but as it falls on others...

Well, turns out some things don't need to be discussed in a public forum, including what was fully said between He and Eye. Ha! Yes. I guess I just told you what I'd told you I wasn't going to tell you if I decided not to tell you....

And I ain't apologizing.

Feelin' mighty excellent after that talk, I don't know what was more excellent to my elevated state of bliss, so that peace reigned supremely throughout my body, stunning not only every memory of other me's, but even astounding the previously unparalleled contentment of old Ccwa! That's a lot of contentment, there! I don't know if I was more enraptured by, lo and behold, stepping into the kitchen through the backdoor and seeing, not only that old used to be totally unfinished room now swankly decked out with every amenity, finished with stately handwrought wood and iron detailing, down to the invitingly non-echoing footfalls, but there at the island counter, amongst several disciples busy with breakfast preparation, and her chopping bunches of garlic cloves, was my own, radiant with life Queen, Jepkemboi!

"What?!" I bellowed, seeing her, utter surprise undoubtedly registering in my still not too handsome, not too ugly face. I first turned to Allah, but He was focused on emptying His basket of vitals on a side countertop. Turning, smiling back at Jepkemboi, it occurred to me, 'Uh-oh,' as I realized I'd completely forgotten to call her. Good to see her warm smile and hear her telepathic,

"*Oh, it's okay, Love...*", informing me, she understood.

I was further overjoyed to greet the forever hard to tell what age they were, Dr. and Mrs. Kattan – and, by the way – those were their names, as their family history had never been cleanly snatched away like We, the Diasporic Originals' history had been. I hugged my wife, hugged them, they all hugged me, and Allah came over hugging Us all, and then introducing about.... was it 6 or 7? I think 8 other disciples, who were real people with their own families either living at the estate with them, or they were only visiting for a short stay. I simply don't want to bog this chronicle down with the massive extent of each person's integral part in maintaining pure utopia.

Asante Sana to everyone of You who participated in that revitalizing repast that robust day. We spread laughter jubilantly, and sustaining nourishment to each of Our group like We used to pass around not so revitalizing flu germs, hence? This contagion not only required no effort, it brought confirmation that We've learned why the Devil must be defeated at every pass. Eternal bliss is so necessary, although, within every detail may hide the Cursed Shaytan, equally, inbetween every breath gasps a yearning for peace. We were so satiated with contentment, the still usually stoic Dr. Kattan was irrepressible, telling all the best jokes at that bounteous table, almost.

Yeah, dude, this is syrupy stuff, here, but, I have a greater point – I'm sharing this small glimpse of what has little to do with the focus of this history, because while this isn't directly related to the time I'm writing about, know that Heaven isn't an address – like real 'love' isn't a word – Heaven is the result of actions where You create it, protect it, plan it, so you can replicate it, and once that's Your reality – every moment's a happy ending of the moment before the next happy one. Yeah, like dreams of love, dreams of Heaven are all fluffy, nice and good and stuff, but, I'm sharing because an abundant life tain't magically perfect. We sang songs, but they were Our latest hit tunes (please don't ask if We have the top hits, as? We're BLACK, smh) – tunes, which included a few raps, some ballads, and some of Us were bad at both genres. None of Us were accompanied by harps or white winged angels, even though all the lyrics were about a good, righteous life, that you've got to get accustomed to living.

When you do? It's just Black Us, happy. Having a good time, like We do.

See? Heaven? Is REAL LIFE, like Gods are REAL HUEMANS. It's random snipets of truly divine gems, wrapped up with common, unextradordinary space, wound about those gems. Folks read those fairy tale books and get all disappointed when they grow up to discover life is quite unremarkable, no matter where it's lived. Here, We're still tied together, dependent on one another, through good and bad, however? We're now tied with golden threads no longer caked in filthy lies and filthier deeds to live a fantasy that's not possible unless somebody suffers. I repeat! There's no Dobby anywhere here, answering some fat cat's every whim. Everybody, including Allah, quite ordinarily, cut veggies, accidentally nicked a finger with a newly sharpened knife, cried over diced onions, set out plates, cups, told tales that were funny, sad; some told not so special tales at all (think I told at least one of those, feeling a bit awkward for a second or two, till I got caught up in someone else's tale) – and We all cleaned up afterwards, joyfully. Dr. Kattan cleaned the downstairs bathroom cause it was his turn.

We're okay with the perfectly fine, inevitability of the ordinary.

For me, the best moment when the plates where pushed away from Our dining table in the grand hall, right before We got to the clean-up, after Our Creator shared a half hour one heck of a hilarious story (the doc simply had more one line jokes, but not the very best stories) – the best moment was when Allah said in one of those quiet pauses:

"Shaytan gathers advocates by addicting them to artificial fun, in every manifestation. When 'artificial'? Well, that was his more pleasing word for 'nothing'. He gave The People nothing and the more artificiality you seek, the more nothingness you reach, until the immaterial becomes the void I destroyed. That's what Satan is. Fake, excessive, intoxicatingly mindless non-existence that can't sustain itself and it hooks onto the fear that You, the person, are not enough for Yourself, in these quiet moments. Yet, this is when You prove nothingness has no power over You. I never commanded any being have no fun. Lion cubs and zebra foals have hearty fun, but to nourish life? You must support life so it lasts forever. You don't fear what's common, what maintains fun when You have a true appreciation for humility. For getting all work done. 'Cause fighting against life's destroyers, sometimes? That's not a movie, most of the time, and it's never fun. But the after working the muscles, comes your strength and then your ease..."

I'm still not sure what that means, but I'm full speed ahead workin', now, having fun writing the way I want to, not the way I was taught is 'proper'. I'm suddenly inspired, which is really, really GREAT, with The Gathering only an hour away. Ha! I'm on page 312! HOT DANG!!! I could do this thing....

Oh! I almost forgot to mention my sister was there, too! Hmmmm. I wonder if that could be subconscious, not remembering to mention her presence and her jokes that were kinda funny — perhaps way back in 1831....

HA! Just kidding, big sis! You know you got skills! (*cough, cough*)

Oh, and by the way? Her new fiancé, the Venerable Mansa Musa, accompanied her. Well, I'll be! Somebody strong enough to attract the Beloved Queen Sita. Will wonders never cease. Wait till you find out, mom and grandma! Guess in a year or two my successor could be entering this world and replacing me, if searching history is his/her calling. I'm not worried about finding something else to do, myself, as I now know, mastering every discipline is my way.

Yes, yes. It was a mighty good morning.

~ ~ ~ ~ ~ ~ ~ ~ ~ ~ ~

I may not reach her in time, I despairingly perceived, instantly. How crushing after all I'd just accomplished, if in the end, I lost her, trying to rescue a princess I may have just killed. But what if that princess was my sister? However, servants, once their task is done, are not to turn around, unexpectedly re-entering a grand arrangement uncommanded, where only royalty are allowed to enter and leave freely – if even they can.

'Cause there's a princess in there who has nowhere left to go.

And I'd arrived in this reality walking through a narrow stone passageway built for menial staff, that left little room for even the free to change their minds, let alone a foreign retainer turning his full grown man's body about to go back the other way. I was certain the passage was narrow so guards could easily pick off multiple assailants, one at a time. Plus, I was sandwiched between 2 large male attendants, bigger than me, the humble messenger who had no reason to linger where I didn't work, thus was being escorted back to the stables to get up on my horse and return to my own master. Before Tyree me popped in, Kurush me been counting on the reason for my visit not being graphically revealed in the lifeless form of the most beautiful woman in the world, who'd just before I handed her a gift from her new husband, had been quite alive. Granted, I wasn't Tyree a-n-d Kurush when I'd handed Kyerah a vile of poison. Why, that might not have even been her.

I could sense, if I was to be found out for poisoning the princess, or cut down for making an attempt to save that deep black royal young lady, and, thus, executed, so be it. There was no fear in this body.

I was Kurush, which meant 'farsighted' and I'd always finished my duties, precisely. My mind was a machine, methodical in my tasks which gave me a comforting pride. Kurush would never deviate from a mission, which is why my master, Massinissa, entrusts me with duties of imperatively sensitive natures. Assassinations on his behalf is what I do, here. Blood, war and carnage is a familiar spectacle to these eyes, although, handing the loveliest woman I'd ever seen the means to her end – even for killing machine me, that was difficult.

However, my mission had been temporarily changed. If I didn't figure a way to get back into that dining hall, this instant?

The princess would not only be dead here, but my sister, too, if she was in that chamber, living as that sovereign woman. Tyree me didn't precisely know where Kyerah was, so I might never find her, again. She'd become one more indistinguishable facet in a memory so complete, the probability I'd locate her, would be astronomically miniscule. Same as Dr. Kattan never found The Bold Mumia Sirius Negus Ra, and he lived with that loss every day.

Death, as I've said, for me in the Orb is not desirable, but if I can be retrieved, it's not permanent. For the unfortunate soul, who's not the Protector, falling i-n-t-o the Orb? Death inside here changes all things where it matters.

That's why, I was gettin' back to that chamber. Yes, there'd been real time death that day when Hell came to an end, but? If I could do this right, somehow? At least Hell wouldn't get my sister, or at least I'd save a princess I might have just killed. Though, in the Orb, she'd only finish what she was determined to accomplish.

~ ~ ~ ~ ~ ~ ~ ~ ~ ~ ~

I'mma be free forming this last section, whereas till now, I've kept my writing in a somewhat orderly style, as I've been taught by my teachers, and also by those thousands of books I've read over my lifetime. Taught that there's only one way to string words, together.

336

Better get used to it, buddy!

But since events in my only one life were now speeding up and condensing into a march...? A procession...? A cavalcade...? Well, after writing all these pages (whoa, I'm on 319!) – after all this? I've learned that rules (which I didn't create or give approval for their perpetual continuation) – rules sometimes need bending, as long as everything forged from the effort still makes sense. There's no other option, especially when even the English language (a highly limited form of expression seeing it's a bastard tongue with nowhere near the number of words nor complexities of the oldest languages spoken on Earth – those being Afrikan, those being the first) – it makes perfect sense to claim the right to step outside the rules. Why, after writing just this paragraph, I've confirmed the necessity in the Thesaurus, in which I couldn't find a single word adequately descriptive for an insane deluge of events which was about to take place. And that's not the only time I've needed a specific word and found nothingness. So lemme get started finishing this epic ending of the beginning, by whatever means necessary.

Comforting Side Note: Apocalypse means the end of an age of lies as its defenses can no longer withstand The Truth....

~ ~ ~ ~ ~ ~ ~ ~ ~ ~ ~

That Sunday, late morn, I couldn't do my research on mom's laptop 'cause she needed it for grown folk stuff – something about a social networking forum for Black professionals seeking to facilitate their return to the job market beyond the confines of racial profiling, whatever, whatever, whatever kinda hyper dull stuff, of which I do remember every detail, but not because at the time I was remotely interested. The minutiae bits and pieces of life were the raison d'etre of the fourth floor of my brain, as my mom carefully explained what only grown-ups must find fascinating, while my basement mind was like...

'Oh, man! Can we get on with this, pleeeeeaze?'

She trailed on with more, "...whatever... whatever... whatever... but why did you wait till the last minute, son? Surely you've known about this assignment for weeks, but you're only getting started now?!"

I was steady as a rock, not wanting to lie, so sincerely I answered, "I'm sorry. Mrs. Finn gave the assignment last minute on Friday."

337

That was the truth, right?

Steadily clicking on links to access her forum, she instructed me to, "Call Dr. Kattan and see if you can use his computer. There won't be another meet-up like this for a month and I've got to find a job, a.s.a.p." – never interrupting her flow, blue light from her laptop screen glowing in the lenses of her reading glasses.

"Mom, actually, I don't think he has one."

She looked up at me with her distinctly unknown to us, Ibo face, incredulous.

"Of course he does! Who doesn't have a computer these days? He just doesn't show it to people. I think...," inquisitively knitting one eyebrow down as if remembering instantly the real Dr. Kattan, as opposed to how regular people behaved – making her add, "Well, most definitely he has plenty of books, that's for sure. What's that topic you're writing about? Kemet?"

She'd always called it 'Kemet', but now it warmed my heart that she would know to call it by its proper name in the first place. Moms are so uncool, by nature, but? I guess she wasn't all that bad, although sometimes she could ramble on in her too grown-up way...

"Yes, ma'am," I answered.

Kyerah, who'd been looking intently out the window, fuzzy orange slippers hanging over the edge of the couch, while grandma dozed quietly in her spot next to her, piped up, "They're not home now, anyway."

We're not a nerd family from the looks of us, as I've said probably a number of repetitive times. But, even without reading each other's thoughts, we all understood, no need to ask Kyerah – we knew if both the El Dorado and the PT Cruiser weren't in the driveway, then the Kattans were definitely not home. No one had to verify that my sister had seen the proof quite competently looking across the street. When everyone's on the same page, you progress forward much faster, rather than wondering if the future Queen Sitamen already had some sort of psychic power at 15, years before we'd gained that independent ability. That's why my mom and I uttered a sychronized:

"Oh!" Rather than a, "How do you know that?"

338

And to that combined utterance, we concluded, "You owe me a coke!" shaking our mutual pointer fingers at each other that we owed a drink we'd never drink. Habits are hard to break once practiced for years, including the habit of having fun with pretty okay parents or a single parent on her own...

I, however, did wonder why Kyerah was staring out at the mansion, which was a practice she'd always poo poo-ed, making fun of me whenever she observed me frozen at the window indulging my keen interest in 'the air'...

I can still hear her laughter after choicely asking, one day, if I could tell the difference between each atom of oxygen, so I could give them names and put them in my last will and testament. I even cracked up! But, oh, she made that joke last forever through the years! Strange, this morning, she was the one glued to the view of that not haunted – but nonetheless disquieting for a reason she knew, now – haunted mansion. Plus, she'd been the prolonged moody one, rather than pre-fall into The Sacred Breath me. Or, okay! Sour me yesterday because my only confidant sister didn't understand what I clearly did, 'cause I'd seen it firsthand through Cletus' eyes.

She was still mad at me?!! Man, I tell ya, it was good to be free to be an immature boy again, 'cause rather than listening to my overly analytical 4th floor staff that wanted to humanely scrutinize the difficulty of being a 15yr old Black girl in these conflictual present day circumstances – 'Ah, *you 4th floor guys!*' – I sided once more with the basement crew who decided girls, especially girls who were sisters, had to be the biggest pains in their brothers' lives...

I'm not literally saying what they'd said, but, b~u~t,

B
U
T
T

...it was funny, dude.

So, that's how I wound up dropping 4 or 5 textbooks upon a long pine veneer table in the bright and cheery Russet College Library, a couple hours later, merely a few blocks away from my no hurricane necessary to look like it'd been through one home. There were no scuffed up, haphazardly and mindnumbingly dull green walls in this school building, despite its location in neglected Newark. For that matter, some of the most revered colleges and universities in the U.S. were within one or two struts of dilapidated poor Black

339

neighborhoods, although their campuses looked like something out of 'Robin Hood'. Though ironically treacherous tax freebees for the rich, not the poor, brought that pathetic state of affairs about, at the moment, it was highly convenient for me, 'cause every public library on the East and West Coasts of the country was closed on a Sunday, along with every library in-between, including the Kattans' (for that morning, at least, with them). The last one of the 2 days of the week when students might need their services to finish assignments, was universally limited, while the liquor stores were all wide open.

Well, alright – it had been my fault I'd forgotten my deadline on Saturday, um? After having forgotten it, beforehand, on Friday. Good thing my mom was a certified teacher who made one phone call, finagling 12yr old me access to the Russet's Carver Memorial Library, since remember (and mom remembered) – ? We, evolved Jacksons, were maniacally on time. Me, too, especially when it came to proving a certain misinformed teacher wrong. The memory of Mrs. Finn's unabashed ignorance still scalded me. That's why I didn't mind entering the nearly devoid of people main reading room, looking extra short and juvenile to the solitary, only moderately dusty librarian, high up atop his entrance desk, but? What if the time my family had always been punctual for? Was over and done with, while the world had begun ticking to another original, yet forgotten rhythm, unbeknownst to us? What if, no matter our plans, there was a bigger, better one?

I knew the Ankh Udja Saneb was on its way, but I didn't know w-h-e-n, nor considered it my particular responsibility, any longer, as I mulled over an assortment of historic whatever, whatever, whatever about Kemet that horrified me with the books' downright deceptions. Bent on using my calculator mind to compose an Ali knock-out blow to Mrs. Finn's assertion that Hippocrates was the 'Father of Medicine', I was shocked that page after page of college level material – textbooks like, 'Ancient Eygpt', written by 'EGYPTOLOGIST' David P. Silverman (Question: Are there British-ologists? China-ologists? Rome or Greco-ologists?!!! WT?!!!) – and other textbooks like, 'The Oxford History of Ancient Eygpt', by Ian Shaw, or 'Ancient Egypt: An Introduction', by Salima Ikram (more E-g-y-p-t-o-l-o-g-i-s-t-s!!!) – all of them containing nothing but the same synchronized dry facts, with not a word of any use about very BLACK Imhotep; nor did they seem to notice Kemet was in Afrika, with the Nile River running upwards, not downwards, at any of its length. I wondered if these historian-ologists shared a toxic Coke amongst themselves after writing such repetitive dribble. I could only pray.

Oh, there were long accurate chronologies of the royal line, but each one mistakenly calling Kemetic rulers 'pharoahs' over and over, making me smh

340

over and over as I read. And there were plenty of modern drawings of the Ancestors depicted as white as Bing Crosby's Christmas dreams, smack up against plates of the original drawings from the Kemetians, themselves – who 'strangely' painted themselves in only Black.

I even found a book (I picked it off the shelf outta sheer horror) that speculated aliens had built the pyramids, spurring my logic lovin' 4th floor to question who would give Afrikans all that technological and architectural superiority simply for the heck of it if We, Originals:

1. Couldn't be trusted to maintain it, or?
2. Weren't the supposed aliens' children, who, like progeny, would be bound to receive their inheritance from their parents?

These aliens weren't aliens. They were Our Ancestral Family. BLACK PEOPLE. Not a bunch of bloodlessly pale, saucer-eyed strangers from another planet. Nah. The only strangers were just the Strange People from a Strange Land right 'chere on planet Earth.

Oh, yes, sir! I was livid because, despite having learned almost nothing about even Ancient 'Egypt', moreso despite the sparsity of my first person memories as young boy Amenhotep (indeed, the recall was scant, choppy and random) – I had a bedrock understanding like an amnesiac retains the full use of language, or a person suffering Senile Dementia can still play a perfect arrangement on the piano, although neither type of afflicted person can recall their own children's names. Don't tell me who you t-h-i-n-k I was cause I...

R
E
M
E
M
B
E
R
E
D

who I was. No, I couldn't speak the tongue I'd spoken to Sitamen, any more, tell you what my favorite meal had been, but the feel of the rooms I'd slept in, ate in, ran through, was taught in – I knew them and the sense of what was reality back then, whether I recalled the day to day details or not. I even

341

vaguely remembered full spectrum lighting at NIGHT, that no candle could ever provide, yet there'd been no electrical wires needed to emblazon those vast halls, nor white people's technology...

(Which, traveling through Allah's Memories, I'd discover wasn't as white as that was made to seem. Whew.)

Doggonit, my mom had been right! I sorely wished I'd had called Dr. Kattan, as I was certain he HAD to have volumes of material with the factual story, and if I must stay up till the wee hours writing my report in his library, after he and Sister Makeba returned, then that was egggggzzzactly what I was gonna do. With this thought, closing the cover on another useless revisionist histor-lie book, I was about to call my mom asking if she'd let me know when they'd returned and that's when my cell phone rang.

Oh, sorry. As I said, I'm no professional writer. Just learning how to be a professional me, meaning, I think I forgot to mention earlier that like many children during that era, I carried my own cell phone so I could reach my mom in the event of an emergency or she, in turn, could find me. Only this wasn't a call from Mrs. Jackson. This was a scream from her daughter.

"Hey," I answered, "whassup?"

"Tyree!" Kyerah's voice put me on immediate alert. Something enormous was wrong sooner than happy to be immature again me would have expected.

"What? What's the matter, sis?" I whispered despite being the only patron in the room besides the librarian, every floor of my complex mind that'd been starting to feel unnecessary suddenly awoke and clicked on my own no battery or electrical company required brain lights. That sharp 4th floor had never forgotten the sense something awful was on the way, reprimanding all the other facets of me with, 'We told you so!'

Not really, but, it's easier to describe this way...

"There's cop cars and police everywhere! You gotta come home!"

Again, I couldda bogged down the convo with a need to verify, or to gossip, but I want you, reader, clued into the slow primary steps of becoming a god. It saves everyone a whole lot of guesswork time when you're harmonized with those you're around. See, I already we had an Enemy. I already knew the Kattans had something valuable the Enemy wanted, whether or not that was the Sacred Breath, the mansion was all the same being watched; and in the time it takes thoughts to travel faster than the speed of light, when Kyerah said, "...come home..." I knew most likely this emergency had to do with what made the air go 'pop' as it came to colorful life, and I'd be there in a little bit more time than it took to say:

"I'm on my way!!!"

And hung up the phone.

~ ~ ~ ~ ~ ~ ~ ~ ~ ~ ~ ~

Siren lights aren't as bright in the daytime as they are at night, except when they're pulsating their beams onto 847 Carson. It was high noon when the glare of red, blue and white arced around upon the mansion's façade, sharply accentuating its pointed gabled rooftops, undeniably taking on a neon intensity which almost hurt the eyes. Anyone at all, even my dad, would have noticed the effect immediately, if there hadn't been such a crowd of onlookers fixated, instead, on 16 police officers positioned behind various cars, guns drawn and pointed at the windows and front door of the Kattan mansion, while everyone squinted.

However, I did overhear one cop explain to 2 others, "Dang! This is one freaky place. Almost impossible to see any suspects lookin' at all that voodoo crap and those lights bouncin' off that reflective paint. That's gotta be some building code violation, don'cha ya think?"

Too bad nobody noticed how the glare of the strobes was even more luminous, nearly as radiant as the Sun, itself, when they bounded off the dilapidated, murky yellow paint coating of 846 Carson, on the other side of the street where no one was looking, not even me.

I had run home the 4 blocks, leaving my pile of books behind for the annoyed librarian to put away, my backpack, by block 2, painfully thumping against my spine as I ran – but I didn't care. Seeing at least 2 cop cars up ahead, halting traffic flow on the cross street – same one Nyisha had walked with me along till we got to my buckling block – I couldn't care about some daggone back pain that was nothing compared to the racket of my heart which propelled my legs forward like exterior blood cells, thumping with each footfall, in time to the thwacking Northface gear – I didn't care, determined with each labored breath that I close the distance between myself and trouble.

And, my block was truly buckling, now, with black uniforms, shouting commands, and I didn't know if I could fix any of that as quickly as would be necessary.

Although, I let go a cautious relieved sigh, arriving at the scene, not seeing barricades or police tape which made me assume whatever was happening had only recently begun. No one was shouting, "Oh my GOD, they killed him!" – quelling my fear that somebody'd gotten shot, already. Unless somebody was about to g-e-t shot, as there was the distinct energy of panic you didn't need superpowers to sense. I pushed my way through the crowd of gawkers on the corner, refusing to be stopped by warnings I'd better not get too close.
"Boy," said an old woman, who in hindsight, I recognized was my kind neighbor with the exuberant grandbabies, "you'd best stay here. You know them policemen don't play around."

But I wasn't hearin' her anymore than her grandchildren would have, 'cause I was Cletus.

"I don't play around, either," and without pushing her out the way, I determinedly weeded through the last line of congregating neighbors to where I saw my mom and grandmother in front of 846's Acme fencing talking to an officer. Officer Terechinko-whatever, whatever. He was motioning them, I figured, to get back inside our house and off the sidewalk. Tempers, like that split second before a struck match flares up into a flame – tempers were clearly on edge. Mom and Grandma were refusing to go back indoors, which (to my enhanced insight) was enraging the cop.

"This sidewalk is part of our home, and those are our friends," my mom insisted. "What exactly have they done wrong?"

He answered, testily in his Russian-like frosted voice, "I don't know who's who or what's what, Ma'am! All I know is we got a call about an intruder in the house and when we got here, we heard gunshots. We're tryin' to protect the safety of the community so you're gonna hafta go back inside your home! Now, Ma'am!"

His aura was nearly an exact replica of Mr. Lewistein's, showing no friendship for me or mine, plus? Clear to my eyes, he knew this whole event was a hyper ludicrous lie. However, same as my sister, I couldn't yet read his thoughts to discover the details of what he knew. I didn't know that if each melanated person there could have eliminated the negativity from the site, such a mind reading feat would have been possible, that very second. Officer Terror..? was a more open book than he or we would have ever realized.

Mom, calm as a cucumber, answered, "I didn't hear any gunshots, just your sirens, and now you've got one owner of the house in handcuffs and the other pinned down in his own home. How could they be intruding into their own home?!!"

'Go, mom,' I and my memory of Cletus thought, but with my one mind, I wanted everyone to survive this minute to defeat these people once and forever.
I reached the two elder women of my small family the moment the officer raised his arms to physically push both women back through the open gate door.

I wanted to protect them by bashing his head in, but, instead recognized, with the calm I'd felt after waking up from my exit out of the Orb – I knew I could only say a forceful, useless:

"Hey! That's my mom and grandma! Leave them alone!" while peripherally across the street I saw Mrs. Kattan, hands behind her back, being shepherded into a police car, parked in front of their wild vacant lot, yelling her own "Leave my husband alone," at another officer. "He's done nothing!"

"Tyree!" mom cried, motioning to grab me while being pushed through the gate, the same exact instant the Kattan's front door opened, the doctor stepped out hands raised, with police starting to shout,

"HANDS UP!! DROP THE GUN!!" several times... but there was no gun. Just a Black man's hands, waving insistently in clear and plain sight. But, the on edge, like new springs in a playground bouncy ride, officers repeated that several times, with no more desire to see the world than the painted eyes on that kiddy ride and with no heart, either.

"HANDS UP!! DROP YOUR WEAPON!!...

345

... and like that? 5 or 6 of those little popping sounds, I now knew intimately, terribly, set off like a packet of fire crackers after the fuse has been lit.

Again, it wasn't a movie 'cause I couldn't rewind, despite a cold sensation as if it was. As if reality was a photo I could rip from the clouds down, tearing it apart and recomposing a more pleasant version than this horrifying mistake no one could take back as it bowled Dr. Kattan down like a grown up rag doll. His frame collapsed in ways the human body doesn't fall, with no conscious regard to hitting your head or smashing your knees or soiling your stylish Afrikan garb, which he always wore. Nobody falls like he did, then, face first tumbling down the three steps out his green front door, onto the black tarred circular driveway, his body nothing but dead weight, his torso taking the force of the drop.

Somebody screamed first. I think it was Mrs. Kattan, who was spontaneously joined, like a choir in that asylum I no longer needed to be committed to, because the whole world had gone insane – she was joined by the screams howling out of patients who didn't know they were patients standing there on Carson. One joined with another becoming a madrigal crescendo, no theatrical lighting shining the way, any way to understand what had just happened. Screams came from my mother, my grandmother, other women, and children I still didn't know by name. And one came from my sister, whom a part of my mind had worried where could she have been in all this madness, having meant to ask somebody as soon as I got a second, which I didn't – she was then screaming from our living room window, above – horror in her face, to be sure, exactly as when I'd come out of the Orb, after she'd seen me getting shot. Only now she was seeing the inanimate body of the doctor better than I could, between the cars and police, poking out behind them – all I could see was he was prone face down, head turn crookedly to the side, a small stream of blood beginning to flow from beneath him, pooling around his chest.

"Holy"... expletive, I said.

"Alright, that's it!" said the officer I hated fiercely so I won't bother to try spelling his name anymore – "You, are under arrest!" He meant Ruby Larchmont and Renee Jackson, but, as far as I was concerned, he meant me.

"For what?!" We all roared.

"Inciting a riot!" he shrieked in turn, calling for another officer to assist with manacling my 37 year old mother and my 61 year old grandmother. Was he out of his mind?!!!

346

"Mom!" I tried to get between the officer and them, not thinking this would never be effective, yet thinking my force of will, alone, could stop him. Mom, who'd never been angry with the cop, merely intent on understanding his reasoning even if there'd been none on his part, she told me:

"Son, go upstairs."

"But mom?! What are we gonna do?!"

They both were in cuffs, now, and I had been easily pushed gruffly back in the direction of the crowd, none of whom had any inclination to get involved. I wasn't looking at them, though, but at my grandma, who was in such a state of confused shock, I felt as if I could read her thoughts, and those thoughts, as plain as the nose on her face, said this was never in her gentle vision of herself. Never. The threat of tears seared the bottoms of my eyes with a far too familiar sting. However, since Sister Ruby remained silent, if stunned, I held my emotions, also, not wanting to give any inkling of victory to this most disagreeable of people.

My mom, cast hateful gazes at the cops, and then turning to me, softly said, "Call Brother Gainde," as the no-name officer shoved her and grandma along. "You have his number, right?"

"Yes."

She looked me so piercingly in my eyes, there was no need to say, "I love you." Instead she finished with a careful, slow, "Good. I'll call you the instant I can. Now go upstairs with your sister and this'll be put right in no time. I'll call Aunt Brenda, just in case. Don't forget to call Gainde and don't you worry, you hear?"

"I will, and I won't," I said as both were forced into the waiting police car parked right in front of our house.

Mrs. Kattan was already in the back of the other, sobbing loudly while pleading to see to her husband. The officers paid not a wit's worth of attention to her, nor Dr. Kattan's motionless body, with about 10 yards between husband and wife. Newark's finest strolled back and forth, confident they'd done their best. Black and white, men and women, busily chatting, even laughing with one another as if they were at a weekend barbecue, or? A picnic.

347

Mrs. Finn couldn't hope to compete with the outrage I felt, realizing the same scene had taken place millions of times, only rather than police cruisers and glocks, there'd been whips and auction blocks, white crowds and sizzling black bodies. Damn. Damn. Damn! I was going to become a cap crusader, full sized super hero costume worn in my soul, simply to defeat the real thugs on this Earth, and for all time. Yes, I was a child, but that had never mattered to the Enemy, before.

Racing upstairs, I called for an ambulance, immediately, using my cellphone, concluding the villainous authorities probably hadn't. If there was a chance, though I wasn't sure how, if EMS and that morgue of a hospital could save the doctor's life, then so be it. Even Satan's gotta do some good to do greater evil.

And that made me ponder, taking in the coldness of the officers' auras, no matter what their skin tone? Well, from Designated Special Negroes to full blown freaked out replicas of Mr. Lewistein, with sizzling hot hatred hidden within their Yurugu hearts (oh, I could see it like one could see a mountain) – I had a psychic certainty that gunning the doctor down hadn't been a case of mistaken identity, in the least. And it would be an assassination, if he was already dead.

911 made me stay on the phone with them, getting my name, address and relationship to the 'injured 'party', until an ambulance came whining down the block, in a matter of minutes. From all I'd heard about them? I must have been the only person with such luck. Apparently, there'd been one close by in the neighborhood. Hanging on the line I saw cops swarming the now vacant estate, as I fumed that they'd be touching sacred artifacts they couldn't begin to comprehend. I couldn't comprehend them. I watched dreading they'd soon find Allah's Sacred Breath, hurling existence into the oblivion of the carnage I'd seen inside. But, once I saw the medics, having talked to the cops and then walking over to the doc, stretcher in tow? Once they'd lifted him, carefully onto the stretcher, then placed him gently into the back of the ambulance?

It occurred to me, '*Where's Kyerah?*'

Checking the rest of our home took only seconds to verify ('cause it was that small) that my big sister was nowhere to be found. I called to her in case she was hiding out, filled with fear or shock - heck, I felt, not fearful, but definitely traumatized - finding a quick check under both beds and in every closet (including the linen closet, shelves and all) proving utterly useless. There was a plastic storage bin blocking the backdoor, on the other side of the bathroom, between the bedrooms and the kitchen. Why would she leave the house, I pondered, when – oh... I remembered how she'd snuck into the Kattan's backyard to spy, just the day before yesterday. Could she have gone to the mansion?... But, how could she have slipped by me and all those cops outside in the chaos of that melee?

Thoughts rolled through my head in something more than panic, as I'd had enough catastrophic events, and life changing revelations in one week to fill several psyche wards. Then seeing the good doctor go down, well? Regular people panic, but my brain, with every floor finally feeling overwhelmed, was having one gigantic multi-dimensional conniption fit. Thank goodness I remembered I'd promised to call Gainde like mom had directed, only...

to reach his answering machine.

"Brother!" I blurted, every dreadful despair in me, and the world's despair, too, hoping to find comfort (ironically knowing I'd only spread my despair to him). Sadly, the voicemail was an inadequate champion, clicking lifelessly into action after the line had rung 4 interminable 'brrrrrrnnnngs'. I was beginning to not like phones, as emergencies proved their limitations.

Anxiety gave way to a disappointment which had a strange calming effect, helping me catch my breath, like counting to ten does, before making a drastic decision to jump off the Golden Gate Bridge. My tumultuous emotions were still on autopilot, but taking one action made taking another, rather than panicking, far more logical. It was almost like falling in the Orb, on the way out, only, there was no hint of joy. Just sorrowful dread.

I knew Gainde would return the call. Thus, in the meantime, I decided to do something productive by searching the apartment, from hard to reach corner, to on top of and underneath overstuffed furniture, from cracked living-room ceiling, down to the span of the floor. I searched one room after the other, no square inch neglected, not sure what I was looking to find, but hoping some clue would jump out and smack not a detective me over the head.

It didn't.

No, I wasn't panicked anymore, but almost 2 hours had passed with no word from Brother Gainde or mom or Kyerah, and knowing darkness would fall in another few hours, and me alone in an empty apartment, my situation molded over into the hopelessness I'd read about happening to my ancestors, making me miss the days when unmitigated agony had been a unknown mystery. Yes, my dad had been killed, but I hadn't realized how much my mom's, my sister's

349

and even my grandma's presence provided a warm threading of reassurance that I belonged someplace, whether I'd have sworn differently if you'd asked me or not. Feeling crest-caved-in, which was something far more awful than being 'crestfallen', this was the catalyst behind my decision to call one more number, 'cause I had nothing else to lose.

The line rang and the gentle sound of her real life greeting contrasted heavily with the sorrowful state my heart, and the unnatural quiet of my surrounding; but I needed a friendly voice from someone who'd demonstrated wisdom and kindness in the face of overwhelming odds.

"Hello? Is anybody there," she repeated before I recalled, I was supposed to make an effort to say s-o-m-e-t-h-i-n-g, despite my pain.

"Nyisha?"

"Yes, this is she. Can I help you?"

'Whew, I pray...'

"It's Tyree." There was no joy in Mudville and even less in my own voice.

"Tyree? Is something wrong?"

I was sitting in grandma's spot on the couch more inertly than she ever could, suddenly coming alert as I noticed a tiny 'hole' on the far left side of the doorway to the kitchen, almost hidden by the floor length blood red drapes.

"Uh?" I said, absentmindedly. Again, tain't it funny how emotions, like rolling water, will span out to fit the shape of whatever container they're poured into, although they remain just as wet? 'Cause I had my familiar ocean of woe, when suddenly seeing the complete blackness of that hole that hadn't been there before? I know because I'd searched that doorway, thoroughly... Well, I still had problems, but now I had a clue to drain most of the problem into a more comprehensible bay and keep them there, at least, for the moment. Well, I could keep MOST of the problem at bay, as near that hole – which I hadn't see there before, there'd been not sight nor hint of either Aanda.

'Oh, no. Don't let the worse have happened. How will I explain that to mom?'

"Tyree? Are you okay?"

"Uh?" I repeated, wanting to jump over the portmanteau before the hole maybe went away, but wisely I decided to answer my friend's question, "I'm okay... no. I mean, I'm not okay. Nyisha, the police shot Dr. Kattan."

"What?! You mean that man who owns that..." momentary hesitation, "... house across the street from you? Oh, wow! That's horrible. I'm so sorry to hear that. He's your friend, I remember. Awww, Tyree! That's awful! Is he okay? Are you in any trouble?"

"I don't know if he's okay or not. I don't even know how many times he was shot, but the police sure gunned him down like he was their target practice bullseye. It was awful. Yes. It was the most awful thing I've ever seen, in this lifetime," as the horror of the doctor and Cletus' family came back for what both sights were – not remotely tolerable. "And no, I'm not in any trouble, not like that, but..."

That's when an idea, perhaps one that'd always been brewing in my imagination on some floor of my head, but a new floor under construction that was taken even less seriously than the basement – an idea came in full battle gear into my mind.

"Nyisha!" I yammered, suddenly, slowing down to add – "My sister is missing, and I need your help to find her."

"She's missing?! What?! What happened to her?"

"I think I know, but it'd be impossible to explain over the phone and we gotta find her quickly or she'll be lost for good. Look, I know this sounds weird, but how many friends can you get together to meet me at the schoolyard?"

"The schoolyard? What?! Tyree, is this another trick of yours, 'cause I ain't got time for no foolishness from you!"

"No, I swear. I have no reason to lie to you now that I told you the truth. Well, maybe that means you shouldn't trust me, but, I'm not lying now. My sister, Kyerah, is really, really missing and I need help finding her, and now. I need a bunch of people's help." Same as happened when I'd had that talk with Dr. Kattan, telling the truth is always the most believable tactic 'cause your whole energy lines up with what's right so your every word harmonizes with the truth in others who're listening and?

Nyisha heard me.

351

"Okay," she still reluctantly conceded. "This sounds weird, but if all this were truly wacky, you wouldn't want a bunch of witnesses to the fact that you jes' might be crazy. Which means your sister is actually in trouble. Dang. What an awful day. Alright, I'm there. I can call some of the guys and my friends, see who can make it. Should we meet you right now?"

"Right the minute that just past."

"Got it. I'll make the calls on my way, and see you, then. So, long."

"So, long..."

~~~~~~~~~~~~

Late noon dominated the sky with its transitory glow, the Western singe of magenta-ed gold strips, a beautiful woman's scarf that was recalling its waning love, allowing the bedazzled Eastern half of her fringe to kiss the long and heartbroken shadows goodbye. That's the vista that reigned when I arrived the distance it took to reach the scene of my almost crime (well, yeah, I admit, it was downright wrong to have even thought up that pretend to be a bully scam), so? I reached the scene of my complete crime against my Brother Howard, from several days back, that felt like years ago. Nyisha, Reggie, James, Terrence, Maxwell, Lisa, Kenya, Shantay and the sister I'd seen hangin' with Von and his friends when Kyerah and I had gotten back from the dollar store, were all there, along with one more guy and girl I'd never seen before. This time, I noticed, Nyisha didn't bother to do the polite thing and introduce me to anyone, but?

'There's no Von, here, thank Heaven,' was at the front of my office tower mind, on every floor. I had enough worries. If only I'd known what had really happened that day, I'd have thanked Heaven if he'd had been there.

That said, swiftly approaching the crew, one after another, they turned their bodies or heads to face me as I entered the yard, the building-sized coffin school at my back. I was greeted, but unlike the first time, there not only was no excitement, there was plenty of outright distrust. I could see it in their energy. Anybody could, actually.

I heard Von's girl, who leaned over to Nyisha, say, "Yeah, I remember him.

352

He's that midget bully."

My hands went inside my jean pockets and I kept them there, as I looked from face to face. Gratefully, my whole face agreed with what I felt and I felt desperately determined.

Didn't need to fake nuthin' this time.

So, "Thank You," I began, nodding my head, sincerely. "Thank You, all, for coming."

"Yeah, what's up, dude? Your sister's missing?" Reggie, as always began; but there was no humor in his comment, nor friendliness anywhere in his delivery. He was almost a different person, stonedfaced, no chance there was a wise crack on the tip of his tongue. I concluded, yeah, we'd parted on good terms, Friday, but as I'd already pulled one caper, he and everyone else must be thinking – this was another.

Remembering the warning from the Kattans that nobody would believe a word of what I was about to reveal, but knowing hesitation would win me no friends that minute, nor help keep the ones I was hoping I'd made – I let the truth roll, telling them what had happened to the doctor, to Sister Makeba, to my mom and grandma. Turns out you can't fake real pain as my fear for Kyerah clenched my words in my throat, and it turns out none of them were heartless thugs, making inevitable empathy rise in their eyes, rolling out with headshakes and commiserating groans.

That's how I got to:

"... and when I got upstairs, Kyerah was nowhere to be found."
Tentatively, Terrence suggested, "Maybe she went out?"

"But I'd just seen her at the window." I responded, "She was looking at the doctor laid out on his front steps. I heard her scream and then she was gone. There were too many cops for her to come outside and our back door's blocked by a big old bin for our coats. It was still there when I went inside. She couldn't have closed the door and put that back in place, magically."

Each conceded with puzzled looks and nods, before Nyisha and several others, predictably asked, or stated –

"So, what are you saying? What? She disappeared into thin air?"

353

This was the point in the testimony I'd patiently been waiting to reach.

"No. And yes..."

Kenya and Shantay put hands to hips, while everybody else looked merely seconds from truly leaving me alone to be 'Crazy Tyree', only this time, for real...

I'd wanted to explain more, but I had to keep their faith, so? I pulled a rolled-up napkin from out my right pocket, drawing at least cursory interest, as everybody stepped closer in to see. Short me, to anyone strolling past, disappeared in the gathering of those older, taller children.

"What's in that?" Maxwell asked.

I nodded, mutely asking patience, napkin set in my right palm, unwrapping the content with my left hand. The bone white of the opened paper, fully unfolded, made a sharp contrast against the absolute blackness of the nothingness it held. There never was such a black. That anyone could tell.

For a moment a hush ensued as the throng tried to determine what the heck each was looking down upon. It was the older girl I'd seen with Von, with nearly the same almond eyes as Nyisha's, who cocked her head to the side, and utterly exclaimed:

"What kinda ten cent magic trick is that, child?" She flipped her head back, snapping her teeth, finishing with: "You surely don't expect us to believe your sister disappeared in a napkin with a hole in it?!"

There was a perimeter of trees on the end of the courtyard before the residential houses spread out beyond, heading along Garvey Avenue towards Carson, and in those bursting with springtime trees, the cacophony of bird chirps was instantly drowned out, or more likely, startled into silence by the uproar of laughter from a gathering of teenagers who towered over my head like leafless trees with eyes, gazing at what they thought was an optical illusion, cause their education never taught them the impossible could be possible.

I upped my bid to keep their attention, saying, "Wait. Lemme show you...", and placing the napkin with its content on the worn down, cracked black asphalt, me adding, "You gotta step way back and whatever you do, do NOT touch what you're about to see, no matter how much you want to."

I looked up at them, catching each set of eyes, their faces taking on their returning curiosity. Good thing everybody had been taught to love magic tricks, at least...

"I gotta repeat this, guys, and you've each gotta swear, you WON'T touch what you're about to see."

One by one, they all promised, some still a bit skeptical. Maxwell and the girl I assumed had to be Nyisha's sister wore full face smirks.

Despite the doubt, bended on one knee, I was about to give the Orb the gentle push with my palm as I'd been instructed, when I jumped up, having almost forgotten the most crucial, 'Thank You,' of them all.

"We have to say 'Grace', first!"

"Are you kidding, me?!" complained my usual backup Reggie. "Man, I don't do religion, 'specially for no hole in no napkin! I can think of holes I would pray over, but that tain't one of them. Man!"

More laughter, but this time no bird was left after the initial racket, except the pigeons. Takes a hurricane to make pigeons leave.

"This is some daggone game," the boy I didn't know said, turning to leave. "Yo, I'm out, ya'll! Stay here with this crazy fool if you wants to, but I ain't stupid."

Everyone, grumbling, maybe would have left with him, but when I started to pray, closing my eyes and putting my faith that The One and Only knew what He was doing, even if I didn't? That maybe He'd brought these young men and women here on purpose, not by accident? That He knew them better than stereotypes, better than me, better than they knew themselves? I let my gratitude speak loudly in prayer, starting wobbly at first, to soon, as I reached the 2nd verse – I felt someone else's hand take hold of mine on one side, and another take hold on the other side. Then I heard rising voices joining me in time with the only prayer not a Christian me knew by heart –

"Our Father, who art in Heaven, hallowed be Thy Name. Thy Kingdom come. Thy will be done...."

You know that one, I'm sure, without me disrespectfully saying 'yadda, yadda,

yadda' or 'whatever, whatever, whatever' to end it quickly here on paper...

When I opened my eyes, everyone, even the boy who'd almost left, was there, in a hand clasped circle of teenagers and pre-teen me, around a wrinkled napkin with a very, very black hole in it.

"Okay. Now," and kneeling back down, I took a moment to think of how to correctly push on that eyeball and gently doing so, real quick, I stood back up, sharply.

"Okay, form a circle, holdin' hands, everybody – but stand as far back as you can. And don't..."

My words were too low to overcome the airplane decibel whoosh of the Sacred Breath expanding in 0 to incalculable speed of light spontaneity, as it'd done in the Kattan's kitchen. It zoomed right up to the height of the top of my head, over which I could see my rescuers eyes expand in their sockets, almost as instantly and large as the Orb had burst into size, accompanied by that unexpected wind vortex, blowing t-shirts, beaded necklaces, and earrings which clattered upon the sisters who wore them.

"WHAT THE?!!!!" nearly everyone yelled (even the guy who'd almost left), and all jumped back, straining our grip to one another, yet we didn't break the connection, and gratefully, the Orb seemed to know when to stop expanding.

"HOLD ON!!!!" I hollered, though I won't keep capitalizing my screams, 'cause I know you, reader, understand we had to scream to be heard. "This is The Sacred Breath of Allah."

"The what?" cried Nyisha.

"It's all the memories of Our Creator as His recall is perfect to the subatomic level, so much? It's a 3 dimensional photo album."

"What the?"

"Holy dog crap!"

"Whoa, dude, you aren't crazy...."

That last comment was Reggie's, and there were more, but to save time in this recollection, lemme get to the part where I let go with my right hand, flowing it across the sphere's surface to shrink it back to marble size, resting on the napkin like nothing unusual had ever happened, besides that hypnotically dime sized black hole in reality. I was concerned one of them would find its magnetic pull too much to resist, like I'd had, initially, so I'd collapsed it right away. But, looking 'round, I could see my warning had been taken seriously, since nobody was missing, very gratefully. Obviously, there'd be no more doubts, anymore, or perhaps the Sphere only called my soul's name.

Talking in normal volume, with their 100% and more secured attention, e-a-s-i-l-y, I quickly filled them in on what the Orb did, including that a person could fall in, and forgetting who they are, stay in there for hundreds of generations, so never, ever (over-emphasizing, to be sure) – NEVER let go of each others' hands. I told them, avoiding the long story about what the heck I was doing with such an item (though they did ask that and I promised to tell that part later) – I told them about the vital Aandas, which were missing, too, and that's why I needed their help. I told them everything, pretty much, consciously leaving out that white people are Our Avowed Enemy stuff, so I could get to..

I think my sister wanted to find our dad, or maybe she'd been curious enough to touch it, and it swallowed her whole. That's why I called Nyisha."

"And what the heck do you exactly think we can do?" asked James. He was willing, I could see, but he was still doubtful.

"I'm counting on us being the Aanda with a human chain. Ubuntu style...

=

I wasn't completely ignorant, back then, having been taught a little bit of something about our Afrikan family by mom and dad, and also, in that Black run institution for exceptional boys and girls, Medgar Evers Prep. For a small example, I'd learned the concept of 'ubuntu', which is a Zulu term for group compassion, or the act of connecting one to another beyond blood family; while just like in a blood family, harmony is sought and when achieved, it's protected and thus amplified. Why, you may have heard the story of a white man who'd offered a basket of fruit as a prize to a village of, I'd imagine, hungry Afrikan children (made hungry by encroaching White Supremacy, to be sure, as what Afrikans didn't know how to put seed in dirt, watch it rain and then harvest dinner grown in the richest soil on the planet?) – this white guy had challenged them to a race and the winner's prize would be the basket of fruit.

To only his shock, the children huddled together, whispering, and when ready, they joined hands at the starting point to then run together, leaving not even a toddler behind. They reached the basket as ONE, sharing the prize amongst everyone of them. I repeat. Only the white man was shocked.

And I'm walking with my colleague, Sister Sitamin, this minute, into the Epidome, to attend the 35th Annual Gathering of Creation's Re-Birth. Attended by the most powerful People on Earth, with accidentally impressive me, handily carrying pages 1 thru 339 and a half, the whole unfinished firmly enscripted tome, inside my briefcase, as I think-script the next dozen or probably more pages to the finish that I pray I do reach before my scheduled address up at the rostrum. Walking through the assembling throng, directly outside the auditorium entrance...

I need 4 things, today.

1. No one call on me before I get to the last page.

2. Each speaker take his/her sweet ta' Betsey time.

3. I don't fall asleep until I've finished the book, and?

4. If I don't finish, I need my Venerated Elders to have learned Ubuntu, too.

358

Chapter

5

"But if you walk into that thing holding our hands, you can't go far, unless you drag the rest of us inside with you. Even then? How can you use your hands or anything else if we can't let go?" Nyisha brought up some great points that I hadn't quite considered. That was frustrating. And yet? For some reason, the answers made perfect sense to my new floor number 7. Maybe 7 was just as wacky as the basement. Maybe 7 was pre-telepathically smarter than all the other floors, as it was thinking way ahead...

"I've a feeling it's what it's supposed to be. The Most High isn't a magician up in the sky. He made the science and used it to birth Himself from nothingness. Well, We surely are meant to create Heaven and we've got each other, while He had no one. Our numbers have got to have its own power."

Maxwell shook his head, warily, questioning, "As black as that thing is, how will we see anything, so we know when to pull you outta there?"

"Oh, you'll know. If I'm right, you'll see what I see."

Shrugs of shoulder accompanied with slow nods of head after head said they weren't sure, but?

They'd give it a try.

Nyisha, put her brown hand on my shoulder, warmly asking, "We'll be here, Tyree, but are you sure you want to do this?"

Lookin' confidently into her eyes, I answered, truthfully, "Yes. I have to do this. It's my sister."

Couldda said, "GULP!" truthfully, too, but since feelings don't kill, no matter how many you have, I was certain I'd be okay, with no danger that my emotions or the Orb were too much for me to navigate.

"Alright, then," I added. "Here goes."

359

I started that triple black marble up, pushing with a bit more pressure, igniting it into a full-force near 7ft high wind machine of extra-dimensional wonder.

'This is bound to attract a crowd,' I thought, but concluded, *'Kyerah I sure love you, bad jokes and all...'*

We formed our Ubuntu chain – boy, girl – boy, girl. My faith in hand, along with Kyerah's and Lisa's, I signaled with a nod as I stepped inside, only to remember I'd forgotten to pick a destination. Which? Didn't turn out as disastrous as my sudden dread told me it might – that I'd really screwed up this time, and would surely be tumbling back into the dark nothing, dragging 11 innocent people, each with families who'd never know what happened to them – dragging them to their doom with me.

But, no. This wasn't a repeat, though I had to wobble a bit, once I'd stepped into that complete blackness, to catch my balance and stand upright.

And yes. I said I had to catch my balance and stand upright, in the unfathomable depth of the Void. For, from all observance, it was the same exact place that had swallowed me up before, as infinite as it'd been then, coils radiating out into the eternal distance, soothing tonal humming flooding Our perceptions.

Yes, I said, Our perceptions, but more on that in a couple paragraphs.

This go round, there was a cooling breeze, but no hurricane force backdraft since I wasn't falling. I wasn't floating, though, as if there was no footing. Matter of fact, my Carson sidewalk was less solid. Plus? Nobody was holding my hand. I was all alone standing, with my back to a glowing coil. Standing, I repeat, on nothing at all, in the middle of that endless blackness, festooned with those kaleidoscopic glistening looping ropes, near to far off in the distance, as though I'd opened a doorway and had stepped into a confetti forever.

Worried I'd made a horrible mistaken leap of faith that would leave me stranded in this empty limbo till I died of thirst and hunger, my fear was brushed aside upon hearing...

Hearing?

Hearing in my mind, a whole bunch of familiar teenaged voices, collectively saying,

"WOW!"

Yep. This is where that 'Our' came in, for We were thinking like an oversized mind party.

"Listen to the music...," Shantay sighed.

"That's not music," said Reggie. "That's God's heartbeat..."

Oh, I smiled that second, for the first time in what felt like years, but had been not even most of that day. Hey? Gimme a break. I was 12. A minute feels like a month during childhood.

"It worked!" I shouted, and jumped from sheer joy.

That's how I learned, in the Void, I could bounce beyond the laws of gravity I'd always understood. Startled, but feeling very astronaut, I floated a good 2 stories upwards, coming to a standing halt, near the coil I'd assumed was mine.

"Whoa, dude!" I could hear Terrence say, "Now THAT? Was freakin' COOL!"

I turned, expecting to see my friends right behind me, but there hovered this enormous wall of organically flowing colors, like a liquid prism reflecting back inside itself, no prismatic confine limiting its bandwidths of brilliance.

"You guys can see this?"

"See it? Dude, I can feel it!" That was the guy who'd almost left. I suddenly knew his name was Omar, he was an excellent cook, already – at only 15 – he was bored senseless by school, and overall, he was a terrific hueman being. I sure couldn't tell any of that from first glance.

"You got that right!" shouted Reggie, while others clamored out similar sentiments. "Like I'm right there, only I can't tell your body what to do. Not that I wanna know that much 'bout your body, bro'!"

Funny how fun has a way of removing all doubt. And, um? Telepathy, too, 'cause I could read escalated confidence in their thoughts. They knew everything I knew and I knew everything they knew – up to a point. Seemed those emotions that desired privacy, automatically, kept my expanded view

361

from seeing any details meant to stay private, cause I didn't know a darned thing about what sort of toilet tissue anybody used, where they used it, nor any other facts that would make me nauseous, disgusted or embarrassed for the girls sanctity.

Whew. And I didn't want to know those details, anyway.

Oh! Nyisha's sister's name was Rekia, and she was one amazing songwriter.

Then the other girl was Meighan. She hadn't told a soul, but she wanted to be president, although, she'd settle for mayor.

We were incredible in Our own unique fashion, with no need to know each others' secret details, as I certainly had no desire for anyone to know Nyisha's eyes were as captivating to me as the Orb...

I, and We, too, decided to experiment, touching my palm to the coil, feeling a familiar warmth – the same temperature one would expect from a living body. The surface wiggled a bit, sort of like solid jello. Silence took over, as We dared to explore, everyone's fascination coming through to my spirit, making words unnecessary. That's why, I put my whole hand inside, not knowing if I'd pull back a hand or a bloodied stump.

There was cool fresh air tingling my skin, and I could see a muted rainbowed shadow of my hand through the film of the coil's exterior.

Heck, I took a whole step in.

Did I say, "incredible," a few lines back? Well, I mean it this time. I saw, We all saw the schoolyard, only a misty dream of it, with perhaps several thousand people filling the court, like transparent ghostly visions if an alien had never seen humans and tried to imagine a bunch at once, based on a written description. There was nothing horrific about them as they were full of color, but the color didn't stay in the lines. Not cartoonishly, but if in real life some child had colored a black and white photo of people. The image wavered, too, with persons standing here, then over there, with no definitive continuity or pattern, nor was it the only image.

The scene would, randomly transition from multitudes of persons, split second, to no one at all.
When there was no one, it became disturbing.

See, the colorful scenario, filled with smudge-y bright people, smelled like refreshing Spring, with if not a crayon blue sky, then a decidedly cheerful one. But the barren momentary setting smelled strangely like wet concrete, which is pleasant, but here it signaled, that's all there was. Concrete wafting on wind eddies as dry dust. No life. This bleak reality appeared for a fleeting half a second, so I had to concentrate on it, almost remembering it more than seeing it – the schoolyard becoming an Armageddon-ish nightmare of grays, and barren trees, with a slow cold wind blowing over the emptiness. Catching a glance beyond the courtyard, too, I could sense...

... there'd be nothing but death out there, on the lonely, abandoned street, inside the houses across the road – their grey wooden paneling rotted, and falling off. I knew this vision was an introduction to something gone tragically wrong, everywhere, on every street, not merely my own. Not wanting to see anymore, though it was a split second before the happier vision returned, I stepped back out of the life coil, understanding the doctor had been right – no one could predict the future, but without any doubt, something was on its way.

I knew what it was, too. I knew, We all knew, if I looked up? The Ankh Udja Saneb would take all Our breaths away, but it wouldn't be interrupted by fun. It wouldn't be interrupted by anything but more defeat, and I had no idea how to thwart that, so? I dared not raise my head.

The guys understood this, as our silence was shared more quickly than words. Yet, we were no ways tired, as finding Kyerah had become everyone's number one priority. Not to mention, unlike me? They thought her jokes were funny.

Will wonders never cease....

"Okay," James, broke the quiet, "Let's get to work."

Shaking the foreboding off, We agreed.

"Try another coil, Tyree," Kenya suggested.

Hmm, never thought of entering another coil, since I'd never had the ability to do anything but fall in here. Never had the opportunity to stand up in the nothingness before my friends had offered their help. Kenya's suggestion sounded viable, so I strode further out, in the direction of the nearest band, theorizing the closest coils would probably be my blood family. I started walking quite ordinarily, as one would on any solid flooring, however? The further away I got from what I guessed was my own coil, the slower I got and the more whatever the heck I was walking on felt like cracking ice on a shallow frozen lake. Or, like Carson, but rather than stumbling on solid buckling concrete, with my next footfall, and no benefit of accompanying cracking sounds, I fell right through something I couldn't even see! One leg wound up dangling off the edge of what wasn't there in the first place, leaving my hands frantically scrambling to hold onto what wasn't there in the second place.

Flailing about for surer footing, We got to see the carnage above – a sight that magnified the yawning danger I was in.

Gratefully – I should say GREAT-fully – I didn't completely fall, but there was a giant, "Whoa!" out all our mouths, followed by one sharp tug which yanked me back into the waning light of the real schoolyard. Only a newborn baby, I was sure, could have received such a shifting smack from darkness to the light; my transition made easier only because I knew where I was, and now I knew, no matter where I went, I could be pulled back to this timeframe instantly.

Good to know, on top of that, nobody in the circle was pulled further inside with me, and I wasn't nauseous.

In unison, we said, "More people," although our telepathic connection had ended.

Taking in the periphery of the yard, despite my suspicion we'd attract a crowd of the curious, the basketball court remained deserted. Seems a dozen Black teenagers, no matter how unusual the event, was a warning, not an invitation to the wary onlooker. Nobody had wandered over as common passersby, since same as I had been, everyone strolling the streets was filled with harrowing tales about how rotten ghetto 'kids' are. They couldn't tell the goal of our efforts anymore than I'dda known that Omar wasn't a jerk, or that Howard would one day make my sister very happy, let alone that his name was really Mansa Musa.

"I know!" Terrence interjected. "Who's got cell phones?"

7 phones were yanked out of pockets, backpacks and a couple purses.

And right after the second it took to re-shrink the Orb, calls were placed, young folks speaking about an emergency in the schoolyard, to every relative and friend they knew. Call after call. Musta been 20 made, with me, hanging back cause I had nobody to contact. Decided jealously knawed at the back of my emotions seeing how many friends and family they all knew, and when one person was done, the people without phones borrowed the free ones to call their own. Sorrowfully, in this town, all the people I knew were here in the schoolyard, or in jail, or I was praying silently, recovering in the hospital. Reverberations of Kyerah's warning pinged on every level of my thoughts.

Was I a weirdo?

Looking at my own phone, yeah, I was happy Aunt Brenda had left a message, from 5 states aways, but, happier seeing Gainde had called me back, leaving instructions to call him, A.S.A.P.

"Peace, Brother," he formidably greeted me when he'd answered my own, "Peace."

I explained the worse, quickly. I'd done this before when my father'd died, with each person who asked why I'd been out of school for a week, so long ago. However, given Gainde knew maybe more about the Orb then I did, I didn't have much to explain.

Hearing enough, he asked, "Where are you?"

I answered.

"I'mma contact the Ascend leaders," he replied to my answer, "and knowing them, they'll be there pronto. Matter fact, Brother Xolani lives just a couple blocks from there. I'mma find the Doc, but I'll be your way, soon as I can." He paused, then added, "Tyree?"

"Yes, sir?"

"This is a terrible day, but? From great sorrow may come great good. Now, I'm on my way, but if you can? Don't wait. You've come up with a brilliant idea in a desperate situation. Good critical thinking, brother. Now, go find Kyerah with your friends. I believe in you, young man."

"Yes, sir! Yes, SIR!"

Children, with the right approval? Can accomplish miracles that take grownups a whole lotta resuscitated faith...

~ ~ ~ ~ ~ ~ ~ ~ ~ ~ ~

My, I haven't had this feeling in dozens and dozens of years. I almost wanna turn around in my seat to make sure a very young Brother Mansa Musa isn't sitting behind me, tapping his pencil on the armrest of his chair, having a little fun at my nervous expense. Like I said, before, gods aren't robots with no emotions, so that Heaven is an automated soulless factory more similar to the grave than what makes life panoramically invigorating. No. Gods have sensations, good and bad, because even the devil comes from...

Black Us. And a truth is, We dropped the ball at the Devil's birth.

But, while the potential for devilment is here, even if defeated, Howard isn't here at The Gathering, as he's a young god like me and his fiancé, Sitamen. None of the original 'crew' is here. Only me and my sister – she, on the women's half of the cylindrical theatre, and me, seated in the other with the men – both youth in the midst of this intoxicating assemblage of the greatest heroes, thinkers, inventors, creators, w-r-i-t-e-r-s (one of whom I'm beginning to believe I am, though I'm not the greatest for daggone sure, although? I ain't as shabby as I thought I was, when I started this assignment...) – here are history's most ingenious scientists, mathematicians, builders, artists and overall heroes of the triumphant and perpetual maintenance of Heaven. Only my initial accidental fall into The Orb, decades and decades ago, comes close to the awe inspiring brevity that I'm feeling, now, (although I felt much the same way last year, too, without the worry I'd epically failed at finishing this book). Believing I'm about to go under the tow for the last count, again, as I sit in this breathtaking venue, having located my pre-selected seat (cause I'm a guest of honor, by gum!) – I can't help feeling like a child.

Hang on, reader...

Ah. I'm on page 349 and the opening ceremony's beginning. Cool. The house lights are dimming and now a floor to ceiling screen, centered in the levitation zone, fully visible at all angles (we control more dimensions than your 3, don't forget) – the screen's now projecting a documentary spanning humanity's progress, worldwide.

Yes. This'll take a while and today's speakers haven't even come to the stage yet.

I'm waving to my sister who's several levels above me, directly on my left.

Oops. She's glowering at me.

So? Where was I....?

~ ~ ~ ~ ~ ~ ~ ~ ~ ~ ~

We were ready, now. Ready for what, nobody could guess, but the assembled 47 people, wondering what the hot tar and green feathers was going on, were screechingly, narrowly gonna trust that these teenagers couldn't have all gone stark raving mad, and none of us looked like we were on crack.

That's why a real reverend, Lisa's dad, actually, indulged his daughter's request to offer a more knowledgeably significant prayer. I'd repeat it, but it took so daggone long, that about 15 lines in, the other gathered grown-ups (it wasn't only grown-ups, but plenty of children, our age and some younger, too) – the other grown-ups started to coughin' and gripin' about the more important things they had to do.

Once I'd expanded the sphere, for the final time that day, you couldda heard a pin drop from a mile away. Even the littlest baby hushed up.

"What the?" was a comment heard from a lovely lady I knew to be called, 'Sandra', cause I'd stepped back into that hypnotic blackness, while all of Us capable of holding hands, held them, some capable of watching the babies, watched them, and Sandra's beautiful spirit came with me along with the spirits of the rest. I discovered personalities, brilliance and talents that revealed my publicly acclaimed 'gifted' ranking to be the charade it was. Why, I wasn't anymore gifted than a single person there! I could finally understand that I'd only been carefully instructed in how to excel at submitting to nonsense that insulted the innate talents everyone has in equal abundance, if they searched.

So, Sandra said what We all felt, also, glimpsing the inner fire that burned in every soul, she added,

"What the? We really are beautiful..."

'Cause here were the living Black facts that no Western Society has ever shared, in any manner, be it textbook, movie, news program or any assorted entertainments I'd run across. Oh, yes, there were a few formerly triflin' folks joined with Us (though their secrets were their own), however, We, each, knew? They'd be triflin' no more, as they were seeing who We predominantly really are, for themselves. Who they really were, under the trifle. Thus, same as

367

my breakfast with Allah, please forgive me, Family, if I don't take the time necessary to describe the preciousness of each being assembled in his or her totality; as in no way was Your uniqueness deserving of awe one decibel less than that given to any object on Earth, no matter how costly, no matter how amazing to the eye. Tain't no material possession as invaluable as You. Each of You deserve Your own book.

Hence, (who uses the word 'hence' anymore? I just need something besides 'now', which I've probably written 700 times, by 'n-o-w', dangnamit) – hence, understanding each needed detail of handling the Orb was instantly understood. Newcomers knew precisely as the original crew had upon my entry, every new addition of Our chain's collective knowledge, for more kept coming even when I was within the Orb. Every new set of joined hands became a rising thinking river of Our ever extending Family, with no threat of overflowing its banks. Ha! We shared a laugh that Tyree me and everyone, else, had an army that was better than friends.

I hit the darkness running in the vast ocean that was no danger, any longer, getting a quarter way straight ahead, till together, We started flying, as effortlessly as in my dream, with no threat of falling this time. I reached the nearest coil within the blink of an eye to unflinchingly step through the wall of collaged hues. So it **was** possible for me to step into someone else's perception!

It was my mother's life coil, as I immediately found myself within her being, seated next to grandma, my grandma's head down, and she was softly sobbing, mournfully. My mom had her arm, which was my arm that I had no power over, placed soothingly on her shoulder, usual impatience replaced with supportive concern. I wondered if she'd hear Us, if spoken to, gently?

"Mom?"

Her head popped up. I was seeing all around from her eyes, now. I perceived the small holding cell they were sitting in, looking out on a mundanely unimpressive police office, mundanely less impressive police officers busy about it. I noticed, unlike those helping me, every thought my mom was thinking was her own, as I couldn't hear not a whim, not an impulse and certainly not her plans. Strange, I pondered – however? She could hear me.

"What the?" she blurted.

Grandma, taken out of her grief, looked up at her daughter, tearfully asking, "You alright, Renee?"

368

"I swear I just heard Tyree's voice!"

"Aw," she sniffled. "This is too much for you, too," and grandma put her hand on my mom's.

I focused all my tenderness, We focused all Our tenderness into her being, whispering, "I love you, mom."

"Love you, too, son," she whispered back, no fear in her, anymore.

Grandma tightened her grip on my mom's hand which I felt, too.

We gotta keep looking, everyone agreed. We understood, the more time elapsed, the more chance We'd never find the actual physical manifestation of my sister. I kept my eyes... my eyes? It was my soul that kept an awareness of the two women, abandoned in a cell they didn't deserve – as I left them slowly, walking backwards, returning to continue Our search inside The Void.

This time, although I couldn't see anything but the Void, and the Ankh Udja Saneb about which seemed a mile above, the longer the Ubuntu chain grew in the schoolyard, spilling onto the street, the stronger I felt. I reached the next closest coil, a cool, softly hued living ribbon in the darkness, the diameter of a NYC skyscraper (New York had been a frequent money supported family vacation spot). Almost uniform in its somber amber pulsation – I reached it in what seemed the time it took me to notice its presence and turn my body towards it.

That's when, as I was about to stride through the wall of undulating burnt sienna, russet, interspersed by flashes of electrical jolts, I noticed nobody had said a word about what lay up above. It was so forlornly depressing I didn't want to see it, either, hovering up there like an infinite storm cloud, but I knew sooner or later, whatever it was, it would be Our fate.

Good thing I didn't need permission to use my eyes, even with about 50 minds conferring simultaneously on the next best thing to do.

I concluded that was to look up, and wish I could tell you, reader, there'd been some change, but sadly, the jeweled carnage was larger and closer than I'd thought, as if it'd grown a bit since I'd entered both that day of my fall and right then. For a more adequate description, reread page 76 (or was it 77 – I don't have time to check myself, which I know you understand), and picture

369

that times 5, so you'll be mentally looking at what sucked the very breath out my lungs.

Sandra, Brother Xolani (he and the other Ascend leaders had arrived, but not Brother Gainde) – and Reggie, Nyisha, plus, 123 other people by now were holding hands and together, We felt a collective shudder, up and back down the chain. Speculation flew round, but no one could agree on exactly what those dead ribbons flying out of nowhere might be, nor how to stop them from doing what they were doing to every coil in sight – strangling, draining, extinguishing the vibrancy out of each band of radiance till nothing remained but shattered barely glistening remnants – no one could figure out how to stop 'Gotten Worse' from getting even moreso.

"I feel your concern, little brother, but, We must find Kyerah, Amenhotep," an Elder and poet, named Roscoe, interrupted. He was there with his poet wife, both having joined the chain about a block from the schoolyard entrance, and without having ever met him, We knew he was a giant of a wise man, more than any of Us would have realized passing gray haired, inconspicuous him on a neighborhood street. Yes, yes, We were all intelligent, but there were some who were wise beyond the reach of understanding the obvious.

It was comforting to me to know, despite the Hell ahead promised by the Ankh Udja Saneb, there were now others who knew and could offer farther reaching vision.

"We can come back to this, after," I conceded, stepping into the diffused coil, straight in front of me.

Sigh.

It was dad's coil, only he wasn't there in one physical body to greet me. His aura was there in a swirling essence of earthen tones punctuated by looping electrical surges that broadcast his uniqueness, everywhere and nowhere. If I didn't have the Ubuntu to support me, this time, I would have collapsed, again, as I'd done, that first day I'd tripped and became a hero who'd dissolved in a flood of tears on a stairwell.

That's why I stood there, supportive condolences from every participant – I stood in an oscillating vortex of colors, only on nothing solid, like it was in the blackness of the Void, with the lights turned on. Yet, whereas out there everyone could sense the majesty of The One, here was the signature of one of His creations, without form, self-awareness or music. It was my dad; though, I

370

still couldn't talk to him, still couldn't see him, whether in a new face or not. I'd seen Kyerah in Sitamen, first glance; but here, I could only feeeeeeel his nearness. I doubt his nearness could, in turn, recognize me without eyes, nor hear me without ears when I pushed back a lone tear, murmuring, "I love you, dad."

"Time to go, Tyree," appeared Nyisha's no nonsense voice, extra understanding, again. She didn't doubt me, anymore, making me glad to be alive, spurring me to answer, with assurity:

"Yes. Let's find Our sister..."

=

"I attest – this step towards my singular solace is not the agonizing legend cowards and the vainglorious vow it to be. It is a simple choice for the determined, who know their answer is one of action to thusly ensure a cessation of all further actions by any party they'd ever known or would know. This step's infamously unendurable agony is the vestment of fables that only giants and dubious creatures of legends entertain, and yet – deemed fragile womanhood in this body, in this useless in any way that's considered societally useful body, will submit to my courage this hour, this minute. For, I have emptied the contents of my wedding gift from a golden goblet into my obsidian sacred temple over which I am the sole master. Thusly, neither I nor my troubles will tarry upon this rugged soil any further, with no interest due to whatever future legends shall be woven over my grave..."

~ ~ ~ ~ ~ ~ ~ ~ ~ ~ ~ ~

Funny, huh? I would have thought my lifecoil would be more astounding than my sister's, e-a-s-i-l-y, but? Eh?

Mine, suspended in the blackness same as the rest, was quite matter of fact, with an albeit hearty, no nonsense shine that actually befitted a male, I'm quite proud to admit, in hindsight. A lot like my dad's. Plus mine, although I'm younger, and I guess was why it wasn't as mountainous as my dad's, was much larger, circumferentially, than Kyerah's. She might not even know what 'circumferentially' means, HA! Yeah, so much for this little boast, 'cause Sitamen's spiral?

Was a reverberant ribbon of coruscating intensity that dared any but the steelhearted to risk hovering near. In other words, it was an inferno of light's definition. Guess since I know her, I never paid that much attention to her admirable qualities to perceive them as anything more than a girl's.

Oh, OKAY! So girls can be pretty excellent, but, who would have believed this fire's origin was a 14 year old and my sister, for goodness sakes – who wore purple curlers and fuzzy orange slippers – who'd have thought she'd be anything but goofy, having been the brunt of far more numerous embarrassing moments I could tell ya about, but?

I won't, 'cause I respect her and know it's okay to keep some things private, about everyone. Here's to you, my cherished big sis'...

Why, who couldn't acknowledge her strength's existence now, when all that luminosity was shining on me bright enough that I had to squint?

We were all momentarily stunned arriving at this, the next nearest spiral to the one that'd been my dad's. After seeing it from a distance, in the speed of thought – that's faster than the speed of light – even those looking through my eyes squinted simultaneously, as they stood, hand in hand, along Garvey Avenue. Hundreds, by then, several blocks long, people with their eyes closed in order to view my side of the Orb – they shut them reflexively tighter, Black fearless beings streaming across roadways, holding up the beeping, angry traffic. I knew this because in my own squinting, I'd shut my eyes long enough to see the epic vista of what We were experiencing...

...which was not all joy and laughs and wonderment, indeed, no matter the serenity We collectively felt having connected soul to soul with each other.

~ ~ ~ ~ ~ ~ ~ ~ ~ ~ ~

I'm enscripting this section quickly, because Venerated Elder Queen Nzinga has stepped up to the rostrum to begin the most important latter half of the Epidrome's opening speeches, (meaning, somebody's bound to mention my name, sooner than later [oh, man...]), so, I'mma break down the havoc happening on the outer skirts of Newark that evening, in a shorter time than the facts probably deserve.

~ ~ ~ ~ ~ ~ ~ ~ ~ ~ ~

Un-initiated regular folks all around the immediate neighborhood, on cross streets and up and down Garvey, got real curious, looking out their windows that overlooked tangled greenery and the school across the street, until the

373

chain, through word of mouth, gained more links and inevitably crossed a populated avenue. That's was when dozens and dozens joined, having attracted random people on about their business through the evening washed neighborhood. Black folk ain't shy when it looks like they're missing out on the party or sumthin' free's being given away. And who wouldn't inquire what the heck was up, now that it wasn't merely teenagers but young people to elders? They were warmly informed (cause each person in the chain could still hold a full conversation, while paying attention, as long as they held hands) and those brave enough to link up with the last persons in line on either side, were immediately gifted with complete knowledge and understanding. Then? Tens and tens would jump off to call friends to come lengthen this blossoming hue-man daisy chain that wasn't rescuing merely one little girl (which was enough), but was rescuing all those who participated.

I had wanted to visit other people's homes, one by one, to hear their living history; only it wasn't taking so long, now, as it would have individually. I and everyone got to grow from the living history, herstory, theirstory, Ourstory, from 8 teachers sharing their truths; 5 janitors and 6 bus drivers theirs. If I'd previously thought I'd been granted an office tower mind, well, in this no longer my solitary consciousness, I went from a stairwell building, to a single elevator to a bank of elevators in a universal engagement. No traffic jams, no desire to be anything but on time in multi-logue of conversation. We were a skyscraper city and the rent was no problem.

Why, there was medical staff, who, with Us, lost their fear of losing their jobs as they shared unencumbered truth, which was more along the lines of what I'd spied that commute past the hospital. Students told whatever they knew, discovering that most of what they should have known, they'd never been taught in any P.S., J.S. or H.S. There were cashiers, the unemployed, lawyers, (even homosexuals, who afterwards were cured of wanting anything but the perpetuation of life). There were solitarily homeless men, women and whole homeless families with children. Although, We didn't know how, We knew they'd be homeless, no more. We would help them, only for real. There were artists, carpenters, rappers, cashiers, electricians – and one brave councilman whose innermost thoughts revealed, despite instantly realizing the uselessness of his advocacy, his heart and soul desired nothing but the unapologetic empowerment for Us, all. He apologized to the assembled that he simply didn't know how to achieve it. We told him We'd help him and he felt powerless no more. There were hookers and pimps, yes, who'd cover up and desist, now that they saw their precious value, however? There were regular folks who realized they'd been living life as hookers and pimps, not professionally to pay their bills, but for free, out in the community in their actions.

No more.

And there were men and women who looked like 'thugs', which just one touch told everybody, it was merely a look. If it was more than that, after this evening, being a real 'thug' would be job experience for becoming an entrepreneur. Yes, there'd be no more foolin' ourselves, 'cause from one man, We collectively learned 'thug' was the white man's new word for 'nigger', when We'd never been either.

Then, though it would take much longer than a prolonged handshake to sort through the who did what to whom, when, where and who started it first? The Brothers and the Sisters were determined to work it out, together, cause they now and henceforth saw they were worth the effort.

Don't misunderstand me, though. The people assembled weren't only Black People. Many Latinos proudly offered up hands, wanting to save a child, only to discover through one of their own who was schooled in their true history, there was no land called 'Latin', nor any of their Ancestors who'd hailed from Spain. Even a few Asians had dared to come out from their various franchises, while most tried to shoo Us away; but those who did? Held Our hands with discomfort when they realized they were in the wrong community if they weren't there to free those who put a roof over their family's heads. Yet? Those Asians held on, as they, too, were thirsty for truth and shocked to discover everything they'd believed about their customers was a complete fabrication.

We, most importantly, as I took a breath before stepping into Kyerah's lifecoil – We discovered We were meant to be separate tribes, each race unto itself, not meant to hate each other, nor dissolve back into the bland nothingness, from whence We'd each been tricked into believing was humane, wherein every tribe dispenses with its refreshing uniqueness in favor of a flavorless 'American-ness'. That was progress in Our broad thinking, but, I still kept my secrets about the Yurugu despite the hue-man being to hue-man being acceptance of the truth of who We were. It was a communal healing that left none afraid.

Too bad, that's when the trouble started, and I know the following because Eye could see everything...

Understand, reader, We were seeking nothing but life, so? No single being of this one particular tribe, after that death, was permitted to join hands in order

375

to protect them, whether they deserved personal protection or not. Who knew? Maybe there were bunches who could survive the connection. Maybe their inner energy was of a caliber that We could have learned from meeting, however? That first white person, who wasn't even trying to help Us? I ain't cryin' no tears for him.

As for why it happened? Hmmmm.... years later I theorized, in my very unscientific way, the difference was in the melanin. I'd have to give you a physiology textbook inside a history textbook and that's too much book to write in the next 7 hours (the time I'm hoping I have, so I can finish this whole assignment). Thus, to summarize the facts, without vitriol or easy crass insults?

All beings, all life has melanin. It's the substance that permits the conductivity of energy cell to cell to support animated existence. Plants' melanin is chlorophyll, and that chlorophyll is green because they don't require the color green to transform sunlight into fuel for growth. Yet, you ever wonder what power's inside that power of 'green' outside of the mythical might of money? Our Black melanin, absorbs all frequencies of light, be that seen or unseen, so much, even green is absorbed. Well, the darkness of space is in truth, filled with pure frequencies, including photons of light, which is only seen or felt as these emissions bounce off an object such as the Sun, the planets, the moon and the stars. They have to travel to you and I to bounce about, so We see each other. But when you see Black? You're not seeing a color. You're seeing a body to whom light has been magnetically drawn, where all its supercharged healing left you behind. The very vista of space is itself –

IS MELANIN!

The lighter the color, the less magnetic, the less conductive, and the more of that original energy gets deflected, never being fully absorbed. You don't need a lot of melanin, though, for the melanin to work properly as there's many materials that conduct electricity at different rates, while still allowing the procession of electrons through to their destination. However? Of all the races of the world, except white people? Our melanin is structured around selenium, which is an efficient, stabilized conductor of electricity. The Tamahue's melanin is built around sulphur, which has a level of conductivity that in no way compares in intensity to selenium. Well, magnetism, the substance of that Triple Black Sphere, like a black hole in space absorbs all light, the Orb required near perfect transportation to be positively absorbed by those in extended contact. That said?

I believe Officer Alexi Tereshchenko (the instant he grabbed that sister's hand, she being that moment's last person in line) – the minute he grabbed her hand to pull her away, We learned everything We needed to know about him, good and evil, from the second he'd been mixed together 51 years ago to form a zygot. His circuitry had no ability to resist complete immersion before it was, it was... smh...

Well, I believe the officer experienced an organic short circuit that exploded every organ as every organ requires light to survive, except Cancer cells, and they mean death, as they eat themselves.
That evening his circuitry got too much and turned every cell in his body self-cannabilistic...

~ ~ ~ ~ ~ ~ ~ ~ ~ ~ ~

This isn't Alexi's story, but he didn't know that, unfortunate only for him, after receiving the call on his cruiser's radio about an unauthorized demonstration on Garvey Ave. It was dusk, he was only an hour from the end of his shift and he'd already had a long and stressful day. Appears, he'd killed the wrong man.

"Damn gorillas are 24hr trouble," he said to his partner, Officer Green, who laughed, out of habit, no longer totally agreeing as Alexi could easily tell. He'd been thinking of getting a new partner, no matter what it took, as he'd never trusted Green to truly comprehend the difficulty of their situation as white people on a planet overpopulated by darkies. Sure, he'd had to tweek the evidence now and then, in full view of Green, who co-operated because he wouldn't not only not rat out another white officer on behalf of some escaped slave, but because this was Tereshchenko who was quietly understood to have special 'privileges', plus? Sometimes doing dirt in front of Green couldn't be helped, and a lot of dirt was necessary in his assignment. Pity dumb dolts like his partner didn't have enough education to accept that black people could never, ever be allowed to rise too high above the gutter they'd been dragged down into, even though Green had once been a member of the Aryan Nation, himself. Officer Green had drunk the White Supremacy Kool-Aid, since trailer trash were easily hoodwinked by groups like the Aryan Nation who recruited using the upper class constructed legend that Black People were inferior, and were dragging the white man down. That made Alexi wanna laugh..

What a useless campaign 'cause, after the overkill of unarmed blacks by gleeful
377

rank and file, especially shooting the doctor, today, his partner was goin' a little soft in the heart, questioning how could white people be superior and be so barbaric? Green wouldn't put it that way, but Alexi knew he was an idiot.

See? Officer Tereshchenko also realized black people may be gullible as Hell, but too bad, they weren't dumb as Hell. Thus, you couldn't pity them like an abused tabby cat. Dumb creatures didn't require direct oppression to be kept in a powerless state. If blacks were incapable of higher thinking, the ruling power could let them set up their own self-ruled township to watch it fall to pieces, no crushing necessary. He knew from years and years of finally reaching the status of a 33rd degree Mason, if he and hundreds of thousands of others with the same information didn't maintain the current oppressive status quo, the civilization his white people had built would come to a screeching halt far more quickly, as...

...the Black Man was God.

No tabby, nor lion sized opponent could be as dangerous as a thinking man who had the ear of the The Original Creator.

Not that he could tell Green any of this, as he'd never believe it. Not at that dolt's adult age, since he'd been carefully spoonfed the legend of white people like all the rest of humanity during the highly brainwashable childhood period spent learning about George Washington and the cherry tree. Alexi, on the otherhand? His Ukrainian born parents had been spies in various clandestine organizations even the CIA didn't know about and Mr. and Mrs. Tereshchenko had the sort of literature not available in any Reader's Digest collection. Madame Helena Blavatsky's 'The Secret Doctrine', Manly P. Hall's 'The Secret Destiny of America', Elijah Muhammad's 'Message to The Black Man', and many more 'secrets' revealing books; especially his father's hidden stash of Aleister Crowley's liberatingly demented visions that had stoked Alexi's boyhood curiosity. After which, his young man's devotion to the lodge had only confirmed what he'd read earlier. That Madame Blavatsky had been right to conclude the white man's god was Lucifer, if that white man was brave enough to accept it.

Well, that brave man was him and thousands and thousands of others; but he doubted that would be Green or most other white people. Common white folk? They happily ignored the obvious oppression they were exacting because they suffered from combinations of sincerely not realizing their victims were as worthy, maybe worthier than they were, or? They were stark raving terrified of divine vengeance – as supposedly sayeth the Lord, vengeance was His, after all.

378

Yeah. Too bad, their association with original peoples of the world had them forgetting that treachery is white people's number one skill, as it's what got them to the top, and t'would be treachery, alone, that kept them there – even if that led to the destruction of everybody.

In the meantime, to keep the common Caucasian masses willing participants in the slaughter of the aboriginal world population, the Rockefeller ruled educational system had convinced them Western Civilization was forged on virtuous intellect – when in truth, it'd been forged on nothing but avaricious mendacity. But a liar, if successful, is still a successful liar.

His fellow brethren, the vast majority of whom he loathed, had and continued to rapaciously rape the planet in the depraved ways of their true master, (or why would depravity be so easy for them) while being suckers for a religion that bred a dolt's devotion to tactics that always failed. Faith, Hope, Charity and Brotherhood. Yeah, there's a set of dice loaded to lose every time! Like those nigger rappers called 'The Last Poets', whom he'd spent a month studying, had said (Alexi'd changed the words, he was so clever) –
"You can take demons out of Hellishness, but? You can't take the Hell outta demons. Whities, all whities…"

That last line made him laugh, everytime.

If his people had been true Christians, they'd have not only stopped celebrating Roman pagan holidays, they'd have stayed home and been suckers like the Arawaks Columbus encountered. The Arawaks looked strong and friendly – making them, according to Columbus, excellent slaves. This cop, if not his partner, understood white people's dolt headed hypocrisy of preaching righteousness while doing awfulness, with gore lovin' abandon, he understood it had been the result of a definite mistake. In his estimation, a mistake born the day the Byzantine Emperor Constantine stole a religion from Afrikans which proselytized mercy.

Could anything be more conflictual and more despised by The Nigga-lovin' God than hypocrisy? Well, we were the devil, he consoled himself, so all sins were to be utilized.

Too bad, Constantine's original plan to use the cross to conquer had instead conquered white people's dedication to pure death and mayhem, centuries after the Roman Emperor's own death. They went from innocently enjoying mass random slaughter in the arenas and rolling on the open streets sexual romps in any impulsive fashion imagined, to chastity belts and burning witches for having the sense to worship Baal.

No Papal Bull, issued to absolve Columbus and the church, could save the white race from damnation for the grievous sin of doing evil in The Creator's name.

But Officer Tereshchenko was Hell bent on delaying it.

Too bad Satan had such an awful reputation, or he'd have more willing comrades if everyone knew what fun he was. Alexi's was a lonely job he'd been assigned by his leaders – pretending to be a police officer to discreetly monitor Dr. Kattan and get that sphere (even though his bosses didn't believe the doctor had it, Tereshchenko was sure he did). Too bad, cause if treachery were popular, it wouldn't have taken decades to ingratiate himself with those more pliable thugs, and he'd have sped his progress further along by taking advantage of his ignorant colleagues, rather than recruiting them with resistance. Alexi was certain he'd have had lots of co-operation, even from Green, given? The vast majority of the men and women he worked with, including the couple African-Americans, believed mainstream media's portrayal that there was 'something' about black people that was despicable. If a mere 10% of white people could be convinced Satan is their good guy who would use every means necessary, LITERALLY, to maintain white hegemony? There'd be no more hesitation about practicing every whim that entered one's head without that damned uptight Christian guilt.

Not to mention, all the work Alexi'd done wouldn't have turned into such an utter failure.

'Cause he still didn't have the Orb, so his superiors continued not to respect him, wondering why they were protecting his blunders, as the wrong black man had been murdered....

again.

Instead, that stupid fool called 'Von' was dead – that was no problem, but a better corpse would have been Dr. Cheikh Kattan, currently in stable condition in intensive care.

Who called for that ambulance so quickly?! If only this operation had gotten top priority like the one that took out Princess Dianna. Foolish woman had been about to marry a Muslim prince!!!

380

Alexi felt no guilt about cornering the black boy in the bathroom and putting one bullet in his head. Stupid thug had threatened to take what he knew about Tereshchenko to the press if he didn't receive quadruple the $1K he'd already gotten to steal an item – granted, Von only knew that item from a vague description – but the officer was getting nervous for the first time since the nigger had spied that new kid going over to the Kattan house. He'd had to send the thug in, before new complications he couldn't control arose and the Orb was passed into the hands of an unknown factor.

Damn! That smear didn't even find it!

Well, whatever Von (his friends called him, 'Zone', for chrissakes) – whatever he'd done, knocking over cans after breaking a window, unfortunately, the couple had returned the same time, and Zone had hid in the very upstairs bathroom that would be the scene of his death, once Alexi found him, long after the gunned down doctor had been hauled away too soon for Kattan's death to be made a certainty. Whatever had happened? It was a glich in his hastily made plan after the doctor had lived. Dropping the 2 females off at the precinct, he'd raced back to the scene, where the boy had still been waiting. He'd hadn't want to kill Von, yet? No big deal, he'd thought, cause he would have pinned the murder on a dead Cheikh, no matter the discordant details, since extra crooked cop him had his privileges, and the entire system was on the side of the Blue Wall of Silence.

Oh, well. He'd planned on returning after work to retrieve the body sitting on the toilet, slumped over the free standing brass tissue dispenser, but now here's this demonstration taking up the time he needs to go back to 846 Carson. What the *bleep* was this? A nigger séance or another 'Hands Up! Don't Shoot' protest?...

No one had questioned his claim that Green had searched the entire upstairs of the freak house, and Green went along, while Tereshchenko made himself very visible on the other side of the street, and never re-entered the residence once the squad cars arrived. No one, not even the captain, would dare question him, but why tempt fate by being inside should the Zone be found, shaking with fear in a tiny bathroom, waiting for him to give the okay to leave?

"Yo, dude," Von had called the officer earlier afternoon from his cellphone, an hour before his sudden demise.

"What? Did you find the Orb?" Alexi'd taken the call by getting out of the cruiser he shared with Officer Green. His partner over the years had been dissolving into lipid-ness, and was eating his 2nd Subway sandwich of the afternoon that was working with the thousand other sandwiches, fries and half a foodcourt he'd eaten in only the first 3 months of that year. Slim and muscled Alexi didn't eat poison meant for dolts and niggers. His Ukranian girlfriend, wonderful twisted girl she was, juiced at home, exactly as instructed, so he had a fresh green drink, a protein bar and an apple. All organic, but of course.

How he hated the Kattans and their garden. He didn't have time to grow his own, and it would have been so less complicated to poison them, but they didn't eat anything they didn't grow or buy from farmers they knew, personally.

"Man! Do you know how big this house is?" Von harshly whispered.

"You think I give a freakin' rat's behind? They don't go out too often at the same time, so find it."

"Well, they're home now, and I'm trapped here in the bathroom!" Von raised his voice to a harsher whisper to hammer home his position, at the same time not giving away his location to the owners.

Officer Tereshchenko conveyed no emotion, whatsoever. No panic. No anger. No disappointment. He nearly soothingly asked:

"Which floor?"

"Third."

"Don't move till I get there..."

And then he made the call of a break in...

~ ~ ~ ~ ~ ~ ~ ~ ~ ~ ~ ~

We each mourned Brother Von, as if We'd lost a family member, because Sister Rekia was devastated and because We knew how beautiful We, each were. This wasn't some 'bad boy'. This was a forever lost opportunity to heal another one of Us. There were so many tears, even from me, as I felt responsible. We knew it wasn't my fault, yet, that's what I felt. It would take years for that image of him slumped over on that toilet like that, a corpse waiting for Officer Tereshchenko to return to retrieve him – it would take years for it to not pop up in my mind, as a reminder to protect even those I didn't personally know. Right then, about to resume, what in that second seemed my selfish search for my sister. Everybody knew that something, after this day, had to change.

Thus when that cop died, We had to stop Ourselves from cheering, because real death is a serious matter.

First, you could see a small electrical sparkling light emanating from his hand, pulsating with a buzzing sound, after the devilish arm of the law kind of a man had attempted to pull the sister named Devetra (a spirited, peaceful Queen, We each felt extra warm towards, as she'd always suspected We were gods before We'd connected here and saw We were on Our way) – almost instantly after trying to wrench her away, as if Garvey Ave. was a modern auction block, a resonating incandescence flowed from out the fissure where with his hand he'd brutally grabbed onto Sister Devetra's arm. It wasn't a jagged surge of tiny lightning bolts leaping from the contact, but a scrawling, lyrical spiral of searing white ropes growing and enveloping his entire body; eventually; starting from his fingers to then embracing his black uniformed frame, his shiny badges and what-nots covering his chest disappearing in a cocoon of roping white fire. And from the way he struggled, it was apparent to onlookers that although any one of Us could leave the chain (folks do hafta take bathroom breaks, no matter what they're doing) – he on the otherhand, desperately trying to, couldn't break free from his comeuppance.

I admit. We didn't let go.

It would have been an enjoyably stunning display of leaping living vengeance to watch if he hadn't been screaming with sheer terrified agony and writhing to break away the moment he realized he was stuck. Not to forget, if We hadn't experienced Cletus' crystal clear memories of his family burnt to cinders? Even with no one cracking gallows humor jokes? Well, despite knowing everything about that officer's evil and he was gettin' the verdict such guilt demanded – despite the fact his living cremation should have been a blissful satisfaction? Yeah, it was, but only a little 'cause We didn't want death that day. We wanted justice and that's what he got. Our hearts were trained on increasing life. However, Tereshchenko, whose name I knew from that moment on, He was nothing but purified death. He didn't have merely a few bodies on his Glock, he had graveyards in every cell of his own body. The Orb just gave him more of

383

what he already was. No, nobody laughed, but the irony wasn't lost as the officer went from being the slave driver to being driven to the grave he'd made of his life.

His rotund partner, clueless to how much he was loathed by this now justifiably fricasseed man, stood there, his mouth gapping, backing up to take a seat in his cruiser. He got on the radio, although, We didn't know what he said to whomever.

Sister Devetra let go of Alexi's lifeless hand when the magnetic connection had no place to go, no cell left to intensify. The cop's corpse, smokeless, smell-less, dropped like Cletus' bullet riddled shield had done, so long ago.

Before more police cars came, sirens knocking any other noise into background status, We began to warn any clearly white people to stay back. That was easy as there weren't but a few in our neighborhood. The dead officer was retrieved upon the arrival of his fellow cops, their guns drawn and trained on Us. However, this was a gathering of all types of people and all age ranges, as I stated. Discernibly confused, the authorities, conferring with each other in a huddle, weren't sure if they had *the authority* to handle the spontaneous assembly with full out violence.

Their solution was to recruit a Black cop to pull the chain apart, but? As soon as he, Officer Washington (a really confused but no longer confused guy) – as soon as Officer Washington, whom We got to know as Brother Fontaine – when he was palm to palm with a teenager named Aiyanna, who'd joined Us as soon as Alexi hit the concrete?
He was on Our side, too.

The growingly frustrated squadron of former slave catchers could only look on and keep anymore people from joining Us, afterwards – at least, for the moment.

"It's for your safety, ma'am!" one cop yelled at an elderly sister who wanted to join hands with her grandbaby, and was held at bay.

"Stand back, sir," one after another said to the throngs of curious people, almost politely this time. It was obvious, not knowing what they were dealing with, they were scared now, casting nervous glances between each other and Our way, arms out to hold back the crowds.

But there weren't enough of them to cover the blocks and blocks and blocks, with new people joining Us up and down the line.

See, We, as individuals could speak freely, while having multi-dimensional awareness of whatever happened at any point, so some of Us explained the unexplainable to family, friends and the curious in a myriad of ways, such as:

"It's just the community coming together, finally..."

or...

"I gotta do this..."

or...

"We're here to save Our daughter." That was Brother Jerry, a truck driver, in between long hauls up and down the interstate highways. He was ready to deck a few police, but after watching that cop go down, he smiled and he decided there'd be no need, although everyone knew there'd be more trouble, not less.

Jerry was right, though...

=

'Cause We were Ccwa, too, living carefree once again, finally harmonized with the frequency of The Most High, protecting Our own. There was nothing to fear, now. Nothing to fear, ever. The only lingering question in anyone's mind was how come We hadn't known this truth, about Ourselves, already?

Well, I knew the answer to that, but, I wasn't tellin' nobodae, cause not only hadn't I finished writing my report about Imhotep to give to a cog in the wheel of why We didn't know – to hand in a report written to prove who We were to a white teacher who probably wouldn't believe it anyway and would have been lit up like a Christmas tree if she'd dared to touch my shirt – not only hadn't I completed my assignment but I hadn't convinced Kyerah, either, the other evening, despite my best almost a superhero try. So, I was mum in that score, while in the Ubuntu, there were a number of highly educated brothers and sisters (such as Brothers Xolani, Roscoe, and Sirocco, and Sisters Devetra, NaNa and a warrior grandma named Valarie Cutthecrap Castile [it's a long story]) – there were a large number of schooled individuals who knew what up with those pale strangers from the caves and could seamlessly quote the dates, places and names of their historical treachery, like they were their own Orb.

Then, too, there were a bunch of so-called 'regular' folks who, despite having never researched the facts, had always known, textbook quotes or not – they'd known all their lives that the cause of the world's worst chaos was obvious. But not they, nor anybody who thought like them got a whiff of attention, in the light of something that held everybody back, in the final group conclusion. *Shoot!* If what those grown-ups had to offer, freely, didn't rate, then of course nothing I thought would matter to anyone, as I was only a child; which is why the excuses for Officer Tereshchenko's evil, caught fire more surely than that cop had ignited, the second he confronted the truth of who his soul knew him to be.
The first comment from one of Us?

"Now, let's not lose Our heads! Granted, that policeman was one really, really bad cop, but, they can't all be so bad, cause what about his partner, Green? He was trying! We gotta organize a march for better training and bodycams!"

That pack of fetid excrement came from some guy named Don, who was only saved from experiencing a similar fate as Alexi had, by his black melanated

386

skin, cause on the inside, he, too, would have killed a man, but didn't need to as he'd killed his own Black self in more ways than I have the stomach to list – in more way than The Ubuntu could save him. Granted, after his connection with the Ubuntu, his addiction to perversion would, most likely, be removed from his yearnings, but the truly awake could tell, his addiction upon which all the others were created would remain. His steadfast belief that Black People had nothing better to substitute for what he thought was actual civilization, that remained, despite the bold fact that the poorest truth is a better savings plan than a wallet burstin' with lies.

Shantay's dad quietly quoted, "Better is a dinner of herbs where love is, than a stalled ox and hatred therewith."

Nobody heard that, so, Brother Don's doubt was enough to enlist the agreement of the majority, 'cause, although no one else was as bamboozled as Don, frankly, still? We didn't have an alternative nation, or for that matter – We didn't even have Our own schools. Although, with all the murders that had made even Green hesitate, We might have told Don to take a hike, since, it wasn't self-hatred that ensured Our dependence on those who despised Us. It was the kindness in Our hearts that sealed Our financial co-operation with utter chaos, making it seem a nicer choice than defending generationally proven truth. Bible quotes are, after all, only words. A belly requires food. A beat up heart requires resuscitation.

What the heck could I say to thwart that, which was giving even me doubts, since as I've said, innumerable times, gods aren't perfect. We have more complex feelings than there's colors in existence – and principally amongst those feelings is Our bountiful desire to love with never-ending forgiveness. An impulse so innate, no one could reason it away with a history lesson, no matter how damningly detailed.

We weren't even fully gods, yet, or We'd have forgiven Ourselves for hating oppression enough to finally hate the oppressors.

Jeez. Everything happened so quickly, with more left unsaid, here on these pages, than happened there. Why, the prior synopsis took more time to write and time to read, reader, than it took to happen. Only 3 minutes had passed between reaching the coiling brilliance of Kyerah's echo, to squinting to take in everyone else's view and then taking my first step into the divine memory of my sister's soul. 3 minutes is all, despite these details and despite that death.

She wasn't where I stepped into, as I'd figured, since most likely she'd entered the Orb before the time slot where I was standing. Where I'd found my mother sitting, currently, in a jail cell. We decided to jettison downwards within her spiral, starting slowly, just in case it didn't work.

Surrounded by a 3D world of transmuted colors, much like my dad's, only with more vibrancy, the hues flowed one into the other with no defined form and offering no resistance. I pushed myself downwards, like I was set to jump upwards on a trampoline, causing a slurry of ebullience to rush up around me in a collaged frenzy, making me wonder when I'd get queasy, again, same as I had exiting the Orb after being pulled upwards back into my own coil. Remembering that proffered bucket, I lightened my pressure, spontaneously slowing the flood of dappling swirls into a gentle wash going up as I floated down.

I halted on a dime when I bumped into my sister.

It was as if I'd dropped into a straight jacket, rather than walking ahead into one, like when I'd stepped into my mother's timeline. I wasn't Kyerah, but I saw everything from her eyes and knew this manifestation to be no one else.

Or, better said? It was a memory of her, as her soul, her electrical flow, her aura? Had no vibrancy here, as there'd been with Mrs. Jackson. And also, unlike with my mother? I could hear Kyerah's every thought, as if they'd bounced out a hair's second after she'd actively thought them, propelled into the universe, their owner without control of their trajectory, leaving an audio trail my magnetic force could catch, because I existed ahead of the time when they were conceived. My mom and I? Our times were synchronized. I'd never hear any thoughts developed in a being alive alongside myself, without their conscious consent, or?...

... without them being a white person experiencing righteous damnation.

The volume was quite faint, same as a dusty old record would have been played on a turntable that even mixologists have stopped using. We hushed up, as one, since, We, were one mind. Some had to tell bystanders on the streets, to hush up 'cause, "Tyree has to concentrate...". They instantly obeyed, not because they understood what was happening if they hadn't been part of the handholding, but because the word had gotten out about the power of what was now, randomly, being called, 'The Ubuntu'. Later, everyone would call it that, but, the 'cause was still, yet to come.

Oh! Forgive me! I'm getting sloppy, but the chain was ever lengthening since

388

the police didn't have the numbers to cover the line that now stretched out about a mile, if We'd been able to straighten it out. However, curtailed at either end, multitudes were joining in the middle, crowding together, peacefully, into the schoolyard. First there were 50, then 150 and as of this point in my journey into the Orb, there were about 500. Twice that on the blocks. It was an empowered connection, inciting communal interaction like We were wasted souls in a desert, who'd stumbled across an oasis in each other. Everyone was beaming, sharing food, comraderie and love. Why, even old P.S. 47, in the darkness of complete night, was imbued with a vivacity that made it seem new and finally not ashamed.

However, more on that in a few pages, maybe, if I remember to include it in my rush to get this done, and if I get it done. Venerated Malik El-Hajj Shabazz has just taken the transcendent podium, to propose an exploratory journey to the Sirius Dog Star region of space. Who should go, why, plus, the form of transportation, be that vehicular or teleportational. The method of transportation remains in the planning stages, but the legendary for very, VERY, good reason Brother God is utilizing advanced hydra-prismatic graphics, which act like a 3D touchscreen display with the bending of light through water molecules in the atmosphere. The image doesn't simply remain static in one spot, it brushes up against you, in fully independent and interactive people projections – dressed in undulating white robed regalia, (no skimpy Western style futuristic clothing since that stuff was always more like paint on naked flesh) – they appear as passengers embarking on a journey, waving invitingly as they board a model of the proposed spacecraft. Darned impressive, but as always, it's the revered brother's eloquence with which he makes the complicated so joyfully simple, even non-scientific, that I could go home and build my own ship based on his demonstrative inspiration, and despite my math-phobia.

But? There's always a 'but' with the Divine. He'd finished his presentation, and there's family, now, offering their advice, and/or their disagreements. A few are calling the endeavor unnecessary, as Our Solar System is well within the Age of Aquarius, spiraling the whole celestial configuration of every planet towards Sirius, in the first place. Others agree with the project, as it'll take several thousand years for Earth to orbit within range of the twin stars made famous by the Dogon People, and? That makes me think, thank goodness, this debate should take a few hours of those thousands of years, and add to that? There'll be a lunch break!
Though, lemme add, decades ago, Our Sirius Family visited Us here on Earth, but that's for another book. For this one, back to enscripting –

Kyerah was sitting on our green couch, in that tiny Carson apartment, breathing heavily, the tiny marble sized Orb in the palm of her hand, as she clung to her desperate conclusion she could fix every family problem if she could find our father. If she could go back far enough she could stop whatever had started the cascade of deadly accidents – both our dad's crash and the gunning down of Dr. Kattan, a slaughter so shocking she'd fallen from her perch looking out the window as if her body had been shot through with red hot terror, losing its ability to hold itself without upright support.

After a few minutes of slumping in our grandma's spot, she remembered what was in her pocket. She took out all 3 marbles, placing the 2 Aandas around her neck, and the Orb, which she'd then taken last out of the satchel, she'd placed on her outstretched right hand. I could see in her mind the image of Sister Makeba, secretly handing the bundle to my sister, Our sister, earlier, in the bustling confrontation she'd had with the police. Kyerah had gone over to the growing frenzy on the front lawn of the mansion, after having called me on the phone. The doctor's wife, as Kyerah walked non-chalantly back to our empty shack, gave her a knowing nod, and the future Queen Sitamen gave one in return, her hand holding the parcel in her right jean pocket.

It wouldn't have done a darn thing for me to pray that Kyerah would have known what to do with that hole in her hand, as it wasn't guesswork realizing she'd made some mistake which led to her disappearance, and I could only look out upon the scene before that mistake was made. But I was surprised to hear in her thoughts that she knew she'd have never found our dad by simply expanding the Orb and plunging inside. I'd told her of my near extermination from this life and of that she had no doubt. She knew she'd be lost within without any last minute rescues from anyone. However, Kyerah Myloni Jackson was no Cletus. She wasn't resigned to her dilemma with practiced calm. What she was feeling, what, as a result, We each were feeling, was her renewed grief and a gaping terror that she was in the middle of a reality which might kill her, too, without hesitation. Without remorse.

She had Allah's Sacred Photo Album, afterall, but no Allah, there, to protect her, that she knew.

That's why I knew the sound of a creak on the stairwell, feet bounding breakneck pace up to our 2nd floor landing, I knew in another reality that noise wouldn't have troubled her in the slightest, but here? Being startled by what would have proven to be her brother, and not more murderous policemen, only him opening the door with his key? Instead made her jump with a start, clenching her grip over the Orb which within a nanosecond, cinched her fate to be swallowed up whole, like her body had been consumed into a tiny insatiable black hole.

And then there I was, once again – not as I'd been, entering a vacant apartment about to wonder where my sister was, but repeating a now familiar falling, falling, falling. I didn't feel the same personal horror I'd had the first time, but since Kyerah was, fear was what We all, in the Ubuntu, experienced – as a little girl who didn't know what she'd stumbled into. That massive, ravenous expanse of nothing she could stand on, pulled her freefall, and gratefully I'd explained enough of the experience that she wasn't as surprised at what she saw, as I'd been. She wasn't as frightened as I'd been, either, but that didn't mean she was in the mood for dying, and certainly not headways, sideways, feetways, tumbling uncontrollably-ways – she wasn't in the mood for hurtling downwards at supersonic speed to her death.

That's why, when it stopped, suddenly with once again no crashing, and I then found my consciousness in an immobile state of darkness, no movement in a body which echoed it was my sister's aura and not merely a memory, but her very soul nearby like a perfume lingers after the wearer has exited the elevator; that's why finding her eyes closed, as I could feel she was face down on a table of some sort, but I couldn't see it, nor where she was – that's why realizing Kyerah, no matter how many wisecracks I'd ever made, I knew Our beautiful sister was dead. It hit me like I'd fallen into a furnace of molten steel, this time, without her gentle laugh to tell me, 'It's okay...'

"NO!!!!" I screamed out of lips that couldn't move, so I don't know who heard me in whatever world this was, but up and down the line of those who were there with me?

Everybody, dropped to the ground on bended knees, tears flowing, and there was not a word said, not even the need to say, 'Hush'.

Pain speaks louder than words, including the quieting pain of agonized despair.

=

There's no more time.

Wow.

There's not a half of a half second left, but? Ain't it crazy, how I forgot in Heaven, We're here for each other? Remember? I'd told you about that. Told you about not being perfect, either...

Well, I'm hovering, at the podium, with The Most High. The Best of Planners. The Most Merciful. Master of The Day of Requital. Judge Over All His Creations...

and He's smiling at me.

Wow.

I'm okay. I'm okay.

~ ~ ~ ~ ~ ~ ~ ~ ~ ~ ~ ~

After We'd finished a most resplendent but light buffet at individual tables set up by volunteers in the outer vestibule, after We'd each gregariously returned to Our seats, to a few more astounding speakers, lastly, The Honorable Elijah Muhammad, himself, introduced Him, to thunderous applause and sound barrier challenging cheers.

Now, The God of Creation is a Man, not a rock star. There were no flashing lights, no waving of His arms in practiced greeting, while he ran onto the stage, shouting, "Thank You, Abjerusalem!" Nah. He walked and His magnetically black face wasn't alight with superficial smiles. There was love in His eyes and I knew Him, but His no nonsense expression reminded me of every Self-Sustaining Black man I'd ever known, and I'd known none like Him. There was no impulse within Him to impress, cause Allah has no partners. He says a thing and it is done. Thus?

392

He doesn't need Our approval.

He moved with perceptible strides, brushing His white robes in waves, reaching the black granite podium, as if on a conveyor belt of air, but He walked somberly and slowly, nodding with understanding, before the Humbly Gathered. There'd be no arguments from any being within this vast amphitheater, spread out behind, before, above and below Him – there'd be no disagreeing with Him, and there wasn't a whisper heard from any mouth, nor in any thought.

"Beloveds," He began, matter of fact-ly, in that rumbling voice that would be heard with a microphone or without, "The journey continues, uninterrupted, if We remember the path."

Allah has no need to make long speeches...

"When We do forget, We forget Our destination, which depends on defending Our Immortality. We forget, evil won't hesitate seeking the life within Our youth to divert Us even further from Our goal. We must protect them if We're to maintain this moment's existence, let alone the continuity of Our serenity. But We can't protect that which We don't hear and thus, don't value. It's not merely Our Sisters and Daughters and Wives and Mothers We must honor, but the only true immortality which keeps life worth living. Our youth, Family, must have Our ears, too."

And that's when, without adding more, He called upon Dr. and Mrs. Kattan to the lectern to join Him. I hadn't seen them, way down there, in the dignitary section out of my eyeshot. Then, after nodding approvingly at them, finishing with embraces, He invited, from within that same area, one after the other, Neguses Lokman (Reggie), Endybis (Maxwell), Memnon (James), Taharqa (Terrence), Aesop (Omar), and Negists Sitamin (my sister, as you know, reader), Amanirenas (Lisa), Daurama (Kenya), Amina (Shantay) and Candace (Rekia). I realize I've never fully explained the name changing We'd underwent, but more on that in a few moments as, The Most High is calling my name, right after having summoned my Beloved Jepkemboi (Nyisha) to stand in His presence, and with all of Our friends.

"This Beloved Warrior Brother, Akhenaton, Keeper of Knowledge, for a moment has forgotten he's not alone on Our path. He has a mighty task to chronicle the history of Our beginning, but We are patient, for We are One. None of My Chosen are alone, any longer." With this, The Creator now clasps

393

my forearms and shakes my hands, and is ending His greeting with an embrace.

"You have done well, son. I'm proud of you," He's saying to me, now, quietly, so only I hear the same words, with the same vastly calming aura as I'd heard them, long ago, that day in the desert, and remembered that same magnetic promise with that call from Jepkemboi, as I fretted in my hotel room.

I want to thank Him, but He's embracing my original crew, and I'm overcome with the joy that my home spans the entire planet, and loves me, pillar to post, even imperfect as I am. I'm reaching out to hold my wife with all the love that's in me.

'I thought you didn't want to be around a crowd of fastidious old folks?' I think at her, specifically, keeping our thoughts to ourselves.

She's looking up into my eyes (I grew a whole lot in the years between meeting her and marrying her), her own somber expression filled with love, soundlessly replying, 'If you can become more well-rounded, so can I! Plus, I got my own gold leaf invitation. Why bother going through the lesser gods when I can speak, all by myself, with The One?..'

I'm laughing, thinking back, 'And there you go! It was so easy, after all!'

We're joining in the embraces, and The Gathering of Gods is participating with a thunderous ovation.

The ovation I'd gotten in the Orb has met its reason for clapping...

~ ~ ~ ~ ~ ~ ~ ~ ~ ~ ~

I can take my time, now, which? Makes writing this history no longer my appointed duty, but a much needed healing, and I admit, almost a pleasure. It's certainly an honor, knowing I'm a part of a great time in Our-story, and not another cog in a wheel of endless stagnation, nor destruction. I'm a supporter of life in every realm I touch, including my wife's and my son's lives, who're laying beside me on our wheatgrass rooftop, overlooking the terraced ripple of edible wealth we've grown rising to the horizon of the Heavens above and feeding the Heaven that is our happy home.

It's a couple months after The Gathering, and I took that time to relax, then get back to my hands on, hands chopped off duties as Protector, but, no my son hasn't been born yet. My Queen is now 6 months pregnant, as I'm enscripting, which no longer worries me, either as I don't have to reveal everything, although, I'll still reveal enough. We have more feelings than there's visible colors the human eye can see. And I'm okay with leaving the All Knowing as the best guide for each of Us.

My, my. This soothing late Summer air invigoratingly agrees – what an interesting continuation of my journey this new addition will be.

But that's for another book. I'm not finished with this one, nor all the others inbetween, yet. You see, reader. Back on The Ubuntu, We didn't, know Our Enemy had his own name, his own plans, and yet? His appointed time was coming to an end, while We had all the time in the world...

~ ~ ~ ~ ~ ~ ~ ~ ~ ~ ~

Have you ever been faced with what seemed an insurmountable impasse, and you knew, before you'd even gotten beyond it that you were going to find a way? That there was some item, some tool you didn't see, but you knew you had, and you'd use it for a key hole you'd lost the key for – a imagined up use for a tool that no matter what it was designed to do, w-o-u-l-d trip the inner pins, and you'd successfully open that door to the room full of food for you, the previously starving man?

Well, I was just a boy, but I knew, I wasn't going have any more death that day.

Plus, I had a brain about the size of the Western Hemisphere, as it'd been exponentially enhanced by the army of brains of a few of my closest friends. 2,348 thinking warriors, exactly, and by the moment – it had to have been maybe 10pm – by the moment I realized my sister was deceased in that yesteryear timeframe, my expanded ability to think spontaneously through every conceivable probable way to open this lock concluded:

A whole bunch of Us had to enter the Orb, putting each being right inside their own coil, using, hopefully, Our combined might to jettison back in time, collectively, so somebody, s-o-m-e-b-o-d-y had to have been right there in that room with Our sister *before* she'd died. And We had to hold on for dearest life, cause this saving folks was time consuming and:

CONSPICUOUS!!!

There were police and army forces everywhere. On foot and in helicopters flyin' overhead, a battery of army vehicles stationed on every block where We stood, including in front of the schoolyard. They daren't touch Us, though; instead deploying screechingly brash searchlights, illuminating the blocks and blocks of the Ubuntu expanse, making Our black faces glare blue green, Our brown faces gleam lemon yellow and Our so-called 'yellow' faces glower translucent white.

But, We didn't need their approval to pick this lock, and to their chagrin, they couldn't stop Us.

Apparently, a critical number of participants had joined, after about 1,500, We calculated and they'd tripped some hyper energetic fluidity between Us, a satiation of circuitry that revealed its force without Us trying to impress those who meant Us harm. The same coils of white strands that had given Alexi a taste of his deadly soul, were freely, now, encircling Our mini gathering, reverberating what was inside of every person holding hands. For those not acquainted? That was Pure Love, so, the burst of lyrical, capering ribbons, streamed blissfully about the line, but, it didn't affect Us, nor those who approached Us with genuine interest. However, love is an action, not merely a feeling. Love defends its right to exist, to share itself without fear. So?

With a look, from any one along the line, those spiraling coils snapped outwards to spark the fear of Gods in those with harm in their heart. It's not like the person looking at a wrongdoer knew that other being meant Us harm. It's that the energy was magnetically drawn to obliterate that which was negatively charged, thusly? No threat came any closer than 15 feet. Let it be known, We didn't hurt anyone. We didn't need to. We just explained Our mission to the police chiefs, the generals, the politicians, the media who came to ask, without giving too many details. And Our Love gave the arrogant ones with demands a friendly jolt. Hence, We told the gathered militia, step aside, to let anyone who desired to hold hands do as they wished. 'Cause We knew, when the idea to go back further in time hit Our mind, in order to find a second party in that space my sister was in, and We didn't know where the heck she was, We'd need a whole lot more people.

A whole lot more.

And as We thought it? It was done. Ha! But there's no need to explain what the cops and the soldiers (who'd been dispatched too quickly to deny the United States was ready to go to lock down mode at the drop of a false flag) – there's no need for me to chronicle the minute details of what those who opposed Us were doing, like I did with Officer Tereshchenko, since they had no choice but to concede, because Our guns were bigger.

"Everybody ready?" I called out. I'd had left Kyerah's coil, reluctantly, to make the short trek across the Void and stand beside my own, which I recognized from its more muted aura, although I was miles and miles from my real time presence.

"Ready," said Reggie.

"Good to go!" came Nyisha.

"Okay!" was exclaimed in various forms, in a multitude of languages, such as, of course Haitian Patois and Spanish, then smatterings of Mandarin, Korean, Kiswahili, Amharic and Hausa, everyone of which was universally understood, up and down. We pre-established only half would enter and nobody would let go of a single hand. For your better understanding, reader, I couldn't feel Nyisha's nor Lisa's hands, per se, within the Sphere, but same as I could see people's auras and the interflowing colors above the Kattan mansion, without definitive proof, I knew I was holding tightly to my rescue, because that's what my soul wanted. Everyone understood this necessity without needing to say, "Don't let go."

But I said it anyway.

We were 5,094 when about half that number, one after another, incrementally stepped into that hole in the middle of a forgotten schoolyard in the middle of a so-called forsaken city. In the hot barrage of searchlights, the Orb seemed flatly 1 dimensional, as if folks were stepping into a child's circular construction paper cutout, and disappearing. But We understood, finally. And if We needed more volunteers, well, with handy cellphones ready, recruiting more would be no problem.

Hey. We were trending on every social media around the planet.

We were okay. We would have been having a ball if We hadn't come to get business done, and FAST...

Everybody, We theorized, would arrive within or directly outside their own coils, as I should be the anchor inside the Orb, holding it steady like the engraved script on its surface would have done if I'd remember to consult them, from the beginning. If, IF this proved correct, no one would forget who they were in real time, no one would plummet in the vastness of nothingness as I'd done and Our empowered magnetism should prove unbreakable.

Well, that worked. We couldn't see the broad result, but through Our thoughts We saw the replica of everyone's aura, surrounding each person. We began the count to propel back into ancient times...

"10, 9, 8, 7, 6, 5..."

"Wait!" a young bright faced teenager name Trayvon shouted, halting Our count. "Remember Tyree got queasy, ya'll! Go, but go slow, or We'll be cleaning up an ocean of what everybody ate last!"

There were chuckling yeses, in assent. Thus, nobody would descend faster than would cause the first hint of squeamishness. Agreed, We resumed, reached, "1" and began Our downward ride, all persons under their own self-guided direction. Ha! No one got squeamish or queasy or sickly or any of the other synonyms I could find for wanting to hurl right before you hurl. That unity is one powerful cure-all.

So, We sped it up. Breakneck speed. Seems, We be superheroes like that...

~ ~ ~ ~ ~ ~ ~ ~ ~ ~ ~

I, Kurush, knew how to take both these guys out, with martial skills that would have taken Tyree me probably the next 20 years to learn. The question was?

'What if these guys were better than me?'

There was only one way to find out, since loyal retainer assassin me had been trained specifically for combat in difficult small spaces. Assassinations worked better where they weren't expected and few planned on one lone humble servant sent to end their days, pre-maturely, in a hallway. I figured modern me would work better, too, as I was here to rescue, not to kill. Love of life is a stronger motivation for gettin' ish done.

As for everybody else who'd entered the Orb, We stopped when We could sense the true aura of Kyerah, like discerning that scent of her lingering perfume, once again. But most of Us were in diverse places all over the globe. Same Orb time. Different Orb stations.

It was a little chaotic, too, with a flood of hundreds of unique settings, vistas, sights, tastes, smells, sounds, all Afrikan or Afrikan derivatives thereof, all free, hitting Our five senses as one. I think I could see James fishing from his humble boat in a bay, mystified by the unsullied blue of both sky and water, yet I didn't know how far or how close he was to me, nor anybody else. Kenya was a toddler running through a mosaic imbedded colonnade, alongside an inner courtyard garden. Brother Xolani, I think that was him... he was a herdsman, guiding his white cattle as numerous as gnats in a circle of sunshine. There were wives, laughing, husbands forging, some tears, some pain but mostly there was safe peace, and everybody remembered who they were through the Ubuntu. Many ran into that motley colored miniature void inside their coils, as it turned out, they hadn't been physically alive in that particular past moment at all.

The entire panoply was nearly intoxicatingly riveting and if I'd had more leisure, I'd have dropped down in that stonework passage and drank every manifestation in, like a living television set, yet? Inside my head, I couldn't fixate on the shock of locales and not lose concentration on my ultimate goal.

The man in front of me was dressed in a servant's garb of some status and was a full head taller, but he was no warrior, I could ascertain from his bearing, thanks to Kurush's expertise with assessing every element of a challenge. But the man was carrying a long scimitar at his side, although I noted it was sheathed, with his hands in swinging pace with his stride. It'd take him a moment to retrieve his blade, after the first moment it took to get over his surprise at being attacked. A warrior would have operated on reflex. Shoot, a warrior walks expecting attack, but not a common man, enlisted for ordinary never surprising duties. His blade was for show, and would have been enough if I'd been a mere servant, myself.

Unfortunately, I couldn't see the other attendant behind me, which was of no concern as Kurush's mind had pinpoint recall. I remembered this servant as a powerful brother, when I'd seen him back in the dining hall, but despite that, he was only a lumbering man to the smarter servant before me. He was even taller than the man ahead of me and he, too, had a blade – a small one.

However, I doubted he'd have mastered its use if his commander hadn't mastered his own.

Or so I hoped, because my weapons had been confiscated, and were waiting for me at the front entryway, a place I'd noted, when I'd arrived, was brimming with actual fighters. Best not wait to arrive there at the end of this walkway. Good thing my best weapon was Kurush's skill.

Not wasting a movement, with muscles that could have performed precisely while I slept through the exchange, I dipped down, delivering a simultaneously smooth combo of a pivoting sidekick to the small of the leading servant's back, (which pushed a gust of air out his lungs making him gasp as he faltered and went down) and with split second timing, I lashed a targeted backhand punch to the weak jut of the taller man's chin, having gaged where his chin would be based on the air currents his movement made on my back.

I was shorter than both, but I was lean and sinewed, handily bringing them to their knees as I sidestepped out the bigger guy's falling way. I then spun about, relieving the groaning giant of his cutlass and the other, with another foot to his back – I relieved him of his scimitar, before his clarity returned enough that he might reach up with his hands to dislodge my foot.

That's when I heard the, "Oh, man! Tyree! Yo, dude, you almost knocked me out!"

Springing off the downed leading servant's back, blades pointed directly at him, as he achingly got on his knees, I shot a quick glance towards whom I thought had been a mere rather large obstacle behind me, to see the impossible to not recognize visage of Reggie Turner, in a grown man's face. His eyes were winced shut in pain and he'd risen rubbing his stinging chin.

"Oh, wow, dude!" I blurted. "I had no freakin' idea that was *you!*"

I attempted to help him stand up straight, forgetting the blades were in my hand, clunking them nosily together in that echoing hallway. Child me would have put the knifes to the side, but Kurush made me turn in time to see and thus stop my first opponent, who'd regained his standing posture – Kurush saved me from getting jumped in turn. I stepped back, not wanting to skewer the man with the long blade, and he, gratefully, wanting to live one more day, he halted.

Not that anything that happened here would have been permanent for either

400

myself or whoever this guy was, but it wouldn't be the same for my sister if We didn't find her, and now.

Talking with my servant assassin's authoritative voice, which didn't include, 'hems', or 'justs', or 'ums', or 'uhs', or 'whoas', nor even a 'harrumph', I advised the defeated brother servant to remain where he was. If he could have slit my throat with his eyes, I'd have bled to death at the scene, but he conceded by putting his hands up. Good thing for Us both, my name wasn't Alexi...

"Okay," I addressed Reggie, though our two minds were in total synchronicity, now that we knew we'd been in the same daggone place, "One of Us has ta go get Kyerah. If I go, it's gonna look strange. If you go, she won't know who you are and you know nothing about her, other than as possibly, a princess. So, I'm not a murderer, here, but this guy can't be left to go alert the guards."

Everybody was paying attention now, throughout the Ubuntu. We were close to Our sister, but, it wouldn't be easy.

Don, still outside on Garvey Avenue, suggested, "Deck him, Tyree. There's no time for diplomacy. He'll be living the same life as if nothing ever happened. It's better than killing him."

I wasn't feeling that. The vast majority of Us weren't either.

"Oh, please," snapped Don. "You already hit the guy. There's no time to play fair!"

"Tie him up, and mute his mouth," Nyisha, interrupted. She was in a village, pounding millet in a huge wooden mortar bowl, with a baseball bat length pestle.

Lots of folks questioned, "Tie him up with what?"

But I knew what Nyisha saw out my eyes. She saw the long plain sackcloth robe the servant was wearing, and that it was cinched round his waste with a doubled over cord. Looked like hemp from the texture of it, so it'd be fibrously super strong and flexible. My dad had told me you could use hemp to make clothes, cure Cancer and fabricate darn near indestructible vehicles. Selectively Black loving him had said, "The white man outlawed it because it can be grown by everybody."

401

My father surely loved truth, even if he hadn't known enough of it.

I looked at Reggie, who'd sufficiently recovered, and he instantly pulled the cord off the seething brother from an ancient time, whilst I wordlessly pretended I'd do the real slitting any minute if the man tried anything. Reg tied his hands behind his back, then from the bottom of the robe, tore off 2 strips which he used to secure our captive's legs, after sitting him down, back against the wall. Reggie finished the job by stuffing the last strip in his mouth.

Then looking at me, as if for the first time, he blurted, "Dude? Yo, you look like Tyree and at the same time you look like a ferocious warrior! Weird!"

I laughed, telling him, "If you guys weren't living at the same time, I'd think you were the reincarnation of Mike Tyson!"
Turning back to the trussed up man, stifled any further laugh from anyone, 'cause it wasn't a good feeling tying up Our brother. And as Don was warning Us, it wouldn't allow a whole lot of extra time as the man could wriggle this way or that. But it gave Us the chance We needed to:

...walk back into the dining hall as if We'd been summoned. After that, We wouldn't need that much time.

=

She was here, somewhere, as I could sense her living presence, but? I was wondering if I'd just given her poison that would end it.

Kurush told me what to do, otherwise I'd have been struck immobile by the sights. See, I had his pinpoint memory of the dining hall, but anybody's memories besides Allah's are never quite as impressive as the real thing, and Allah's are so precise, you can't tell the difference between Orb's real and, um? Real real. That's why if Kurush, and that was me, mind you – if I hadn't already been acclimated to opulence through my experience as a retainer assassin to kings? Though I remember walking into the hall to deliver the poison to the princess? Actually seeing the palatial setting I hoped to find my sister within, as an equally 12 year old not a 'kid' child, I'd have stumbled or taken a mindless moment to go,

"Whoa..." And that might have gotten my fool self killed.

But swinging back the thick wooden door and striding in past the 2 guards stationed there on either side, Reggie and I were both Black Men cool.

That means, I said an internal, inaudible, "Whoa!" with a thousand other minds.

This space was not only so far removed from my family's little shack on the ghetto, it made Sandstone Hill look like it was the shack, and the Kattan mansion, a house.

A dollhouse.

This mere dining hall was a Moorish waking dream of twilight blue, epically sweeping from embellished tiled flooring to the chasmal carved and painstakingly frescoed dome above (no need to have seen them fabricate a square inch as the labor left its calling card chiseled on your eyeballs). The expansive space was a manmade apogee, from floor to laboriously detailed ceiling, tastefully exclamated with glistening zaffre blue gems set into every turreted alcove, each alcove further capped with golden scalloped arches. The room was operatic where the fat lady would look skinny, capable of fitting 2 or 3 Kattan libraries, one beside the other, with room to spare, and 2 or 3 more

403

on top of one another before they touched the raised inside of the cupola.

It must have been night, because though opaline glass filled windows surrounded the left and right wall banks, fronted by a squadron of red marble pillars, I could see their opalescent luster only due to the hanging grandeur of 6 Moroccan chandeliers, the size of small economy cars, fully lit, draping their light upon the room and a table. Yet, despite that glow, the table was plunged into shadows emanating from the one diner seated all alone in the middle of its near half a football field length.

One person sitting alone at a table like that was bound to look out of place, but her manner, her slightly lowered head suggested a separate heavy burden was on her heart. With some utensil I couldn't see, she was moving items around in front of her, so I could tell, despite her dour appearance, she was still alive. Having entered from a side door close by one end of the table, even from afar, the perfection of her features, intensified by the depth of her blackness, was as obvious as the sky is big. I wondered how could the most beautiful woman I'd ever seen in my short life (mind you, a life spent alive during the digital age, giving me 75 years worth of acquaintance with women's faces compared to any male from whatever age this was – because Kurush wasn't an elder but he sure was a very experienced man) – I wondered what could ever make such a sublimely perfected young woman so sorrowful?

'Oh!' I laughed, privately, to myself, seeing no other woman in the room. '*It's Kyerah! Geez, what a drama queen! Only she could be in the middle of saliva dripping wealth, look like high fashion model Iman's darker more beautiful twin sister and still find something to whine about. Wait till I kid her about THIS!*'

Oops. To accomplish that I knew I'd better get her out of here, without alerting the guards' suspicion, 'cause I'd given her poison, only minutes ago.

Damn! I'd killed my own sister! Yes, I knew here she hadn't been related to me by blood, but the fact stung because it was now obvious, We're all related by souls.

"Lemme follow after you, Reggie," I said to him, separately realizing, he and I had been speaking two different languages to one another, languages which these physical memories of whom we'd been, long ago were more acquainted with using. Our vocal chords remembered those familiar tones, while never having learned the movements, nor had our brains developed the neural circuitry to speak English, at least not very well. It was only Our telepathic connection that allowed he and I and the entire Ubuntu to understand every word said. There was a U.N. conference of hundreds of languages going on, but nobody was confused, like We'd all soon discover – confusion was the order of the day in institutions like the United Nations.

"Gotcha!" he answered and started walking ahead, not alongside.

Surprisingly, there weren't as many guards as Tyree me would have assumed, but, I was quickly put up to speed by Kurush, who's mind contained countless images of vanquishing a thousand of the princess's father's army, and thousands of soldiers from the armies of multitudes of other kings. Massinissa was as legendary a leader of battle as Sophonisba was the legendary beauty of the world.

Sophonisba. My big sister, in any realm.

Ah. No wonder her palace lay barren of protection. No wonder she was utterly despondent. The Romans were demanding she be presented to Scipio, as his slave...

Following Reggie, without being questioned by the few attendees or sentries, who all stood in waiting, we reached the table. It was empty, as said, except for a bounteous meal spread out in the center before her; too much for one woman to eat. Kyerah's black pearlescent face had only increased in perfection, now that we stood directly on the other side of the span, the sole gulf. But there was no doubt it was the living her, as she had that glow, that scent of existence I'd come to recognize was the difference between Allah's memories and Allah's creation.

Reggie had it, too, but he'd been behind me and he was no ways 'cute'.

Cheek resting upon the small of her fist, elbow planted on her chair's armrest, she listlessly looked down upon a shining silver plate, toying with the uneaten food there, giving no indication she'd seen either of us. She, nonetheless, did ask,

"Is there a second course to this gift?" Fork in hand, she pointed it towards an empty red gold goblet on her left. My big sis, without doubt, had forgotten who she was.

"Kyerah," is all I said, in a heavy, battle-tried, Afrikan man's accent.

Raising her eyes, inquisitively, she seemed puzzled, as if wondering where she'd heard that name before. Then she looked at me like a psych ward patient coming off of a prescribed opiate high – the distinction I once thought would be my fate, but never again.

"Sister, it's time to go home," I warmly added, doing my best as a warrior, servant assassin, not to cry.

"Tyree?" she sleepily asked, tilting her head at an angle, wondering how come reality had become the dream, and the dream had become more believable.

"No. I think I'm too late..."

From the waning intensity of her aura, there was no doubt, the drug would soon prove more believable than anything. So, used to be proper for all the wrong reasons me; used to be upper middle class Black, but would have never have hung out on the family's front porch me; used to be uptight I? Lunged clear across the broad width of that mahogany top, spilling dishes, still full goblets, plateware, cutlery, startling guards and servants into shouting action, shattering the cavernous silence of that hall and time and to grab hold of my sister's hand before her spirit might leave, going someplace where awaiting souls went till born again.

Ones doomed to be trapped within the Orb.

Four guards sprung into action, but they were stationed too far aside to reach me or Reggie – too far to catch us before I'd said, "Pull!" and then the all of Us, with my sister and I, together, Reggie, and the several thousand others, We each tumbled out of a time none of Us had been taught about, back into the Void. 4,562 persons, hovering at separate positions in the depths of complete blackness, in no danger of falling here, or falling anywhere, no matter where We'd roamed.

That was a whole lotta folks, yes, but, We'd have felt like failures if Our number had been 4,561, minus one New Black Girl...

~ ~ ~ ~ ~ ~ ~ ~ ~ ~ ~

Kyerah didn't need to know what had happened. She was holding my hand and that way, everybody told her in a touch. In turn, she instantly told Us a terrible tale of the Blue-Black Afrikan Princess who had transfixed every man who'd ever seen her, inspiring whole nations to go to war to secure her hand.

406

Whole nations, including a twistedly degenerate one that only desired her humiliation.

It was funny, many contemplated, how similar this story sounded to the ancient fable of Helen of Troy. There were those who thought it yet another innocent accident, called coincidence, that only white people seemed to commit on a regular basis, but there were far fewer convinced this was purely happenstance, anymore.

Beyond this, from that day forward, my sister has never doubted who the Enemy is again. How did she achieve such a diametric change in thinking? Cause Sophinisba's agony had been hers, with no memory of there being any other choice. She'd have rather have died than let a Roman practice their sickening perversions on the flesh she understood was her temple, in a land wherein whose people had practiced sacredness and didn't question their right to defend it.

=

We could have physically picked up a dozen or more cops with Our conjoined power, in a spiraling electrical fishing net, if We'd wanted, effortlessly tossing them into The Sacred Breath, to then watch them free-fall in the blackness, but their importance in, over and around Our lives had ceased and desisted. We were in charge, by order of Ourselves. Plus?

We were having too much fun, to give a fart! And We weren't even holding hands, for the moment. One after another had been pulled back into the actual present time, out of the Orb, onto the worn asphalt tar of the schoolyard – a yard that had never known such a winning team. Only 2 hours had passed while We'd been hurtling through the stuff of what'd taken place, eons ago, and it took a half hour, only, for the sum total of everyone to exit, till I and Kyerah, the centers of the Ubuntu stepped out behind Nyisha and Lisa, and them behind Reggie and James, with the throng of those before filling every space block after more blocks than ever. We were heralded with thunderous applause, up and down Garvey, in a mini Million Man crowd that had extended all the way to my neighbors on Carson.

Well, okay. It was only about 8,300 people. But? We were just beginning, remember, 'cause We had yet to 'officially' become 'The Ubuntu'...

The police and military hadn't known what the heck was going on. They, their SWAT teams, sniper sentries, tank operators, helicopters and remote drone units had collectively resigned themselves to waiting patiently till We were finished; and anyone who left the line, for whatever reason, they weren't talking to folks We no longer recognized as deserving of authority over Us, no matter how that Original Person felt about why none of Us had been taught the histories of Sophonisba, Manykeni, John Horse, Amenhotep, all the people the entire Ubuntu had been, and then all that those people We'd been, in turn, had personally known. Nope. For Us, the 'authorities' had lost Our respect.

What did matter, was several planets worth of knowledge in less than one square mile. Who needed the whole of the United States, if all We got from them was baldface lies, obfuscations and half-truths, which were worse than the lies since, half truths made you want to believe. Granted, the vast majority of participants calculated if We made the Enemy 'fess up and do better, he'd

408

stop committing so many 'accidents' and finally become Our friend...

But that was for a future day, even those folks decided. For now, We were on a hashtag unnecessary first name basis, in an honorable Afrikan manner that understood the blessing of societal structure (the more elder a person, the more respect he/she received and the younger, the more patiently loving the guidance). There were no strangers in this crowd, if you weren't wearing a uniform, or weren't a curious (most called 'em 'nosy') white person who'd been gently kept at a safe arm's length during our Ubuntu. Thus, nobody who hadn't participated understood what the heck would turn ordinary citizens into apparently – now, the very best of friends. Thousands of us were jubilantly hugging, conversing with each other with no shyness, fluidly, en masse, like We'd grown up in a single household. A rather huge one.

All Praise Due to Allah, His mansion has many rooms.

"It's going to fall apart, Tyree."

In the throng of congratulations, I want you to comprehend, I'd started with a select crew, but We'd wound up family close with everybody in that courtyard and those streets in either direction. In Western literature, be it fiction or non-fiction, the intricacy, the threads that build the society are trivialized as if one thread doesn't matter to the rest. As if there's one hero, and nobody else except him, or except her. But on a luxury garment, pull one strand from a seemingly indistinct end and the quality and thus worth of the outfit is destroyed. Meaning? Yeah, I was the guy who'd started this, so people were enthused to meet me, but I wasn't the most fascinating, nor the most knowledgeable person there. This celebration didn't center around me! Folks were having a good ol' time discovering one another, as all knew all, upon first glance. Whilst? The whole assembled crowd was my very best friend, with no notion that no one person could talk to everybody, and certainly not all at once.

So, having collapsed the Orb, securing it in a new red velvet satchel, which kindly Sister E-Queen had brought me (something she'd sewn up quickly and expertly in her home a few blocks eastwards, after spending a good half hour on the line) – with the Orb in my pocket, and the Aandas in safe keeping around my neck and then Kyerah's, Our crew had spread out all over the place, in the depths of their super extended Ubuntu.
Being spread out, I might have missed what Kyerah was saying with maybe 25 people between her and I, with passionate discussions all around. This is why I'm daggone sure, her statement was the first purely telepathic thought I'd ever

received. I turned in her direction, and through the assembled, I caught sight of her returned to being a regular girl, with her regular almond face self, head shaking back and forth with concern, and this time there was no disagreement between us.

We both knew nobody had given a second thought to the Ankh Udja Saneb.

Good thing I and my own once again regular office tower mind conceived a strategy to keep this amazing moment from falling to pieces, like Our unity always does, as Brother Xolani had shared when We were one fearless mind.

"I'm sorry, brothers," I said, interrupting a throng of brothers surrounding me, who'd been examining the very dialectically Afrikan analysis of the modernized context of Our problematic conditioning, under imperialistic religious indoctrination versus the cosmic syntactical precision of the Black Conscious physiology...

...um? Yeah. My thoughts, exactly, reader – at that time. We weren't gods yet, by a longshot, and though the conversation with these brothers had been, um...? Kinda fascinating, I wasn't ready, or at the time I was certain I wasn't capable of being a scientist, yet. Maybe, after I returned to the school that was now, happily leaning to the side.

"I'm sorry, but, I gotta find the original crew."

"Oh, yes, little brother, of course," everyone said, ankhs, beads, and kente clothe flapping as I and they saluted Black Powerfists at one another. They were genuine warriors, no doubt, as I knew them, personally. They offered regrets I had to leave, but no resistance. There was plenty more talking for them to get into with those who better understood what, the heck, they were saying.

Using my cellphone, I confirmed in a call to my sister what needed to be done, quickly, as this time she knew before I did. Then, I reached Reggie, Nyisha, both of whom had been contemplating the same conclusion, and one by one, the first crew gravitated back together and opening a circle in the block party gathering, we asked our people to quiet down so we could have a community meeting, much bigger than my Carson kitchen would fit.

'Cause Our work wasn't done, but I couldn't tell anybody that outright, since?

We wanted the revolution to be easy.

410

Chapter 6

Negist Jepkemboi: I still can't believe We all forgot about the Ankh Udja Saneb hovering right on top of Our heads, like that! I mean how crazy were We?

Negus Memnon: Folks were worn out by then. We'd rescued you, Sister Sitamin [motioning her way], so? We were done!

Negist Candace: More likely We wanted to be the first to upload pictures on Instagram.

[laughter...]

Negus Taharqa: Or to World Star Rap Up!

[Peace, Family. My Queen and I are having a little get-together this afternoon, with our own family and friends, lounging on the patio deck, overlooking our cozy sunken peristyled garden. It's no palace, as what I'd found Queen Sitamin within, but the small bubbling brook and the naturally arranged flowers and ornamental shrubs, make for a tranquil environment to hold an informal group interview. I don't know what will be said, but I'm enscripting it all, without censure. Anything can happen, but don't expect 'The Real Ratchet Gods of Abjerusalem'! lol! No, really. Wrong dimension, dude...]

Negus Lokman: [laughing] Nah, it wasn't that. It's was still not having any substitutes for Our Enemy's infrastructure. With no cash, ya might as well keep selling drugs on the corner. Folks forget that about economics. It's a hell of a master.

[lots of all around agreement and nods...]

Negus Mansa Musa: True, there, brother! It's about faith. How can you believe in what you have no proof will work?

Negist Daurama: Yes, but when does one begin to duplicate The Almighty's faith? To birth Himself, well? It's not like He'd had proof He could create

411

anything, before He actually did.

Negist Hatsheput: But, unlike Him, We did have Satan in Our midst. Hard to ignore his constant oppression.

Negus Endybis: Yes. Like Our constant faith that the white man was the one meant to fix anything enormous, when he was the one who created the trouble in the first place.

Negus Ahkenaten: But wasn't the nothingness The Creator's oppression? I mean not in a physical form, but in a precedent form?

[puzzled looks]

Negus Ahkenaton: [continuing] I mean it's difficult to do something unheard of in any environment. It's difficult to even conceive a different thought pattern. So what We faced? Was what He faced, with no encouragement. While by His mercy, He gave Us each other to stem the loneliness.

Negist Zenobia [my maternal grandmother]: That's the Devil, in any realm who promised Us the same nothing. We were addicted to his nothingness, and didn't want to know there was any other way that meant doing work.

[all around agreement]

Negus Aesop: And when you find another way exists, you gotta to defend it like a newborn child by realizing that's your God given right.

Negus Lokman: Heck, We were a nation before We knew We were a nation.

Queen Sitamin: In that case, We'd always existed, and so has Allah. He has no birth, merely an Awakening.

[hmmm's from many]

Negist Jepkemboi: That's the difference between Heaven and Hell, then. When you know you exist beyond the minute staring you in the face, you protect yourself for all time. Otherwise you behave like you're not even there and soon enough, you aren't.

Negus Memnon: Even more? The catalyst is Self-Acceptance. You defend what you love no matter how much money you have or what addictions you're suffering. As soon as that light of tenderness towards self is begun...

Negus Endybis: [interrupting] But don't forget, you establish that acceptance through having an opponent. When Allah gave Us this planet, there was no white man anywhere, so when he showed up, We were sitting ducks. Without the Devil, We'd have never learned how to protect Ourselves.

[silent pause]

Negus Aesop: But having an opponent doesn't mean you continue to need that opponent unless you forget the past, exactly as Elohim explained. When you know who you are, what you and the value therein is worth? Well, who needs a friend who keeps smacking you down so you can remember how good it is to have a friend? Allah doesn't need the nothingness, once He birthed Himself. He doesn't need Satan to remind Him of His power.

Negist Amanirenas: That why, once awakened to love of self, nothing can stop you, not even fear.

Negist Amina: Because all you desire is more of yourself...

Negus Akhenaten: The moment you defend your right to be, and mean it? Satan remains behind, and you have claimed what was always yours.

[head nods]

Negus Lokman: [inquiringly rubs chin, looking at me with a smirk] So, is your self defense finished, yet, brother?

Negus Akhenaten: [chuckling, looking at my wife who's only weeks away from giving birth] Just about. No rush, as now? I embrace my right to perfect my existence.

Negus Taharqa: [amused] And what does that mean? You know We can't wait to read your book, despite Our pretense at patience.

Negus Akhenaten: It means I'm having a great time writing, unlike when I started. So it'll be finished, no doubt. [shaking my head in hindsight with a laugh] Oh, and you guys are pretending, huh?
[more laughs, and humorous looks of innocence]

Negist Hatshepsut: Well, at least you're in a good humor about it. Remember

413

when you were so cranky, nobody could say a word to you. Nobody did.

Negus Akenaton: Yes. Even We gods are a work in progress, as there's always the next level to learn how to defend, till it feels like second nature before it becomes Our nature.

[We're gonna clean up Our lunch mess, now. In another hour or two, our guests will depart, kindly, but eagerly pushed on their way home, as I finally can't wait to finish this story, so, I'll be right back with my conclusion...]

~ ~ ~ ~ ~ ~ ~ ~ ~ ~ ~

Side Note: After that initial Ubuntu, I didn't perceive any change in people's sense that they were regular beings, with regular understanding of the world around. Maybe being Knowledge Protector enhanced my perceptions, alone.

Maybe it was even something within that made me a natural Knowledge Protector that had had me obsessed with the Orb and its maintenance, but it wasn't within anybody else. I mean folks surely weren't against re-entering, but they weren't clammering for it, either. Oh well. Some love roller coaster rides and others, throw-up.

I did both and still wanted to get back in line.

Now, maybe the experience had been a bit unusual, to say the least, especially for the goin' to meetin' 7 days a week at the Chu'ch types. I heard a few mention 'witchcraft' and the like. Heck, I could understand as I came out wondering if I were a superhero, my first time.

It was a darned good thing I didn't say a mumblin' word about going back in to fix the Ankh Udja Saneb. I'dda collected a paycheck from the police department and the military for doing their job of clearing the streets much better.

'Cause there wasn't a soul asking me how to fix that problem, even though they knew it was there, let alone begging to return. Long story short, though if you've reached this far along, why stop now? Long story sorta shortened? I realized, Houston, WE STILL had a problem. That's why standing in the spot where the Orb had once been expanded, I proposed to the more

414

adventurously minded, We have some fun, visiting random places 'cause We were all due for much ease after such hardship.

"I'd like to ease myself to some sleep," Brother Williams, the soon to resign officer said. It was about 2:30am by this time.

Understandably, without hesitation, lots of folks agreed. That was too bad 'cause for what I had in mind, We'd need maybe the whole of Newark.

Crazy, it was the basement guys who suggested to entire me that I suggest going to visit newly departed loved ones. Dang, when I proposed that? Ya couldda heard a pin drop, so many of Us had newly departed people We dearly missed. Me, included. One thing Hell is generous with, it's death.

"I hadn't thought of that," Sister Devetra, pondered out loud, sparking a conversation between everyone about family and friends they would give their eye teeth to see, touch, hear again. Some wanted to search for precious valuables they remembered the last time they'd held them, but not where they'd left them.

I warned everybody in earshot, and repeated when Our hands had linked up and I took a step into the re-expanded Orb, these were only visions and nothing could be brought back that belonged inside here. Everybody understood, but as I've said, pain speaks more volumes than books, even photo albums.

That's why, Kyerah, transported with me to a barbecue our dad and family had been invited to attend, in 2007, by his brand new boss, Mr. Ganderheist, head of the engineering team at Lochan Marchlin Nuclear Power and Waste Management Facility. And that was why she'd said, right before we arrived, still before the Orb, holding my hand, and Nyisha holding my other hand:

"I can't believe I'll finally see him, again.

"You know this isn't him, don't you? You know we're here to figure out a way to fix the mess up above?"

She distractedly pivoted her head from side to side, in bemused denial.

"Nope, I haven't forgotten, but, seeing is believing, right?"

"You are joking?" I blurted.

415

"What? Don't tell me you don't want to see him again! You know that's not true. You're just afraid to find out the truth."

"No. I'm afraid nobody, including you, wants to face the truth."

"Oh, don't worry. Something will come up about how to fix everything. I have faith."

And with that, she nudged me into the newly expanded memory of everything, no opinions welcomed...

Upon entry, which took only as long as it took a person to cross into the hole in the fabric of time, space and physicality, each being could then jettison themselves anywhere they chose, in their own timeline. Nobody had to wait, and having already seen each time another person joined the Ubuntu, the stronger We all got?

Well, I had no concerns, as everyone agreed, We were not going to linger longer than 2 hours, and anyone staying outside set their alarms, if they had phones, so they could telepathically remind Us. It was apparent nobody connected with me forgot who they were, but still? All agreed, seeing long lost loved ones or long yearned for past moments had to be magnetism of its own kind, maybe pulling each of Us in the wrong direction, however?

We were together, and thus, no one would be left behind, whether they wanted to be left behind or not.

But, speaking of phones, I'd asked everyone to call anybody they knew, within range, to join Us, whether you woke 'em up or not. Given this was the biggest event trending in history, on the internet, given the 'authorities' were frozen with confusion as to how to respond, not merely to Our conductive power, but to the sheer numbers who'd long ago outnumbered any armed officials – given all this, We now covered a 3 square mile range, with hundreds joining every half hour, now. We were, even, ever so close to the hospital, Dr. Kattan had been admitted to (did I mention it was the zombie one I'd seen on the bus?) – We were so close, I specifically, warmly asked if those in that area could make a beeline up and through the ER admittance ward, to his room. Same tombstone hospital I'd seen along my bus ride, but from the dozens and dozens of doctors on the line, I knew when it came to traumatic wound care? They reassured me the Dr. of history was in good doctors of traumatic injury hands. Perhaps the best, and, yes. A whole bunch were white. Though, um?

416

Not on the Ubuntu line, however, out of concern for their own potentially traumatized beings.

Maybe, if We reached him, I prayed, We could send some healing his way, although? I hadn't sensed any healing happening with anyone on a physical level, not outside, nor with those who'd gone inside the Sphere. Only what'd happened with me. That was troubling, as, perhaps, somebody could get killed in there, but?

It was the carnage above which troubled me most, for that vision meant everybody dies. Thus, in We stepped.

~ ~ ~ ~ ~ ~ ~ ~ ~ ~ ~

Mr. Ganderheist was white, and I remembered him as a truly friendly guy, although here at this barbecue I'd only been 7, so what would I have known? But he'd been a mainstay throughout my father's career, championing his meteoric rise in the company, till the board had appointed my dad head engineer upon Mr. Ganderheist's retirement. I remembered that's when all the problems began. But here?

I'd entered the memory standing next to the smoking high tech barbecue pit as this slightly rotund, prickly red faced man had flipped a burger onto my open white bread bun, spread out on one of those good quality paper plates. I don't know what I'd said just before I'd arrived, but something about the manner I now spoke, slightly hesitant in delivery:

"Um, Thank You,"...

made Mr. Ganderheist's face take on a quizzical look. I couldn't discern anything unusual about him, no aura negative or positive, as the spirit that had once given this memory life, was busy existing someplace else.

Taking the meal I'd never eat, wondering how a memory of food could sustain the bodies of those spirits that'd gotten trapped within The Sphere – unless? The spirit was sustained by a different kind of nourishment...

I saw Kyerah, who'd jettisoned through her own life coil, and we'd agree to halt here, after propelling back in time for merely a fast 20 count – I spied her on the other end of the lawn, playing with the Ganderheist's daughter, in her

417

princess house which was nearly the size of 346 Carson, only much, much nicer. She suddenly stopped, I guess as I must have, so as to seem strange to my dad's boss, she looked in my direction, nodded a goodbye to her blonde haired buddy and came over.

"Where's dad?" she asked.

"I don't remember," I answered, turning as nonchalantly as I could in the sparsely peopled backyard lawn. Yeah, I was 12, but I didn't remember how to be 7, I had to admit, so I'm sure the both of us looked a little 'off'. Definitely, with the knowledge of 10,443 people, ranging from 5 to 87, rolling around in my head, one third of them getting a chance to see their loved ones, again, I couldn't begin to fake clueless.

"There he is," I saw him, standing in the kitchen with mom, hidden by the contrast of bright sunlight out here, bulb-less lighting in there, and a closed glass sliding door between. My heart jumped. Or I should say, my photo album of a heart jumped.

I put my burger I no longer wanted in this stage of my life down on the wooden picnic table, and we walked across the lawn, ascended the stairs of the patio and slid open the back door.

Stopping their conversation, my dad, mom and Mrs. Ganderheist, happy faced each, turned around to smile as we entered.

I knew it wasn't truly him, but

D
A
N
G
!

It was hard to believe he was a figment from even The Creator's mind, looking so complete in every detail, from his non-milk Ashanti blackness that we didn't recognize in him, anymore than Our derivation was known by Us, to the ways an individual does little movements nobody else you'll ever know will. Why, he was even picking his teeth with one of those flat end toothpicks he'd used which I'd forgotten were signature Marcus Jackson. Like my post it notes, he used to leave those toothpicks all over the house. Drove mom crazy as they were pokier to sit on than a crumpled up piece of paper between sofa

418

cushions.

"Hey! Did you guys get some of that good grill? Oliver's a pro!" he said in his melodically fluctuating Atlanta rhythm, after snapping a pop of air between his teeth. No actor alive or dead could have mimicked him more precisely.

Mrs. Ganderheist came out from behind the island counter with a platter of what looked to be potato salad, only it looked like mostly dry potatoes, with very little of what our family would have described as potato salad.

"Well, you are too kind, Marcus! Don't ya tell him, though, or he'll be barbequing till the middle of January! Hey you genius little kids! Stand back so I can put this on the table outside."

There was only a sliver of space between me and the marginally opened door. Slipping right up next to my sister and I, a cord of lyrical light jumped from our bodies to hers. Just a hair's width wide and at the point her skirt was closest to our clothes. Mrs. Ganderheist was almost as tall as her husband, and as kind, as we remembered. But I wasn't thinking about that. I was taken back by that surge of electricity which was gone as fast as it'd appeared. Gone as she moved through the door. It snapped me back to the reality of Our mission, and that wasn't roaming thru family albums.

Kyerah's and my eyes widened towards one another. WT?

"Woo!" The Mrs., herself, responded. "That surely was some amazing static. Dij' ya'll get some food?"

"No ma'am," my sister replied, as I tugged on her arm. "We'll go get some right away, though. It surely smells great!"

Apparently, big sis could pretend, too.

The lady was already out the door, paying no further attention.

I wanted to go over that coiled little light burst with Kyerah, but she'd shrugged my 7yr old grip a loose to walk over and give my father a hug.

"Whoa! Well, Keekee! I love you, too." And he hugged her back.

Nobody called her that, anymore...

419

I joined them, for a moment that must have lasted several seconds past what time any child would ordinarily hug their parent. My mom placed her glass of iced tea down, and gleefully came over to add her embrace.

"Awwwww," she said, "I'm so glad your dad and I didn't send you guys to the orphanage, after all!"

"Hey!" Keekee protested, pulling back teasingly, but laughing.

"Well, hon," dad quipped, "We can still change our minds. They'll be open, come Monday..."

The three of them laughed, while the good natured humor couldn't erase my objective now. I'd loved our all day ribbing, maybe best. We'd been jokes all day folks. That was my family, and it felt like the home I missed, but? As Kyerah, kept holding on, I remembered?

This was incredible. It looked just like him. Smelled like him. Laughed like him, but my very scientifically based non superhero instinct could tell, crying over what I missed about him, just a couple days ago was more real than this memory that didn't have his living soul.

Even more real was up ahead in the Void, and it wasn't the slightest bit funny, even for fake. This moment was?

Just a pleasant rest on the way to business, and I could not be veered off by a distraction, no matter how superficially amazing.

So, I grabbed my sister's arm and pulled her back outside onto the lawn, smiling at her protest and as our parents glowed indulgently, but slightly disquietingly, back.

"What the?" she protested. "Why'd you do that?"

"Shhhhhh..." I hushed her till we got to the far side where no ear would be in range.

Then I said, low voiced, "'Cause! That's not dad, and we didn't come here to hang out. We came here to find a way to get help with the AUS!"

~ ~ ~ ~ ~ ~ ~ ~ ~ ~ ~

Putting you, reader, up to speed on the Ubuntu, everybody who'd entered the Orb was too busy catching up in their individual reunions or goals to pay attention to not at all important little us, and we could sense that. So, big sis and I were in touch with each other's thoughts and maybe it was that narrowly focused connection that led her to nod affirmatively, while nobody else holding hands, soul to soul, could have cared less.

"Alright, I agree," she replied.

"Then, that light spiral! We, both, caught that bouncing off of us towards Mrs. Ganderheist!"

"You think that's what was richocheting up and down the Ubuntu?"

I firmly nodded my head, answering, "Yep, you're thinking what I'm thinking. That was the exact same kind We created outside the Orb, only tinier."

"Maybe? Hey, li'l brother, what if?"

"Sis, you don't have to say another word!"

"Oh, but what if I wanted to say, hmmmm?... 'Circumferentially', huh, as in circumferentially, you got a big ol' head? How 'bout that," and she bopped me on it.

Mimicking my dad with expertise, getting into a boxing stance, I exclaimed, "Don't mess with me. I almost know how to fight back."

We laughed like we were a healed up family, in real time, finally.

"Hey!" mom called out from the seat she'd taken on the deck, "No fighting, you two! These folks think you're nice children! Let's not let them know the truth!"

Mr. Ganderheist laughed, saying, "Ha! You haven't seen ours go at each other!"

The various grown-ups, all white, shook their heads at the state of children that day and age, in their grown-up knowledge about the secrets of life. Why, there was such visible mirth, here? One might assume there would never be another problem in the world.

421

If you've guessed I couldn't see auras from memories in the Orb, you'd be scientifically correct.

"Say, Kyerah! I'mma try something out..." and I headed back towards my abandoned burger, up to the side of Mrs. Ganderheist.

"Now, we're thinking!" my sis said, following after me.

I had to know, but, as I got up close enough behind her, I spied another small spark arcing between myself and this woman who'd never been anything but nice to me. Now, clearly I could tell she hadn't noticed a thing, yet, I, on the otherhand, felt nothing but guilt...

~ ~ ~ ~ ~ ~ ~ ~ ~ ~ ~

Making me step back, because at the speed of thought, I'd changed my mind altogether. What if the electrical charge hurt this woman, someway I couldn't predict? The tendriled arc disappeared, and with no turning around in shock, Mrs. Ganderheist seemed unaffected, calming my concern that I might somehow harm only a memory of her. Instead, I put my hands up turning towards Kyerah, her emotion of disappointment reaching me before any of her own thoughts could.

Luckily, none of what I or my sister felt, thought, did or didn't do would matter, as? Mr. Ganderheist made the connection for each single one of Us.

Only a half foot from his wife, heading towards her, not looking at me or Kyerah standing behind, he tripped over? Was it a stump, a rut – was it his own 2 feet? I'll never know as I was about to disappear from that setting, forever, never viewing what propitious obstacle catapulted the mildly rotund pink man into his wife with a thud, and then, her paper plate and its contents of pale potato salad, and empty bun flung up in the air, propelling Mrs. Ganderheist backwards onto me.

I fell, then, too, but I don't mean onto the ground, though the body I'd been did that.

Me? I was squashed into Mrs. Ganderheist's lifecoil.

YEEEEEECH. CREEPY CRAWLIES!!!!

And gross, dude! She'd only landed head, back and shoulders on my lower torso and legs, knocking me down with her full weight; however, metaphysically? Her entire being splattered onto my living energy, and I found myself absorbed, no sparks evident, as they probably didn't have time, into an unknown woman's body that I was controlling. Oh, barf fest...
since, there was nothing hidden from me, within her being, whatsoever.... shudder, shudder.

That was **way** too much information flooding my senses, as if I'd plunged off a high ravine, smacking upwards into a rapid force of water that was an open book of this memory's soul. Every single

F
R
E
A
K
I
N
G

detail, with no censor. No filter. No privacy. No pity.

I didn't want to know any of it. Later, thinking about the magnetism of melanin, I further calculated I could step into my mom's or my sister's timeline and not discover personal secrets because Our lifeforce still had some force, even if We weren't the living soul within them. But there was no hint of resistance here, and so?

Beseiged by sheer horror, instantly repelled, I pushed Mr. Ganderheist off what had become my body, now. Someone he still considered his 'wife'. He got back to his feet, apologizing to me, his 'Honey', and to the visibly Tyree me, still on the ground, who was looking more confused than hurt. That's when he, making sure his wife and photo album me were okay, he reached out to touch her/my shoulder with concern, making me mentally shriek, forcing my spirit with that touch from Mrs. to Mr.!

Oh, the horror – or did I use that word, already? But that's what it was, and I gotta explain, this is not meant to be comical, except to the lost. See, there's a reason for the 'No Homo' in my temperament, and I haven't touched on it in depth, nor will I here, since it'd be another book. But this is one of those exceptionally imperfect moments I didn't know whether I'd write about. However, having decided pages before reaching this one, for edification purposes, due to the war that's being waged upon you, reader, be you male or female?

I'd better.

In my personal Black family, there'd been no love, let alone indulgence of any of those Black directors, actors and sports personalities who were pushing the modern notion that Black Men looked amusing demeaning themselves by dressing like women. If there was one battle Marcus Jackson had effectively taught his son to wage, it was against the constant attack on Black Men (he'd said it was called, 'The Effemenization of the Black Male'). He had not minced teaching about that aspect of white people's fear of the might of Our Men's unapologetic manhood. Now, he'd also talked about the attack on the Black Woman and thus the Black Family, but? Like I said, the Man's duty to be the protector was sacred to my dad, and to my mom. We, their children, were shown certain things were for girls and certain things were for boys, period. So, I'd been no homo since the day I noticed I was a boy. Everything around me and my sister had been strategically framed to encourage our love for the way The Creator had made us, but? It was framed with kindness and we absorbed the lesson, straight into our very DNA. That sort of training explains the relief I was experiencing...

... looking at this woman, now, through her husband's eyes, who seemed unharmed by my using her like an open doorway. She softened her look at me, while she did appear a tad disoriented. She probably thought my expression conveyed love, when it only conveyed planet sized contentment to no longer be in the midst of female confusion beyond anything I'd have ever imagined possible. Now, as the steward of Mr. Ganderheist's movements, despite the fact, I was sensing not all was correct in his Dodge City, either, his chaos revealed itself slowly, cause I was so daggone *relieved!* For the moment, I felt thoroughly more comfortable pretending to be him than even when I'd been pretending to be 7yr old me. Worried there'd be sparks which might incinerate both these bodies, but noting there were none, I continued brushing his wife off, who suddenly was shorter than me. Avoiding her bump of a behind, I left bits of dirt, and small leafy matter clinging to her floral print skirt, trusting she as a memory would soon return to whatever her lifecoil should be doing, soon enough.

Mind to mind, I told Kyerah exactly where I was.

Heck. I told Everybody.

It was gonna be a whole lotta cokes that a surprising number didn't drink, either, 'cause, Kyerah and a hundred thousand other people across the photo album world and outside the Orb, up and down the streets, cried, "You're where?!!!" in sync.

There was a loud, "Oh, snap!" from Terrence, a half second off track, in a solitary thought. Oh, the laughter as We were laughing with him. All of existence was Imbo-ing.

Except for an unconscious, but still connected through the unique signature of his soul Dr. Kattan. We'd picked up his and his son's presence the moment I'd fallen. Brother Gainde and a nurse held his hands along the Ubuntu when it had finally roped its way up stairwells, through corridors, to his comatose body lying in his hospital bed, hooked up to dozens of blinking, bleeping machines and ventilators. The emergency surgery had successfully removed 5 bullets which had all missed major blood vessels, meaning, though a very ill man, the doctor was gonna be okay.

Brother Gainde didn't say a word, but was sending waves of approval to Us, all. Yes, I know I say it a lot, but it was funny; in all this excitement, and after all the unique amazing souls who'd joined, You couldn't help but notice there was something extra serenely intense about that brother.

So, just like that, We officially, by Our right to determine it, became'The Ubuntu' – kinda. Almost. Alright, there was still a little ways to go, but, to this day, consensus concludes – this was the moment when a nation woke-up. When We verified beyond doubt, what was in the hearts of Our Enemy had to be defended against.

Now, several dimensions of reality were occurring more complexly than this linear book form can convey. Reader, I can't wait till you can command multiple layered physicality, with which You'll be able to see length, width, depth and then around and behind things. In the meantime, think of a party, not of people, but of distinct experiences; a simultaneous interplay of sight, sound, action, thoughts, and time, itself happening more compactly than a few stylistically well written paragraphs can convey. Or? Better than my paragraphs, whatever you may feel about them.

Thus? For the most accurate portrayal, gather your own friends and ask each one to read an upcoming particular setting that I'm about to write, and have

425

them read each paragraphical grouping at the same time. Plus, read it real fast. There! That's the ticket!

"Are you okay?" my wife was asking me, as she put her hands up to my chest. This was the moment I started sensing something off within Mr. Ganderheist's memory, though I was grateful he was a man. Yes, he was similar to the magnetic racket of his wife, but, with her I'd been screaming the whole time till I exited her memory, not trying to learn more. Seeing no sparks, sensing no injury, feeling perfectly confident remaining where I was for the moment, while We were collectively holding Our breaths, waiting for the man's body to ignite like the meat grilling on the pit? Some of Our Family pre-emptively advised me to get back into the Void, for my safety, but I figured, 'Why'? Everybody could pull me out, on a dime.

"Oh, I'm great, Agatha!" I chimed with extra Bavarian turned into American charm. Tyree didn't know all the places he and his family had come from but Oliver knew most of the details about his own. Not as many as I was gonna discover about him, but he knew a disturbing amount.

While, I knew everything. Everything about Oliver Ernst. Little Ernst.

"I'm just clumsy as hell!" I, secret psychopath, said for the amusement of my guests. And then attending to my wife, I asked, "Are you alright, sweetie?" Oliver would have left her, years ago, if it were not that she was the daughter of head CEO of his company, Robert Marchlin.

Then I looked to the children standing there, little Tyree utterly confused, and before this moment to these eyes I was looking through, little Tyree was such a handsome boy. Granted Oliver was workin' hard on putting his problem to the side that unremembered by him, he'd inherited from having had a father who'd worked with Alfred Kinsey, using 2yr old Little Ernst to verify horrors no licensed by any school 'doctor' should need to know. But more importantly, Mr. Ganderheist had plans for the boy's brilliant, yet, clueless father.

'FRIGGIN' EXTRA GROSS, FAM!!! I CAN HEAR EVERYTHING THIS MAN HAS EVER THOUGHT AND...'

... everything he'd encountered in his existence from his first consciousness to the current 2011 day him, snoring cozily in his Atlanta bed, and to my, I may have to use the word, 'horror', again.

'*Those Yurugu are nasty as sin!*' cried Sister Cutthecrap.

She was joined in resonating consensus by, at this point, what had to have been hundreds of thousands in an Ubuntu that had reached 250K.

That one lone voice that'd lost so much credibility, Brother Don, the instant Ganderheist's existence as a slug entered Our mind and minds, (oops, almost used the word, 'horror-fied') – he felt r-e-p-u-l-s-e-d to the point of wanting to throw-up, himself, urging me to:

"Get the Hell out of there, son!" He didn't even think it. He said it out loud on Garvey, while holding hand to hand with the throngs, outside, in the cool nighttime surroundings.
There'd been a slight distrust of Don, but, decidedly We considered his suggestion sensible, as I was currently walking through the brooding den of an Alien's film, with grotesqueries waiting to hatch any minute and all at once.

Automatically, We wanted to consult the most luminous soul We could see amongst Us, for which direction would lead Us, forward. Even Brothers Roscoe and Xolani humbly sought the advice of –

Brother Gainde. I mean, luminous is luminous.

To which, the doctor's son answered, '*Remember, you're not alone little brother. But let's consult someone with vast experience within the Orb, whose 126 years,* (there was a gasp up and down the line, but when We'd sensed the doctor's awakening spirit, We'd already experienced every day of those years) – *most of them lived within the Orb? He might provide the best expert advice. What do you say, venerated Elder Kattan? Does Tyree have your permission to continue and do you have any guiding words?*'

A telepathic '*harrumph,*' weak but clear, emanated from the soul of a doctor who only kept his eyes closed, at this point, so he could see what I saw – that double gust of audible air never sounded so welcomed to my no longer spoiled American boy ears, because:

1. I knew I was part of a Great People and you don't need to get everything under the Sun if your nation has what you need and doesn't hate you, so it shares.

2. I knew I would never want to be an American anything, again – forever...

427

Yes, Sir. Yes, Ma'am. That harrumph never sounded so welcomed.

'*Go, with Allah, Tyree,*' his thought voice whispered, merely a tint of its old sonorous depth, even telepathically.

The meaning of what he said was all We needed.

'*Go, see what We can see, and remember – you are in charge, not your Enemy.*'
Whoa. What a concept We thought. I'm in charge. We are in Charge. The Ubuntu had taken a basket of fruit from a disagreeable people, ate the pulp and now We'd sow the seeds to produce a planet wide harvest of freedom. We'd become a nation in progress.

So, with that? I began selecting what I would see and what I would not. Simple, since all manifestations of filth have an odor, from olfactory to psychical, to, thus, spiritual. Before any of Us endured the distastefulness of Mr. Ganderheist for another second, I shut the HORROR of this strange man, from a strange people, off.

Now, simultaneously, in that multi-dimensional reality, I was attending to those around me in the backyard, Sun at its full apex, laughing with my 'wife' over some of our many spills and chills, which I remembered then, as if they'd happened to me, because, yes, it was Oliver me, still donning his whole persona effortlessly, after getting rid of his more objectionable nastiness. I was sifting through the details of Oliver's lifecoil like it was a twirling file cabinet in the nothingness, and I could fly.

2/3rds of a million people wanted to join me, it looked so exciting delving into Mr. Ganderheist's past lives all the way back to the Caucas Mountains and before that, but figuring that many souls might kill him in real time, so he'd never rise from his rest the next morning?

Each of Us who had walked into the Orb to find loved ones or lost valuables, found the nearest non-selenium melanated being and stepped on in, being We were the key that We'd discovered a new use for. We stepped right into the closest white person in Our individual timeframes with no arcing lights, no resistance. Why? With this first Yurugu, We found We could walk in and out of whichever white person We encountered at any point along that initial person's existence. Enter in the 1990s? Exit at the 1450s. Merge with a stockbroker on the trading floor if you'd been the janitor? Converge with the owner of a Fortune 500 whom you'd never gotten anywhere near. Some tried the same with other more melanated folks, standing right nearby, for the

428

curiosity of it, only to bump into memories of solid bodies, and offer embarrassed apologies. Guess, one could only enter through a direct coil, confirming it wasn't the amount of melanin, if you had that selenium – it was the intention, and, overall with the Caucasoids? Inside their realm, there was no defense, no secrets, from whatever We saw behind their eyes, to whatever of their thoughts We heard within their living minds.

Memory or not? Every one of their secrets was revealed...

=

Despite the several planets of increased activity along the entirety of the line, it was easy for me to remain focused on Oliver, and for the gathered to stay focused on their individual explorations. I can't say with certainty if that was because running from pillar to post within Allah's memories was simpler due to that lighter magnetic pull that made any movement We each made hundreds of times more effective than it'd been within all the other manifestations I'd had within the Orb, or if white folks?

Weren't as smart as they thought...

HA! Just kidding!!! That's a jibe, reader, 'cause, gotta hand it to Oliver Ernst Krüger Ganderheist – the man was a slitheringly brilliant foe. Too bad my dad didn't know he was his Avowed Enemy, sitting across from him, me in that portly man's body, and like a script laid out in my mind, I knew exactly what Bavarian I would say, that would eventually, inevitably, lead to my father's demise.

On purpose, which makes it murder.

"Mr. Ganderheist," my dad stated calmly, though his features were knitted with marginally visible disbelief, as if he could barely disguise his disgust. "Respectfully, sir, I don't know if you realize the enormity of the danger to the community, but, those pressure tubes in the containment vessel are way past their prime,..." he repeated, "... sir. They shouldda been replaced 15 years ago, and if they're not, right now? They can't last another 3."

In this real conference office, lacquered oak tables, swivel leather chairs, enough for anyone attending – but that day, 3 years after the barbecue, it was only Oliver me and my dad – the newly appointed head of the nuclear engineering department – there we sat, alone, while I knew the Bavarian man's thoughts – oh, I knew.

Dad was right. Those tubes and the whole daggone plant was being reduced to radioactive rubble, one atom at a time. It was called the Wigner Effect. Like battery acid, only a million times worse as the radiation ate away at every piece of equipment coming into contact with the plant's bread and butter, turning pipes, walls, chimney stacks into their own nuclear echo.

430

Yeah. Oliver knew and understood Mr. Jackson knew, too. Unfortunately, his employee was proving too childishly over-optimistic with a big mouth. That was a problematic combination. Yes, it'd been a public relations coup d'etat having a black engineer front for the rickety plant at those pesky community meetings. All plants leak radiation, permanently polluting the environment; but, the gullible public figured, as pissed on as blacks are, for one of 'em to get up at a podium and lie nothing but the lie? Made that public more easily believe the lie must be true. Oliver saw how well it worked with the President of The United States, so why not use the same tactic to ricochet his own flagging status at the plant?

It's not like Marcus didn't know the plant was a ticking timebomb, as he was too smart not to, but?

'I'd have sworn this nigger wouldda appreciated his steep paycheck increase a bit more humbly,' pondered Mr. Ganderheist.

My dad's on-time, well-spoken demeanor had duped his boss into believing Marvin would submit same as the 100% white staff had, and even more as Oliver'd been the only one to offer him a job in Mr. Jackson's chosen field! Not to overlook, Jackson was threatening his own chances at getting cushier positions, seeing the heavy pushback he'd endured hiring a black man for a white man's job. You'd be a fool to think he'd allow some nigger to upset his career, seeing how Mr. Ganderheist could never be satisfied being CEO of only one company.

In the midst of this flow of despicable thoughts about my father, I could have punched him square in the face with his own hand, decked him cold, boxing skills or not, if I hadn't known I'd be hitting myself, too. Not to forget, Tyree me couldn't change an iota of the future which had already happened. I was along for the ride of what this man's every muscle was enslaved to do. I didn't need to make any of this up; was simply saying what had been said that day by a man I hated for more reasons than I can put on paper without writing an encyclopedia of profanity.

"Are you calling me a fool, Mr. Jackson?" was one of those automatic responses, Tyree me let out.

Looking the German in the eye that I was borrowing, my dad replied, "I would never call you a fool, Mr. Ganderheist. A man of your knowledge must realize the data doesn't lie and that's the problem."

"You've got a lot of nerve, boy. I took you under my wing, groomed you for leadership and you repay me with flagrant insubordination."

"Sir, I appreciate the confidence you placed in me, but when I accepted this position I was under the impression I could help this plant run more safely. I can't do that if with every repair, I'm told, 'There's not enough money.' Tell that to the men who work this plant and then take their irradiated bodies home to contaminate their wives and family! Tell that to the community that's breathing hot rads with every inhalation of Uranium 238, spitting out the damned steam vents!"

My dad's eyes narrowed and his downhome voice got real low, and much slower, as he became, unbeknownst to him, perhaps, or maybe he didn't care – as he became a dangerous negro to his boss.

He continued, "Tell them that there'll never be a safe place to put this radioactive crap."

Disgusted (not by the truth I heard, but by the uppity-ness of this nigger), I forcefully stood up, splaying my hands out on the table, and leaned in, hoping to make my point (cause in truth? The Bavarian was scared...), I shouted at him, "You do the job the way you're told or get the hell out."

Mr. Jackson's usefulness was coming to an end, though the black man, not comprehending the change in his fate, laughed and replied, "Oh, I'll get out, but this won't be the last you hear from me."

Didn't take but a second after my dad had closed the door behind him, that his former boss was on the phone working soon to metamorphize into a murderous schemer with his own non-melanated Ubuntu chain.

~ ~ ~ ~ ~ ~ ~ ~ ~ ~ ~

"The size of the lie is a definite factor in causing it to be believed, for the vast masses of the nation are in the depths of their hearts more easily deceived than they are consciously and intentionally bad. The primitive simplicity of their minds renders them a more easy prey to a big lie than a small one, for they themselves often tell little lies but would be ashamed to tell a big one."

-- From Benito Mussolini, contributing to the "London Sunday Express," December 8, 1935.

~ ~ ~ ~ ~ ~ ~ ~ ~ ~ ~

The initial intended victim had merely been 'Money', the other family member that was the first to be taken out or I should say, assassinated, with commands begun on high, handed down from coldhearted to complicit-ly agreeable, to scared of homelessness white people, which apparently was everyone of them, including one or two black folks working in the same industry, if not for the same company as my dad had, before he'd resigned. I witnessed job applications torn to pieces if they dared carry his name, bank loans denied, credit frozen, old coworkers become impossible to reach. Potential new coworkers were told to keep a long distance from that Crazy Marcus Jackson. That monetary murder would have been enough to make any man give up hope, but turned out?

Not this Black Man. He had a plan, even if a bad one, which he shared over his intercepted cell phone. They'd been listening to him for years.

Stepping from one white person to the next had been easy enough, and that's how I, within seconds, had put the puzzle pieces together. I'd merely step out of one white guy's coil into whichever useful one was standing next to him, anywhere along his timeline. I found thousands of lifetimes of information that way and my sister? Having stayed in telepathic touch, searched the white women's side of their puzzle, of their assembled contribution in the destruction of our beloved father, and everybody else.

Add to this the collective investigation being conducted by every member of The Ubuntu who'd entered the Orb and yes, We knew who Our Enemy was, now.

But, before I tell you, reader, about that most terrible day of my life, before We get to explaining the depth of what We all found, without taking unneeded time to retell every detail, let me describe the place Kyerah and Eye agreed to meet up within, by exiting our forays into the strange world of a Strange People to instead? Re-enter our former selves, arriving the same minute, evening time in our Sandstone Hill McMansion, nervously doing our homework in that living room where the furniture fit precisely, not overwhelmingly, including the Black Man statue, frozen in a winner's stance, without benefit of having a mind, yet? If we'd only known he was a faith-filled monument to a time we had no idea was inevitably up ahead.

433

~ ~ ~ ~ ~ ~ ~ ~ ~ ~ ~

Giving a head nod, acknowledging we'd both arrived, my sister and I closed up our school books, leaving the comfort of the coach, to walk past the kitchen entrance (it was a 3 storied loft house that had started out as a traditional southern home before my mom and dad removed all the unnecessary walls and adobed the outside) – we walked past the kitchen, through the dining area to the doorway of the office where my dad, we knew, would right then be on the phone. We'd heard him, plenty of times through the lifecoil of others, but?

We simply wanted to confirm what happened next when there'd been no white men near him in the last moments of his life. Perhaps the pressure had been too much for him, even Kyerah agreed.

Putting our ears to the solid mahogany door, we couldn't hear a daggone thing; so, very carefully, I pushed the old world styled handle, moderately slow, as I'd done this many times in the past. Too fast and it'd audibly click, too slow and the latch would never clear the socket before the hinges of the door squeaked.

My memory heart was racing, as if I was following Dr. Kattan and his son down the hallway.

I triumphantly relaxed, nodding at Kyerah when the gap silently appeared, divulging the burgundy carpeted luxury of my father's man-cave. He never used to spend much time in here, prompting my mom to ask, once years ago, if she could remodel it into her studio. She had 2, already – the shed house in the back and a separate factory floor she rented closer to town for crafting her larger sculptures; but having this room would mean she didn't have to go outside to get her work done and care for us, children.

Obviously his answer had been, "No," and good thing as he'd used this room, nonstop, now, to make those calls, all those bugged calls necessary to keep difficult from becoming disastrous, and disastrous from then becoming impossible. This night, he was on the last stretch of that effort, his words taking on that slur that can become typical of a man using intoxicants, trying not to succumb to the dark feeling of defeat that comes on the other side of 'disastrous'.

"No, you don't understand, me, Oliver! I know who's behind all this! What? You think I don't? You think I'm stupid? You blacklisted me and you have the nerve to think I won't..."
Pause.

"What? Are you threatening me? Oh, lemme tell you sumthin', mister. You're gonna get yours. Yes. I've been patient, but no more."

Pause, and we could see him walk past the narrow thread of a view we had into the room, but he had his back to the two of us.

"That's no business of yours. Nothin' I do is gonna be your business anymore...."

After ending with words I'd best not repeat in this book, reader, he forcefully hung up the phone, and we could hear him taking his seat behind his desk, with a thud, out of our peeping eyesight. That's when my mom's voice struck our ears, comin' up behind, and I nearly jumped out of my skin, which, coincidentally, I was thoroughly capable of doing, but didn't want to, that second.

"Get away from your dad's door!" She said vehemently quietly, though, as if she didn't want her husband to know his children had been spying on him. And rather than responding angrily, she tenderly put her arms on each of our shoulders and guided us away.

"Go," she nodded in the direction of the couch, "do your homework. Let me talk to your dad, okay? I'm sure he'll be fine, guys."

We, nodded, not saying a word, knowing she was a nice mom who didn't know what the future held, not a hundred years from now, so certainly not an hour, either...

~ ~ ~ ~ ~ ~ ~ ~ ~ ~ ~

I was glad my dad had given me the rudiments of how to drive, sitting me on a phone book so I could see over the dashboard, while I circled around our own ample driveway, or I'd have discovered early on that you can crash The Creator's perfect remembrance of a car and suffer the excruciating consequences before your several hundred thousand friends could pull you out, most especially if the car goes real fast.

See, I'd left my sister in the livingroom and had crossed the gulf of the Void to return to my father's coil, which was seconds away when you can fly. Well, I'd flown up only an inch above, and now, I was seated in the Jaguar F-type Coupe, and those 6 cylinders were humming like a swarm of bumble bees performing a Zeigfield Follies synchronized dance. Oh, how Mr. Jackson loved this car, taking me back and forth from dealership to dealership while he'd gotten down to dithering between this and the Porsche. The Jaguar salesman had finally convinced him by droning on about how a vehicle like this would make anyone who saw it smile from ear to ear, with admiration, not merely envy as it was a smartman's car, but?

Driving it in the being of the most important man I'd ever known eclipsed the relevance of anything all the salesmen had said. I thought to myself, 'Who cares after 5 seconds of lookin' at it, whatever kind of car you drive? The real value gets in and then gets out of the interior cab, while never depreciating.'

I didn't know when I crossed into his 3 dimensional reflection that I'd end up here, smack at the wheel of a heralding super vehicle, which could go 0 to 60 in 3.4 seconds, had apparently passed that 5 miles back up the road – I didn't know because my drunken dad's thoughts were so chaotic, he'd pushed this streamlined monster to half of its 200mph capacity – though by law it wasn't allowed to go faster than 186 on the open, truly open, somewhere in a desert, road. Interstate 85 surely wasn't that. Usually throttled with traffic, the highway was deserted, if not in an actual desert, or there would have been far more death, when We couldn't have stopped it.

All I could think as I grabbed control of that steering, cause his muscle response wasn't on automatic, meaning I couldn't command his memories unimpeded – all I could think pivoting that wheel on the winding 4 lane highway, maintaining control for dear life – cause I'd already learned pain in the Orb was just as painful – all I could think was...

'All Praise Due to Allah that we couldn't afford to buy the Jaguar V8!!!'

I let up on the pedal, and not needing phonebooks since I was in a body tall enough to get a view of the dark road ahead, I shifted gears down, slowing my

436

speed from a hundred to 55mph in double the time it took to build up to that rate right after my dad had driven out onto the sidewalk-less road in front of our house, my living sister's spirit, once again watching him go.

What the heck was he thinking? Good question and the answer broke my heart.

Reader, men are universally straight forward beings, but mark my words – not all men are the same, even among Us, darn near immortals. You can't apply a cookie cutter template and believe, 'Oh! This is the way men think!' anymore than you can apply a template or predict the rules and habits of one family based on what another family does. These are men, not robots, same as We, Gods are not without the depth and scope of souled entities. Even for white men, whose compartmentalized thinking lends them to make the dumbest of shortsighted decisions – and boy! I'd gotten too extensive a lesson on that reality to easily explain (maybe later on, if I recall) – but even white men are not all alike.

As for this Black man, moments, seconds, I didn't know how long he had left, but, this man coming to the end of his life, of his rules, of his brilliance, of his reasons for his action, tonight, this unique man wanted to...

live.

And here's where I wonder, should I share his truth, because? I know I don't have to, but I accept I want to warn even my own progeny that there are ways to live and ways to not. I'm heavily sighing, recalling that my father wanted to exist for reasons I've learned aren't the best part of life. See, he thought success was proven through things, through accolades, through the opinions of those around him who didn't really care about him; and though he wanted to save the people in the community who lived near the nuclear plant? Even more he wanted to be a hero, as if that's the reason to become one, cause most times? Heroes are best when unknown.

Wow. Seems as I write, I've answered my own beginning question.

What makes a hero?

Every way that's necessary to rescue those in need. Whether by planning, by accident, but definitely? What you rescue should be worthy beyond the momentary envy of anyone but yourself and your Creator. It doesn't matter how it happens if it saves the people inside the fancy car, inside the swank

437

house, or inside the rickety shack that would have been a better place to begin all over again with one more person living within ours at 846 Carson. We could have built from scratch, handily, with the brilliance of the mind I was absorbing the full contents thereof, amazed by my father's mathematical, scientific mastery which made nuclear physics look like pick-up stix, while misdirected he was certain regaining his white approval (though his mind explained it in other terms), the Jacksons would be reset on their generational rise to glory once found worthy by those who still hated them, on a great enough average to make merging with them, the death of what made Us great.

I'm not saying the stolen schematics and photos he'd taken from his former place of employment, showing exact locations and magnified depictions of those dematerializing pressure valves, that were in a briefcase in the car's trunk – I'm not saying they shouldn't have been delivered to the hands of that reporter he'd contacted on his cell phone shortly after driving up the road. I'd never say that, as wouldn't it have been nice if the common man, woman and child, no matter what race, what nationality could have been told the truth?

That all nuclear reactors hemorrhage cancer escalating radiation which the nuclear industry hides.

Wouldn't that have been fantastic? I'm just saying, my father severely underestimated his enemy, cause I knew, from having been in their minds, they'd been waiting for this dangerous negro who knew too much to be allowed to gain the upper hand. That's why, when it had pulled up alongside me on that several laned expressway, I'd been expecting that V8 Jaguar's driver, who wasn't drunk and his bosses weren't living off their last dollar – I'd been expecting him to roll up close enough to shoot out dad's tires, cause I'd occupied that heartless timeline a few white guys back.

"*It's time to leave, Tyree,*" came the sonorously calm voice of Gainde, still seated at the side of Dr. Kattan's bed, where I could hear the rhythmic beeping of all those life saving gizmos, that would be of no use to me, here.

I didn't want to leave, though. I hadn't driven that ever so faster car, so I could verify the trajectory of Marcus Jackson's cherished prize possession, carrying him in it slamming across the lanes into and through the center divider and directly into the path of that freight truck, which had been carrying another worthy being, named Leonard Mason.

A white man. A very nice, non-despicable or nasty in anyway whatsoever white man. And a great dad, too.

438

But that other white guy, driver? In the V8? He couldn't have cared less, braking his vehicle up beyond the screeching wreck, the explosion, the smell of burning everything that added new scents to Cletus' ancient simpler ones. For that white man, this was what you did to stay on top, and believing it could be any other way was? An infantile mistake only suckers and Black people made...

I hadn't driven that V8, viewing an accident I couldn't stop, just to punk out now. I wanted to comfort my father, somehow. Wanted to die in his stead, cause I wasn't scared. I knew daggone well, I couldn't bring him back this way, anymore than his thinking could have produced another outcome. I'd only have confirmed, there's a bigger plan that I didn't control, no matter what my desires.

"Come on, brother. You know what happened. This is unnecessary. It's the Yurugu who have no balance, but You? You don't have to see it all, knowing it's never going to be healing. Sometimes? It's okay to walk away and move on."

Yes, The Ubuntu could have pulled me out, but they wanted me to decide for myself.

"I understand, now, little man. We must be about life, together to ensure nothing but life," added my Senegalese accented predecessor's voice, the good doctor. "We have everything to fight for, making victory assured. Let's build, Tyree, not wallow in the filth."

And like that, I trusted the wisdom of my elders, letting my Family pull me out, as We glanced the headlit grill of that more expensive jet black death knell, driving up to do its damnedest. Yeah, it was the color 'black', but it wasn't the truth of Black, so its owners could never catch me or mine in their traps, not ever again.

=

This is it. It's over, as it was that day, only morning had happened by the time We'd all filed out the Orb, everybody cheering, congratulating one another. I was emotionally exhausted, though happy to have rescued Kyerah and pieced out what had really happened to my dad. I hence could mourn him with pride, knowing if he'd learned what We all now knew, he couldn't deny it anymore than We could. Well?

The vast majority of Us. There were some – some like Don, who exited still making their excuses.

Now, reader, I know what you're thinking. You're like, '*Dude! But something else happened, cause there's still a couple more pages for me to read and, uh-duh?! Homie?! There's the Ankh Udja Saneb!!! What up with dat?!!!*'

Granted, you have a good point, but? The moment I left old thinking in the past? The Ubuntu was finished, cause I hadn't been the only one discovering every secret which revealed, Our Enemy was an ancient one, whom Our Ancestors knew exactly what they'd been describing when they'd called him the Cursed Shaytan. The Devil. The Goat People.

The Doer of Evil, whom We'd know by his deeds.

See, from loose and dangling thread to thread, faster than the speed of light, We'd repaired Our golden robes by unraveling the web of deceit of Our lawful captor had woven, cause like I said?

We be Gods, and, Gods roll like that!

We surely did discover what the AUS was, and thousands of other facts such as:

1. The Jews in Israel weren't the real Jews. They hailed from Khazaria.

2. The real Jews, accurately called 'Hebrews', cause there was no 'J' when We'd become a nation way back in the day - the real Hebrews were Black Us, who'd been abducted and brought here exactly as stated in The Bible.
3. The True Religion of The Creator is as natural as breathing air as it's

440

submitting to His will. That has nothing to do with a church or mosque or temple that's not preaching truth.

4. White people were made, not part of the Original Creation, cause there's no such thing as 'Natural Selection'. That's a theory around so long, it should have been proven, BUT? It's never been proven cause it can't be....

5. The public education system had been modeled on the Prussian system, set up after the end of World War I, to create a more docile citizenry. Hence, it taught nothing that would encourage independent thinking.

6. Fritz Tee Meer, once the commander at Auschwitz, developed the plan while in jail, serving out what wound up as only a 3 year sentence for genocidal war crimes against Ashkenazi Jews who were sacrificed on purpose by other Ashkenazi Jews during WWII, cause nobody had believed they were slaughtered during WWI (funny, the Jewish owned major media newspapers were ordered to report that 6 million Jews had been killed, but no one believed it, yet) – Fritz Tee Meer developed the plan to kill off the world's population by systematically poisoning the food supply. He went on to found Codex, working with the United Nations (yes, the U.N.) and to use Monsanto which created GMOs.

7. GMOs turn the human gut into its own pesticide making factory, slowly but surely poisoning the liver, giving rise to exploding rates of Leaky Gut Syndrome and Liver Cancer.

8. All the modern nations were owned by a select cabal of families, working through the Zionists, the Black Nobility (the royalty of Europe), the Jesuit Priesthood, and the Catholic Church. They'd carved up the entire planet like a 3D basketball cake, without asking any of the inhabitants. They'd developed more mechanisms of population control than there's words in the dictionary, including the words I don't know. 'Holly' wood, as a matter of facts means 'to cast a witch's spell'...

9. Every war waged, every pogrom concocted had been deliberately instigated by the very white persons who then would pretend they'd been honestly attacked by those they then had the means to obliterate. As a matter of fact, the world wars were first concocted in 1905 in a publication claimed to be fictitious, but a court of law ruled it was a forgery of an original. 'The Protocols of the Elders of Zion'. Later, long before the start of WWI, Freemason Demigod, Albert Pike, described 3 of them, started for exactly the same outcomes that occurred with the first 2.

441

10. Vaccines were equally part of a deliberate genocidal attack, begun by eugenicist Jonas Salk, who'd written hundreds of volumes on how to kill the population using the premise of saving them. Margret Sanger, best friends with Hitler, postulated the same with her advocacy of 'Planned Parenthood'. Medicine itself, was an allopathic soft kill strategy to make loads of profit while never curing the disease. Ancestor Imhotep had been right that food was the best medicine, which is why increasingly the movies, the supermarkets, the doctors had been pivoted as far away from cure as East is from West.

11. There was no such thing as brain chemical imbalances. The psychiatric industry is run by men and women who wish they could be taken seriously, so they make stuff up, to then ruin people's brains with pharmaceuticals that cure nothing, once again.

13. Teaching a child lies, any lie? Causes permanent loss of faith as soon as that child, at whatever age, learns he can't trust the world around him to value his need to trust. It's the biggest crime to commit to lie to a child as it lays that being's acceptance for never demanding anything better.

Oh, goodness, Family, there was so much more We discovered that would make this document as enormous as the the Netjer Tebeqa, perhaps bigger, breaking any poor cart picked to hold it, let alone making that cart squeak in protest. You must do the research on your own to then confirm you have an Avowed Enemy, because he surely won't tell you everything he's offered is a lie. On his part? That would be insane.

So what's the AUS? Whoa.

Turned out it wasn't white people, themselves, which is what We'd suspected. Matter of fact? We found those mythical 'nice' people in Our vigilant study of the white man's ways, and there weren't millions of them, but there were thousands on a planet of a billion whites.

What was Our standard for that measure?

Which white persons wanted to see the rest of the world, especially the most hated People – Diasporic Afrikans in the U.S. – which among them wanted to see Us free to command Our own destiny without their constant nosy intervention. Yes. A daunting search, but We did it. We found a few, in a thoroughly disheartening reality We could no longer tolerate being an existence of neverending disenfranchisement and violence. Yes, there's Black on Black crime, but as Brother Roscoe said:

442

"There's French on French crime. Japanese on Japanese. Danish on Danish. And with millions of whites killing whites with toxic everything from medicine to food, We, the Originals are nowhere near as barbaric. But, never in the history of man do a people lose their sovereignty if a baby's lollipop gets stolen."

These people were no more than spoiled brats in the playground, calling everyone else idiotic names, while they were the hogs, commandeering every apparatus for themselves and whining if they had to share, like being civil to those who weren't trying to harm them was a threat. We were numbed by the overwhelming monotonous bullying of White Supremacy. A mythical creation that came with reams of names, faces, addresses, bank accounts and was principally Ma and Pa Kettle white folks who didn't know Satan eats his own. And Satan's fork was sticking out in the heart of the dying Pacific Ocean.

Brother Xolani shook his Muhammad Ali head in sorrow.

Sister Devetra's jaw drop, and she cried.

Men and Women and their Children, OUR CHILDREN, not only held hands, they cuddled up closer, and bowed their heads. Nobody texted. Nobody pushed any digits, cause it'd be hard for anybody who wasn't seeing that, through the eyes of the white scientists who were lying to the public, the beach combers who were soon to see millions and millions of once living breathing gifts, whales, seals, fish, birds, gifts from Allah to everybody – from the eyes of the beach combers, residents and tourists who would day and day see nothing but death up and down the coastline – We all knew explaining the murder of the largest ocean in the world would be believed less than telling the world about the Orb, unless you'd understood radiation like my dad had. Or?

Unless you were some of those truly 'nice' white folks who understood an Extinction Level Event had occurred, the minute they, all alone in the world, had begun talking about the explosions at Fukushima, Daiichi Nuclear Power Plant on 3/11/11 (the Devil had a fascination with detonating false flags on 11 numbered days) – they'd posted videos, screamed their heads off, whilst White Supremacy wasn't concerned. Their newspapers were saying nothing cause they understood the world trusted Satan, not his renegade offspring – offspring who deserved everyone's respect, no matter their color.

Cause, lemme repeat. TRUTH HAS NO COLOR, but only the brave have the nerve to pick it as their armor, and Our armor?

We're Our own Separate People. Finally.

But about that radiation....
A bunch of Us, gliding through this treasury of eyewitnessed facts, We'd investigated the German specialists being brought over to the United States, along with Nazi icons placed throughout American governmental structures, in Washington D.C. – We'd seen they'd been brought in to continue the formulation of the atomic bomb, the so-called best weapon the white man had ever devised. That's what he'd taught the public in all those 'Duck and Cover' drills and advisories of the 50s. It's all about the BOMBS from those pesky Russians, when the real death was coming from all those nuclear plants and now? The whole Pacific Ocean was doomed, as it took more than a single bomb to usher in extermination. One bomb had nothing compared to the nonstop Hell pumping out of facilities that provided the poorly educated with jobs.

Although, even more chilling, it only would take one measly radioactive atom of radiation inside any living organism to eventually bring on a significantly shorter lifespan. One atom is the equivalent of 1,440 X-rays per day, from inside out, while the victim never suspects his days, the days of his offspring, the days of his DNA's existence on this Earth can be counted in single digits.

No. Inside the minds of those who knew, no lie the white man has told has ever been as great as, "Nuclear is good for the environment." Not when one building, alone, can kill everything for a thousand miles around.

The entire Pacific Ocean was doomed to die, simply because that much radiation hemorrhaging out of the destroyed 4 reactors of Fukushima had no choice, as it didn't think, any more than any statue could. As the most majestic achievement white men had created, it killed, and killed, and then killed and killed even after its creators were dead. It was gonna kill every race, every nation, every age, especially the young and the elderly. From those white people who were feared, to those the Enemy swore he loved. Radiation doesn't discriminate. There was the chance Our melanin could save Black Us, long enough that We could stop the complete genocide, but not if Our People kept eating Fritz Tee Meer's cooking, mixed with anything from the Pacific or areas soaking up the nuclear fallout. Not as long as We lived a life of lost gods, steeping in a pot of negativity. We, like the Ocean, would soon be People Stew.

However? There's no way to adequately explain a catastrophe as incomprehensible as what lay up ahead of those hovering coils, in a book meant to keep dumbed down Us frivolously entertained. This task has been excruciating, extensive, and finally empowering and enlightening, but if it doesn't enlist, You the Reader to investigate for Yourself, then?

It is a useless tombstone of a tome in a dusty vault in a cavernous library that nobody uses, cause, there's nobody left to take heed and do better.
Remember, Sister Makeba had said the Ankh Udja Saneb could be a welcoming to a beginning, or a firm goodbye.

And that's what Brother Gainde had been planning for...

Epilogue

There's a physics law that says energy cannot be created or destroyed. Well, We, Gods, like to say, energy cannot be created or destroyed except by The Creator.

Humbly I'mma refine that to:

Melanin is thinking energy which when harnessed in a righteous way, is the Image of The Creator through moving ACTION, and thereby it can never be destroyed as equally as it is the energy which then has the protective structure to withstand all forces arrayed against it.

This is what Brother Gainde and then every other Sacred Healer in Our midst taught Awoken Black Us. Allah, gave Us, His power to Self-Heal and then Self-Thrive. We didn't need every white person to be the source of evil, cause it'd have been far more wonderful if they'd all been nice, seeing's how evil is not the partner of The Almighty, but? If You don't know You're the source of Your own rescue, as We, Originals didn't know, then ugliness nipping at your heels will do for a Season, till You understand there's nothing in existence more lovely than anything made by the Direct Hand of THEEEEEEEE GOD. Especially His First Creation.

There's nothing more amazing than that which He imbues with His own power.

That's all it is. The choice to be powerful. Doesn't require evil, doesn't require approval, doesn't require anything but faith...

Faith is what We are.

We're all We've ever needed.

~ ~ ~ ~ ~ ~ ~ ~ ~ ~ ~ ~

The sidewalk would be in a state of disrepair for another week or two, after about a hundred of Us, using sledgehammers, and a couple donated jackhammers, broke Carson's jutted slabs into rubble. It was frustrating, as my whole family, and every family on the block would have to use the wooden planks laid down from the roadway to the walkways of our homes, for a while, because We didn't have vast resources. Our change was gonna take time, but waiting for Our Enemy to change?

Was no longer necessary.

Our small beginning was more valuable than all the gold in the world, because it was Ours. Yes, it'd be a year or more before the shacks were torn down and better houses had been built in formerly abandoned lots, or the plentiful abandoned dwellings that could be repaired, were repaired. So 2 months after The Ubuntu, my family's house was pretty much still a hovel, but it was my hovel, filled up with love and on a regular basis, and even prayer!

We'd pooled together, between our organized cottage businesses, and collective contributions without need to beg (We just gave) – We'd pooled together enough of a downpayment to buy these and several blocks worth of structures. It was a small area, but it was a start, and nobody who owned them, from city landlords to degenerate fat cats several cities away, dared to challenge our honestly fair offering. No, they didn't give them to Us. Not that year, yet....

After I'd reshrunk Allah's Sacred Breath that morning in the schoolyard, these crackers and their cracker lovers who didn't know what the heck had happened, still, they knew enough that they'd realized that whip wasn't gonna work, anymore. Even though We'd returned to ordinary non-superhero-ed people, they didn't know what the Heaven was up, thus they dared not risk retaking what used to be theirs, and only asked for compensation. As We were still a vulnerable, not entirely self-sustaining territory, We paid. It would be many, many hard fought years before We reclaimed Our original gift of the entire planet. In the meantime, seeing's how they'd only witnessed 'Magical Black People On a Rampage', on whatever media outlet broadcast, or on whatever device the rest of the world had seen, their innate fear of Us, which We'd gotten personally acquainted with, did all the propaganda We required to mythologize Our prowess. I mean I could expand the Orb whenever needed, and I continued to learn its secrets from both Dr. Kattan (who healed up

447

slower than he would have as the Librarian, but he healed up completely, eventually) and I learned martial arts from Brother Gainde and learned how to be a man from both. Now, it takes time and effort to reach out, gather up and then hold hands with a million people...

but nobody required convincing to restart any future Ubuntus, as We knew We had an Enemy. Ya didn't have to ask twice.

Shoot, yeah, I'd been the accidental catalyst of all this change, but even I was impressed by the sight, myself, sitting crunched up in our super cramped living room, watching it on big screen, streaming hand held Youtube uploads of that profound Blackness, out of which a nation was born. Broadcast straight from the People who made it a reality, cause the mass media coverage didn't dare report The Ubuntu the way it'd actually happened. Man, when We finally built Our own Youtube, now wasn't that freedom...

So, we watched the real coverage of the tail turning into the Head, on shaky vids but rock solid truth from Us.

Ordinary beautiful Black Us.

My, there'd been thousands of sparks, and coils, and ropes of light contrasted against the night sky, which floodlights couldn't dim, and Our adversary couldn't thwart. The Enemy, We learned later, even tried to use an EMP – Electro-Magnetic Pulse to disarm Our energy and wound up shutting the electricity they used for their own equipment. The legions, about a thousand soldiers, marines, airforce strong, were made weak by their own desperation. If they'd have been nicer?

We'd have shared with them that the side they were fighting for was about to fry them with red hot isotopes (another word for radiation) spewing from a little power plant in Japan with a funny profanity sounding name. However? We knew they needed to bow their every head in the way Allah saw fit, and on that night, into the early morning? None of them were. Heck, from that day into these 97 years later, most couldn't stand Our Awakening.

But there was more fun that day, as We made sure there was no more death, not from Us. Okay, We singed a couple police cruisers, downed several unmanned drones, disintegrating them before they reached the tops of any buildings or power lines and melted the lids on a couple A1 Abrams Tanks. Some of the brothers got so precise with their concentrated aim, they burned the pants off any 'authority' that got too close. Now that? Was *hysterical!!!* I

448

think it was those Ankh wearing kings who nearly spontaneously calculated the numerical frequency of the power in Our hands, surging soul to soul. Yeah. They were Super Black Man, Big 'S' Cool.

Hence, no landlord, when We made a bid for those first homes dared argue the price, and a bunch even lowered it, throwing repairs in at no extra cost. About 3 gave Us the buildings for free, out of gratitude for Our proving evil is not the owner of anyone who refuses. Even one white guy who, was extra inspired. He wanted to stay, but no white person was allowed to enter Our new little world. So he went back to Europe to wake up the 'gods' in his fellow Caucasoids. Maybe I'll describe some of his efforts in my next book, but as it didn't have anything to do with Us? I doubt it.

I didn't want them to start with my block, but those hyper aware beings didn't pay attention to a single protest from still 12yr old, REALLY Black Boy Me (We were all on Our way to that beautifully intensified deeeeeeeep darkness). With community trust as natural as a seedling growing into a tree if given the right guidance, We opened Our own bank, after negotiating with the surrounding government to create a sovereign territory right here in Newark. I mean it was tiny, no doubt – only 4.5sq miles – but it was OURS, to rule, to protect as Our wisdom understood would be good, not merely for the few, but for each and every one.

What cottage industries did We develop? Well, small ones, to start with. Many of Our People had already been toiling away at their modest entrepreneurial endeavors, helping to advise the community with Our business plan to eventually become self-sustaining and organically based in everything We did. We used Afrikan manufacturing villages as Our models, as they produced without benefit of heavy industrial equipment. We started making soaps, detergents, clothes, packaged foods, and?

To grow Our own food, clearing the lot was gonna take effort. But We tore down that jumble of an unkempt mini-forest on the side of the Kattan mansion, from day one – tree by tree, garish piece of litter, almost never to be drank again coke can by coke can. Our food, seeing that We had to strengthen Ourselves against the radiation, would be free of anything that would hamper the life inside. But before We could possibly build up to that level of production, in the meantime to ensure We had enough food, We rationed whatever wasn't utterly toxic in the neighborhood supermarket (there was only one), sold Our products to a highly sympathetic larger public beyond, bought staples to store in the empty buildings We guarded, and grew tons of food in container pots or any patch of land with even a couple teaspoons of dirt. We began gardening on rooftops! There'd even been knowledgeable farmers who'd

449

taken part in The Ubuntu.

See, it wasn't magic that prolonged Our lives to near immortality – it was good, healing food. It was going to take a while before We left all the old addictions (there was still a thriving business at the various fastfood joints). See, I was The Librarian Keeper, so, I could walk out of the Orb and my muscles would be stronger, or any of my injuries would be cured because I reasoned, it was by Allah's permission. He wanted more for His Chosen than just to be given immortality. He wanted Us to earn it and thus cherish it.

That's why, after that day was done, Our brains, Our bodies were in the same weakened condition they'd been before. If that much instant repair was possible, Folks would have exited 10, 100, 200lbs lighter, no cravings for anything that was killing them, but it didn't happen like that. Nope.

Reaching perfection is a journey, but it is a destination, not a fable.

"It's looking mighty fine, Brother Amenhotep," said my smiling grandmother in a full, gentle but clear to my ear voice, when We'd begun breaking up the buckling sidewalk. She'd come out with a tray of my mom's lemonade, handing it to me and the dozen other folks who were laying down the wooden planks over the exposed dirt where the sidewalk had once been.

"It's a mess, grandma," I replied.

"It's a beautiful mess, son, cause it's Ours'."

Now, my grandma of all people? She walked straight, because she no longer suffered her arthritis, but our family had been among the first to take healthier eating lessons (yes, even for us, Jacksons – oh! OOPS! We became the Muhammads, by the way, and prayed every day – or at least, every other...) – we learned natural healing from the Kattans and all the other community sages. And Mrs. Ruby Muhammad was, also? No longer a shut-in having united with those other family members after she'd been reached, palm to palm, in the precinct jailhouse, along with my mom and Sister Makeba. That'd been a planned and easy takeover, the moment The Ubuntu rounded the corner and coiling lightning bolts frightened every officer into vacating the premises, immediately, while the last one handed Us the keys. Ruby Larchmont wasn't quite laughing yet, these days, but hers was one of the brightest smiles in Our little growing Abjerusalem.

"Oh, yes, ma'am," I answered. "That it is, grandma. That it is!"

450

Don't get me wrong. If it didn't get torn down, that droopin' porch would surely still commit murder, but worst houses in Newark, amazing to believe there was worse – they needed major repairs, first.

My mom waved at me from the brightly repainted sunny lemon façade with white frames around the window, above. Kyerah, sweatin' with the rest of Us, grabbed her own glass, wiping her brow, as over strolled the Original Crew, dressed in work clothes that weren't a fashion statement. I'd asked her about her experience as Sophinisba, but she shook her head sadly and told me:

"Never again."

Whatever age, We, collectively did what was necessary the first couple weeks, as, at the beginning, there'd been no school in session back at P.S. 47. Why? Well, Dr. and Mrs. Kattan, without hesitation, volunteered their mansion to The People as Our new school location, which included the members of Ascend, who began teaching fulltime, far better and completely truthfully as almost no child had ever been. The Event didn't reach the Wisommm Center, but that didn't matter as the life I had felt there was far more effective here, no matter the plain-ness of the surroundings.

Plus, initially, most parents didn't want to return their little ones minds to the Enemy. Good that it turned out We had so many certified teachers, including my own mom, who were driven to share Our truth so ferociously, one might worry there'd be more educators than students. However, as the thousands and thousands signed up, from even surrounding neighborhoods, We took over a dozen school buildings, including, eventually old not as ugly, with no metal detectors, P.S. 47. The teachers found themselves duly needed.

We knew it'd be very difficult given everyone involved was immediately fired from any job controlled by white folks and those who believed the mainstream media. It was even dangerous to travel outside the safety of Our community, cause it was one thing to be amongst Ourselves, while one walking all alone in the territory of Our foe? Well, you were taking your life into your own hands.

But that was okay, as We didn't mind being a fixer-upper and with 24hr community patrolling, especially on the perimeter of Our little world, We didn't suffer any fools bringing that old world thinking nonsense.

Which brings me to the Dons in Our community. If it was gonna take time to shut down the last burger joint, of course it was gonna take time to convert,

451

and/or expulse the last braindead negro. But, We had plans for those among the People who meant Us no good.

Hmmmm. I'm feelin' this writing thing, now. Looks like I'll have to chronicle what happened next. In the meantime?

I, myself? Well, I was the new Knowledge Protector and my sister was my assistant. If not her, because she could put the Aanda down while I wandered Eternity, I was too busy protecting Our small Heaven to have time for school. You'd be amazed how much there is to learn from history when You have to rebuild a civilization that actually civilized everybody else, yet, they taught you nothing about how you did that.

Wow. How We DO that.

~ ~ ~ ~ ~ ~ ~ ~ ~ ~ ~

Excuse me, but my wife – only 2 weeks to go before my true immortality arrives in the person of Baby Mumia Sirius, although until he decides his name, he's our little Kanefer – Jepkemboi has just brought me my morning tea. I'm gonna end this here, cause life is good now that the future has a past that's protecting it's right to be....

The End

No, for real this time. Go home. Build something, 'cause you might be wondering why I never mentioned Jesus. Well, he's YOU. So resurrect yourself with knowledgeable action.
Why, even God me? I'mma go learn some Sacred Math and Sacred Biology from the Science and Mathematics Protectors. Not surprisingly? They're two of those Ankh wearing Brother Gods from 97 years back.....

All Praise is Due to Allah.

Resources

Learn more about the very real, ongoing hemorrhage of radiation from the Fukushima Daiichi Nuclear Power Plant from 'The Radical HomeGoddess' Youtube channel, for as long as I'm allowed to participate on that forum. This is NOT information the Nuclear Industry wants to get out. For the moment, and I'll do my best to share any new forum I go to, and upload the playlist, 'FUKUSHIMA: From A to Z'. You can find, as of 2018 on 'The Radical Sister' (changed the name, recently) – and it will give you what you need to prepare. This novel was written to make it easier to fortify Our Youth and Our Elders, with everyone in between – to give them the courage to make those preparations Our new reality.

Never forget, We have already won.

I Love You!

Sister Ajali Shabazz

93248802R00255

Made in the USA
Middletown, DE
13 October 2018